I0818008

A FOREST OF FIRE

A FOREST OF FIRE

THE TERRULIAN TRIALS
BOOK TWO

CHLOE HODGE
REBECCA CAMM

This book is written in Australian English.

First edition: October 2023

Find us at: www.chloehodge.com | www.rebeccacamm.com
Instagram: @chloeschapters | @readingwritingdaydreaming
TikTok: @chloehodgeauthor | @readingwritingdaydream
Facebook: Chloe Hodge Author | Rebecca Camm

Reading Groups:

ASOS Discussion Group — https://www.facebook.com/groups/asosdiscussiongroup

Chloe Hodge's Reading Coven — www.facebook.com/groups/chloesreadingcoven

Rebecca Camm's Reader Group — www.facebook.com/groups/rebeccacammsreadergroup

Printed in Australia.

Hardback ISBN: 978-0-6456250-6-6

Special thanks and acknowledgements to:
Editor; Emily Morrison
Cover Design; Cover Dungeon
Character Art; Simarts_
Formatter; Rebecca Camm

THE TERRULIAN TRIALS

A Sky of Storms

A Forest of Fire

A Sea of Secrets

A City of Smoke

A Desert of Despair

A Kingdom of Conquerors

Content Notes

A Forest of Fire is a why choose urban fantasy romance novel. It contains cursing, sexual references, violence, assault, bullying, sexual assualt, and other adult themes.

A full list can be found on rebeccacamm.com or by scanning the QR code below.

There's fantasy and then there's fantasising. Whatever–or whoever–your fancy, we've got you covered.

Terrulia
Tritosa City
The House
of Ascension
The Palace
The Crimson Steppes

Verdant Plateau

Stormcrest City

Damascon Hollow

THE HOUSES

HOUSE JUPITER

STORMCREST CITY

AUGER FAMILY

Victrus and Eliana

Victoria, Fallon, Ethan, and Hadley

HOUSE NEPTUNE

TRITOSA CITY

LOCH FAMILY

Zale

Zane, Zuri, Zara, Zeke, Zach, Zion, and Zariah

HOUSE CERES

THE VERDANT PLATEAU

HAWTHORN FAMILY

Gabriella and Rosa

Wren and Noah

OF TERRULIA

HOUSE PLUTO

DAMASCON HOLLOW

THE DRAKES

Cormac

Ace

HOUSE MARS

THE CRIMSON STEPPES

HALE FAMILY

Barrett and Myra

Kayden

NOTABLE CHARACTERS

Kendra Reynolds - The Crimson Steppes
~~Flynn Stewart - The Crimson Steppes~~
Dick Jobs - Tritosa City
~~Mark Leroy - The Verdant Plateau~~
Lou Bellona - Stormcrest City
Celeste, The Overseer - The House of Ascension
Master Nolan - The House of Ascension
Master Luna - The House of Ascension
Master Jeremiah - The House of Ascension
Julian, Advisor - The Palace

ACE

My head throbbed like a bitch, welcoming me back to reality. Pain rippled through my gut and the rest of my bruised body as I slowly regained control of my senses. Someone must have worked me over whilst I was laying in the dirt out of it. It was nothing I couldn't handle, though. My head was the real kicker. I reached up, feeling the slick blood dripping from a cut near my hairline.

The cunt who had taken my bionic hand and tried to eliminate me from the Terrulian Trials was going to pay. Danger Dog—the rat from Hallow's Griff—thought he'd gotten one up on me. The coward attacked me from behind, stole my hand, and then must have knocked me around for good measure. The fucker was at the top of my revenge list now, and there was nothing I liked more than vengeance. How dare he take my hand? How did he know disconnecting it would render me defenceless? There were more fingers on that shiny thing than there were people who knew that particular detail. I'd find out who ratted me out, and then I'd make Danger Dog regret the day he got on the wrong side of a Drake.

But first, I needed to finish the trial and get out of this hellhole.

I dragged myself to my feet as the world spun, trying to throw me off its orbit. I held my ground, gritting my teeth until the need to vomit left me. Which was a feat, let me tell you. On top of my head spinning, the marsh within the crater stank like death. The already foul water was only worsened by the corpses the monsters had dropped in it. It was basically a mixing pot of shit, mud, and guts.

The world steadied slightly, enough for me to look around at the depressing marshland and contemplate my next move. The red beacon shone brightly above in the misty skies like a light at a brothel, informing outsiders that everyone within was currently being fucked. The dark form of the dragon flew overhead, no doubt searching for Potentials to fill its stomach.

I crept towards the cover of a few creepy-looking trees, determined not to end up in the creature's sharp teeth. But I stumbled through the mud more than I'd have liked. At this rate, there was no way I was getting to the finish line in time. I leaned against one of the trees and shut my eyes, taking a few deep breaths while waiting for my head to clear. After a few moments of giving myself a piss-poor pep talk, I opened them to spot a helicopter rising in the distance.

Shit.

The sight of it did a better job of spurring me on than the little chat I'd had with myself. The spinning blades mimicked the speed of light, moving way too fucking fast for my liking.

I patted myself down, searching my pockets for the golden coin, only to find it missing. I swore, making a sailor somewhere proud, then kicked the nearest tree. Fucking rat had taken that, too. Nothing was ever easy in life. I was an idiot for thinking, even for a second, that he'd left it. Instead of standing around taking my anger out on the tree or wallowing like some chump, I trudged back towards where the chest had been at the centre of the crater.

As much as the rat pissed me off, I was furious at myself, too. I'd gotten complacent with the others around, and that was a mistake I wouldn't make again. I needed to watch my own back. The only person I could rely on was myself.

I hauled ass through the marsh, my boots like weights thanks to all the mud. The shouts of dying Potentials mixed with the piercing shrieks of the giant bats rang ahead, and being the opportunistic guy I was, I kept moving. Dead Potentials could still carry coins.

As I drew closer to the centre, I lowered myself to the ground. There was no bat in sight, thank fuck. Only a Potential lying in the mud. She was face down, so I rolled her over as I approached. Her lifeless eyes looked up to the skies despite the mud splattered all over them. Her guts were spilling out of the giant gash in her abdomen. It wasn't my finest hour, but I searched her body and swore beneath my breath when I couldn't find any gold.

I left her in the mud and kept trudging in the direction I was pretty sure the chest was in, passing a few more bodies. Some were missing limbs, whilst others looked as though more than just giant bats had feasted on them. Between the monsters and the fighting between Potentials, this trial had been a massacre. I was looking forward to seeing how many people made it to the finish.

If I could find a coin, that is.

I needed to hurry if I wanted to keep my place at the House of Ascension. Losing this trial meant failing the job Cormac had sent me to do. He would punish me creatively if I returned to the Drakes without infiltrating the treasury.

Movement caught my eye, and I hurried over to another body. The guy was in bad shape. Blood oozed from the claw marks on his neck and chest, and his arm had been completely torn off. He muttered incoherently, his blue eyes darting around in a panic. I put him out of his misery, then searched what remained of his body, grinning like a bookie on race day when I found the shiny coin.

I would have kissed the thing if I hadn't smudged blood and dirt all over it.

Shrieks echoed through the air. I jumped to my feet and got my ass into gear. If I could avoid the bats and the dragon, I could get this fucking trial done and dusted. I moved through the marsh; the mud becoming a watery soup as the disgusting liquid rose to my ankles. My head had finally stopped being a whiny bitch, the spinning no longer an issue, so I shifted into a jog, only to catch the attention of a giant bat. The screeches grew louder, and I chanced a look behind me to see the ugly thing close on my tail. Its black wings flapped furiously as it flashed its pointed teeth. I threw myself to the side in time to avoid a swipe from its razor-sharp claws. It circled, diving for me again, but I dodged the bastard. I had no weapon, so I bolted, ducking and weaving to lose it.

The fucker was eating up my precious time.

A cluster of mangled trees was in the distance, and I sprinted to them, zig-zagging beneath their cover. A branch caught my remaining arm and sliced a gash up the inked skin. I hissed under my breath, trying not to make a sound as a river of blood dripped down to my fingers.

Shrieking sounded above me.

I grinned as an idea hurtled into my mind. With a grunt, I hooked a branch under my arm. Then, using my weight, I snapped it from the tree. It wasn't the best defence, but it would have to fucking do.

I stepped beyond the trees, brandishing my weapon. The bat took no time hurtling towards me, its beady red eyes fixed on mine like a good old cowboy stand-off. I waited until it was close enough for its claws to scratch me, then thrust the branch upwards, piercing the bat's furry chest. Its vampire-like fangs flashed as it howled. The creature's talons dug into me as we both fell into the muddy water. I rolled on top of it, leaving the branch in its chest as I beat the shit out of it one-handed and tried to drown the monster with my weight at the same time.

It eventually fell still, and I slid off, panting as I looked at what was left of its piggish snout and ugly face. If it could even be called that anymore.

Sure it was dead; I took a second to inspect my arm. There was a nasty red line through what had been a tattoo of a vicious electric eel. It made it look more vengeful if you ask me—mirrored how I felt towards Danger Dog, that's for sure.

As I rose, I noticed the bat wasn't the only body lying in the ankle-deep water. The princess from House Jupiter lay motionless nearby, after what had clearly been a fight she hadn't won. My gut clenched as I looked down at Fallon. Not because I cared, fuck no. I wasn't some sap. It was simply a knee-jerk reaction to the possibility I'd never get the House Jupiter ring. Though, just because she was dead didn't mean I couldn't get it.

I dropped to my knees and ran my gaze over Fallon. Despite the blood and filth covering her body and the blade protruding from her abdomen, she looked peaceful. Without thinking, I pushed the hair from her face and to my surprise, a breath escaped her lips. My heart rate spiked, and I pressed my fingers to her neck, checking for a pulse of her own.

She was still alive, though judging from the stab wound, it wouldn't be much longer. I should leave her here. Fallon was my competition and, not only that, but we also hated each other. I shouldn't have even been contemplating saving her. She was everything I hated about the world.

I shook my head. *Focus on finding the ring, then have an existential crisis.*

I rummaged through her pockets, coming up short. Where the fuck was the ring? It had to be on her. It was too valuable to leave lying around. To the right buyer, the House rings were worth more than someone could make in a lifetime back in DH. The Drakes would make bank on the thing. If I gave it to Cormac, that is. My boss had a lot of questions to answer before I handed anything over. I didn't appreciate being left in the dark about his dealings with Mark and whoever else was involved.

"What are you doing?"

My head snapped to the side to see Kayden storming over. He looked like shit. Mud covered him more than any real clothes, but he didn't appear seriously injured from what I could see. His red hair was in vibrant contrast against the dirt and his brown eyes looked at me with accusation, which didn't sit right with me.

"Weird time and place to feel her up, Twiggy," Kayden continued with a frown.

"I'm not some fucking rapist," I spat, shooting him a glare. "I'm looking for her coin. Can't get her over the line if she doesn't have one."

"You're helping her?" Kayden raised a brow. I knew he didn't fully believe my lie; I wouldn't have believed me either. I'd made my disdain for her well-known. "Bit suss. You don't exactly have a good track record for giving a shit about others."

"She's worth more to me alive than dead."

"There it is. Twiggy's actual intention revealed," Kayden drawled. "And people say I have a heart of stone."

I hadn't elaborated on why, but judging by Kayden's reply, he'd once again known what was in my head. I needed to keep my distance from him. The brick head was way too comfortable around me these days.

"They're not wrong," I replied with a grunt. "Fuck off now, Pebble. I don't have time for your shit."

"Don't plan on sticking around," Kayden said, shouldering me as he moved to pick up Fallon. He dropped two coins in front of me. "Be a good little boy and carry the coins. Let an adult do the real work."

I elbowed him in the side, my anger rising as he put his hands on Fallon. "I don't see one around. Only a guy who's injected so many roids that the juice has affected his brain." I looked him up and down and smirked. "Probably shrivelled a few body parts, too."

I didn't see his fist—just flew onto my ass into the muddy water. Fuck. The guy hit hard. I'd give him that. And now the fucking spinning was back. I clenched my jaw, spitting out blood as I sat up and watched Kayden scoop Fallon up, carefully cradling her in his arms. It was weird to see such a big, muscled guy, who could easily break a skull in his fist, be so gentle. A walking contradiction if I'd ever seen one.

"If that's your lame attempt to see my dick, then you're gonna be disappointed, bro," Kayden said without looking at me. He clicked his fingers. "Coins, Twiggy."

"Fuck you," I growled, snatching the coins from the muddy water and rising to my feet.

He hadn't won this fight but brawling with him now could mean losing the trial, and I wasn't going to let that happen.

I rolled my shoulders and fought back the need to tell him to stick his order where the sun didn't shine. Instead, I moved out of the way, shooting daggers at him all the while.

We wasted no time racing towards the finish line. We were so close I could taste it. The skies were dark, the monsters invisible within the clouds, yet their shrieks let us know they were still there, waiting. We pushed on, battered by a sudden downpour of heavy rain. It pelted down on us like it was trying to settle some score. Even as the water rose around our legs and the vision of our way forward became blurry, we kept going. The Overseer was throwing everything she had at us, but she wouldn't stop me. Even though my body ached, I'd experienced worse and then some.

I had a job to do, and I started nothing I couldn't finish.

The rain, which I'd thought would keep the monsters at bay, only drowned the shrieks out. A giant roar burst over the storm, and Kayden swore loudly beside me. I looked behind me to see the dragon flying toward us. It gnashed its teeth as it drew closer, scaly skin glistening in the rain.

The dragon roared again, forcing us to zig-zag through those creepy trees for some form of cover. It didn't give a shit about them though, smashing into the trunks and throwing wooden debris all over the place. It was too fucking close to me, the wind from each beat of its wings shoving me in the back, along with branches and shit.

How poetic. A Drake killed by a dragon.

Unfortunately for the beast, I didn't plan on dying today. I could feel its hot breath on the back of my neck, ruffling my wet hair as I forced every drop of energy into forcing my feet forward. The finish line was in sight, and I gritted my teeth as we inched closer. The Overseer and Potentials were only a few paces away. I shouted at the skies as I raced forward, then threw myself in a last-ditch effort, Kayden by my side the entire time.

We collapsed over the finish line. My heart pounded in my chest as I looked back to see the dragon do a sharp twist and fly up alongside the protective barrier. The rain was gone, and the dragon roared at the loss of a meal. We'd cut it fine, but we had fucking made it.

Now it was a matter of whether Fallon had joined us.

ZANE

"This is discrimination!" I shouted as the petite nurse ushered me away from Starfish's room and down the brightly lit hallway of the med bay. Ace's bionic hand jostled in my back pocket, getting handsy with my butt cheek. "Crabs have rights too, you know."

"I will not have you turning my med bay into an aquarium, Mr Loch," the nurse snapped, her hands pushing on my lower back. "The Potentials here need to rest and recover."

She shoved me a few more steps and then ended her physical removal, standing guard instead, seemingly happy now that I was far enough away from Fallon and Noah. They'd come out of the trial alive, and whilst I had had a chance to see them, it had only been brief.

The nurses had refused me entry nonstop just because I'd brought catfish in with me one time. How was I supposed to anticipate someone would get so scared of the majestic fish in a bowl that they would fall and knock over a bunch of expensive equipment? I'm not psychic and yet, here they were, blaming me for something I couldn't have predicted.

I wanted to see my bestie and my Starfish and be there when they woke up.

It was bogus.

"I know, that's why I brought Seb here," I replied with a heavy sigh, clutching the little crab close to my chest as I turned to face the woman. "Having an aquatic buddy nearby boosts mood and therefore healing."

"We have our own methods," the nurse said. She popped one hand on her hip, the other pointed directly behind me. Her dark brows drew together and she pursed her lips expectantly.

"Outdated methods."

"I'm not having this discussion with you, Mr Loch."

"But—"

"Out."

"Alright, alright," I said, shoulders slumping as I began my retreat for the time being. "Your archaic medicine has won today."

The nurse took a step toward me, her face twisting into a nastier expression. "What did you say?"

"You heard me!" I called as I spun on my heels and darted down the hall. There were other rooms off the hallway and I wondered whether there was a way between them. The nurse hadn't followed, so maybe if I slipped into another room—

"Watch it, Merman," Ace growled, narrowing his grey eyes at me as I rounded the corner, causing us to almost collide with each other. He was dressed in loose white pants and a white t-shirt; standard med bay clothing.

I threw an arm around him, drawing him close as I held on tight. He was so rigid; it was like hugging a tree. A very broody, angry tree, but I didn't care. Ace was alive and by the looks of him, completely healthy.

"Get. The. Fuck. Off. Me."

"Oh, shit." I quickly jumped back, remembering Seb clutched at my chest. Poor little dude was being sandwiched between Ace and me. "Seb," I said, grinning as I held the crab out to Ace so that they were at eye level. "Meet your Uncle Ace."

"No way in hell."

"Don't listen to him. He's just grumpy." My smile dropped as I quickly drew Seb back to my chest and whispered to the crab. I looked up at Ace and tilted my head to the side. "Were they treating you here?"

"Obviously."

"But I asked and they said you weren't here," I replied. "At first I got worried because then I thought you were dead but they told me you were alive just not here, but you are dressed like that so…" I gasped then glared off into the distance. "The nurses."

They've been keeping me from Ace, too.

I looked back to Ace to see him striding away from me. "Wait! I have your hand!"

Ace froze mid-step, his head turning slowly to face me. "How'd you get it?"

"Some cheap knock-off version of you crawled out of the trial with it and because we are besties I couldn't just let him have it. No way. That would have been breaking the friendship code and what kind of person breaks that? Not me. I have honour and—"

"Give it to me," Ace said, cutting me off as he strode back towards me.

"Oh yep, right." I reached into the back pocket of my boardies and pulled out his bionic hand. I didn't trust just leaving the thing lying around so I'd kept it on me at all times. To be honest, it was kind of nice having it cupping my ass cheek all day. "Here you go."

He took it, his gaze adoring as he examined the metallic hand. I couldn't help but grin at his expression. Ace was all hard lines and frowns, but right now he looked like he was staring at a baby sea otter, not a mechanical limb.

"Are you going to put it on?"

Ace's head snapped up and he shook it, pocketing his hand in one swift motion. Without another word he stormed off, leaving without so much as a thank you, but it was okay because I'd gotten a hug and I'd seen his face in something other than a smirk or scowl so I was calling it a win.

Instead of following Ace out of the med bay, I decided to try my luck and see if I could sneak between the rooms. I hurried to the closest door and quietly stepped inside, only to find a cleaning closet. Frowning, I moved on to the next room, finding a lab. There were tall benches with people in lab coats hovering over them, large screens with scientific stuff on display, as well as rows and rows of glass jars filling the shelves on the walls. I spotted a few sea creatures within them.

From what I could see they were alive, which made me sad because there was definitely not enough space in those jars. Poor little dudes were prisoners.

"Don't look," I whispered to Seb, retreating from the room. "I promise, we will set them free."

I decided to try one last room. The door was ajar so I stuck my head in to look around but once again I was as lucky as a salmon trying to befriend a hungry bear. No way through to my Starfish or bestie, only more injured Potentials sleeping in their beds.

I was about to give up when I spotted a familiar face. Kendra was standing beside one of the beds, looking down at a dude I didn't recognise. Frowning, she whispered something I couldn't hear before drawing a tiny bottle from her pocket and pressing it to the dude's lips.

"Mr Loch!"

Banging my head as I whirled around, I squeezed one eye shut and rubbed the sure-to-be bump with the palm of one hand. The nurse from earlier was back and she was not impressed.

"I told you to leave," she snapped, grabbing my bicep and dragging me down the hallway. Her nails dug into my skin and I winced, but she didn't loosen her grip. "Don't make me ban you entirely."

"I can't imagine it would be much worse than this."

She glared up at me. "It will be a long trial if you have no access to healing magic."

Behind us, sirens sounded and the nurse instantly released me to head in their direction.

"What's that mean?" I called after her.

"Code Blue," she shouted back and I hurried after her, panic rising in me like the tide. Starfish and Noah better be okay.

The nurse turned into the room I'd just come from, relief flooding me, and I stepped inside behind her to see the dude Kendra had been standing over seizing on his bed. His mouth spilled froth as he convulsed, while the monitor beside his bed flashed and beeped noisily.

I looked around but Kendra was nowhere in sight. More nurses hurried into the room, rushing past me and soon I was no longer able to see the dude, though I didn't need to. The monitor went silent. I didn't have to be a genius to know what that meant.

The dude was dead.

"What happened?" one of the nurses barked. "He was stable an hour ago."

The image of Kendra slipping him whatever was in the bottle flashed in my mind, and my thoughts went to a dark place. I shook my head, holding Seb close. The idea that Kendra would have killed the dude was absurd. She had probably given him a vitamin tonic or something.

Silly shellfish, I scolded myself. No jumping to ridiculous conclusions Zaney. It was just a coincidence.

FALLON

I woke to sunlight streaming through an open window and a throat as dry as the Crimson freaking Steppes. I groaned, rolling over and burrowing beneath the light cotton sheets and quilted blanket, appreciating the soft fabric against my cheek as I closed my eyes, hoping to drift back to the sweet escape of sleep.

Wait, back the fuck up.

I jerked, straightening and sitting up as I realised I was in the med bay back at the academy. Safe and sound and *alive*. Not bleeding out in a stinking bog, not being eaten by bats or dragons, and certainly not sprawled out next to a murderous, backstabbing bitch.

I looked around the room for the latter, just to be sure, but nope, I was surrounded by other Potentials. Most of whom were still asleep.

My eyes caught on Noah in a bed near mine and I breathed a heavy sigh of relief, feeling some of the tension leave my bones. He'd made it, which meant Zane must have passed the trial, too.

Well, shit. Not only was I alive, but I was at the House of Ascension, which meant someone had saved me. My brows creased as I considered who would have cared enough to drag my dying ass over that finish line and to the safety of the academy. Kendra might have, but then, I hadn't seen her once in that last race to the finish.

I bit my lip as my mind drifted to a certain sexy, rugged redhead from the Crimson Steppes. But surely not. Even as his name popped into my mind, I barked a laugh, shaking my head. Kayden had nothing to gain by saving me. He might have been crushing on me in his weird, big brute kind of way, but the guy had always made it clear the competition was all he really cared about. That and disposing of Victoria after she'd killed his best friend, Flynn, and usurped his base in the trial.

Ace wasn't even in the same ballpark. The guy would just as likely have sunk that sword into my gut as Victoria.

Ugh. That bitch had a lot to answer for. My fingers curled into fists as I thought of my sister. Was she alive? Had someone saved her too? I doubted her fake friends would care enough to go back for her, but maybe that mysterious hooded guy got her out? Either way, I wasn't sure which I'd rather—being able to exact my revenge on her traitorous, miserable ass, or knowing she was dead and would never bother me again.

A problem for another damn day.

I rubbed my eyes and yawned as I prepared to snuggle back under the covers. After a month spent traipsing through marshland battling beasts and Potentials, I just wanted to sleep in this comfy-ass bed.

"Fallon?" An excited shriek followed, tearing a few disgruntled Potentials from their sleep. "Shit, sorry," Kendra said, appearing anything but apologetic as she navigated the row of beds to come careening towards my own. Not much quieter, she said, "Thank fuck you're awake. I was going out of my mind waiting for you to return to the land of the living. How are you feeling?"

She crashed into my side, wrapping her slender arms around my shoulders before sitting back on the bed and crossing her legs.

"Like sunshine and daisies," I croaked, cracking a wry smile.

"Girl, you scared the shit out of me. When Zane came back without you, I thought you'd—"

"Died?" I supplied for her. "Almost. I ran into Victoria on the way out. We had a little … disagreement."

Kendra gasped. "*She* did this to you? Your own sister?" She narrowed her brown eyes, swearing under her breath. "Of course she fucking did. I'll kill her."

"You might not have to," I admitted, chuckling at her button nose all scrunched up in rage. "I don't know if she's alive, but if she is, that bitch is mine. Victoria Auger is going to rue the day she was born because when I'm done with her she'll wish she'd stayed dead."

Kendra clucked her tongue, then looked up with interest as Noah hobbled over to the bed.

"Uhh … hi," he said awkwardly, wrapping a palm around the back of his neck. "Can I…"

He gestured to the bed, then sat on the edge as I nodded. He'd looked better, but even after the damage Victoria had done, he was still hot as fuck. Maybe even more so, with no shirt on and some bandages bound around his torso, his muscles on full display and the green shimmer snaking around the top of his broad shoulders. He ran a hand over his shaved head, and I almost salivated at the movement. If not for the cuts and scrapes that the nurses hadn't bothered to remove with their healing ability, he looked like a freaking magazine model.

"Glad to see you made it in one piece, Hawthorn," I said with a playful grin. "I take it Zane is doing okay?

Honestly, I was surprised he wasn't here, half-draped over my body or fussing over Noah.

Kendra snorted. "The guy's been badgering the nurses nonstop since you were both admitted here. He barely left your sides until he got banned from visiting."

I shared a look with Noah that conveyed zero surprise over that.

"That doesn't sound like Zane at all." Noah rolled his eyes. "What did he do this time?"

"Tried to bring a bunch of lake creatures in to keep you company," Kendra replied. "Said everyone needed something cuddly to help them get better."

A laugh burst from my lips. That was Zane to a tee. I could only imagine the mayhem that must have caused. Bless his sexy little socks. The guy had no idea how to act normal, not that I'd change that for a second. Though, I was kinda glad he'd not succeeded. A cute doggo or a cat, I'd welcome, but something slimy and wet wasn't my idea of a cuddly companion.

Something hard and happy to see me, on the other hand, was exactly the pep rally I could go for. Something with abs, a jawline for days, and just a hint of vigorous aggression. Okay, maybe more than a hint. There were a few people who fit that description. I had to wonder if Noah was one of them now that he had some skin in the game.

I wasn't the only one who had a reason to want Victoria dead—if she wasn't already so lucky. Which brought me back to how the hell I was sitting here at all.

"Do you guys know who brought me back?"

Kendra shook her head. "It was chaos out there, what with the dragon enjoying a fucking buffet of Potentials. But I did find Dick Jobs and another girl, and we finished the trial together."

"Dick Jobs?" My mouth dropped open. I snapped it shut and shook my head. "Damn, the skinny shy guy has got some guts after all. Good for him."

Noah snorted. "Wouldn't have made much of a meal anyway. All sinew and bones."

Playfully, I punched his arm. "Well, whoever my mysterious saviour is, I'll have to send them a postcard to say thanks. That dragon? The whole damn trial? It was no joke. I probably wouldn't be alive if not for them."

I could still see, still *feel* the blood raining down as it clenched its massive jaws around other Potentials. Not to mention the feeling in my gut when my own sister stabbed me. That shit was rough.

"Fallon," Noah rasped, clearing his throat.

Kendra shot me a quick look—more of a sly smirk, really, the little shit—and rose from the bed. "I'm gonna grab us some coffee. Be back soon." She blew me a kiss for extra measure, and I smirked at her retreating form.

Once she'd left, Noah's brow crinkled, and he moved to face me more directly. I shuffled in the bed, sensing whatever he had to say was important. His knuckles scraped against my hand, leaving it burning in the wake of that touch.

"I wanted to thank you for freeing me from Victoria. I wasn't—" he swallowed audibly. "I wasn't expecting to make it out. You and Zane turning up was a surprise, but an appreciated one that I won't forget."

My heart cracked a little to hear the sincerity in his words.

Something told me Noah was no stranger to violence, but Victoria had fucked him up pretty good. If Zane hadn't dragged him to the finish line, I had no doubt he wouldn't have made it. I placed my hand on his, looking into his eyes. "You don't have to thank me, Noah. It was basic human decency." I shrugged. "I think you'd have done the same if it was the other way round."

He hesitated at the contact, but after a beat he twisted our hands, interlacing his fingers through my own. I had to bite back my surprise at the action, but I didn't pull away from his warmth. "Maybe. But that's beside the point. You almost died in the trial, and I can't help but wonder if that's partly because I held you back." He uttered a long-suffering sigh. "I guess what I'm trying to say is that I'm sorry. Rescuing me got you hurt."

My lips parted. "Sorry? You've got nothing to apologise for. Victoria is a psycho. My whole family is. If anything, I'm the one that should say sorry."

A growl ripped from his lips, and his calloused hand tightened as he leaned forward. "Don't," he said, a command in his tone making something inside me perk its ears up. "Don't you dare take on that burden. You helped me when you had nothing to gain from it. I'm not stupid. I know you'll stop at nothing to win that crown, so I'm going to help you get it."

What the shit was happening? Noah *wanted* me to win? I pursed my lips, my eyes creasing with amusement. "We're all competing for the same reason. Why the hell would you do that?"

"Guess I'm just a stand-up guy."

I raised a brow and snorted. "Uh-huh, because you entered these trials for shits and gigs."

All I could do was stare as he leaned even closer, his other hand softly trailing against my cheek, which felt a little bruised. Noah sighed, relenting. "Let's just say I have other incentives for being here."

I tried to ignore the stupid organ in my chest that kicked up a fuss at that small touch. "Like following your lead on Mark?" I smirked. "Sorry, not sorry about that, by the way."

His teeth clenched together, a murderous nerve pulsing in his neck.

"He deserved everything he got and worse. There are several things I would have liked to do to Mark before he died. I had questions for him, but if he were alive right now and standing before me, they would be the last thing on my mind."

"Noah Hawthorn," I said after letting a low whistle loose. "Total hottie and a murderous bastard. I knew there was a reason we got along."

"Sounds like two reasons to me." He arched a brow, a rare smile on his face, his eyes sparkling.

I suppressed a laugh at my *slight* error being the one thing he focused on. "Okay, two reasons, even better."

That smile widened a fraction as he drank me in, his gaze stripping me bare. Fucking hell. Hot didn't cut it. He was sex on legs.

"Maybe there's more. Maybe I want to see what other things we have in common. But I just thought, with you and Zane…"

"That I was spoken for?" I grinned, stretching my arms above my head and popping my chest out, wondering if he'd take the bait. He absolutely did. "Nah. I like to keep my options open and I don't do possessive. At least, not outside of the bedroom."

Okay, maybe I was baiting him and loving every minute, but this was a side to Noah I hadn't seen before and yeah, I absolutely wanted to see how deep it went. I appreciated how kind and respectful Noah was, but I'd be lying if I didn't want to push his buttons and see if this connection between us sparked.

"You're in a bed right now," he said in a low voice, his implication sending a wave of heated awareness through me. "In a room."

Wow. And here I was thinking Noah was some innocent guy on his moral high horse. Maybe that darker side just needed to be tugged out from beneath all the good. I gasped in mock surprise. "Are you flirting with me right now?"

A small grin formed, and he moved closer, so his chest was nearly touching mine. "Is that what you want me to do?"

Oh, gods. This walking dictionary was really busting out the moves right now. And it was freaking working. I bit my lip. "Do you really have to ask?"

His mouth was just an inch from my own as he moved in, ready to capture my lips, when a piercing sound echoed through the speakers, causing us both to grit our teeth and cover our ears.

A scuffling sounded, followed by a muffled curse until the Overseer's voice echoed out through the speakers. "Greetings, revered Potentials. You have battled with body and wit to survive the first trial, facing-off beasts of burden and Potentials most dangerous. Yet here you stand, marking the pages of history. Ready to face your next challenge."

I rolled my eyes and Noah just shook his head, apparently as fed up with the Overseer's ridiculous speeches as I was. Somewhere in this academy, Zane was probably doing push-ups, pumped up from her stupid pep talk.

"The hardest part is yet to come, dearest students, and you must rally every ounce of perseverance to prosper in the coming days. Your next trial shall be one of magic, and you will need all your skills to survive. To ensure you get the most out of your training, classes will resume tomorrow, where you will be pushed even harder." Overseer Celeste paused dramatically, and I realised there was some spooky music playing in the background. "See that you make the most of it," she said in a ghostlike voice, before ending cheerfully. "That is all. Have the best day, little cherubs."

Fuck's sake. She ruined an almost-kiss with Noah for that? I shook my head, feeling a wave of fatigue come over me. Noah must have seen it too, because he pulled away, patting my leg.

"Get some sleep, Fallon. Maybe I'll see you at dinner?"

If I didn't know better, it sounded like there was a hint of hope in his tone. Unsure what to make of this mystery man, I smiled and rested back on my elbows, flashing him a sly grin. "Sure thing, Hawthorn. Sweet dreams."

His lips quirked at the slight implication in my tone, but he ambled back to his bed and was out in like five seconds flat. How did guys even do that?!

Sighing, I rolled over and tucked my face into the pillow. One trial down, what felt like a fuck-tonne to go. The only positives, in the meantime, were Kendra and a few sinfully good-looking guys to distract me. *And that's just what they are,* I reminded myself sternly. *Distractions.*

Zane, Noah, Kayden … even, dare I admit it, Ace. They were all just snacks to keep my appetite sated until I reached the main course. I couldn't let myself fall for anyone, not when I had bigger game to hunt.

But before I even came close to the second trial, I had some answers to chase, starting with finding out whether my sister was alive and who had saved me in the trial.

I hated feeling like I owed someone a favour, 'cause that shit had a habit of biting one in the ass later down the line. I may have saved Noah and welcomed fresh faces into my inner circle—and okay fine, my panties—but I still had my goals.

Destroy Victoria, win the trials, take down my parents, and make this academy my bitch. I would be queen, and nothing was going to stand in my way.

NOAH

I lay there with my eyes closed, breathing in the sterile air of the med bay. Hopefully, Fallon bought my sleeping act. What an idiot. Who tries to kiss a girl who's injured? Me, that's who. She'd looked so beautiful sitting in her bed, the pale blue of her patient's gown making her appear more vibrant than usual. Especially her copper eyes. And then she started flirting with me, making me want to not think things through like I usually did and just act. It had been reckless on my part; she probably wasn't in her right mind and didn't need me to be pushing myself on her like that.

She deserved better than me being an absolute muppet.

To be honest, I didn't know how I felt about Fallon. I was attracted to her—that was a no-brainer. But was there more to that?

I had too much shit going on in my life to think about it further. My city was relying on me. Katie and Rena were relying on me.

Subtly, I lifted my arm and saw Fallon laying there with her eyes closed. When I told her I'd help her win, I'd been dead serious.

It's important to think of the bigger picture, beyond what I was doing in the trials. At the end of this, someone was going to be crowned as the ruler of Terrulia.

Fallon had already proven repeatedly that she could stand her ground against those who wanted to tear her down. Whilst the trials pitted us against each other, they also shone a light on our humanity. Fallon was a decent person, and she would no doubt make a great queen.

But if I wanted Fallon to get the crown, I couldn't lie around in bed all day. With a wince, I slowly sat up. My injuries ached with the movement, and I cursed the oh-so-wonderful Overseer whose stupid chip blocked my healing powers.

I sighed. I should just grin and bear it. There were worse things that could happen to you in this world, and if the pain was what it cost me to try and put a stop to those things, I'd pay the price.

Not bothering with shoes—I wouldn't need them soon anyway—I left the med bay, determination stealing my spine. At first, I'd thought Mark's death had brought me back to square one, and I'd been left with the decision of whether to leave the trials or find someone else to investigate.

Instead, I now had two leads to look into. House Jupiter was involved in the disappearances from the Verdant Plateau, and Victoria had shown a lot of her cards when she was torturing me. She'd been worried about what I knew of Mark's dealings and had verified that Ace was aware of the Drakes working with Mark. I just needed to delve a little deeper to prove the hunch I had about House Jupiter. If Mark and the Drakes were selling people, then someone had to be buying them.

I rounded a corner, picking up my pace as I headed to the dorms.

Victoria was one suspect I would investigate; the other would be the Drakes by means of Ace.

When I'd followed Mark's map, the helicopter at the meeting point had been stamped with the Drakes' emblem. Despite his excuses and denials, I didn't trust that Ace wasn't involved, especially after Victoria dropped his name. I felt like the biggest idiot. I thought we'd turned out to be friends or something along those lines until that moment. I'd given him the benefit of the doubt and it had blown up in my face.

From what I'd heard, his gang was as thick as thieves ... which is exactly what they were. You didn't become the most renowned gang in the world by being a nice person. My bet was the authorities were catching on to the Drakes' little kidnapping scheme in Damascon Hollow so they'd ventured out to other cities.

Opportunistic bastards.

Ace had taken advantage of me, and now I'd do the same to him. I'd let Ace think I believed him when he said he knew nothing. That way, I could monitor him more closely. There was a reason why keeping your enemies close was an age-old saying. And if I was going to do that *and* what I came to the trials for, then I'd need allies.

As I pushed open the doors to the dorms, leaving the med bay, I almost collided with another Potential. My side burned as I deftly shifted out of the way.

Fuck, I hated not having my healing magic.

Ignoring the guy's complaints, I clutched my side and hurried over to the reading nook that had been built into the bottom of the stairs. I made sure no one was around to see me before stripping to my birthday suit, then stashed my clothes behind some cushions. I let my camouflage flow over my skin before heading back into the entryway. I grinned that no one looked any wiser.

I raced up the stairs, ignoring the pains in my muscles, heading toward the dorm rooms I needed to investigate. Time was of the essence, and I needed to move fast. The Masters had probably cleaned up already.

Hopefully, having allies would mean I could do less of this sneaky shit. At least alone.

Fallon was already on board in that department, so the next obvious choices were Zane and Kendra. Despite Zane's sea-obsessed quirky behaviour, he was surprisingly astute and loyal when it counted. It was still a shock that he'd helped rescue me from Victoria, even leaving Fallon behind so he could carry me across the finish line.

It wasn't just his rescue that was gaining my favour.

Kendra was an interesting one in that she was far from intimidating, which I think was her whole deal. She was unassuming, though if you paid close attention like I did, you could see she was clearly very intelligent and could hold her own in a fight most of the time. And when her competitor was out of her league, she had friends like Fallon who would protect her. Kendra may have a very sweet and petite exterior, but there was a cunningness within.

As for Kayden, he was a no-go. He was a dark horse whose loyalty lay wherever he saw the best outcome for himself—even joining those he had been against. Case in point, Ace and Fallon. He had outwardly stood against them up until when it suited him, then he was at our doorstep. As far as I was concerned, he offered nothing more than brute strength, which wasn't what I needed, so he was off the cards for me.

Besides, Zane and I combined would have at least half of Kayden's muscle … or maybe a third. Regardless, we had enough to fight anyone in our way, which was beside the point. My job during these trials was too important to not think critically about who I lay my trust in, and like Ace, I had zero confidence in Kayden's word.

I ascended the top of the stairs and approached the room Fallon, Zane, and Kendra were assigned.

My heart pounded in my chest. This part always had my nerves up.

Despite being invisible, opening a door when people were around to see it was a dead giveaway of my presence. I counted to three and hoped no one was in the dorm as I turned the handle and stepped inside.

I sighed, my shoulders relaxing when I found the room bare. I didn't know which bed was Mark's. They all looked the same, except for the one with PJs laying on it. Images of Zane riding dolphins covered the fabric; a pretty big clue as to who slept there.

I dropped my invisibility, not wanting to tire myself out unnecessarily. Wasting no time, I started toward one side of the room, searching the belongings around each bed. I ignored Zane's, checking the bunk above him to find a few familiar items of feminine clothing. I may have no issue rummaging around in Mark's stuff, but touching Fallon's things was a line I didn't want to cross. I quickly left her bed, moving to the bunk opposite.

There were the usual toiletries and clothing, as well as a hot pink bra wedged under a pillow. The bed above was empty, which meant the next bunk over must have been Mark's. There were a few personal items, but on closer inspection, I realised the haphazardly tossed objects were Zane's.

A sickening feeling told me I was too late.

Mark's belongings were gone. They had taken away any potential evidence of his illegal activities—all effects indicating he was ever here—and most likely disposed of them.

I startled when the door swung open and quickly returned my

invisibility. Zane walked in, dressed in light blue boardies and an open shirt that showed off his muscled abs. Careful not to make a sound, I froze, standing in the middle of the room, unsure whether he'd seen me at all.

But Zane was so preoccupied with whatever he was holding in his hands that I probably shouldn't have worried.

"The med staff are discriminating dories. But don't worry, you can hang out here. Everyone will love you," he said, talking in a soothing voice as he held his cupped hands close to his face. "You'll fit right in."

I raised a brow, wondering what the heck he was on about this time, only to jump back when Zane shouted in surprise. He shook out his hand, blood dripping from his thumb, and then he frowned down at the little crab sitting in the palm of his other hand.

"Not cool, Seb," he scolded the crab, his brows crinkled. "Rule one of being in the dorms: don't attack your roomies. Don't make me tell you about the last guy who got too handsy in here."

He lifted the blankets on an empty lower bunk and gently put the crab down, tucking it in like a kid being put to bed. I rolled my eyes with a reflexive smile tugging at my lips.

"Sleep off the bad mood, little dude. You have roomies to impress," he said, winking at the crab. "I'm off to check on my Starfish."

I shook my head. Bloody Zane. The guy was quirky as anything, but, strangely, I found him putting a crab to bed endearing. He was wearing me down with his overt affection, too. His declarations of being best friends and weird-ass stories were growing on me.

Make of that what you will.

Zane left, and I was about to follow him out when something stashed within the head of Mark's old bunk caught my eye.

As I stepped closer to the window, I spotted the refraction of light on the glass coming from his bedhead. Hidden as it was, the item would have been almost invisible if it weren't for how the light was hitting it at this moment.

I jimmied the glass slide out and twirled the item between two fingers. These things could hold so much—from data to programs to memories. A universal storage device.

It might not have anything to do with Mark, but I knew one thing for sure; whatever was on it was important enough for someone to smuggle it into the Academy and keep it hidden.

Now I just needed to access whatever was on it.

———— ✦ ————

As I pushed open the door to the caff that night, I was shocked to see how few Potentials were there. I hadn't seen many people since leaving the med bay and had passed that off as pure chance with everyone either recovering from injuries or resting. Now, I realised chance had nothing to do with it.

I'd expected the numbers would be down, but shit. The casualties were worse than I'd imagined. I gazed around at those who remained and wondered whether any would leave before the next trial. It would be the smart move. The chances of winning the Terrulian Trials and becoming the next ruler were slim, despite the rapidly declining numbers. Surely, the embarrassment of going home was minuscule compared to the threat of death?

Fallon and Kendra were easy to spot as I scanned the room. After grabbing a plate of food, I headed over to their table.

"How are you feeling?" I asked, looking Fallon over as I sat down. She had a few cuts and bruises on her face and neck, but her being out of bed was a good sign. My eyes went to her lips, and I could feel my skin heating at the reminder of the almost kiss we had earlier.

"I've been better," she replied with a shrug.

"You almost died. I think you're allowed to feel like shit for a few days," Kendra said, offering her a warm smile.

"The only thing bothering me right now is not knowing who helped me finish the trial *and*—" she turned to Kendra, raising her brows. "Who you were getting coffee with."

Kendra blushed. "Easy, tiger. Who says I was getting coffee with anyone exciting?" She tucked a strand of her dark hair behind one ear. "As for your first problem, I've asked around, but no one knows a thing. I think they were all too preoccupied with staying alive to notice anyone else.

Fallon pouted her lips, but let the former subject slide. My mind was already back in the trial.

I had barely been conscious at the end, and a large part of my memory was made up of blurs, strange smells, and screams.

"I see the angel bitch and nudist are friends now! Is that because you both like to get naked and fuck everything in sight?" one of Victoria's lackeys called as he swaggered towards the table.

"Gods dammit, Kayden," I muttered under my breath, giving the rumour spreader a filthy look. Kayden just gave me a shit-eating grin in response. "I don't fuck grapefruits," I told Fallon quietly.

She looked at me sympathetically and patted my chest. "I know, baby."

The guy reached our table, puffing his chest out as he grinned, glancing over to the table where his friends sat before looking back our way, his gaze landing on Fallon. "Do you fuck fruit like your friend here, or is a real dick a requirement?"

I slowly rose to my feet, anger coursing through me as I clenched my fists.

"Why?" Fallon said, raising a brow at the guy. "Did you want to join? You can bring the banana, seeing as your dick is too limp to count. Hell, why not make it a fruit salad?"

"You bitch!"

"This is your one and only chance to run along," I said through gritted teeth.

"Noah, I can fight my own battles," Fallon retorted.

But I couldn't let the guy's disrespect stand. If I was going to work with Fallon and help her get the crown, then we needed to eliminate threats. It was time to make people think twice about coming for us.

My hand snapped out, grabbing the guy's wrist, and I spun him around in one quick movement. I forced him to his knees beside Fallon, angling his arm behind him until he cried out in pain. Leaning forward, I spoke in a low voice. "Apologise."

Angling my head towards Fallon, I watched her glance at the guy on his knees, then up at me. Her cheeks were flushed and she bit her lip.

"Sorry," the guy whimpered.

"Sorry, who?" I prompted calmly.

The guy hissed through his teeth, but he wilted. "Sorry, Fallon."

I released him, not bothering to look his way as he scurried back to wherever he came from.

"Okay, even I found that hot," said Kendra, fanning herself with one hand.

"Uh-huh," Fallon agreed, looking deep into my eyes. I grinned at her as I sat down again. That was an unexpected yet welcomed outcome.

"Starfish!"

I swear everyone in the caff turned as one to see Zane shoving open the door and hurtling himself in our direction. He was completely oblivious to the rest of the room as he ran with his eyes fixed on Fallon and collided with another Potential.

"Shit," I breathed as the poor guy fell backwards onto a table, his tray flying from his hands.

Zane followed but manoeuvred himself like some sort of interpretive dancer, keeping himself from going down. The other guy wasn't so lucky, hitting the table hard and causing all the plates, as well as the occupants, to fall to the floor.

"Oh my fucking god!" Kendra burst out laughing, her brown eyes wide, and we watched as the tray soared through the air before landing upside down on some other Potential's lap. That guy jumped up and screamed about his burnt dick, whilst the first guy groaned where he lay crumpled on the floor.

Zane didn't seem to notice or care; he just kept moving even as the guy who'd insulted Fallon slipped on a banana and landed at Zane's feet. I chuckled. Cosmic karma. Zane simply leapt over the asshole and continued towards us, leaving a path of destruction in his wake.

"For the love of—" Fallon began, cut off as Zane descended upon her and wrapped his tanned arms around her. He pressed his lips to hers, squeezing her body tightly until she managed to get a hand free and slap him away.

"I went to the med bay, but they said you'd left, which I didn't believe because they are lying lionfish," Zane said, his words coming out a million miles a second as he casually dropped into the seat beside

Fallon. "So then I did my secret slippery seal move, only to see your bed *was* empty."

"And what move is that?" Fallon asked, tilting her head to one side.

"Can't tell you. If I did, it wouldn't be a secret anymore, would it?" He winked then sighed heavily. "I wouldn't have had to use it if they'd just let me pass."

"You *did* try to bring sea creatures into the med bay," Kendra said, barely containing her laughter. The fallen Potentials around us shot several nasty glares in his direction as if to prove her point.

"It's a medical fact that fish are good for your health," Zane grumbled, still oblivious to anyone not at our table. He hunched over and frowned at Fallon's plate, his chin resting on his hand. "It's not like I was trying to bring a tiger in there."

"Were you hoping people would eat them?" Fallon asked, frowning. I contemplated whether Zane wanted the med wing to incorporate fish into their patients' diets.

"Of course not!" Zane looked at her, his eyes wide. "They were for petting."

"Yes, because *that's* what the studies showed," I said, stabbing a carrot with my fork. "The health benefits come from petting them."

"Exactly!"

Fallon rolled her eyes and laughed. "How silly of me."

I grinned at her. She was gorgeous when she smiled, her face lighting up, though deep within her copper eyes, a sadness lingered. The contradiction made her even more alluring.

"So, is this our crew now?" Kendra asked, looking between us all.

"I think it will be good for us to stick together," I said between mouthfuls. "Forming groups increases our chances of survival and making it to the last trial significantly. Looking around, you can see the data backs it up. Victoria and Kayden's groups are still in higher numbers. And many of those no longer here were people who went it alone. Obviously, there are a few outliers, but that's expected."

Fallon hummed in agreement. "Noah's right. Things are only going to get worse. It makes sense to have allies."

"We can battle it out at the very end," Zane said as he stole Fallon's fork and began helping himself to her dinner. "And when I'm king, you can all be my advisors."

"Who says you're going to be king?" Fallon scoffed, snatching back her fork.

Zane pouted. "I'm king material, remember? Now give the king back his trident. I'm hungry."

"That's not how things work in Terrulia," Kendra said, chiming in. "Crowns, or in this case, forks, aren't just given to you."

"She's got a point, Zane." Fallon grinned mischievously, twirling the fork at him before holding it to her chest. "You're supposed to *win* them."

Zane's green eyes gleamed with the challenge. Then he was on her. Zane's hands were all over Fallon as he tried to kiss her into submission, but, of course, Fallon was way too stubborn to give up the utensil. She held the fork in an iron grip to her chest, laughing as he practically groped her. She eventually ceded to his lips, and the two started making out. I couldn't take my eyes from them, wondering what it would be like to kiss her. I'd been so close to finding out in the med bay. Not only that, but I wanted to explore every inch of her and discover what other sounds she made. What sounds she would make for only me.

I shook my head and noticed Kendra watching me. She sent me a knowing look, paired with a smirk. Shit. I needed allies in this place, but I had a feeling I was getting more than I bargained for, and I'd be lying to myself if I said I didn't want it.

KAYDEN

Whoever invented the burger was a stand-up bro or chick. I groaned as I bit into the beef patty. The cheese and bacon goodness tasted like carb-loading heaven after the scraps we'd had to survive on in the marshland. It had been a few days since we'd returned to the academy, and I was glad to be back. I reclined on my makeshift throne, feeling every inch a king with a girl in my lap and my minions around me. One of them was currently massaging my feet. I hadn't even asked, and she'd hopped straight to it.

"I knew you'd win, Kaydikins," the girl on my lap was saying as she wriggled to face me, stretching out so her tits threatened to fall out of her top. She was pretty, with long blond hair and big blue eyes, but she was nothing compared to a certain black-haired bombshell. "That Victoria bitch hasn't got shit on you."

"For fuck's sake, Chrissy. What did I tell you about mentioning that name?" I growled, slamming my burger on the table and accidentally squashing it, the patty oozing between my fingers. I looked around for a napkin, but there was none in sight.

Instead, I nudged the girl off me, and she pouted. "It's Crystal."

"Close enough." I waved a hand, and she scampered to a nearby chair, sulking. The red-haired girl at my feet grinned triumphantly, and the blond glared at her with daggers.

"Maybe he'd remember better if you didn't have the personality of a fucking rock," the redhead said snidely.

Casey's spine stiffened, her blond hair whipping as she turned on the girl. "No one asked you, Rayna," she snapped. "And besides, he *likes* rocks. Enough to go for round two."

A mistake I wouldn't make again, that was for fucking sure. The two of them were about as dull a lay as the desert I lived in, and that was saying something.

"You fucking whore," Ronda yelled, jumping to her feet.

Amused, I watched the girls get their claws out, resorting to hair pulling and slaps. It was laughable, but also undisciplined as fuck, and that just wouldn't do. "Enough," I barked and the women instantly stopped their bickering. "One, we don't lay hands on our own. Two, if you're going to resort to slapping and hair pulling, then what the fuck have I been training you for?!" I shook my head in disgust. "Drop and give me twenty. Next time you want to act like children, you can think twice about returning to this group."

They saluted me and hurried to do as commanded. I nodded in approval. "Honestly," I said to my other minions, "the bats make better company than these two."

They sniggered, agreeing with me easily. Too easily.

I sighed, looking at the empty chair beside me. The one reserved for Flynn, even though he wasn't around to fill it anymore. A big brute had already made the mistake of trying to sit there, and I'd thrown him across the room for his insolence. Fuckers.

These Potentials were mindless sheep. No one pushed me or bothered to do anything at all except sing my praises. Rightfully so, but fuck was it boring. Since the trial, I'd felt lost, even a little … lonely. It was absurd. The only way I'd staved off the emptiness was by running myself into a ragged, sweaty mess in the gym each day.

I'd never had a problem being alone. I was good at it, used to surviving any way I could. But after working with Fallon and the others, plus losing Flynn, things had changed.

With one last lingering look at the vacant seat, I scrubbed a hand over my face, searching the room for the angel herself. I spotted her sitting with Zane, Noah, and Kendra. They all laughed at a joke Zane had made, and something suspiciously resembling sadness pinged in my chest. *Weird.*

"This shit's getting old," I said to the guys at my table. "How about some wrestling in the gym? You"—I pointed at a dude as wide as a truck—"Show me what you've learnt under my watch. One on one."

The guy gulped audibly. "I, err, pulled a muscle on my morning run."

"Coward," I said, chuckling. "Anyone else? Come on weaklings, I ain't got all day."

They all made excuses. Every. Single. One. Since when was I commanding a bunch of pussies? And how the hell had they survived the first trial? I pulled my lips back in disgust. Mummies' boys, the lot of them.

I just needed to *feel* something. Talk to someone who bit back, pushed back. "Fuck this shit." I got up so quickly, the table screeched in protest as it slid across the floor. With a huff, I sucked up my pride and started making my way towards Fallon's table when I bashed into something hard and grumpy.

A big grin slid across my face as I saw who it was. Perfect. "Well, if it isn't Twiggy himself."

"Call me that one more time and I'll rip your fucking face off and feed it to you for breakfast," Ace said, his steely eyes fixed on me.

"What crawled up your ass and died?" I asked, folding my arms over my chest. Dude was angrier than usual, which was saying something.

"My sanity," he said with a scoff. "Disappeared the moment you rocked up. Now get out of my way."

My mouth quirked up on one side as I waited for him to take the bait. Because, of course, he wasn't about to back down. He was rearing for a fight as much as I was, and I could tell when someone needed to let off steam. Really, he should thank me for pushing his buttons. "And if I don't?"

The nerve in his neck pulsed. "You know I've killed men just for looking at me wrong, right? Don't test me, caveman." He rolled his neck, his stance shifting slightly. "Then again, I think I'd rather enjoy giving you a real red smile."

I snorted, gesturing at myself with a thumb. "Stone body, remember? I'll pummel your ass before you even get close."

"The same way I pummelled your mother's pussy last night?"

Oh, low blow, you slinky fuck. My chest puffed as I stepped into his space, the angry lines of his face tightening as he bristled at me. I flexed my fist to throw the first blow when someone walked into the room, stealing away my anger in one breath.

A fist cracked into my cheek, but I didn't even stagger, too distracted to care. Ace looked between my eyes, then stepped back. "What's the fucking problem now?" he snapped.

I turned his head slowly, to which he responded with a vicious growl. I ignored him, too focused on the blond as she strutted into the caff like she owned the place, a bunch of her groupies surrounding her.

"Victoria Auger," I said in a low voice. "She's alive?" The woman looked at me, her copper eyes narrowing as she slid one finger across her neck in a silent promise. "How the fuck did she make it?"

Ace punched me in the gut, making me drop my hand from his head. "Who the fuck cares?"

"She killed Flynn, took my garrison, and tried to kill some of our own," I said, raising my brows. "Bitch signed her own death warrant."

He looked at me blankly. "And you're telling me why?"

"We've gotta kill her, Twiggy." Like what wasn't the rakish little drake getting? I'd have thought he'd be first in line to take her out, psychotic as he was. I saw him take out Potentials in the trial. Guy killed with brutal efficiency and those were the skills I needed on my side, not those useless cretins back at my table.

He laughed coldly, shoving me out of his way, which was a mean feat for someone so much smaller. "Let's get one thing straight. We're not friends. Just because we helped each other in the first trial doesn't mean we're going to be best buds. I still hate you, and I couldn't care less about Fallon and the others."

My gaze hardened. "Glad we're on the same page."

Ace raised a brow. "Are we? Because two seconds ago you wanted to be chummy and bond over murder. Let me make this perfectly clear, I don't do shit out of the goodness of my heart because there is no good there. I do nothing that doesn't benefit me, Red. Get it through your thick skull. You are alone here. Your little friends that you care so much about?"

He looked pointedly at Fallon's table.

"I don't see them making space for you over there and, to me, they seem to be just fine with that." He patted me on the shoulder with three hard mocking slaps, then walked away, chuckling under his breath. "You're on your own shithead."

I stood there with my chest heaving and my skin growing hot as I mentally shook myself. What the fuck? Nobody spoke to me like that and got away with it. The guy was miserable and clearly had mummy and daddy issues. Yeah, that's all it was. He was just jealous I had people in my corner.

So why did I feel so crap? I looked at my followers, not giving two shits about the people there. When my gaze trailed back over to Fallon's table, I found it empty. Something clenched in my stomach, and I gritted my teeth, walking away.

Fine. I'd take care of Victoria myself.

I was just about to make my way over to her when my cuff pinged, alerting me to my next lesson. Magic theory. For fuck's sake. I threw a long look at that cold-hearted bitch before I left for class.

I passed Fallon on the way out of the caff, who'd stopped to chat with some rando. She looked perfect today, her long black hair bound in a messy bun, a black tank tucked into a short, check skirt with combat boots to top it off. The perfect blend of sweet and sexy.

"Looking good, Angel," I said with a sly grin, lifting my hand to salute her, only to realise there were still bits of burger smooshed between my fingers.

She laughed, waving back with a little wriggle of her own fingers, those luscious lips lifting in amusement.

For the love of fuck. I growled under my breath as I made my way into a bathroom. Everyone high-tailed it out immediately as they damn well should. After washing my patty-covered fingers clean, I slunk into the classroom. Apparently, Kendra, Zane, and Noah were allocated a different class, so the angel was on her own. I dropped into the seat next to her just as Victoria walked in, not even sparing me a second glance as she took her seat near the front.

Ace sauntered into class right after, looking even grumpier than usual. I looked pointedly at Victoria and then at Ace as if to say, 'I told you so', but the grumpy asshole just gritted his jaw and angled away from me.

Luna sighed, looking paler than usual. Her long hair was dishevelled and her usually sexy and pristine clothes looked ruffled. The look on the instructor's face and the coffee in her hand suggested it had been a long night. In fact, she almost looked … scared.

"You're late, Mr Warner, and my patience is wearing thin. Take a seat so we can get started."

The only remaining seat was on Fallon's other side, and Ace shot me a sly smirk as he slipped into it. The bastard was baiting me but he'd be eating that grin in a few seconds. For someone who claimed he didn't care about her, he sure seemed to linger conveniently close in classes we shared with her. Lying asshole.

Then I saw Fallon's face. She didn't even seem to notice Ace's presence. Her olive skin paled, those copper eyes tracking her sister's every movement. I didn't fail to notice her hands curling into fists as she squeezed them in her lap, and I grabbed one before she could split her skin with her new forest green nails. The colour reminded me of Noah and I wondered if he was the new flavour of the month.

Fallon snatched her hand out of mine, rolling her eyes as I scooted my chair over and draped an arm around the back instead. Ace shot me a murderous glare, his own seat shuffling the slightest bit closer to her.

"Miss me, Angel?" I said under my breath as the instructor started our lesson on magic theory. Today's class was about the growth of magical power over the decades. It was elementary stuff that anyone with a basic education should have been taught anyway.

When humans first developed magic, they weren't that strong, but now we were considerably more powerful. After we used up all of Earth's resources, effectively destroying the planet before we found our new home, humans had to make eco-friendly changes—harmonise with our surroundings. When first utilising the energy and magical properties of the crystals in Terrulia long ago, humans began to evolve. We developed adaptations according to our habitats—the five cities—and then we learned to harness magic. Now, we were the ultimate species.

Fallon's lips twitched like she had almost broken a smile. "Should I have?"

Saucy little minx, always playing hard to get. I grinned. "Don't play coy with me. You started something in the trial, and I'm waiting to continue where we finished."

She snorted. "You'll be waiting a while then, boulder boy."

I flexed my muscles, enjoying the way her gaze caught on my biceps. "That's not a very nice way to thank me."

Her nose crinkled. "Thank you for what?"

Luna began addressing the class, bringing up a graphic of telekinetic magic which showed its gradual progression in strength and area usage since humans first arrived to Terrulia, to the present day. I ignored her, leaning in to whisper in Fallon's ear. She had already turned her attention to the teacher.

"For saving your perky ass back at the end of the trial."

She gasped under her breath and her head turned to mine, giving me the perfect opportunity to claim a kiss. Her eyes widened even more as I pressed my mouth onto hers, my tongue sweeping over her lips in a promise for more.

It took her way too long to push me away, which I knew she eventually would. The girl had too much pride to allow anything less.

"What the fuck, Kayden?" she hissed under her breath.

I just chuckled, shooting Ace a shit-eating grin over her head. His eyes narrowed into slits, pure murder flashing in their depths.

Fallon shifted into view, and I watched as she cocked her head, the rage rushing out of her.

"You're serious, aren't you?" She shook her head. "Why?"

I shrugged, searching for an excuse. "I thought it'd piss Victoria off." She looked at me sceptically, and I just couldn't help myself. "And maybe I wanted to help you."

A bang sounded next to her, and she jumped, turning towards Ace, whose bionic hand was threatening to snap the table in half from where he stood, pressing down on it. The class looked at him with wide eyes but quickly averted them when seeing his lethal scowl.

"I helped too," he blurted, which only made him seem to get angrier at the slip. "Just thought you should know," he growled, sitting back down.

I scooted my chair closer. "It was mostly me, though, so I'm thinking you owe me."

Fallon turned her beautiful face back my way and rolled her eyes. "What do you want, Kayden?"

My name sounded so good on her lips. I wanted her to scream it while I was buried inside her. But first things first, I wanted something I had never really wanted with a girl before.

"A date."

Her eyes shot up, and she smiled slightly. "I—"

Ace scoffed, then moved his chair closer to her, scowling. One of his hands lifted to curl a strand of her loose hair around his finger almost possessively.

My chest rumbled with annoyance. He was throwing off my game and he knew it. "What? You think she'd rather go on a date with you instead?"

Fallon burst out laughing as though the idea was absolutely appalling to her. "Why the hell would I want to go on a date with a guy who'd happily murder me in my sleep?" she said accusingly.

I grinned. 1-0 to Kayden. Ace could eat my dick. Or not, because I hoped that would be Fallon soon after I gave her the best date ever.

"Yeah, Twiggy," I agreed with her, scooting my chair as close as it could go and putting my hand on her arm. "No one wants a permanent storm cloud raining on our fun."

Fallon swivelled. "I didn't say I'd go on one with you either," she snapped.

Ace shot out of his seat, his eyes like twin blades stabbing into me. The entire room turned to look at him, but the fucker took his time like he owned the place. Before he exited, he leant down, whispered something in Fallon's ears that made her cheeks redden, and rested a hand on her leg, dangerously close to the apex of her thighs.

She wriggled as his hand climbed her leg, the tiniest squeak escaping her as she looked at him. What the fuck? Had he … had they?

Red coated my vision, and I leapt out of my chair. "Take your fucking robot hand off her," I roared.

"Kayden," Luna said with a gasp.

Ace's lips curved. "Make me, you stony prick."

"Ace," Luna snapped, trying to control the situation.

We both ignored her.

"What the fuck is happening?" Fallon said, sliding deeper into her seat.

I puffed my chest and Ace squared his jaw, his hand reaching for something in his pocket. Before either of us could take a swing, we were blasted off our feet and out of the door.

"Both of you take it outside," Luna shouted.

Ace and I glanced at each other. I looked him up and down before he sneered and walked off. The classroom door closed, leaving me alone in the hall.

The fucker had lied to me. He *was* interested in Fallon. Well, he could get in line, because Fallon was going to be mine, and anyone who had a problem with that had an appointment with my fists.

My chest heaved for a few moments as I stood there, my hands curling into fists. I needed to let some steam off or my minions were going to have a very bad day. Just before I turned towards the gym, though, a flash of blond caught my eye, and I grinned.

On second thought…

I followed Victoria as she slunk down the hall, swishing her hips like she owned the fucking place. She must have snuck out of class or made an excuse, which meant she wouldn't be missed. And for what I had planned? The backstabbing bitch had it coming.

Before I could grab her wrist, she spun, somehow pinning a blade at my throat in less than two seconds. The sharp metal drew a bead of blood where she pressed it to my skin, but I ignored the sharp sting. I'd been itching for a fight all morning.

"Come to get revenge for your long lost friend?" She sneered, and the utter satisfaction on her pretty face made my blood boil.

"His name was Flynn, and you'd best remember it."

She smiled coldly. "It was so easy to dispatch him, but I'm not so easy to kill, Hale. You should know that by now."

It was amusing, how tough she thought she was. I shot her a cocky smile, then grabbed her hand holding the blade and squeezed until the joints crunched against each other. The weapon dropped and her back was arching from the pain.

"I know a roach when I see one," I agreed. "You should have died on the battlefield, but you just keep crawling back. You were right about one thing though. I do want revenge, and if your sister doesn't kill you, I will."

She smirked. "Aw, how sweet. The dumb brute feels the need to protect his damsel in distress."

"The dumb brute could break your hand and wrist without a second thought."

Victoria's face contorted, and she lashed out with her free hand, trying to punch me in the throat. I blocked the attack easily, then grabbed her by the neck and lifted her against the wall. She scratched at my hand and tried to kick me in the balls, but I lodged my thigh against her legs.

"I'll say this only once. Stay away from Fallon. You and me? We have unfinished business, but unlike you, I don't get others to do my dirty work, nor will I cause a scene at the academy. We'll settle this in the next trial, Victoria, mark my words."

Her face was bright red as she flailed, and I eased my grip just a little. I could crush her so easily, watch the light go out of those cold, dead eyes. I had never hurt a woman before—at least, not outside of the trials—and certainly had no trouble putting those who did out of their misery, but Victoria Auger was an exception. She was a stone-cold killer.

Today was her lucky day though. Revenge could wait and at the very least, I'd bought Fallon some time away from her psycho sister.

"Kayden?"

I turned, finding Zane and Noah watching with wide eyes. With a huff, I let Victoria go. She immediately began gulping deep breaths of air. Just to be safe though, I picked up her small blade and pocketed it. Unsurprisingly, by the time I turned around, she was gone.

"What was that about?" Noah asked curiously.

"Who cares?" Zane said, patting me on the back with a laugh. "That shit was gnarly, and Kayden was defending Starfish's honour. The pod is back!"

I sighed and shook my head, not even bothering to figure out what that meant. "Victoria and I were due for a little chat, but Zane's right. She won't be bothering Fallon for a while."

"Or you've just made things worse," Noah pointed out.

The notion had my stomach twisting. Maybe he was right. I wouldn't put it past Victoria to retaliate harder now.

That uncomfortable thought followed me around for the rest of the day.

FALLON

It was a quiet, balmy night, the light of the moon shining down through the open windows in my dorm room. During my fitful sleep, Zane must have tucked himself into my bed, because he lay sprawled out beside me, one arm snug around my waist.

I stared at his beautiful face, admiring the curves of his jaw and cheeks, the ash-coloured brows arching over those pretty eyes closed in sweet sleep. Utterly gorgeous. Model material—even boyfriend material—if we weren't fighting for a throne.

I'd never dared to hope for such things. Not with my parents and the underworld I'd grown up in. Inviting strangers into my life was as good a way as any to get a guy's throat slit. Too many curious questions or glances, and Victrus and Eliana wouldn't hesitate to end a relationship before it had even begun. They'd taught me that lesson very early on.

So I'd stuck to fucking, fighting, and being alone. It's what I did best. No distractions, no guilt, no ruined lives because of me. I had enough blood on my hands as it was. They'd just keep getting bloodier with the trials to come, which is why, for one hopeful moment, I stopped to consider … what if? What if I just enjoyed whatever this was between Zane and me, or any of the others? There didn't need to be strings attached, and it's not like my parents were watching.

I scowled.

Victoria, on the other hand, would likely report back on everything she saw. I nuzzled into Zane's chest, burying my head in his shoulder. He sighed softly in his sleep, a few muffled snores escaping those luscious lips as his arm tightened and pulled me closer.

The bitch just had to survive, didn't she? Like a roach, she just kept coming back to haunt me. Seeing her in class was playing mind games with my head, throwing me off kilter. I felt paranoid, looking for monsters in the shadows, hearing danger in the small sounds of everyday life.

I needed a drink, or a fuck, or maybe just … shit, I dunno. Some fresh freaking air. Sleep certainly wasn't coming to me tonight, so maybe a short flight would help. With a small sigh, I wriggled out from under Zane's arm and crept down the bunk ladder, sneaking a look at the empty bed that had been Mark's. At least I had one less ballbag to worry about and could feel relatively safe with Kendra and Zane as my bunkmates.

Speaking of … Kendra's bed was empty, nothing but a pink, glitter hair clip on the pillow which was so not her usual style. I raised a brow, checking the bathroom, but nope, dark and quiet. Where was my ninja best friend? I smirked. Hopefully, having a better night than me. Either way, she was damn well keeping secrets, and I had every mind to dig some answers from the devil. Later though. For now, the open sky was calling my name.

With a yawn, I slid on some sneakers and padded to the nearby window, cracking it open and slipping outside onto the small balcony. The warm air was fresh, smelling faintly of the grassy fields and flowers in the nearby woods.

I conjured my wings, readying to dive off the balcony, when a strange sound ruptured the stillness. It was silenced as quickly as it came. I frowned, screwing my nose up. Was that a scream? It was too quick to be sure, but whatever it was, it didn't sound good.

Naturally, I had to investigate. Against my better judgement, of course, but shit … this academy was nothing if not interesting. And yeah, I guess if someone needed help, I should probably do something. I could pretend that's why I went looking for the source, but nah, I was definitely intrigued more than anything. I guess a life lived in crime will do that to a girl.

At this point, nothing would surprise or scare me.

I free-fell off the balcony, enjoying the giddy feeling of the ground rushing up to meet me, beating my wings at the last minute and soaring into the sky. I had keen eyes, used to night runs when Victrus had forced me to run drugs or crystal caches to esteemed clientele like a freaking pack mule.

No one had ever dared touch me when I'd stepped into those dens, but then, I'd never given them any sign that leering faces or the dozens of pulse guns flashing in their holsters had done anything to scare me. I was an Auger, and even I could admit that the name gave me strength. It gave me power over my enemies, and I had plenty of those.

The sound had come from somewhere near the Damascon Hollow training arena because, of course, it was in the darkest and most dangerous-looking spot. I huffed a breath, doing a fly-over to check for any possible assassins sneaking around, but it looked clear. Instead, I found a body sprawled on the ground, and my heart surged as I spotted the slick, wet substance pooling around it.

Ho-ly crap on a cracker. I fluttered down, dismissing my wings as I cautiously tiptoed towards the body and crouched. A slim, tanned guy with brown hair and blue eyes, dressed in gym gear. Handsome, beneath all the blood and gore. His throat was viciously sliced, and more than a few holes riddled his chest and stomach from stab wounds. From the way he had fallen and the one hand lying near his throat, I'd bet he didn't even see the attack coming.

Poor guy never stood a chance. I had to wonder what he'd done to deserve such a cruel fate.

My gut churned.

I'd seen this kind of violence before. The sliced throat I could accept was efficient, but the brutality of the rest suggested whoever did this had damn well liked it. Or had a bad day. Who's to say?

I swallowed the lump in my throat and made to stand. A firm hand clamped over my mouth, stifling my rising scream as I was dragged back into the shadows. I lashed out, but my attacker had a powerful grip, and only when I was swivelled around to meet familiar brown eyes and a finger to their lips did I relent.

The hand over my mouth eased, and I glared, shooting daggers at the handsome face before me. “What the fuck, Noah?”

“Quiet,” he said, nodding over my shoulder. “Someone’s coming.” He pulled me deeper into the shadows, turning me so my back slammed against the wall and his mouth neared my own while he covered me. Unnecessary, and dare I say a little possessive?

I couldn’t help feeling a little turned on by the dominance in this quiet, calculating man. And after that near kiss the other day … I suppressed a shiver as his hands shifted from where they grasped my wrists, still restraining me.

Our breath mingled, and I had the sudden realisation that he was naked as *something* skimmed my threadbare shorts. He seemed to realise too, because even in the dark, I swear I could see his cheeks flush.

My lips quirked as I prepared to say something catty, but he slapped that hand over my mouth again, whispering in my ear, “Be still.”

Voices met my ears, and I stiffened, falling silent as the most unexpected group of people walked into full view of the moonlight. Holy shit. I shifted Noah’s hand. “The Masters,” I mouthed, watching his eyes crinkle with confusion, then narrow as he listened in.

“Oh, dear. Oh, this isn’t good. Not good at all,” the Overseer mumbled as she looked down at the body along with the Magic Master Luna, the Combat Master Nolan, and the Mind Master Jeremiah beside her.

I rolled my eyes at her batty behaviour because *no shit*. The four looked suspect as hell, and not what I’d call surprised, either. What on earth was going on here? I shuffled to peer around Noah’s shoulder, feeling his junk move against me as I did and suppressing a grin as he stiffened.

“What are we going to do about this?” Luna hissed, chewing on one of her long, scarlet nails. “If the student find out…”

“They won’t,” Nolan snapped. “We’ll dispose of the body and get this mess cleaned up before morning. The other Potentials will just assume he died in the first trial.”

“And the message?” Jeremiah asked, his face blank of emotion. “Our network is encrypted—there are security measures in place to prevent contact from external lines. How did they get our numbers?”

Nolan swore under his breath. "I don't give a shit how," he said with an irritated shake of his head. "I want to know who, and when I find out, I'm going to rip their fucking head off."

Damn. The combat trainer was psychotic. Probably all those failed dreams haunting him every night. I'd come to expect his bad moods now, alongside Luna's creepy wraithlike qualities—haunting beauty aside. I knew little about Jeremiah except for the fact that he was much too handsome to be a freaking teacher. Short brown hair, green eyes, muscles … a sex dream on legs, if not for his age. Okay, even then.

"Whoever it is has all the power right now," Luna whispered, tilting her head as she looked at the dead guy. "We all have secrets. They can blackmail or strong-arm us into doing whatever they want at this stage and we have nothing to hint at who they are. Let's face it, right now they have the upper hand."

"So we'll change our numbers," Nolan said with a huff. "Improve our systems."

Jeremiah arched a brow. "This hacker bypassed some of the best security measures in Terrulia. They murdered a student, tipped us off, and scrambled our systems. You think changing our number is going to protect us?"

"Silence, all of you," Celeste said, massaging her temple, then breaking into a serene smile. "One problem at a time. First, let's dispose of the body. Speak of this to no one. As far as I'm concerned, we never saw anything tonight."

Nolan grumbled something under his breath, but before I knew it, he and Jeremiah had carried off the body. Then Luna and Celeste used their combined magic to wipe the scene clean of any evidence there had been a murder at all.

What. The. Fuck.

When they were gone, my shoulders sagged, and I released a breath. Noah was still caging me in against the wall, looking at me intently. I wriggled my fingers, then batted my lashes. "You gonna tie me up, or are we just going to stand here all night?"

He shook his head, then let me go and stepped back, much to my disappointment. "Shit. Sorry." My eyes immediately travelled to his exposed dick—gods damn, it was impressive even now—and he shuffled, the smallest hint of a smile curving his full lips. "Give me one minute. Don't go anywhere."

I huffed once he'd left, looking at the space he had been not moments before. Only then did it really sink in. These people had let someone get away with murder and barely batted an eye. Whoever it was, they must have some pretty big shit on the Masters to make them so compliant. Blackmailing the teachers of the most esteemed academy in Terrulia? Murdering someone on campus? Whoever this was had them tied around their little finger. If word got out to Terrulian officials that Potentials were dying at the academy outside of the trials, there would be a full-scale investigation and uproar among the Houses. Dying in the trials was one thing, but at the academy where there was nothing to gain or prove—no honour in it at all—was another thing completely. Scandalous even. Celeste and the Masters would lose their jobs at best if this got out, and who knows what would happen after?

Murder outside of the trials was, of course, against the law, so I had to wonder how the Masters and Celeste would cover this up. It made no fucking sense, really. When it came to the trials, Houses were informed of their candidates' progress via a ranking system and were provided limited footage for their viewing pleasure. Worse, the elite could place bets on Potentials. It was sick, and one thing I wanted to remove asap when I became queen. Who the fuck thought it was a good idea to make us compete like this for the crown?

Noah jogged back to the clearing, dressed in shorts and a tank. Double disappointing.

"We'd better get moving," he said, eyeing off the arena warily. "I don't want to be found at the scene of a crime, not that you can tell it was one anymore."

I grumbled in agreement and we walked towards the woods. "So, we're going to talk about what just happened, right? Because that was some intense shit."

He grimaced, shaking his head. "What I don't understand is why the culprit would tip off the Masters in the first place."

"It's a scare tactic," I said simply, not even having to question that.

My parents were well-versed in threats, or just plain chopping up victims to serve as reminders to the people in their dominion. "Their way of warning the Masters just what they're capable of, and what will come if they don't comply with his or her terms." I smiled slightly. "Honestly? I kinda want to know what they've got on the Masters now. Must be pretty big."

Noah looked at me. Something I couldn't read flitted so quickly over his features, I almost missed it. The guy was damn near unreadable when he wanted to be, and it was infuriating.

"You're not even phased by what we just saw, are you?"

I sighed. "Noah, when your parents are the leaders of a country-wide crime syndicate, you sort of just … stop noticing."

His brows raised like he'd never understand that. "Damn, that's fucked up." Then he shot me a look suspiciously close to pity, and I felt myself harden, the cold, dead thing in my chest remembering it didn't—shouldn't—care what he thought. The last thing I wanted was anyone's pity because of who I had been born to. My blood didn't define who I was.

"It's getting late," I said quietly. "I should get back to my dorm. Later, Hawthorn."

"Fallon, wait," Noah said, grabbing my wrist.

I looked pointedly at my wrist, but the fucker didn't let go. In fact, his expression tightened. Oh? He wanted to play with the big, bad Auger girl, did he?

"I didn't mean…" He grunted in frustration, something primal in that tone making me straighten. "Just stay. Please."

I looked at his hand again, and he let go, allowing me to cross my arms under my breasts and glare at him. "What do you want, Noah?"

He sighed. "There's something I've been meaning to tell you."

When I didn't say anything, he just cleared his throat and continued. "You already know Mark's little lackeys had gathered a group of Potentials in the trial."

My brow rose. "Go on."

"What you don't know is that Mark was planning to sell them to another buyer outside of the trials. He and several others have been trafficking humans for slavery long before we came to the academy."

"What?" The statement was so unexpected I had to press my fingers to my temple. "How do you know this?"

His face darkened, his eyes narrowing. "When Victoria was torturing me, she let it slip. And she was involved, Fallon. House Jupiter, too."

My body jerked. Oh, fuck. I wanted to believe what Noah was saying wasn't true, but it made way too much sense not to. The workers at the crystal mines in Stormcrest? Suddenly, the idea of human trafficking just fit perfectly in the larger puzzle. I'd thought the 'employees' had signed contracts without knowing what they were getting themselves into, but it would seem they had never signed anything at all. It was all just a front to make the business appear legitimate.

"Say I believe you," I said slowly. "What does this have to do with the murder? Better still, why are you so invested in this? It fucking sucks, but what had you hoped to achieve by following Mark? You already said you don't want to be king."

He looked away, and I got the sense he wasn't ready to tell me his real motives. "All of this … it involves some people I care about. That's all you need to know for now."

"Fine." I chewed my lip and tossed my hair, choosing to let it slide. For now. "I'm going to go out on a limb here and say you think the trafficking is somehow connected to this murder and the Masters?"

He smiled slightly at my sarcasm, but he shrugged. "I can't confirm anything just yet, but my instincts tell me yes. I might have forgotten to mention that when I went into the marsh to discover the person Mark had been meeting with, I found a Drake insignia stamped on the helicopter."

I rolled my eyes. Doubtful. Smart ass didn't seem likely to forget anything of the kind.

"So my sister, House Jupiter, and potentially one of the most notoriously violent gangs, could all be tied up in some bigger power play and potentially murdering students and blackmailing the academy. Peachy."

"Yeah, no big deal," he replied sarcastically.

I rubbed my temples. "So we continue hunting for answers and keep our heads low. With another player on the board, this is getting even more dangerous. Now more than ever, we need to watch each other's backs."

He grinned. "You scratch my itch. I'll scratch yours."

"Oh, honey," I said with a sly smile. "Be careful what you wish for."

His eyes gleamed, his expression turning hungry as he gazed at the thin pyjamas I wore, right as a cool breeze wafted on through and hardened my nipples. His gaze dropped, and he didn't even bother to hide his blatant stare.

My smile widened. "Are we done here?"

"Not quite," he said, his expression contemplative as he took a step toward me.

"What now?" I drawled, tilting my head.

"Just this."

He captured my mouth with his, grabbing my chin and forcing my head to tilt up as he consumed my every being, owning my every thought as he crashed into me. My lips parted in a soft sigh, and he swept in, his tongue curling against my own in pure carnal need. It was so unexpected coming from Noah. But I rolled with it, my fingers curling in the material of his shirt. Minutes might have passed, or maybe even hours. I lost track of time as this guy possessed my every attention and I drowned in the most amazing kiss.

It was only when a bird or some other critter rustled a nearby branch, nearly scaring me to death, that we broke apart. He chuckled, almost shyly, which gave me fucking whiplash from the sudden change of intensity.

"It's neither a bed nor a room, but I think you got my point. Be seeing you, Fallon," he said quietly, and for once I was the one standing there like a stunned mullet, usually the one doing the ghosting.

"Noah, wait," I called. He glanced over his shoulder, stopping in his tracks. "You never told me what you were doing tonight before you found me."

He cocked his head, looking like a predator, his dark skin gleaming in the moonlight. When he spoke at last, it was quiet.

"I was following someone. Someone whose tail I lost not long before

I arrived at the scene of the crime."

Oh, shit. "Who?" I asked, frowning.

"You really wanna know?"

I almost growled in frustration. Based on what he'd just told me, I had an idea, but suspense was only good if I was the one being all mysterious.

"For fuck's sake, Noah, just tell me."

His next words came as no surprise, but they sliced through me all the same.

"Ace."

ZANE

I swam towards the edge of the lake of the mini Tritosa City, loving the feel of the water against my skin. Nothing beat getting wet at sunrise. Each stroke eased the tension in my shoulders and cleared the bogus thoughts swimming around in my head.

Since the first trial, I'd been down here every morning for a dip to wet my gills and just chill. It wasn't the same without Pip and Delilah, but I'd have to make do without my dolphins for a little while longer. Back home, a swim with them was all I needed to cheer me up when I was feeling crabby. Or I could at least use my magic to mellow out the negative emotions. Unfortunately for me, the Masters still had my power locked behind the chip beneath my skin.

I wasn't a sheltered sea snail, but the trial sure exposed me to some gnarly shit. So I'd started snuggling into Fallon's bed at night. I really needed to mellow; sleeping with Starfish was hot, but the dreams were far from it. And who wants to dream about monsters ripping bodies apart when they are snuggling with a total babe?

Not me. Nope.

Our time at the academy was temporary, but I was starting to think Starfish wasn't. I enjoyed hanging out with her, even when there was no exploring beneath her clothes. And I'd learnt from our shower together that there was a lot to like in that department. I'd even started imagining bringing her home to ride the waves at my beach.

Yeah, I definitely needed to get her out on the water, but right now,

I needed to think of anything other than Fallon. I was nearing the shore and my dick would salute the other Potentials if I didn't get the dude under control.

Think, Zane, think.

Blobfish. Zeke hurling on his freshly waxed board. Sand in my butt crack. Fallon's butt. Shit, no. Overfishing. Zariah's gnarly toes. Giant bats. Dragons.

I sighed bubbles into the water. That was close. My feet hit the lake floor, and I strode from the water, scrunching my toes in the sand with each step. It was such a good natural exfoliator. I bet I had the softest feet at the academy. Probably Terrulia if I was being honest.

I grabbed my towel from where I'd left it on the sand, drying myself off. I was careful not to break any of the shells plaited in my hair as I rubbed my head and strode to the cafeteria in only my boardies. They were a cool lilac colour with eggplants all over them. My brother Zach gave them to me for my birthday, and they seemed fitting, seeing as purple was the colour of royalty and I'm gonna be king and all that. My stomach growled and I pet it with my free hand, calming the beast until I could feed it. It was a quick walk and soon I was stepping foot into the cafeteria. I breathed in deeply, the smell of bacon, eggs, and all kinds of baked breads filling my nose. *Mmm.*

The trials might kill us, but at least the food was good. I filled my plate, then searched the room for my Starfish, spotting her at a table with Noah. My eye twitched at the sight of them together, whispering secrets to each other. Noah may be the shiny new toy gaining all of her attention, but I wasn't about to give up without a fight. I thought we were going to be besties, but the dude was muscling in on my reef.

Growing up with six siblings had given me a competitive streak and the stamina to outlast anyone who tried to take what was mine. One time, I was chilling on the beach with Zion when he told me he could balance a tower of ten shells on his forehead. I practised every day for months until I could do twice as many. When I proved to him nearly a year later that I was the best, he feigned not knowing what I was on about. Must have crushed him to see me beat him at that.

I sat opposite Fallon and Noah, dropping my plate onto the table, and threw my wet towel at Noah's head. Stretching my arms behind me, I flexed my muscles, showing off my bare chest. I looked good, all tanned and well defined. Fallon wasn't shy about looking my way, her copper eyes taking in every inch of me appreciatively.

Yeah, she wanted me.

"Like what you see?" I drawled, sending her a wink. I stretched a leg under the table and wedged it between her and Noah. "Soak it all in, Starfish."

Noah dragged the towel from his face, rolled it into a ball, and threw it back at me with such force that I almost fell off my chair. *Rude.*

"Woah, dude."

"As I was saying," Noah said, adjusting himself in his seat so that he was facing Fallon and drawing her attention away from me. "We need to keep an eye on Ace."

"Why? Are you scared of him?" I scoffed, then raised an arm and flexed my bicep. "I can handle him."

"I'm sure you can. The other Potentials talk all the time about how strong you are. It's a regular topic of conversation," Noah said.

"More often than they talk about you dicking grapefruit?" I replied, doing my best to keep my face straight, which was hard because Starfish was snickering up a storm. "Anyway, Ace was fine with us during the trial, and pumped when I gave him his hand back," I said, looking around the cafeteria for the dude in question.

He wasn't in yet, but that wasn't exactly suspicious. Ace avoided social situations as much as possible. Although not when he was grateful to the dude who kept his hand safe. Ace had practically thrown himself at me, and can I just say, the dude knew how to hug. Odd considering he didn't have any family to cuddle up with, but I wasn't complaining. I was going to remember it as one of the best hugs of my life, and that's saying something.

"What makes you think he's a shark in the waters now?"

"Noah was following him last night," Fallon said in a low voice.

She leaned forward in her seat, giving me a great view of her sweet boobs. Low cut tops should be her mandatory uniform. That and her short-shorts.

"He lost Ace's tail right before someone was murdered."

Murder? That was ice water over the sexy images I had of Fallon in my mind.

"And what? You think Ace did it?"

"Look, before I say anything, I want to make sure that we all agree that what is said between us, stays between us?"

I nodded along with Noah because, duh, we were besties and besties didn't tell each other's secrets.

"We don't know, but he's a suspect," Noah said once he saw we were all surfing the same wave. He looked thoughtfully at his food, pushing his eggs around with his fork.

The dude said once that even when I wasn't talking, I was talking, but he totally did it, too. The only difference was he kept it all in that noggin of his. Thoughts were best shared, or they bottled up. When that bottle popped it was no champagne party, let me tell you.

"We think the Overseer and Masters are being threatened," he continued. "They were worried and covered up the evidence."

"They can't keep it a secret forever," Fallon said. "The students need to know they are in danger."

"There's always danger here."

I nodded, agreeing with Noah. If any of the Potentials here thought they were safe, they were as blind as a jellyfish.

"Yeah, during the trials," Fallon replied, sitting back in her seat and folding her arms over her chest. "But we're not in a trial right now, are we? It's wrong to keep it from everyone."

"You know what else is wrong," I said, looking across the room to where Kayden was sitting with Dick. "The rip that's refusing to let Kayden sail a wave to join us."

"A rip?" Noah asked, quirking a brow.

I nodded, feeling as salty as the sea with Kayden's current choice of seating. "His stubbornness, that's the rip. He needs to give in and settle into our reef. We all know he's part of our pod. What happened between him and Victoria proved that."

"What happened with him and my sister?" Fallon asked, looking between me and Noah.

"He defended you," Noah replied. "Threatened Victoria and told her to stay away."

Fallon frowned. "I don't—"

"Need protecting," I said, finishing her sentence and grinning at her. "But even you would have been impressed with his whole alpha male thing." I looked back over at Kayden. "Maybe I should go ask him to come over?"

"Who are we talking about?"

Crabs at a cocktail party! I almost jumped out of my skin. I'd been too busy watching Kayden sitting with Dick that I didn't even notice when Kendra turned up and slipped into the chair beside me so soundlessly.

"Someone was murdered last night. The Overseer and Masters are freaked out and covered it up. And as a surprise to exactly no one, Ace is up to no good," Fallon replied, filling her friend in. "I think that's it, but it's only morning, so who knows what else we can add to that list? I would have told you earlier, but you weren't in our dorm this morning."

"I was getting coffee," Kendra said with a smirk. "With my new friend."

Judging by the way she didn't look at anyone when she said it made me think she was lying. Kendra was hiding something.

"Can you really call them your new friend anymore?" Fallon asked with a raised brow.

Kendra bit her lip as she smiled. "Maybe not."

Our table fell into conversation, Fallon and Noah recounting the events of the previous night, but I couldn't concentrate. Kendra was up to something. She'd been out all night and none of us had met this mystery person she'd been meeting up with—if they even existed. Who knew what she had really been up to with all her frequent disappearances? And then there was the dead dude that she slipped something to in the med bay...

I stifled a gasp by shoving a piece of toast into my mouth and almost sending it down my windpipe. I punched my chest, clearing my airways. My eyes watered, but I didn't care. My mind was on one thing.

Seb.

I'd searched the entire dorm the other day and couldn't find my crustacean friend anywhere. Then, Kendra had stepped out of the bathroom and pretended like she had no clue where the crab was.

She had been the only one there, so who else could it have been?

Statistics say you're most likely going to be killed by someone you're close to. Well, she had the bunk right next to his.

Was there a possibility I'd lost my touch? I'd wrongly given Kendra the benefit of the doubt.

Buzzing sounded around the room as everyone's cuffs flashed with a notification. Must have been some message from the Overseer if everyone was getting it. I didn't have my cuff on me, so I leant to the side to see Kendra's screen. A picture of a guy with his throat cut and multiple stab wounds to his chest.

Slap me on the sunburn.

"Oh, shit," Kendra breathed as the cafeteria erupted into conversation around us. "I'm guessing this is the murder you saw?"

"You tell us," I said, leaning in closer to Kendra. She frowned at me, and it was almost believable, but I was on to her like a barnacle on a whale.

"Yup. So much for the Overseer's cover up," Fallon said, giving me a salty look. "I wish I knew who did it. Any ideas?"

Kendra shrugged, looking all innocent. She was playing the part to a tee. "I think nearly everyone here is capable of it. I'm sure your sister doesn't need much of a reason to do something like that."

"She's crazy enough to send out photos of her crime, too," I said, nodding, but I saw through Kendra's ploy to point a finger at the most obvious suspect. Victoria was a vicious bitch who loved to gloat.

"She's definitely a suspect." Fallon chewed her lip, which was super distracting. I almost drifted out to the sexy sea in her rip. I shook my head. Focus, Zaney. "The Overseer seemed to think it was someone from the outside."

"Either way," Noah began, taking Fallon's hand in his. He had nice hands—good size—and I bet they were the perfect balance between soft and rough. I would have told him that if he didn't have them all over my Starfish. "Probably best if you stay with me from now on so I can watch your back."

Fallon scoffed. "I don't need a babysitter."

"Not a babysitter. A sexy bodyguard," I said, agreeing with Noah.

Fallon looked between us; her brows creased. "Are you two ganging up on me?"

"Don't act like you don't like it," Kendra said, drawing all our attention to her. She quickly raised her hands in defeat at Fallon's glare. "Shit, sorry, it just slipped out."

I sat up straight, grinning at my Starfish, only for it to slip from my face like melted ice cream from a cone. Ace strode into the cafeteria all crabby, Potentials darting out of his path as he made his way to the front of the queue for food.

"Maybe Ace took the photo," Kendra said, her eyes never leaving the tattooed dude. "Didn't you say you lost his tail, Noah?"

Again, she was pointing fingers at the obvious dudes. She was desperate to cover her tracks, but I saw what she was doing. The water was clear in this bay.

"Anything is possible with Ace," Fallon replied. "As long as he gets something out of it, I'd say he is capable of anything you can imagine."

Fallon may have been right about Ace in some ways, but it was clear she was blind to another little shark in our midst.

ACE

If anything made me feel like I was back home in DH, it was getting on with business after a murder. The other Potentials might be struggling with the concept, but the Masters were behaving like it was the same shit, different day. Which it was.

It blew my mind the way the other Potentials were pissing themselves about a murder outside of a trial. When we were kidnapped into this joint, there were over one hundred Potentials. Now there were less than half. Did they think the others had scurried home to their mummies and daddies?

It may have been illegal to kill someone outside the trials, but the law meant shit all when wealthy families could manipulate it with their credits and power.

What did it matter if you died in a trial or at the academy? Either way, there were only a finite number of people who would walk away from this place. You know who wasn't going to be one of them?

Danger Dog. That rat from Hallow's Griff.

He owed me a debt. Not only for taking my hand, but for losing it to Zane. And the merman had actually hugged me upon returning it—I'm talking wrapping his dopey ass arms around me. I shivered at the memory. He was getting too chummy with me, and I didn't like it.

Refocusing on my task, I kept my expression neutral as I strode forward and draped my arm over Danger Dog's shoulders. The guy jumped in surprise, but I held firm and steered him away from the path he'd been walking.

"We're due for a little chat," I drawled, leading him towards a cluster of trees. He was all jittery and shit beside me. Good. Fucker knew what was coming to him. Not only had he jumped me in the trial, but he'd somehow got his filthy hands on my secrets, and neither of those things could slide.

"We're going to be late for our lesson," he replied, raising his chin, but it didn't hide the tremor in his voice.

I grinned at his failed attempt to hide his panic.

"It can wait," I said, spinning him around and slamming his back against a tree trunk. I gave him my coldest smile. "This will only take a second."

I lifted my bionic hand and slipped the blade up from one of the fingertips. The guy's beady eyes went straight to it, rounding almost comically.

"Look," he gulped, his eyes darting from me to the blade and back again. "It was nothing personal."

"What is it they say?" I stepped closer, schooling my features to appear bored. "'All's fair in love and war'?"

"Yep! That's exactly what it was."

I shook my head. "This isn't a war though, is it, Danger Dog? And outside of the academy, the Hallow's Griff aren't at war with the Drakes, are they?"

The rat's eyes widened, and he shook his head vigorously. "No."

"Unless your little stunt was a notice of your gang trying to start some shit?"

"It wasn't."

"So you acted of your own free will?"

"Yep." He nodded like some bobble-head on steroids. If he continued to move his head like that, he would give his already miniature brain some serious damage. "It was all me."

"I wonder then how your boss would feel if he knew you'd stepped out of line for, not only trying to kill me and start a gang war, but coming to the trials in the first place?"

I was basing it on a hunch, but I figured those in Hallow's Griff would have been touting his nomination for all to hear if they had been aware. Which meant if he'd gone behind their backs, he'd be facing some serious trouble when he got out … if I let him. Perhaps I'd toy with him, get some information—maybe let him think I'd inform his boss about his extra-curricular activities.

It wouldn't be hard for his gang to get someone inside the academy walls and get a little justice. Not that I needed his gang to step in. I wasn't a rat, but Danger Dog didn't need to know that.

His face paled. "We can't communicate with anyone beyond the academy."

I smirked. So his boss wasn't in enough influential circles to warrant a VIP pass to watch the trial highlights or receive Potential rankings. Clearly, he wasn't aware of Danger Dog being here. That and his knowledge of my hand proved he was two-timing. With whom I didn't know yet, but I would find out.

"Maybe for some."

"Are you gonna snitch, then?"

I stared him down, watching as little beads of sweat dripped from his forehead. It was always entertaining watching assholes like him squirm. I could easily have pulled up a chair and watched this shit all day, but he was right about needing to get to that lesson.

"I'm going to let you live today," I said, slipping the blade away and folding my arms over my chest. "And in return, you're going to do something for me."

"Happily." He sighed, his shoulders drooping. "Thanks, man."

"First, I have a few questions. You never would have gotten past the screening for these trials without help. Who nominated you?"

He shook his head. "I don't know. I was sent a message and told I'd be coming here to sabotage you."

I rolled my eyes at him. "Doesn't take much to get you to talk."

"I want into the Drakes," he said, his words rushing over themselves as they escaped from his mouth. "I'll do right by you and then you can vouch for me."

"Why the fuck would I do that? You tried to kill me."

"Disable," he replied hastily, licking his lips. "You would have gotten out and headed back to DH with a bruised ego, that's all."

It was almost too easy. I would use his desperation to be in the Drakes to my advantage. There was no way I'd let him survive until the end of the trials, let alone help him get into my gang, but he'd be none the wiser.

"You'll have to prove yourself first," I said, pinning him under my stare. "I have a job for you."

The guy looked like a kid getting a big fat present on his birthday. Gullible fucker.

"I'll do anything."

"I want you to join Victoria Auger's squad and find out everything you can about what she's up to."

He nodded. His ugly face was so full of hope I had to stop myself from punching it.

"Good." I reached out, slamming a hand over his mouth and holding his head in place. With a flick, I slipped the blade from my bionic hand and sliced his ear off in one quick movement.

The guy screamed, clutching his bleeding head as I released him and stepped back. "That's for daring to cross me." My other hand whipped around to crack him on the nose. "And that's for calling me Atti the Ant."

I turned my back on his whimpering and strode towards my lesson, throwing his ear into the grass.

"You break and spill my orders," I called over my shoulder, "I'll kill you so fucking slowly you will beg for me to end it."

I left the rat to contemplate his life choices. He wasn't the first person I'd tortured. I wasn't fresh meat in this game. Cormac had made me witness a fuck-tonne of interrogations growing up. Whether to get intel or simply to punish some two-timing opportunistic asshole, I'd been brought in to see how the real world worked. There was no sugar-coating life in DH, not even as a kid. We were given front row seats to the brutality of life, and I was glad for it. I wasn't some dipshit, thinking the world was easy. I knew what it took to make it and I was stronger for it.

As I got older, Cormac made me part of the torture, but by then

I was numb to the pain of others. I held no sympathy for those who deserved to be on the other end of a blade or whatever tool Cormac used to inflict pain.

Some might call me cold-hearted or a psycho. If you had a psych degree, maybe damaged.

I'd call it real.

I'd never tried to be anything but myself, unlike the Stormcrest rich dicks who hid behind fake smiles and fake charities.

I made my way over to the combat training area where today's instructor, Nolan, was standing around, looking all self-important. Potentials gathered around him, waiting for instructions.

"Right," Nolan barked, scaring the shit out of a couple of Potentials and making them jump. "You know the drill. One on one, hand to hand. Once you get your partner, get out of my face."

He shouted off names, and I found myself standing opposite the princess of Stormcrest City. I folded my arms over my chest and stared her down. I was man enough to admit she looked hot today. Fallon wore a cropped white t-shirt and skintight black shorts that left very little to the imagination, not that I had to rely solely on that.

Or that I would want to.

I was in these trials for one thing only. To break in and steal a weapon that would help the Drakes and the rest of DH hold our own against the world. Once I got my hands on the thing, the playing field would level out between those with strong magic and credits, and those without. I'd been making solid progress on cracking the security system, but last night it had been updated, setting me back. Clearly, the murder had frightened the Overseer enough to increase security measures, but I'd crack it. The House of Ascension had some of the best defence mechanisms in the world, but in time, it would fall before me.

My deal with Danger Dog was purely for information, so I knew where I stood with Cormac. My endgame was still the same.

"When you're finished staring," Fallon drawled, inspecting her nails. "I'd like to start."

"By all means." I bowed dramatically, spinning my wrist and catching the light on my bionic hand. "Wouldn't want to keep the little princess waiting."

Scuffing our sneakers on the ground and kicking up dust, we circled each other. I watched her closely. I was bigger than her, and though she had speed that she used against guys like Kayden, I could easily match her. I wasn't going to, though.

I may be in a gang, but there was no way I was gonna hit Fallon. The only time to lay a hand on a chick was in the bedroom, and that was to spank her ass raw.

I couldn't help but imagine Fallon screaming my name as I wrapped her hair in my bionic fist and fucked her against a wall. My other hand teasing her, not letting her come until she was begging like a good girl.

I shook my head. Letting those thoughts slither into my mind was going to make me lose.

Forfeiting was not an option either. No fucking way. I could still get her on the ground beneath me without throwing a single punch. Just had to be a little creative.

Fallon halted, and I lunged, only to find that she'd faked and slipped behind me, hitting me in the back of the head. She was too short for it to be hard, but it was still a dick move. Felt like I was being told off by a teacher or some shit.

"Bad girl." I spun around, growling at her as I stormed closer.

Her cheeks flushed, her body stilling for the most minute second, but she quickly recovered and came for me again. She didn't hold back her punches, her small fists jabbing me in the rib before knocking me in the jaw.

"What the fuck is your problem?" I hissed, cracking my neck. "Merman not living up to the bar I set?"

"It wasn't very high," she replied, blowing out a breath. "He jumps over it comfortably."

"Hand in hand with Noah?" I asked as we circled each other.

She raised a brow. "Jealous, Ace?"

I shrugged. "Whatever you need to do to win. Is that how House Jupiter does all its business dealings?"

"Not that I'm aware of, though maybe my family has learnt it recently from your gang." She bounced on her toes and made for me again, but I stepped back, blocking her next hit.

What did she mean by that?

"I want nothing to do with you or your family. In my line of work, I've learnt the most evil of people are the hardest to kill. Like fucking cockroaches during a nuclear war." I angled my head to the far side of the training area to where her sister was fighting. "Case in point. According to boulder boy, Victoria should be six feet under, but here she is, beating the shit out of some poor fucker."

"Don't pretend like her being here pisses you off," Fallon replied, throwing a punch, which I dodged. "You're working with her."

I spat on the dirt at our feet. "Why the fuck would I do anything with that bitch?"

"The Drake on the helicopter," she said, flicking her long black ponytail and placing her hands on her hips.

Either Kayden or Noah was a snitch. Those two were whipped harder than horses on race day. My money was on Noah, and if Fallon thought I was up to no good, then Noah did, too.

If looks could kill, my body would be riddled with stab wounds. I glared right back, then quirked my lips, smiling even wider when her eyes followed the movement. Princess couldn't help it. She might hate me, but she liked what she saw.

I kept my lips shut, neither confirming nor denying the little web she'd connected in her head. She blew out a breath and then she was on me.

The girl could fight, I'd give her that. She targeted each punch, but too bad. I didn't fight by the rules.

I got up in her space, limiting her range. She threw a hit and, rather than dodging, I stepped into it, pressing us close and trapping her fist between us. My chest throbbed from her punch, but I didn't show it, smirking in her face despite the pain radiating through my ribs.

Princess shoved me back, catching me off guard as she spun and punched me in the face. I stumbled back, my gaze fixed on the fire in her eyes as she stood there with her hands on her hips. Her chest moved up and down with each breath, as she grinned.

I wanted to squash that attitude. Wanted to have her begging for mercy.

Spitting blood onto the dirt, I smirked. "Is that the best you have?"

Her nostrils flared. She pummelled me hard and fast, and I continued to bide my time, waiting for an opening. Because I was an opportunistic bastard, I jumped as soon as it appeared.

She would crumble at my feet.

Fallon darted back out of my reach, a scowl on her face that had me smiling. She wasn't used to an even match.

"Does the princess need her royal nap? Should I call your maid?" I teased. "Where is the merman? Or is Noah on duty today?"

Fallon growled then made to kick me in the side, but I grabbed her foot with my bionic hand, dragging her close to me until our bodies were pressed against each other.

"Victoria wants you dead," I said as she wriggled in my hold and threw a punch aimed at my throat. I wrapped my arms around her, pinning her down and holding her to my chest. She struggled, but I brought her even closer until our lips were an inch apart, our eyes blazing into each other's. "Why would I help save your life with Kayden if I was working with your sister?"

I tried not to get too distracted by the feel of her body on mine. Each panting breath she took only made it harder. Fuck.

Her chest still heaved, but she stopped fighting. "You really got me out of the trial?"

"It's that unbelievable?" I scoffed, releasing her and stepping back abruptly.

She stumbled on her feet, but I didn't help her. I'd thought I hated her, but it was nothing compared to the fury I felt right now. It didn't matter that I had worked with her little band of idiots in the trial. They would always think the worst of me.

"You're just like the rest of them. You think because of where I come from, that I'm always the villain. I'm not a good person, but guess what Princess, just because you come from some shiny place in the sky, it doesn't make you good either."

"Never said it did," Fallon shouted, shooting me a glare.

"I saved your life, you spoiled brat, and that's all you have to say?"

"Do you want a thank you?"

"Fuck no."

She huffed. "Then what's your problem?"

I ran a hand through the hair on the top of my head. "People like you will always look down on the rest of us. You're just like your sister. At least she's honest about being a lying, cheating bitch." I turned my back on her, anger coursing through me as I stormed away. "Run back to your friends. I can't stand the sight of you."

FALLON

What the actual shit had just happened? Murderous, standoffish, miserable little bastard. I slammed my palm against the locker and the metal clanged in protest, the sound echoing around the empty room.

Ace was such a prick. I knew he didn't like me, but that guy had a habit of twisting my insides like a knife and riling me up. Everything he said was a special little delivery of bullshit, handpicked just for me. Everyone else knew better than to spar words or blows with him, but it seemed I was the only one who really copped his verbal assholery.

But not without dishing some back.

I sighed, shaking my head. The one thing he had going for him was the teeny, tiny fact he'd saved me in the trial. Kayden, I could believe for making the effort, but Ace? There was no reason I could think of for him to bother getting me out of butt-fuck nowhere and across that finish line.

Why it bothered me so much was an utter mystery to me. No doubt he'd have some reason in that evil little brain of his, but until then I was getting whiplash from the venomous insults he threw my way. Even if we both knew some of them were a lie. Just a backwards way of protecting his shrivelled little heart and pretending he was void of all feelings.

Impossible. The world liked to throw constant curveballs. Not caring at all wasn't the problem, it was caring too much. Ace could pretend—like me—that he was bigger and badder than everyone else, but it wasn't really true.

We were all just waiting for the world to fuck us over, or maybe in Ace's case, to bend it over and slap it silly.

Until then, I'd just have to suffer his indecision over whether he hated me more than he wanted to fuck me. Again. Even I couldn't deny the tension between us was freaking scorching, the lust practically screaming at us to get on with it already.

Nope. Not fucking likely. As much as I liked the heated hands on me and the possessive, almost depraved way he manipulated my body, I would not give him the satisfaction of being some meek little wench for him to use and abuse as he saw fit. He'd like that too fucking much.

And okay, yeah, I'd more than like that in some ways, but screw that.

I had better things to do than dwell on Ace Warner and his stupid, sexy mouth. With a huff, I smoothed back my ponytail, getting the distinct feeling my flyaways were close to lifting me up and carrying me into another realm.

Ugh. There was hot and bothered, and then there was just … this. I stalked to the locker room mirror and frowned at the sweaty mess staring back at me. I gathered my bag full of clothes and toiletries, stripped, then stepped into the shower stall, turning on the tap.

I groaned as the hot water pounded down on my sore muscles, the vanilla and spice scent of my shampoo filled the air as I scrubbed at my sweaty hair. The sounds of other female Potentials trickled in, and the monotony of it helped ease the storm cloud that had settled over my thoughts.

Eventually I tuned it out altogether until a familiar voice broke the serenity. "Out! This place is about to get soaked. A pipe needs tending to and there's only one chick with the skills for this plumbing job."

I peeked my head out from behind the curtain to find Zane strolling in, already naked, his length bobbing around as he ushered shrieking, naked girls from the room and practically shoved them out the door.

A familiar-looking woman with blond hair and fake tits smiled at him slyly, playing with the soap lathered on her soccer ball breasts. The one who lingered around Kayden like a fucking fart that wouldn't disperse. "Well, if it isn't the merman himself. Want to come play with me?"

I narrowed my eyes, my stomach twisting and skin heating as she toyed with Zane. "*My Zane*" I wanted to snarl, but I was too damn curious to see what he'd do.

He stopped, his face bored as he looked her up and down. "No thanks. Anyone with two giant flotation devices permanently attached to their chest screams 'scared of the ocean'. She's our friend, and I just don't have time for your lack of trust."

She pouted, her face crinkling as she looped her arms around his neck. "Actually, I like the ocean. I love to swim."

Zane cocked his head and sniffed. "Do you smell that?"

Her nostrils flared, and she shook her head. "No. What—?"

"It's called desperation, Crestfish," he interrupted, stepping away from her. "See ya!"

Her face twisted with rage. "It's Crystal, for fuck's sake!" Then she saw me, and her eyes were like freaking knives as they narrowed into slits. "Oh, I see now. You and every other asshole here are blinded by the whore from Stormcrest City. I should have known everyone would want ass over class."

I stepped out of the shower and laughed. "Says the woman trying to suck any dick she can get her lips around. Which is…" I counted on my fingers, then moved my hand and flipped her off. "Oh, wait, zero." I smirked. "No one likes a jealous bitch, Cumquat."

She flung herself at me, shrieking as her nails curled into my hair and tried to rip it from my scalp. Her other hand clawed down my arm. Hair pulling? What the actual shit. I ducked and twisted, manoeuvring easily, then let go before I broke her arm.

Breathe, Fallon. Be the bigger person. I took a deep, steadying breath, then looked at her calmly. "We don't like each other, and that's completely fine, but before you lay hands on me, perhaps you could consider a little something like consent? Zane said no, which is zero reason to attack *me*. Walk. Away."

I turned my back, pleased I had dealt with that responsibly, instead of wailing on her like I so easily could. If it wasn't for her cruel remarks and her general bitchiness, I might have felt sorry for the girl. It didn't seem like she had any real friends, which was maybe why she was using her looks to gain her interest instead. Who knew?

Zane's eyes drank me in, looking me up and down hungrily as I walked towards him. I almost shivered as his eyes traced every curve and swell of my body. Gods, I needed this. *Needed him.* Anything to distract me from the chaos of the last two months.

A shriek echoed behind me, and I stiffened, my muscles already responding to the threat as I swivelled on the spot. Before she could hit me, Zane eased me aside and caught the girl's wrist in his hand. His beautiful face contorted, the sculpted planes and jaw tensing, as he looked at her with pure violence in his eyes.

He clucked his tongue and wiggled a finger. "I think my Starfish said it perfectly the first time. Do you think hurting her is going to do you any favours?"

"N-no. I wasn't—"

Zane started advancing, forcing her to back up as his muscled body crowded her personal space. Maybe it made me a total bitch, but the fear now lining her eyes filled me with the tiniest satisfaction. But come on, what kind of coward attacks someone with their back turned?

"Do you want to know what I'd do to you if you did hurt her?" His voice was so low, it sent invisible skitters down my spine. He didn't even sound like himself anymore, but gods, it was hot.

She shook her head, and he kept walking until her back hit the far wall. He caged her in, placing his arms on either side of her head. Then he leaned close. "Let's not find out. If you lay another finger on my Starfish's head, I'll fillet your skin off and feed you to the sharks. They'll eat anything, you know."

The girl whimpered, but he lifted an arm and jerked his head towards the exit, the beads woven in his hair tinkling. With a yelp, she ran out, her giant boobs bobbing as she ran, not even bothering to pick up her clothes.

I smirked. It wouldn't take the academy long to make light of that situation. The people here were brutal. I knew that better than anyone, thanks to Victoria and Kayden.

When Zane turned, his face was back to its usual mellow self. I cocked my head and grinned. "Sharks? I thought you were more of a dolphin guy."

"Of course, I am. I would never betray my Pip and Delilah like that," he scolded, shaking his head. Then his lips shifted into a sly smile. "But I'm also not afraid to show my teeth."

"Look at you go. All possessive and protective when you want to be."

His eyes darkened as he stalked towards me, moving me into a stall and caging me in. "When I want. For the girl I want."

"And … who might that be?" I asked, sucking in a breath as he stepped towards me.

His hand traced the curve of my breasts, then he leant down to suck my nipple into his mouth.

"You know," he said, growling as he pulled back. He trailed kisses down my neck, while his free hand teased back and forth along the space above my pussy, sending me writhing as he tickled the sensitive skin.

A small whimper left my lips as a finger descended, slipping inside of me as his palm began grinding against my clit.

"Tell me," I said breathily.

He pushed me back into the shower, the spray of the water coating us both as he bit my neck and slipped another finger in. The graze of his teeth across my skin had me melting into his touch, my body pliant as he pressed his rigid cock against me.

"You know, Starfish," he said between a few more playful nips. "I'm quite fond of our shower encounters. But it seems I didn't make myself clear the last time we were together. I only want one girl—and I mean to make her mine."

With that, he bit hard on my neck, and I moaned against him as the pain turned into one of pleasure. He sunk his teeth into my flesh, marking me like I was his prey and he the predator, a possessive animal.

Zane's brow rose, his eyes questioning as he looked at me. I nodded. "Yes. Fuck, yes." Because I'd wanted to know what it would feel like to have him buried inside me since the day I arrived and he'd been standing in my dorm, looking like a bronzed god.

He searched my eyes, his own sparkling green ones drinking me in as he lifted my legs and I wound them around his hips. "I want you, Fallon. More than I've ever wanted anything."

And with that he slammed into me, his considerable length stretching me with its intrusion, making me gasp with pleasure as slowly, so slowly, he withdrew to the tip, then thrusted back in to the hilt. Over and over, punishing my soaked pussy, slick from the combination of my juices and the running shower. It felt so painfully sensuous I was writhing in his arms with need.

Sex had never felt so fucking good. He shifted my body slightly, allowing his cock to penetrate at a new angle. My eyes rolled in my head; my orgasm so close when we'd only just begun. I moaned, tilting my head back against the wall as Zane took complete ownership of my body. It felt so right with him, so perfect, our bodies responding instinctively, seeming to know what each other needed without direction.

"More," I demanded, squeezing my thighs around his muscled sides. "Give me more."

He picked up the pace, hefting my weight effortlessly into one arm while he grabbed my neck with the other, just hard enough to hold me in place. His eyes found mine, pinning me under that stare, not once looking away as he thrusted in and out. He growled as he slammed into me. It was so intimate, so intense, that I came undone.

"Oh, fuck, Zane. Fuck."

My breaths came in shallow, quick gasps as he continued thrusting home, faster and faster, riding the wave of my pleasure and drawing out my orgasm. His name on my lips was the final tug that unravelled him. He groaned as his large hand clamped tighter around my neck, his fingers clutching my ass so hard I knew there would be bruises later.

"Starfish," he rasped with one last pump, leaning his forehead against my own, panting as the tension left his body against me.

I sighed contentedly as he eventually let go and I unfolded myself to stand on the tiles again. When he looked up, I kissed him, slowly, our tongues curling together. We continued kissing for a while until I realised this might have been the happiest I'd felt in a long time.

The thought made me jolt back suddenly, my eyes prickling with suspicious, burning heat.

"Hey," he said, lifting my chin. "You're my girl. Part of my super pod. Fuck these other blowfish. We're going to pop their inflated bellies the moment they get in our way."

A small laugh rumbled out of me and I shook my head. "Zane," I said, smiling, "What's a super pod?"

His lips parted in shock. "Only the best dolphin pods in existence. In a super pod, we mate, help each other find food, and defend each other. We're like family. Peak pod material, right there."

I could swear my heart swelled three times its size to know this absolute treasure of a human thought of me as his … as his family. Traitorous little organ. How was I supposed to not fall for someone when they went and said that shit? But Zane was precious, so full of love. I knew.

I knew I would protect this man at all costs. From enemies and certainly from other 'mates' on the hunt.

Maybe I wasn't ready to be his—or *solely* his—but I'd decided right then and there …

He was mine.

KAYDEN

I loved the sound of my minions' suffering. If only because I knew they would come out stronger for it. I found most of them tedious and about as companionable as a cactus in the desert, but they were still part of my team. And Team Hale never quit.

I chuckled as my feet pounded the gravel path winding around the academy grounds. Dick's wheezing was like music to my ears. A soothing melody that put a pep in my step.

"Kayden, s-sir. I can't keep going."

"You can quit when you're dead," I barked, shooting him a stern look. To be fair, the guy had never been worked so hard in his damn life, but that didn't mean I would go easy on him.

His scrawny little legs wobbled, threatening to collapse from where they pinwheeled double time to keep up with my long strides. I eyed his red face, noting his resolve as he huffed and squinted in concentration. Well, nobody could say he wasn't determined.

He stumbled over a pebble as we rounded the corner towards the Tritosa territory, and I whipped out my hand to stop the guy from eating dirt. Okay, maybe he deserved a break. "To the lake," I said, pointing ahead of us. "Then you're done."

His blue eyes lit up with the end in sight, and somehow Dick Jobs mustered his last dregs of strength and sprinted to the finish line like a cheetah, cheering his win as he reached it.

Even I couldn't help grinning as I pulled up beside him. I nodded in approval. "Nice work today, little Dicky. Keep it up and you'll be running circles around me in no time."

"You think so?" He looked me up and down in excitement, bobbing on his heels.

I shook my head at his eagerness, suppressing a grin. "Agility is more your speed. I don't see you turning into a tank anytime soon. It'll take a lot of work to put some muscle on your bones as it is."

"But when I do, no one will look down on me again," he said, hands on hips. If he was going for intimidating, it wasn't quite working, with his blond hair plastered to his head and the face of a tomato.

I clapped my hand on his back. "We'll see, Dicky. We'll see. As long as you're part of my pack, no one will touch you."

The sun already had some bite to it today. I removed my tank top and ran a hand through my sweaty hair as I plonked onto the sandy shore. It was kinda surprising how nice it was to have someone to work out with. After Flynn, I'd taken Dick's training on as a kind of project to preoccupy me, but dare I say I was enjoying the runt's company.

"What's it like in the Crimson Steppes, sir?" Dick asked, plopping down beside me.

I untied my shoes before answering, then pulled my socks off and eased my feet into the sand. Smooth and silky, unlike the coarser grains of my desert home. I grunted. "Dry. Dusty. Brutal if you don't have the skills to survive."

Dick bit his lip. "Is that why you're so hard on us? The Potentials in your group, I mean."

"Where I come from, if you don't have strength and smarts about you, you end up a meal for the vultures." I shrugged. "The strongest survive. That's just the way it is. Do you think I work you guys so hard just because I like it?"

"Well, um…" Dick looked away, guiltily. "Yes?"

I grinned. "You're right, I do enjoy it. It's funny as fuck watching you all squirm. But that's not the only reason. I'm sick of fighting for scraps, ya know? There's more to life than living day by day. When I become king, I'll be able to make things better for my people. And along the way, I'm going to avenge Flynn while doing it."

Dick paused. "He was your best friend, right?"

I blew out a breath, feeling a little awkward at how deep and meaningful this was getting. "Yeah. He was."

"We'll avenge him," Dick said, puffing out his chest. "We'll get that Victoria girl."

Kid had guts. I liked that. "What's in it for you?"

"Keep training me and offering protection from the others and I'll do anything," Dick said suddenly, his eyes a little wild and desperate as he groped at my arm. "I didn't want to sign up for the trials, but my parents made me. I'm not … I'm not cut out for this, sir!"

"Get off me," I growled, shrugging him away. "What do you mean your parents made you?"

"My parents are ashamed of me." He hung his head. "I've never been good at anything. I don't have any friends. Even the aquatic creatures of Tritosa City don't want to be around me because when I transform, they get scared of my incredible…" He trailed off, shaking his head. "My parents said this was my one chance to impress them and live up to their name. And I want to, sir. Just imagine what they'd say if I made it through the trials! 'Dick Jobs. The hardest and biggest member of his family.'"

I snorted. "A little premature, but … sure. I suppose I can help you impress your mummy and daddy. And in return, you got my back, bro?"

"Yes, sir! Little Dick and Big Red, taking on the world."

I groaned. "Don't call us that or I'll punch your head in."

He just smiled victoriously and whispered, "Whatever you say, Big Red."

I shook my head, not sure I was prepared for what I was getting into, even if Dick was growing on me. Just a little. I got up to dip my toes in the water when I spotted a flash of copper in the sky. My angel in full flight. She saw me and saluted, circling down to land gracefully on the shore.

"Angel."

She threw me a stunning smile, her eyes trailing over my slick abs, which I flexed subtly while she looked. "Hey, big guy."

"What brings your fine ass this way?"

Fallon rolled her eyes, but the smile didn't leave her lips. "Walk with me?"

I nodded, strolling to her side as we began meandering around the lake. "Come to beg me for that date?"

"You wish. But I have been thinking about our conversation the other day. Is it really true what you said about saving me in the trial?"

"Every word. Why would I lie about it?"

She bit her lip as she peeked a glance at me. "Honestly, I have a hard time trusting people these days. Besides, we're all in this to win. Why would you risk it to help me?"

"I couldn't just leave you there to die or get eaten alive," I said, scoffing. "We were a team in that trial. No one gets left behind."

She pursed her lips. "And Ace?"

"Fuck knows what Twiggy's intentions are. I wouldn't waste your time dwelling on whatever goes through that whack mind of his."

She nodded in agreement, then laid her hand on my arm, stopping me. "Well, I guess I just wanted to say thanks. I probably wouldn't be around if not for you."

"You know how you can thank me?" I said, winking.

"Kayden, helping me definitely gets you brownie points but it doesn't earn you access to my panties."

"Angel, we both know you want that as much as I do. But I'm serious, just a date. I want to know you better. Meet the real Fallon Auger."

She blanched momentarily. But the look was quickly replaced by a smug smile. "Baby, you wouldn't know what to do with her if you did."

I stepped closer, tipping her chin up with my finger. "I love a challenge. I'm game if you are."

Fallon laughed, her breathing sharpening as I trailed my other hand down her back to rest just above her ass. She leaned in so close our mouths almost touched, and I felt myself twitch to attention as she pressed her tits against me, her hand rubbing gently against my junk. "If we're going to play, who gets to win?"

I pressed my growing cock against her. "That's the point of this game, Angel. We both do."

A soft hum vibrated in her chest, doing all kinds of things to my body. Then she pulled away, a coy smile on her lips. "I do so like to play. And maybe we can work together again as a team in the meantime. There are … some things I think you'd be interested to know. But this doesn't mean I trust you, Kayden. You'll have to keep working on that."

"I'll earn your trust, Angel. I swear it. Whatever it takes, I'll prove that to you."

She grinned. "We'll see. And about that game…" She winked. "Your move."

Her wings burst from her back once more, the copper blinding me as the sun reflected off it. When I looked up again, she was gone. Saucy little angel.

By the time I made it back to Dick, I was grinning like a mother fucker. "Wanna take a dip?" He nodded enthusiastically, almost tearing his clothes off in his haste.

"Bloody hell, the water's not going anywhere."

He only grunted in reply, then stripped until he was butt naked, his fists planted on his hips as Dick's enormous dick wiggled in the breeze. Well fuck me, that was unexpected.

I couldn't stop staring as it jiggled with each step into the lake, even as I wanted to cover my face in disgust. A few girls walking nearby saw and giggled, their eyes wide as they saw Dick in a new light. "You and me both," I grumbled as I waded in after him, my shorts still on. This wasn't a damn strip show, but apparently the bunch of women now gawking at his cock thought so.

"You've got some groupies, bro," I said with a laugh before I dove under.

When I came back, Dick looked as proud as punch. "Do you—do you think they like me?"

"One step at a time, my dude." I paddled out into the middle of the lake, enjoying how the water welcomed me into its depths. Ok sure, I might have paid attention to the merman's swimming lesson one time, but nun on a cactus, I didn't need to think like him too.

I stroked a hand over my eyes and watched as Dick started swimming towards me, when suddenly he screeched like a schoolgirl and his face paled. "There's something in here," he screamed, punching the water.

"Chill, probably just some seaweed or some shit," I said, amused. His screaming sure wouldn't get him bonus points with those girls.

"Seaweed is—in the—sea," he gasped out, then screamed again before going under.

"Stop playing, bro." I laughed, waiting for him to resurface, but he didn't appear. Oh, shit. For real, I was having too good a time to deal with some lake monster.

I swam over to him quickly, but his head broke the water as I got close. "It grabbed me from behind then let me go," he said, spluttering, looking around in confusion.

"Let's go, man. I don't feel like being eaten today."

Before I could turn around, I spotted the top of a blond head poking out from the water several metres away, pausing as I recognised the shaved undercut and beads woven throughout, then the green eyes glaring at us.

"Merman? What the fuck?" I yelled.

He didn't answer. Instead, he pointed in a motion to say he was watching, but he didn't point at us. His finger went beyond, and I looked around to find Kendra taking a stroll in the distance.

I turned back around to ask what his deal was, but he just slunk eerily back into the water, and not that I'd tell anyone, but that shit was creepy.

Not wanting to spend another minute in his territory, I paddled to the safety of the shore. Whatever insane mission Zane was on or thought Kendra had done, I wanted no part of it.

ZANE

I swam away from Kayden and his little Dick, drifting through the lake like a saltwater crocodile on the prowl. My gaze was still firmly on Kendra as she walked around the edge of the lake without a care in the world—or at least that's what she wanted everyone to think. She was my prime suspect in the murder investigations.

Yeah, plural.

First, she killed the dude in the med bay, then Seb and the dude Starfish and Noah stumbled upon.

I didn't know why she was killing people. All I could assume was that she had a taste for blood since the trials, and it was bound to get worse.

It was only a matter of time before Kendra offed someone else. She had been mysteriously disappearing lately, sometimes not even coming back to the dorm at night.

And then there were the trophies.

A shiver ran down my spine. I'd found them around her bed and even in the bathroom. Lots of pink shit and glitter. The girl was killing people who might have been downright fun if I'd gotten the chance to know them. Who doesn't like someone with sparkle?

I lifted a brow, my eyes following Kendra's movements. She was all alone. To the untrained eye, she was going for a stroll, but I was no guppy fish.

I'd been watching her for the last hour as she walked with Fallon, chatting and laughing like good friends, until Fallon flew off. It was all a ruse. All those Potentials that walked by—some even offering her smiles—didn't realise a killer lay behind that pretty face. My starfish may have trusted Kendra, but she wasn't seeing things clearly. It was my job as her sexy bodyguard to protect her from any threat, and right now, that was her so-called bestie.

Kendra turned from the path, and I swam to the shore. I had the speed of a sailfish and the elegance of an angel fish that, combined, helped me glide seamlessly through the waters and keep my eyes on her the entire time. Anyone else would have caused a scene or lost track, but not me. I was an elite spy.

Water dripped down my torso as I reached the sand and hurried after her. I used the environment to keep myself hidden. I was a pro.

"What—"

"Shh," I hissed, grabbing a random dude who had his mouth open as wide as a whale catching krill. Then I turned him so I could use him for cover. I counted to five, then glanced around him before making my next move.

"Hey—" he began to protest.

I sprinted away towards a group of Potentials, manoeuvring a few with a nudge here or there, and peered over one of their shoulders. Kendra was still walking, no idea of the barracuda on her tail.

She made her way towards the main building, and I jogged after her, pressing myself flat like a starfish against the walls of the buildings we passed. I was all stealth, my feet so silent it was almost like they weren't hitting the ground as I moved. Swimming through the air, so to speak.

I spotted Noah, but it was only for a second before he disappeared before my very eyes. When I saw Victoria nearby, I smirked. The dude thought he was good at spying, but he didn't have shit on me.

I didn't have to get naked to hide in plain sight. If I didn't want to be seen, then no one was going to spot me. I'd fooled Zeke, Zach, and Zion so many times when we were kids. My brothers would beg me to play hide and seek, then it would take hours for them to find me. I had to hide in what I'd thought were the most obvious places, and yet those dudes still couldn't see me. Then when I knew they had given up, I'd jump out of my hiding place and scare the shit out of them. Literally. Zeke shitting his pants was one of the funniest things I'd ever witnessed. I'd have to remind him of it when I saw him next.

I was a master at remaining unseen.

Kendra passed the classroom buildings, and I scrunched my lips, wondering where she could be going. There was nothing beyond here but the main building of the House of Ascension and the library. Two places Potentials rarely visited. She was definitely up to something.

"Zane," Kendra stated suddenly, turning around to face me. She had her hands on her hips and a frown on her face. "Why are you following me? I thought you volunteered to be Fallon's bodyguard, not mine?"

I pulled up, placing a hand on my chest and widening my eyes. "I'm not following you. I'm simply walking in the same direction, that's all."

She raised a brow. "Where are you going?"

"The main building."

"Potentials aren't allowed in there."

"The Overseer wants to see me."

"Why?"

"Seahorses."

The lies were coming so easily, slipping off my tongue like slimy fish on a water slide.

"Seahorses?" Kendra asked, her voice flat.

"Yeah." I nodded, flicking water at her as I shook my wet hair. "Don't want to stress the poor things when moving them from one place to another. She knows I'm an expert on all things ocean, so she asked for my help with her aquarium."

She frowned as the water splattered her face. "The Overseer has an aquarium."

"A big one. Takes up an entire wall. She's quite the aquatic hobbyist. Who would have thought?"

"Uh-huh, sure," she replied, then smiled and waved, her gaze looking somewhere behind me. "Overseer!"

I swore beneath my breath but kept my chill expression. Kendra was totally believing the lies of this master spy. I couldn't let my cover slip.

"Good morning, dear ones," Celeste said, coming over to us. "What can I do for two of Terrulia's most valiant Potentials?"

"Zane was telling me about how you're rehoming seahorses," Kendra said, looking all innocent as she beamed.

Celeste frowned. "Seahorses?"

"Yeah, you know, the steeds of the sea?" I replied, turning and gesturing for her to walk with me away from Kendra. "We can't leave them waiting much longer."

"I—oh!" she exclaimed as I slung an arm over her shoulders and dragged her along. "I'm not—"

I waved at Kendra over my shoulder. "See you around!"

"Mr Loch!" Celeste spluttered.

"You look like a knowledgeable lady who knows a lot about everything," I said, laying it on thick and ignoring her outburst. "I thought I'd been taught all there was to know about sea life, but apparently you are quite the aquatic encyclopaedia."

"I wouldn't say that."

"How else would you be Overseer of the trials if you didn't have brains in that noggin of yours?"

"I, well, you make a good point," she replied, a blush colouring her cheeks. "You mentioned seahorses?"

"Yeah." I nodded.

"Seahorses are some of the most majestic creatures," she said, a broad smile growing on her face.

"Totally."

I needed to ditch Celeste, but not until I was out of Kendra's sight. The Overseer was wound around my little finger, a little too much, suddenly enthused to talk about seahorses. Usually, I would have loved to hear all her thoughts of those righteous little dudes, but I had other things to think about right now.

The Overseer opened the door to the main building, punching in some code, but I wasn't paying attention to which buttons were causing the tiny beeps, though it did remind me of a tune I'd heard when I was a kid. Instead, my eyes were on Kendra.

She was walking away, and I breathed a sigh of relief. She definitely believed my story. I chuckled, shaking my head. I was so good at this shit. Celeste pulled me into the hallway, the doors shutting behind us with a thud, cutting off the view of my target.

Celeste was still rambling, and I nodded dutifully, but I needed to lose her and get back to my spying.

She continued up the hallway, and I remained just behind her until a corridor appeared at my right. I sprinted down it before I could get wrapped up in her aquatic conversation, then turned down another corridor.

I was one hundred percent sure I'd ditched the Overseer. The only problem now was that I had no clue where I was. I kept walking, humming the tune from my childhood, trying to get my bearings, when I heard thumping coming from one door along the hallway. Each one had a panel beside it with a keypad and a glowing red light.

The thumping continued, and I scrunched my brow, pressing an ear to the door in question.

A familiar shout on the other side had me punching in a bunch of numbers into the keypad. Nothing worked until I remembered the tune. A few tries and the light flashed green.

Opening the door, I found Ace, stuck behind bars, looking as angry as a shark losing his meal. Was my bestie in trouble?

"Watch out!" Ace shouted, and I had seconds to dodge the electrified baton that flew at my head.

"Dolphin at a disco!" I elbowed the guard in the ribs, avoiding the hit of another before punching the first dude in the face. He dropped his baton, and I quickly grabbed it, slamming into the second guard's paint-splattered chest.

Why was he covered in paint? Did he come from an art class?

Huh. I wondered if all the guards attended classes in their spare time. He fell to the floor, flopping around like a fish out of water before going still. Blood poured from his mouth and the smell of burning filled the air.

Guess he was going to miss the next one.

I crinkled my nose just as the first guard launched himself onto my back. I swung side to side before running backwards and slamming into the bars of Ace's cage. I couldn't see what he was doing, but a growl escaped his lips, and the next thing I knew, the guard went slack and my back felt wet.

I stepped forward, and he fell to the ground with a thud behind me. Turning around, I spotted the torn skin at his neck. Ace raised his hands, showing me his fingers, which were red with the dude's blood.

He'd literally torn the guard's throat out.

"Gnarly." I nodded. "You gotta teach me how to do that."

"No."

"Why not?"

"Just get the keys before someone comes," Ace replied. "I may have sprayed the cameras but that doesn't mean other guards or even the Masters won't come by."

"Alright, alright, you can teach me later. Don't get your speedos in a knot," I replied, grabbing the key card from the clip at the guard's belt and swiping it on the pad on the wall.

The bars rose, disappearing into the ceiling.

"I'll take that," Ace said, snatching the card and pocketing it in one smooth motion.

He led the way out, setting a quick pace that didn't leave room for much chatter, which was annoying. Once we were outside of the main building and had rounded a corner, Ace stopped, his breath coming in pants as he looked around.

"We should be good now."

"What was that all about, dude?" I asked, eager for some answers.

"Nothing," he replied, running a hand through his hair. "Don't say a word to anyone, you hear me?"

"Hiding something from me?"

"No shit," he said with a scoff. "Now move, Merman."

I raised my hands. "No need to get crabby, we can talk about it later."

"*Move*," he repeated, trying to step around me, but I moved with him, stopping my angry bestie from getting away.

"Got somewhere to be?"

"No." He folded his arms over his chest.

"Sweet," I replied, grabbing his shoulder and spinning him around so that we were facing the same direction. I kept my arm slung over his shoulders and leaned in so no one could overhear us. "Kendra is up to something. You can help me spy on her. She was heading this way but then I got side-tracked by the Overseer and you, but I reckon we can find her again."

He wriggled like a tentacle beneath my arm. If he just stopped moving so much, he might actually relax. I sighed, releasing him.

"I don't care."

"Don't be such a crusty crab. We both know you have a heart in that chest of yours, so stop being a mean pirate and keeping that treasure all to yourself."

"What the fuck are you on about?"

"Wasn't that gnarly before? You and me, teaming up like in the first trial," I replied with a grin.

We had such a good thing going in that marsh, and me rescuing him just now was proof it was still strong.

"Spying together is going to be great. Fewer monsters though, unless you count the little monster killing Potentials."

Ace frowned. "Are you talking about Kendra?"

"You have another suspect?"

"I—" He shook his head. "Fuck it."

Ace may have had other ideas he wasn't ready to share yet, but knowing he was happy to go along with my suspicions only solidified my hunch. We were going to catch her. Zane and Ace. Bestie spies. Surfing waves and fighting crimes.

A shrill scream pierced through the air and everyone nearby turned their attention toward the sound. My heart raced in my chest. This was it. I was going to catch her in the act.

"Come on, dude," I said, grabbing Ace by his black t-shirt and dragging him along.

"Fuck off," Ace grumbled, smacking my hand away before punching me in the gut.

I released him, chuckling at his rough play, but he still followed because curiosity killed the catfish, and Ace was one of the nosiest people I knew. He liked to pretend he didn't care, but if he could go invisible like Noah, I would bet my grandma on him sneaking around and listening in to everyone's conversations.

I hummed a little spy tune, giving us a theme song as we caught up with the crowd now forming by the back of the library. *Look at that.* Kendra had gone this way when I'd last seen her. The evidence was sticking to her faster than barnacles to a boat.

"Shut it," Ace said, slapping me on the back of the head and silencing my hums.

Spoil sport.

I rubbed my head and pushed through the crowd to see a Potential lying flat on the grass. There was no blood, not a single scratch on her, and I would have thought she was just staring up at the clouds and daydreaming if it weren't for the way her neck was bent. Her eyes stared blankly at the sky like a dead fish on the sand.

"That sneaky sea snake." I stroked my chin, my gaze running all over the woman. "I've underestimated Kendra's abilities."

"I don't think Kendra—"

"Hush, Ace," I said, waving a hand behind me to shush him. "Don't let her throw a beach towel over your eyes. She wants you to think she can't do it. That's her whole deal." I spun around, coming face to face with him. "Keep your eyes open, dude. There's a shark in the water."

"Back the fuck up." He shoved me in the chest, causing me to step back.

Ahh, Ace, so afraid to get close to anyone.

"So what do we plan to do about it, you may ask."

"There's no we," he grumbled, striding away.

"Good thinking. Don't want anyone to overhear our plans," I said, catching up to him. "Set a trap? Do some more surveillance?"

"I'm not—"

"Oh!" I gasped. "We can do a stake out!"

"For the love of." He groaned, running a hand over his face. Then he turned on me, slamming a hand on my bare chest and shoving me against the nearest wall. I hit the brick as he snarled in my face. "I'm not getting involved in your shit, got me? I don't give a fuck who is murdering people. Let them kill everyone for all I care. There's bigger shit going on."

I gasped. "You think Kendra is working for someone?" My eyes were wide as the dots all connected. Of course, Kendra wasn't acting alone. "See, this is why we're working together! Bouncing ideas off each other like a true team."

My head snapped back, hitting the bricks as Ace punched me in the face.

"No fucking team," he growled, stalking off.

I held my nose, stemming the bleeding, and grinned at my bestie spy buddy. There was a reason he was a Drake. The dude was good. To anyone watching, it would have looked like he was reluctant to work with me—that we weren't friends—but in reality, it was all for show. He'd left enough clues for me to follow to know that he was on my side.

I chuckled, tasting the blood on my tongue.

Kendra and whomever she was working for better watch out because Ace and Zane were on them like octopuses at a clam buffet.

NOAH

Meditation class should have been a relaxing and much needed break from everything happening in this place. The Potentials were on edge, and rightfully so, considering another one of us had been murdered. It was rare to see anyone alone anymore, but if so, they alternated from being jumpy to downright aggressive.

I was a little concerned about the murders. We knew our lives were at risk in the trials, but at the academy, we'd let our guards down. Without the adrenaline rush and the constant fear of death, it was easy to grow complacent. It seemed losing the illusion of safety was now messing with people's heads.

Whilst the latest crimes made the House of Ascension feel unsafe, I couldn't help but wonder who was committing them and what their motives were. I would have been even more curious to find out who the culprit was if I weren't so occupied with my own investigation. I'd followed Victoria for a few hours yesterday with nothing to come of it.

I gritted my teeth. A waste of time.

I rolled my shoulders and tried to regulate my thoughts through breathing. It had always been an effective way to clear my mind and help me refocus. Today, I had a new plan.

Ace Warner was a dropkick, yet I'd been planning to keep him close so I could gather intel on the Drake's involvement with what was happening, not only in my city, but with House Jupiter and the rest of the country.

I didn't really speak to him because I got pissed off every time I saw his face. Today was different though. I needed him.

The glass slide I'd found in Mark's bedhead burned a hole in my pocket, waiting for the class to end.

I exhaled heavily, then took my time breathing in through my nose. I had my eyes closed while I sat on the grass in the miniature Verdant Plateau. The sun warmed me and a cool breeze caressed my skin. It was the perfect weather for it. Luna was using a soft voice to direct us through our meditation, helping our minds find peace and connect with our magic. At least, that's what was supposed to be happening.

This class aimed to align our psyche with our magic and help us with control. I didn't know about the other Potentials here, but I had great control over my healing magic. My mums had always encouraged me to practise using it, not only on myself but on those in our city. Our magic was a gift to cultivate and better the world.

At least, that's what I had been taught. Entering the trials had shown me not all families felt the same.

Nevertheless, this lesson was, to the definition, peaceful.

If only I could focus.

I lifted a single eyelid to see Ace sitting to my right. His legs were spread out in front of him, not crossed like the rest of us. He reclined back on his hands, scowling at the sky. He wasn't even trying, and it pissed me off immediately.

I didn't know why he was getting under my skin this morning. It's not like he was behaving any worse than his usual grumpy, violent self, but something about him today was setting my teeth on edge. I just wanted to smack him around the head.

Unfortunately for me, I needed his help.

"Breathe in, breathe out," Master Luna said, and I closed my eyes once more and tried to clear my mind. She was directing us to envision our magic as a ball of light in our chests, but that wasn't working for me. Unlike fantasy books, healing magic wasn't light. It was clinical. More like a medical procedure, just without the tools or know-how.

I tried to relax my shoulders and settle into Luna's directions. Despite not wanting to actually win the trials and be king, these classes were still beneficial. They helped me hone the skills I'm sure I'd need the further I delved into the goings-on in Terrulia. If I could concentrate on my initial goal, that is.

My focus kept being railroaded by my emotions lately.

"I'd like you all to take one long, deep breath through your nose," Master Luna announced, drawing my mind back to the present. "And as you do so, I will reactivate the chips and you'll lose your magic once again."

Her tone was calm and soothing, though her words sent a buzz of adrenalin through me. It was unnatural not to feel my magic.

"I want you to remain calm and collected. Let the inner peace you have found stay with you for the rest of the day."

Unfortunately, I had only a microscopic speck of the inner peace she was referring to.

She began counting. I breathed in, readying to feel my magic disappear. It wasn't a gradual thing. One minute it was there and then it was ripped away, leaving me feeling cold and half empty. I opened my eyes and looked around.

Most people were slowly returning to reality. And then there was Ace, ignoring Luna, now sitting up and tapping away at his cuff.

Rude asshole.

Rising from the ground, I stretched out my arms and legs, and tried to hold on to whatever scrap of relaxation I could. Potentials left the area in small groups, and I soon found myself alone with Ace. An intentional move, but judging by the look he skewered me with, not one he was pleased about.

"Ace," I called, surprising him.

His eyes narrowed slightly, his scowl deepening. Then he looked me up and down, and the hard lines of his face settled into a smirk.

"Thought mediation was supposed to relax you."

"How would you know? Not like you took part."

He shrugged. "Not my thing. What do you want, Hawthorn?"

"What makes you think I want anything?"

One dark brow raised in answer.

"Fine," I replied with a sigh. I needed his help and acting like a child wasn't doing me any favours. "I've got a question."

He chuckled, shaking his head. "Help."

"Yeah," I replied. "Nothing gets past you."

"Not gonna happen."

My shoulders tensed, my fist clenching at my sides. "Why not?"

"Don't play dumb, it doesn't suit you." He smirked and shouldered past me. "I'm not doing shit for you."

"I'd have thought you'd want to," I snapped. "Show that you're on my side."

Ace whirled around, storming back towards me. He grabbed my shirt, lifting his fist to my chin, his chest against mine. I didn't avert my gaze for a second. He didn't intimidate me. I saw him for who he was.

"I don't need to show you shit. Saint Noah really needs to get the fuck off his high horse, or I might feel inclined to knock you off." He shoved me and I fell back on my ass. "While you're at it, get over whatever little fucking tale you've told yourself in that head of yours." He tapped me on the temple with his free hand. "Your attitude is getting old."

"Says the guy with the biggest attitude in the entire country."

"Don't push your luck," he said standing over me. His tone was full of warning, which I'm sure would have made most people wet themselves. "I tolerate you more than the rest, but if you're going to act like a little bitch, then I'll treat you like one. I promise you, Noah, you don't want to piss me off."

I huffed a laugh. "I'm not afraid of you. I've seen what happens when you let your guard down and you're not as scary as you want people to believe. You're all talk, Atticus."

His face twisted at the mention of his real name. I couldn't help the slight trickle of regret—or maybe it was fear—that I'd pushed too far.

Ace snarled and then his boot was in my side, slamming against my ribs. "Your selfless endeavour to save the world is a waste of time. I didn't think they gave out sainthoods anymore."

"How would you know when you've invested so much time and energy in living on the wrong side of the law?" I glared up at him, my ribs burning.

"Are you looking for accolades?" He laughed, folding his arms over his chest. "You won't win any here."

"Big words there," I replied, rising to my feet. It wasn't my finest hour, but staying on the ground would get me another boot to the chest. "Got yourself a word of the day app?"

Ace eyed me, but I held my ground. I wasn't giving in to him, fear or not. There was no way I'd give him the opportunity to stab me in the back again. He could punch and kick me all he liked. I'd never yield

"Your smart ass will get you killed one day," he promised, tension rolling off him. He flexed his bionic hand, a finger snapping open to reveal the tip of a blade.

I narrowed my gaze at him. "Luckily, I won't be relying on you to watch my back anymore."

"What an upgrade the merman is. I hope you two are happy together." He stepped back and grinned wickedly. "Or should I say three? You're both wrapped around the princess's finger, after all."

"Jealous?" I grinned, knowing Fallon was a soft spot for him. He hated he was attracted to her. It was obvious to anyone bothering to look.

"Fuck no," he growled, his tattooed arms tensing.

"Bit aggressive for such a simple question," I replied, my smile growing. "Almost like you're trying to hide behind your anger. Maybe if you didn't lie and cheat everyone around you, you'd be less pissed off."

"For the last time," he said through gritted teeth, "I didn't lie to you."

"Oh, good," I replied. "Now that you've said it like that, I totally believe you."

He rolled his eyes at my sarcasm. "Whatever. Keep being a fucking asshole."

Ace turned his back and stormed off.

I was done with this conversation anyway. He would never help me, and I decided I didn't want it if this was his reaction. I'd find my own way to access whatever was on the glass slide. I rolled my shoulders and cracked my neck.

Gods dammit, the guy had gotten under my skin. I wouldn't say we were ever friends, but in here he'd been the closest thing that I had. Yet, he'd fucked me over.

Whatever speck of relaxation I'd felt after meditation was completely gone. Ace had made sure of that. There was only one way I was going to take the edge of my current mood.

Visualising my goal, I planned my next move—which involved Fallon. She'd be able to fill in some of the missing pieces and give me a better picture of where to go next.

Her combat lesson with Zane would be finishing about now, and if I jogged over, I was sure I'd be able to catch her before he whisked her away.

I took off towards the training area, giving Ace a shove as I ran past. It was petty, but looking back to see him stumble was worth it.

It didn't take long to spot Fallon, her face bright as she laughed at something Zane said. He placed a hand on her arm, stopping her from walking, and turned her to face him. He was going in for the kiss and, sure, I felt bad, but I needed her. He would have to wait.

I didn't slow, running straight up to her and scooping her into my arms before Zane even realised what was happening.

Fallon laughed as I ran with her, the sound growing louder when Zane shouted something about sneaky seals.

"This is a surprise," she said, as I slowed my pace and carried her off the path. Having her in my arms had immediately calmed my agitation. An unexpected side effect, but I'd take it.

I carefully placed her on her feet. "A good one, I hope."

She bit her lip and raised a brow. "So, what's with the kidnapping?"

"I need your help," I replied with a smile. "I'm hoping some fresh eyes on my investigation will give me much-needed insight."

She grinned, gesturing towards the dorms. "Lead the way."

Fallon sat on my bed once we made it to my room, and I ducked under it, retrieving the notebook from the loose board beneath. It wasn't the most secretive place to hide my thoughts, but even if they found it, I banked on people not being able to understand what I wrote inside.

I sat next to Fallon and opened it to a double page sprawled with a mix of symbols, numbers, and letters.

"Okay," Fallon began. "Am I meant to understand any of this?"

"It's in code," I replied, my lips tugging at one side. "Never know who is going through your stuff. You can learn a lot about a person by what they pack in their bags."

"Noah Hawthorn," she teased, raising her brow. "Have you been a bad boy hunting through peoples' things?"

I felt a little guilty about going through her stuff, even though it wasn't intentional, and I had put everything away once I'd figured out it was hers. I ran a hand over my cropped hair and flashed my best grin. "Oh, you know me, doing what I do best."

"Good." She nodded, then waved her hand over the notebook. "Talk me through this. What am I looking at?"

"Here are my suspects at the academy," I said, pointing to the first three names. "They aren't the leaders, but I believe they'll have information that will guide me further."

Fallon trailed a finger over my targets. "Mark, Victoria, and…"

"Ace."

She stiffened at the last name. I hadn't realised until now how close we sat; our sides pressed together. Now that I was aware of it, I was finding it hard to think of anything else. Her lips moved, but I didn't hear, too transfixed on their shape.

"Noah?" she asked, placing a hand on my thigh and squeezing.

"Yeah, sorry. Lost in thought."

Her eyes crinkled with amusement. "I was just asking for a recap on what we have on these people."

"Right." I scratched my head. "We know Mark was kidnapping people from the Verdant Plateau, DH, and I'm guessing the Crimson Steppes, and selling them. Presumably, to House Jupiter. Both Mark and Victoria were working with a hooded guy, who is also connected to the Drakes somehow. I think the Drakes are acting as middlemen, maybe taking a cut of the profits. I'm not sure what else they would gain, but I'm betting it's more than credits."

Fallon nodded, though her expression showed nothing. After what she'd told me about her parents, as well as Victoria's involvement in torturing me about Mark, I supposed it didn't come as a surprise.

"The Drakes supplied the helicopter in the trial that was supposed to take the Potentials Mark had rounded up," I continued, my gaze scanning down the list I'd created beneath Ace's name. "And Ace had conveniently offered to pose as Mark for that exchange. The Drakes are the transport and muscle."

"Makes sense," she agreed. "The people in charge wouldn't want to get their hands dirty. Which would mean Mark was a middleman too, just like the Drakes. Any ideas who he was reporting to?"

"Apart from the hooded guy, it's anyone's guess," I replied. "But I think your family is further up, heading it all."

Fallon shook her head. "My parents wouldn't employ someone from another city to head a major operation country-wide. Work with them, maybe, but they would hire one of their own if they were running the thing."

"Am I right though? About them potentially being the buyers at least?"

"Most likely." Fallon chewed her lip. "We don't have proof, but the clues are hard to deny."

"Let's assume they are for now. Why would they need them? Where would they take such a large number of captives?"

Fallon faced me, her copper eyes full of regret. It seemed I'd hit on something that caused her feelings to no longer be carefully hidden like a minute ago as she said, "The crystal mines."

KAYDEN

"Water," I barked, holding out my hand. The guy flinched, running forward and filling a cup before returning and holding it out for me with a shaking hand.

"Y-yes boss."

I snatched it from him and downed it in one go. Then crushed the cup in my hand before eyeing off the runt. "And get me a towel and some of those protein cookies," I added, just because I could. The dude ran off on his spindly legs and I huffed a laugh, returning to my set.

I wouldn't call my minions friends, but they sure came in handy when I needed something. Or even if I didn't. Fucking around with them was the only amusement I had these days, other than chasing my angel.

Speak of the feathered devil…

Fallon walked in, looking all kinds of stunning in black and bronze leggings and a rust-coloured crop that made her skin glow. It's as if she was wearing my colours just for me. She walked straight toward me, throwing a small smirk before veering at the last second to grab a bar and do some squats.

Cheeky angel.

I caught a few of my minions looking at her ass as she squatted. I growled. The low rumble in my throat made them scatter like ants. When they were gone and it was just Fallon and me, I sidled over to her, checking her form and nodding in approval.

Her ass was utter perfection as she squatted. I shifted slightly, so I had a full view. I had to stop the groan wanting to escape—had to stop myself from charging forward and taking what she utterly enjoyed throwing in my face.

"Did I pass the gym test?" she asked with a smile as she finished her set.

I scoffed, folding my arms as I leaned against the mirror beside her. "Angel, you could run circles around the other lab rats."

"Hmm." She pursed her full lips and cocked her head. "And what about you? Think you can beat me in a race?" Her eyes glimmered with the challenge, lighting my body up in response.

Casually, I leaned in and grabbed the bar she was repping, then tossed it over my shoulder, not bothering to follow the sound of the *clang* or the hole that the weights had probably left in the floor.

"That depends," I said in a low voice, running a hand down her side. "What do I get if I win?"

Her cheeks flushed, her body angling towards me as she stepped closer, her mouth an inch away from mine. "I'm sure we can come to a mutual agreement." Her lips grazed my own so softly, but before I could kiss her, she pulled away and flicked her ponytail in my face.

I let it slide because there was no fucking way I was losing. Not when so much was at stake. Not when she swished her hips and looked over her shoulder with a sly little smile.

"Are you coming, big guy?"

"Not yet."

She rolled her eyes and patted the treadmill next to her. "A race at the highest speed. Whoever can last the longest wins. The loser has to … grant the other a request."

My smile widened. "*Any* request?"

She stared right back, unflinching. "*Anything*."

I swaggered over to the treadmill beside her, the machine groaning as I jumped on.

"One minute warmup, then we're on. Ready?" she asked sweetly, and I nodded.

The one minute went too fast, then we were off. The treadmill was barely big enough to accommodate me as my shoes pounded, faster, faster, until we were running so quickly my legs may as well have been pinwheeling.

"Fuck," I roared as it kept going, the sweat dripping down my temple and into my eyes.

I risked a glance at Fallon, and she was puffing just as hard. Her chest heaved as her toned legs moved in double time to my long-ass strides. When she smiled back at me, true panic rose. What the fuck? I was going to lose because, let's face it, muscles like mine weren't designed for marathons or sprints.

Determined, I pushed everything I had into staying strong. Maybe a little too strong. As my shoe stomped down on the treadmill, the damn thing sparked, throwing a tantrum as it sputtered out and smoke billowed out from beneath it.

"Oh, shit." I wheezed as it gave one last puff of smoke and then went dead … the belt taking me right with it off the back of the machine and into a rack. "Fuck!"

I'd formed my rock skin before I collided with the deadly weights behind me, but it wasn't the physical pain that hurt me. My ego deflated like a fucking balloon, squashed like roadkill. She would never let me live it down, and I would never get that date with her, let alone a damn blowjob.

Fallon gasped as she crashed to her knees beside me. "Are you okay?" I turned my head away to hide my flaming cheeks, but her fingers curled through my hair to tuck some of the red strands back. "Kayden, show me your face."

I grumbled, allowing her to tilt my chin.

Her eyes were soft as she stared at me, a small smile lifting her lips as she tried not to laugh. To her credit, she swallowed it down. "Much better. Now, tell me, are you okay?

"I hurt my head a bit," I admitted, trying not to wince. May as well be honest, because how much worse could it get?

She bent down—giving me a prime view of her premium cleavage—and kissed me on the forehead. "Better?"

"I hurt my cheek too."

She smiled knowingly, then leaned down, pressing a feather-soft kiss to my cheek.

"And here." I pointed to my jaw.

Several more kisses trailing along the stubble.

"And—"

I didn't get to finish as her lips met mine, her kiss consuming me, burning me up from the inside. She tasted so fucking good, like peaches and cream. Her tongue curled around mine so expertly, so perfectly. My dick twitched to attention. I felt myself instantly harden as I pulled her to me—on me—her barely covered pussy sliding against my cock as she straddled me.

If anyone walked in, they'd get a fucking eyeful. And the thought of that made me growl as I pulled her closer, cradling her ass cheeks in my hands and letting her feel the full extent of my appreciation.

She groaned as I moved a hand down her ass and over the flimsy material covering her pussy, sliding my palm against her. Fallon wriggled against me, her breath turning heavy and ragged as we ground against each other like fucking teenagers.

Fallon broke away, biting her lip as she ran her hands over my chest. "Do you want to—?"

"Yes," I grunted, needing every inch of restraint to not tear those tights off right now.

"In the—"

"Pool room," I commanded, lifting her into my arms and carrying her through the gym. She didn't protest as I claimed her lips again, both of us devouring each other like we couldn't get enough. I stumbled blindly through the room and shoved into the doors with my back to avoid bumping her into anything.

I was a gentleman, after all. Ladies came first.

As I stepped into the pool room, everyone stared first at Fallon, then at me, their faces paling. But one pointed look in their direction and they all ran. All of them but the redhead who'd made it her mission to cling to my side.

Her eyes honed in on Fallon, narrowing, but as she opened her lips, I growled, "Say one word, one fucking word, and you'll be target practice in my next combat class."

Fallon burst out laughing, and the look the girl threw her was pure venom. I'm sure that would end well later, but my girl had nothing to worry about there. She was pure fucking fire and would never back down from a fight. I was pretty sure nothing bothered Fallon Auger, probably because she'd seen and done things that would give that girl nightmares.

The redhead did as she was told and promptly left, shooting daggers the whole way out.

"Where were we?" I purred, bouncing Fallon in my arms. She gifted me a giggle which was like music to my fucking ears.

"Sauna," she said huskily.

"Fuck. Yes."

I almost turned into my boulder form in my rush to get there, but that would have been embarrassing as all hell. I'd be hard for her in a minute alright, and I'd make that angel sing.

The sweat that dripped into my eyes was the only thing that gave me pause. And Fallon would curse me for what I was going to do next, but she wouldn't punish me. Not when her eyes were closed, so focused on our kiss. I had her hook, line, and fucking sinker.

"Hold your breath, sweet cheeks," I said.

Her brow crinkled before her eyes widened a moment later. "Oh, no. Don't you dare!"

Too late, I jumped into the pool, sending a tidal wave rushing over the edges. She broke the surface, her hair over her face. She looked so cute, all angry and dishevelled. "Kayden!"

I shook my hair like a dog and cocked my head. Her little pout turned into a smirk.

"All clean for you, my lady," I said with a mock bow.

She rolled her eyes, punching me in the arm. "You're such an ass. Hurry up and take me, godsdammit, before I change my mind."

My laugh rumbled from my chest as I scooped her over my shoulder and carried her caveman style into the sauna room. "Yes, ma'am."

The door groaned as I slammed it open and sat Fallon's perky ass on the highest bench. She spread her legs wide, teasing, her finger crooked as I strode over.

"Uh-uh," she said, throwing a hand up. "You didn't think I'd let you go unpunished, did you?"

I shot her a crooked grin. "Wouldn't dream of it, Angel."

She stood slowly, peeling off her drenched tights and panties, then the crop top that was glued to her perfect tits. When she finished, she closed her eyes, pulled the tie from her hair, and flicked it out. The stare she gave me when those copper eyes opened was deadly in all the best ways.

By all that was merciful, she really was an angel. That body was sculpted by the gods, every dip and swell a master creation. Water dripped down the planes of her torso, her long hair half-covering the generous curve of her breasts. No, she wasn't just an angel. She was heaven. And I was about to open the gates to paradise.

"On your knees," she commanded.

I dropped to them one after the other, at this queen's mercy. *No one* told me what to do, and yet for her I felt compelled. Like this angel from the sky had some damn sway over me. I would still be king—her king—but for this, I could bend the knee. In private, with nobody to witness, I could be her willing servant. She smiled, nodding approvingly, then sat upon her throne, those legs widening again, giving me a full view.

"Crawl."

Flynn's voice in my head told me not to debase myself, to put her in her place, but I shrugged ghost Flynn the fuck away and told him not to be a cock blocker.

"For you, sweetheart, anything. I'd crawl through glass if only to make you shatter too."

She shivered as, slowly, I crawled across the floor, heading towards that gleaming body. And when I made it there, I pounced, dominating her as I knew she so badly wanted.

Fallon groaned as I grabbed her legs, hauled her towards me, and shoved my head between her thighs, licking up her centre. The faint tang of chlorine hit my tastebuds, but I lapped at her, sucking and kissing and flicking my tongue over her clit.

Her hand latched into my hair, tugging roughly, the nails digging into my scalp immediately making me harder. She was so full of fire.

Not meek and mild, not submissive, but just as rough and tumble as me. *Perfect.*

This was a punishment I could get around. She moaned, her legs stiffening, her back arching and nipples peaking despite the sweat and water trickling down her naked torso. I grabbed her hip and planted her there, pinning her in place until her eyes rolled and her thighs tightened around my head.

Peaches and cream and pure sex. I slid two fingers into her dripping pussy, moving them in and out, increasing my pace as her muscles contracted around me and her moans grew louder.

"Come for me, baby."

I nibbled her tender bud, and she unravelled, her legs shivering as she cried out. The sight, the sound, it only made me harder. And I couldn't wait anymore. I wanted to make her do it again. I wanted to do it with her.

I leaned back in satisfaction as I licked the taste of her from my lips. "Turn around," I demanded, and she complied, still tremoring as she arched her back. I bent her over the bench even further, admiring the perfect view.

I took my time running a hand down her spine, over the curves of her ass, then up to clasp each breast. She wriggled against me, her breathing ragged as I teased her with the tip of my dick. A frustrated noise ripped from her, and she looked over her shoulder indignantly. "Kayden…"

"Say please," I said cockily, shooting her a wry grin.

She growled again, then jerked as I slapped her ass away, preventing her from sinking onto my tip. When she huffed, I knew it was go-time.

"Please."

I slammed home. Her pussy was so wet I slid to the base, groaning at how good her inner walls felt around me. "So tight," I said in approval.

Her only response was a garbled plea for *"More"* as I moved my hands over hers and thrust hard and fast, claiming that sweet spot. She met my every push, grinding against me, until suddenly she pulled away and moved around me. Turning me roughly, I let her push me back until I was sitting on the bench. Then, with a sexy smile, she straddled me again, sinking achingly slow onto my cock. I blinked in surprise, but she grinned wider as she raked her nails down my chest, then bounced, slowly rocking her hips like she had all the time in the world.

"Fuck, Fallon," I said, as her sensual grinding had me nearly bursting.

My hand reached for her breast and she smacked it away with a smirk, pushing me back and moving faster, taking charge. I fucking loved it, mesmerised by this woman who didn't take no shit. The challenger in me couldn't have her winning, though, so I grabbed her ass cheeks and bounced, driving her up and down so hard she began panting, moaning.

I was so close it was an effort to keep from exploding inside of her. But I wouldn't go until she did, not that I had to wait long. I squeezed her ass cheeks, then moved one hand to stroke lazy circles over her clit while she moved.

"Shatter for me, darling," I whispered in her ear. "I want my dick soaked with your cum."

She sucked in a breath and did exactly as commanded. I groaned, exploding moments after, my cum shooting inside her tight pussy. Her legs quivered so much I had to hold her up, her arms winding around mine. Not exactly a cuddle, but something close. A soft, squishy part of me enjoyed that feeling far too much, but I shoved that useless weakling of an emotion down as I pulled her to my chest. She didn't seem to care that I was still seated inside her, just a boneless heap as she crumpled in my lap.

She grinned, her body gleaming with sweat, just as mine was. "Not exactly how I planned to spend my morning."

"Not quite, but it beats the shit out of anything else, right?"

"Mmm." She tapped a finger to her lip, considering. "I don't know. Maybe Zane or Noah might have given me a better ride."

"Those two?" I deadpanned, scoffing. "They swim in the kiddie pool. We both know you like it rougher."

"Maybe." Her smirk grew. "Maybe I'll decide soon which I prefer. Or *who*."

I growled at the thought of her being with anyone else, even if the chase turned me on just as much. The thought of what I'd gain if I captured her once and for all. Fallon was one of the most powerful women here. She'd already proven to be a good ally, and she'd look smoking on the arm of a king. But more than that … I wanted to spend time with her. Something I didn't really understand yet.

Without thinking twice, I kissed her firmly, ravaging her with my tongue and biting down on those plump lips. She didn't seem to mind tasting herself, and it only made me want to go for round two.

I pulled away, looking into those molten copper eyes. "Baby, you can pretend to be a good girl, but we both know you like them bad. I can give you what you want."

She grinned, flicking me on the nose before stepping off and pulling her clothes back on. "We'll see."

When we were dressed, I took her hand in mine, surprising both of us with the action. But she didn't pull away, and I took that for the win that it was.

"So, I'll see you tonight then."

Her brows pulled up as she looked at me. "What's tonight?"

"Our date, gorgeous." I threw her a wink. "I'll pick you up from your room at seven."

Her eyes crinkled as she laughed. "And what should I wear to said date?"

"Wear something … sexy."

"Of course you'd say that." She rolled her eyes, shrugging as she opened the sauna door. "I'll think about it."

"You play so hard to get, Angel. I'm going to—"

I stopped as she ground to a halt, her spine rigid and warm where she pressed back into me. I placed a hand on her shoulder, immediately tensing, shifting to shield her from any Potential stupid enough to start shit.

The only one I found was face down in the pool, blood clouding the water around them. That shit was a real mood killer. I sighed, figuring I'd better find someone to clean up the mess, but Fallon's face had gone white.

I stepped around her, cupping her cheek. "What's going on in that pretty head of yours? I know it's not just seeing another dead body."

We'd seen plenty of those. What was another one? It's not like this one was one of her friends. But I wasn't dumb enough to ignore what was happening. Was another Potential trying to change the game? Even the odds by taking some competition out?

Her lips pursed as she finally looked at me. "That first murder on academy grounds? Well, Noah and I found the body. It's … complicated."

I shrugged, curious as hell, but figuring that maybe she'd trust me enough to tell me when she was ready. I knew she, Zane, Kendra, and Noah had gotten closer since the trial, huddling together like groupies, whispering and laughing and flaunting their buddy-buddiness.

I'll admit, maybe a small part of me was jealous and hoping I'd be invited into her group. Noah, Zane, and Kendra were powerful, annoying as they could be, but they'd sure beat the whining of my Potentials.

"Guess I'd better get someone to come help," I said, scrubbing a hand over my face.

Fallon nodded but didn't answer as she studied what remained of the body. I couldn't tell much from afar, but it looked like someone had tried to make it into a sponge or something, with how many holes were in it. Damn psychos in this place. Maybe Ace took some of his anger at me out on the dude.

I grinned at the thought. Sucked to be him.

It immediately soured as I remembered Fallon had already been with him. With a sigh, I stalked out of the room and headed towards the Overseer's office.

Halfway there, my cuff pinged, and I checked it lazily, expecting to find a video or photo of some prank on a Potential.

My shoes almost tripped over each other as I stopped at the photo that popped up from an unknown account, posted on the Acadameet app.

Fallon, looking all kinds of sexy, standing over the dead body in the pool, her face thoughtful as she gazed at it. Almost as if admiring the work. I looked back to see if the one who'd taken the photo was in the room. But there was no sign of anyone. How did they get a snap of her without either of us noticing? The murderer was craftier than I imagined.

Worse, the way they'd taken this photo made it look like *she* had done it. Was that their plan? Had they left the body here intentionally, knowing Fallon was with me in the sauna and waited for her to come out? Fuck my rocky balls. This was not good.

I stood there and uttered another long sigh. "I guess that's a no to our date, then."

FALLON

"How many times do I have to tell you? I didn't fucking do it."

"Language, Fallon," Luna admonished, but her eyes were apologetic as she gazed at me. She knew I hadn't killed anyone—at least not today—but it wasn't so easy to convince Dumb and Dumber as they grilled me. They may as well have been prodding me with a hot freaking poker.

I'd been trapped in Master Luna's office all afternoon as Nolan and Jeremiah had taken their sweet ass time, asking me the same stupid questions about the dead boy in the pool. They hadn't seemed to care that Kayden had made it to the Overseer a few minutes after we'd found him, informing them it wasn't me and would attest to that as my alibi that I hadn't been involved nor saw anything to suggest who had been.

I had no clue where *she* was right now, but I'd bet she was busy cleaning up whatever mess the Masters had made of things. The first kill had been an obvious threat, so I had to assume they'd either failed to meet the blackmailer's expectations, or they were now just doing it for sport. Hell, for all I knew, the Overseer might be the killer.

My curiosity was piqued, that was for freaking sure. Someone had set me up, painting a guilty sign on my back, and I had no plans of letting that go. Apparently, the academy wasn't done with screwing with the Augers. Or one Auger at least, seeing as Victoria would likely chop people's heads off for trying something like this with her.

The funny thing was, had it been anyone else in this academy being bullied or targeted, they could go crying to their mummies and daddies about it. Well, not fucking me. My delightful sperm donor was probably off brutally murdering someone right now and having a grand old time. It was more likely my parents would be offended that I was only framed for the murder, not the cause of it.

Until the second trial arrived, I would have to use what precious time I had to find answers. Once I got out of here anyway. Little old me had some big ass prey to hunt. A blackmailer and a murderer. Both, I had zero issues with using my skills against.

"Miss Auger, are you listening?" Master Jeremiah was saying, his dreamy green eyes drilling into mine.

"What?" I shook my head. "Sorry."

The door burst open at that moment, nearly blasted off its hinges, followed by Kayden's booming voice, "She didn't do it, officers."

Jeremiah raised a brow. "That's Master to you, Hale. We're not in some damned city district. And we got your point the first fifty times you mentioned that this morning."

I bit back a laugh as Kayden's brown eyes swept to me, his brows creasing. He *really* didn't want it known he cared. Or maybe he just hadn't admitted that to himself, but no guy went out on a limb just for good pussy … did they?

I didn't know, but I was starting to think he was a little lonely, and it was no wonder with all the ants building his colony. They were freaking terrified of him.

I yawned, leaning back in my chair and feigning indifference as I looked between the Masters. "So what's it gonna be, the stocks or a prison cell?"

Luna jerked. "Good grief, girl, we aren't locking you up."

My glare lingered on Masters Nolan and Jeremiah. "Could've fooled me."

She sighed, running her fingers over her temple, then eyeing off Kayden. He was waiting impatiently in the doorway. My heart warmed a little at what Jeremiah had said. An exaggeration, sure, but Kayden had clearly battled with them on my behalf. Brutish or not, I was right about that little marshmallow centre. Oh, and how I'd roast him for it too.

"How do we know you're not bloody well covering for her?" Nolan said finally, his gaze suspicious. The guy looked like he hadn't had a good night's sleep in days. His under eyes looked like freaking ball bags drooping down.

"Because." Kayden huffed again. "I was … we were…"

"We were fucking," I said, crossing my arms and smirking as they all looked at me in shock. I shrugged. "What? Did you want me to phrase it differently? We were in the sauna, having raunchy, filthy sex"—I winked at Kayden—"and then found old mate floating in the water. I didn't touch the guy and barely got a look at him before someone snapped the photo and posted it, like I have already said."

Nolan rolled his eyes. Luna had the grace to bend her head, and Jeremiah just stared at me curiously, just about undressing me with his eyes as he studied me. Or at least that's what it felt like with that handsome face and assessing stare.

"Let her go," Jeremiah said.

"What?" the rest of us said at once.

"But, Jeremiah," Nolan began.

The Master shot Nolan a bored look. "There was no weapon found, no evidence of a fight on her person. We can't hold her."

"He's right," Luna chimed in, tapping her nails on the sleek wooden desk they sat behind. Like the rest of her office, everything was neat, orderly, and minimalistic. "You're free to go, Fallon."

Nolan leaned forward, scowling. "One toe out of line, girl, and there will be consequences. No matter who your parents are. I'll be watching you."

I sized him up and shrugged. "If it helps you sleep at night, I can arrange a meeting with Victrus and Eliana. Just to smooth everything out."

Nolan's already pale skin turned ashen. "No, no, that'll be fine. Everything's straight and narrow."

"Of course," I said, smiling sweetly and dipping my head. Okay, so maybe my empty threat was cruel, but he deserved it, and it's not like he was a real danger. Not to me. Not after the things I'd seen and done.

The Masters ushered me and Kayden out without a word, except for

Luna who, attempting to close the broken door gave up with a stern look at Kayden, and whispered, "For what it's worth, I believe you, Fallon."

I gave her an honest smile. She was strange, but I liked her. Luna seemed genuine, like she actually cared how well her students did. Even though we both knew there wouldn't be many left at the end of the trials.

Kayden fell into step beside me, the warmth of his proximity seeping into my body. I was dry now, but I hadn't been allowed to change and was still in my clothes from this morning. I cringed, not wanting to think about how I'd sat in sweat—among other things—all day. *Gross.*

"You didn't have to step in on my behalf," I told him. "I'm a big girl. I can handle it."

Kayden shrugged. "I know you can, sweet cheeks. I just wanted to watch you knock Nolan down a peg."

He bumped my shoulder, and I smiled through a yawn. "The highlight of that meeting, for sure."

"Get some rest, Angel. I'll see you tomorrow?"

It was a question, not a demand, which was so unlike Kayden's usual domineering persona that I lifted a brow. "What, no offhand remark about this morning or mention of our date?"

"I'm confident you'll want to pick this up another time. Besides, you'll need your beauty sleep so you're at your best the next time I own your ass."

I snorted. And there he was. "Not happening, big guy. I'm not yours to own."

"Not yet, but I will claim you. I always get what I want, Angel." He winked, throwing a hand up as he turned and walked away. "Sweet dreams, sugar tits."

That insufferable little … I blew out a breath, which turned into a small laugh. Kayden was quickly becoming a lot more interesting, and not just because he was an absolute demon in the sack. Damn near impaled me this morning, and even I could admit I was a little eager to do it again.

But I was more intrigued by this new side of him. I'd seen the longing glances and the puppy dog eyes when he looked at my group in the caff. Kayden wanted allies, yes, but he *needed* friends. Maybe the big guy had gotten a taste of working together, and realised he didn't need to be some lone wolf. The tough guy thing? It was just an act if I was judging right. Although there was no denying he immensely enjoyed training his minions.

I shook my head, telling myself to get a grip as I began walking back to my room. What had started off as a great day had quickly spiralled, and after playing the role of Miss Murderer in that fun little post today, I wasn't in the mood to face any Potentials. What I needed was a shower, a good night's sleep, a merman who made a hell of a big spoon, and snacks. Please, gods, let Zane have all the snacks.

I trudged back to my room in silence, going the long way around the grounds to avoid Potentials, which of course landed me smack bang in the middle of Victoria's war path.

"Murdering people now? Didn't think you had it in you, little sis," she said, sneering as she popped into view from behind a tree.

What kind of weirdo just hung around in the forest at night? But even as I thought that I realised the bitch was probably waiting for me, knowing I'd have been with the Masters and wouldn't want to deal with a crowd afterwards.

"Go find someone else to torment," I snapped, sidestepping her. "I'm really not in the mood."

She held an arm out, then locked onto my wrist as fast as an asp. "But I want to play with you," she replied, pouting her lips. "We had such fun the last time."

"Victoria, remove your hand, or I'll do it for you," I hissed. And I meant it. If she fucking riled me up any more, I'd rip the whole damn limb off.

She released me, but not before her other palm slammed into my chest. I stumbled back with a snarl, shifting into a defensive stance. She just looked at me in disdain.

"Who got you out?"

I glared at her. "What are you talking about?"

"The trial. Who got you out of there? I know you were dying. Someone had to have rescued you."

"Why the fuck do you care? More importantly, what makes you

think I'd tell you? You'd just add them to your long list of people to torture."

She clucked her tongue against her teeth. "I will find out, Fallon. And they will be punished."

"Go ahead," I roared. Victoria blinked, but I was done with her games. My hands balled into fists, my whole body trembling with rage. "You tried to kill me! And when you lost, you tried to kill me the coward's way. You're the disappointment, Victoria. Victrus would have left you in the mud to die had he known what weakness you showed. And the mistake I made of feeling any empathy towards you? It won't happen again, so I suggest you leave me the hell alone. Sound good?"

My sister's face grew redder with every passing second, and when she came for me, as I knew she would, I was ready. I latched onto her fist, angling my body and twisting her arm behind her back. She grunted, but I held firm against her wriggling.

"I'm going to enjoy killing you, Fallon," she spat. "Slowly. But not before I find all your friends and make you watch as I tear them apart piece by piece."

I leaned my head to her ear and whispered, "Wrong fucking answer." I twisted her wrist and a satisfying crunch of bone filled the air. She shrieked, the sound piercing the still night.

"You bitch," she cried out, a half-sob of pain wrenching from her.

I twisted harder this time, and some other ligament or bone snapped in her arm. Tears trailed down her cheek, but I had no fucks left to give for her pain.

"Touch me again, touch *any* of my friends, and I swear I will do to you what Victrus has made me do to so many others. I will run my blade through you again and again, so slowly, so carefully, you'll be alive the whole time as I peel you apart from the inside out. You're not the only one he taught so many lovely little tricks to."

"Fallon." She whimpered in my grip, but I'd become so twisted from our family's games, so blindsided by her before, that the humanity in me just winked out. Her cries meant nothing. Her pain, even less.

"Beg," I told her, keeping my grip locked tight around her limp wrist. "Beg me to let you go."

It was cruel. So fucking cruel, but a part of me wanted her to hurt for all she'd done. For all our parents had done. Red filled my vision. Every awful thing I'd ever committed raced through my mind.

It took me a while to snap out of the angry haze she'd put me in. But I eventually dropped her to the ground, horrified by what I'd done. I sucked in a shuddering breath as I stared at my sister curling in on herself. Then I turned away.

As I headed down the path towards the dorms, I didn't look back. It was only when I burst into my room, Zane staring at me in shock, that I let myself slow. But not until after I'd sprinted into the bathroom, locked the door, and hurled my guts up in the toilet.

"Starfish?" The doorknob jiggled, and my heart sagged even further at the sound of Zane's worried voice.

I'd asked her to beg. I'd hurt Victoria. The worst of it? Some small, sick part of me even enjoyed it. Tears tracked down my cheeks, and I sat there for a long time, my head hanging over the toilet bowl as I sobbed. Because what I'd done to Victoria … it didn't come close to the things I'd done under Victrus's watch. The things he'd made me do under the threat of punishing my siblings or hurting other people. Innocent people. I didn't want to be like that anymore.

After several minutes, I swallowed down the bile in my throat and finally dragged my sorry ass into the shower, clothes and all, until at some point Zane was there. How he'd gotten into the bathroom, I didn't know, but he undressed me slowly, washed my hair, my body, then tucked me into a bathrobe that had two dolphins on it.

Pip and Delilah. Delilah and Pip.

They looked so happy, with their over-exaggerated smiling faces. It's all I could focus on as Zane tucked me into his bed, then wrapped himself around me. I nestled into his solid, warm body, feeling myself slowly returning to reality, my breathing steadying out to match his.

"Fallon?" he asked quietly.

I swallowed. "Yes?"

"Don't worry about that photo or the murders. We'll find out who's behind all this and I'll keep you safe, my little dolphin. No one will ever hurt my super pod."

Fresh tears pricked at my eyes. He thought I was upset about the murder today. If only he knew all the things I'd done, he wouldn't be saying that to me. And maybe it made me selfish, but I didn't care. I didn't have the heart to tell him I was probably worse than that murderer … that just a few minutes ago I'd been the one dealing out the hurt.

ACE

Sitting in Master Luna's chair, I ran my hands along the leather arms as I stared at the computer screen and my cuff, the only sources of illumination in the room. It was late. I'd managed to sneak into the Master's office thanks to the key card I'd snatched off Zane the other day when he found me stuck with those guards. I'd stupidly got caught the first time trying to gain access to Luna's office. This academy had made me complacent, but I wouldn't make that mistake again. I learned my lesson and had taken a different route to find a way in this time.

The screen on my cuff scrolled through code as it transmitted to Luna's laptop, which had the user interface of the security system at the House of Ascension displayed on it. I was seconds away from seeing whether my code worked.

Up until now, I'd had a sort of ghost-like view of the security system, able to see some shit but not interact or delve further beyond the surface. Literally haunting it. Then the system had been updated, and I'd lost even that much access. Until now, that is.

The wall between me and the security system cameras fell, and I grinned like a fucking madman. I was in, but where to start?

I'd check out how to turn the cameras off later, but first I needed a better layout of the place. If I was to find the treasury and steal the weapon for the Drakes, I needed to know this place like the back of my hand. I'd had to physically scope out the halls of the main building, without much luck. Ended up getting myself trapped only to have Zane rescue me. Fucking embarrassing. But also frustratingly fortunate. Zane's cover story when we'd been questioned after the guards had tracked us down was ridiculous yet somehow, they'd believed it. Or maybe they just thought he was on drugs. One positive from that mess was the key card, which had proved more than handy tonight.

Finding no blueprint of the place, I opened the security footage and an entire page of tiny live feeds flickered onto the screen.

The fucking things were so small. How the fuck was I supposed to see anything in these thumbnails? Selecting one at random, I clicked on it. The live footage filled the screen, and I dragged my finger over the scroll wheel, skipping through each feed.

I flicked through video after video, looking for footage of inside the House of Ascension, and deleted anything of me where I shouldn't be while I was at it. I found the footage of me the other day before being apprehended. I'd had my hood up and sprayed the cameras with paint I'd snatched from the supplies shed. You couldn't tell it was me, but it was better to be safe than sorry. I continued my search until one video in particular caught my eye.

I paused the screen, then slowly dragged my finger to the left, backing up the clip. In one of the storerooms, Victoria Auger stood with someone dressed in a black hooded cloak. The video lacked sound, but there was no doubt they were up to some dodgy shit when the unknown figure handed her a pulse gun.

I knew there were hidden weapons amongst the Potentials here. It didn't take a mastermind to know that the Houses would not send their favourites to compete without some leg up. Guess those without weaponised bionic appendages had to be a bit more old school and ship their shit in under mediaeval cloaks.

Speaking of which. I clipped the top off my pinkie finger and pulled out the cord to connect my bionic hand to my cuff. I had a script on there that ran image recognition. If I installed it on the laptop, I could scan the videos and see who else was getting help from the outside.

Once plugged in, the install took less than two seconds before I was running the thing. It would take some time for the program to scour through all the videos—even longer if I searched the files manually—

which meant it was the perfect opportunity to sit back and relax. Unplugging my hand, I retracted the cable back into my finger, then shifted in the seat until I was comfortable.

On second thought.

I pushed back the chair and started going through Master Luna's shit. The woman had to have something worthwhile in here. Booze or pills.

Something.

I rifled through the drawers and grinned when I found a bottle of whiskey in the bottom one. I grimaced at the label. It was cheap, and there was nothing in the office I could add to mask the flavour.

Beggars can't be choosers. So I sat back and took a swig as I watched the screen. The alcohol burned on its way down. Vile stuff. If Luna checked the bottle, she would know someone had been here, but I'd be long gone by then and the cameras would be wiped clean.

With each sip, the burning eased, as well as the tension in my muscles. I was wound tight, but it was nothing compared to the time after the first trial, before I moved to the secluded miniature DH.

My old room had too many annoying Potentials in it. After seeing the desperation to not only win but survive on so many of their faces, I decided I wasn't keen on staying among any of them. Not that I thought they'd get one up on me. But I wasn't interested in being woken in the middle of the night and having to beat the shit out of some fuckhead trying to knife me.

Plus, I liked my alone time. I think I'd die from my brain exploding in my skull if I had to listen to any more of the Potentials talk about their mundane lives or the other petty shit going on that they deemed worthy to discuss.

After the script finished running, I'd be heading back up to my new home away from home. No one bothered me there. Just how I liked it.

I breathed in deeply as I shut my eyes and could almost make myself believe I was closer to feeling some semblance of happy since arriving.

———— ✦ ————

I awoke to the sound of a beep and lock whirring outside my

room, only to realise I wasn't in my dorm or my new pad in mini-DH. I shouldn't have fallen asleep. I looked at my cuff and saw I'd slept until early morning. I quickly slammed the laptop shut and hauled my tired ass beneath the desk just as the door opened. Not the smartest move, but the desk was solid on one side. As long as they didn't come around, then I'd be set.

Slim fucking chance that I wouldn't get caught, but miracles happened. Occasionally.

"I don't like it either, Nolan, but Celeste gives the orders and we have to follow them," Luna said irritably. I'd be annoyed too if I had to deal with Master Nolan this early in the morning. Fuck, I hated speaking to him full stop.

"We can't ignore the murders of Potentials outside of the trials," he pushed. "It is illegal and I, for one, will not go down for aiding and abetting a murderer because that dotty woman thinks it's better to pretend nothing is happening."

"No one is going to jail over this," Luna replied with a heavy sigh. "There's no need to be dramatic."

"No? We are being blackmailed! And for all we know one of us could be the next victim. On top of that, are you also going to ignore all the shit going on outside this place?" Nolan spat. "These murders aren't the only thing happening and unless you want to wake up in prison or find yourself next, you'd best get on board."

The door slammed, the walls rattling from the impact. I didn't move an inch.

Luna's exasperated breaths filled the office. After a moment, her footsteps approached the desk, followed by the rustling of papers. Then the door opened and closed with a thud. I let out my breath and stretched my legs, groaning at the aches in my joints. Before I could get out of there, I needed to check my script.

I got up into Luna's chair, flipped open her laptop and checked its progress.

The script had picked up several videos with the same cloaked person. Looked like they were having nice little chats with a handful of people here—some they gave weapons to, like they had for Victoria.

I recognised her, a couple others all from House Jupiter, and Mark. Their clothing spoke volumes of their vanity and credit accounts. Most of the videos were obviously old as Mark was six feet under, or heavily digested by some monster after the princess diced him up.

I clicked on the last video. Footsteps sounded outside in the corridor. Luna must be back. I closed the video file instantly and charged to my feet. Leaning over the laptop I quickly opened the most recent camera footage for this part of the building, setting up a loop to run from now on. I shut the laptop, stuffing it under my arm along with the cables and flask I'd found in the drawer before looking out the window. I couldn't see a soul.

"Time to go," I muttered to myself. The office was on the ground floor, so I swiped the keycard and unlocked the window. I jumped out, racing away to the sound of the window slamming shut behind me.

I kept up the jog until I was sure I'd put enough distance between me and the main building, making it to the mini-DH before I slowed.

I grinned at what I'd achieved, but of course, the smile was short-lived. Like all good things in my life.

"Ace!" Danger Dog called.

I clenched my fists at my side, not in the mood to deal with that shithead today. He pulled up beside me and I wasted no time grabbing him by the shirt and throwing him against the nearest wall so he knew I wasn't in the mood.

"I was looking for you everywhere. You weren't in your room," he said, panting. His body hunched over as he slipped down to the ground.

Had the fucker run here? He was wearing leather pants, and that shit had to chafe like a bitch. He looked around, a puzzled expression on his punchable face.

"Why are you out here?" he asked.

"None of your business," I barked, towering over him. "You better have a good reason for ruining my morning."

He tried to get up, but I shoved him back with a boot to the shoulder. He lifted his hands up, and I allowed him to slowly rise to his feet.

"I've got intel," he said. "On Victoria."

"I'm listening."

His eyes darted around nervously, and I recognised the look immediately. The fucker may have been scared, but he was cataloguing my surroundings and where I could have been this early in the morning.

He knew too much.

I lifted my bionic hand and let my blades flick out, inspecting them casually. "*Now*, rat."

"She accepted me into her little group." Danger Dog grinned slyly, puffing out his chest, his acid-washed black t-shirt straining at the movement. He wasn't the muscliest guy, but he clearly wore shirts that were too small, hoping it would make him look bigger. Fucking tool. He continued, "Piece of cake, but I knew it would be."

I rolled my eyes. The last time we'd talked, she wouldn't let him near her. "You'd better have something better than that."

The rat licked his lips. "Word on the street is she's out for blood."

"Your street filled with old news reports?" I snapped. "Victoria is like a fucking vampire. Blood is all she wants."

I turned from him and strode away; aware the fucker followed after me.

"Don't you want to know who she wants dead?"

"Let me guess, her sister?"

His grating chuckle made me pause.

"Who?"

"Zane Loch."

My jaw ticked. Victoria must want to hurt the princess, so she was going after one of those closest to her. It pissed me off. Not because I gave a shit about Fallon or her feud with her sister, but because … fuck…

The merman.

Zane was a means to keep me in this joint, that's all. If I needed to team up in the next trial, he was the best option, especially now that Noah had an agenda against me.

I ran my hand through my hair. *Yeah, that's why I gave a shit about the merman.*

"What about me?" a cheery voice called.

My head snapped to the side. Speak of the fucking devil and he will arrive.

Zane popped his head out from behind the corner of the building, a smile on his dopey ass face.

Danger Dog opened his mouth. "Only that—"

"Shut the fuck up." I picked up a rock and threw it at Danger Dog's head. He whimpered like a little bitch, clawing at the fresh spray of blood on his temple.

"I was following him," Zane said, his voice lowered as he moved closer to me and wriggled his brows. "I remembered what you said about Kendra working for someone, and this dude has been looking all shades of suss."

"Kendra isn't working for this asshole."

Zane rolled his green eyes. "Obviously. Maybe he is helping her? Bottom of the bucket fish are always desperate. I saw him getting credits off Victoria. The whole thing smelled fishy."

"Are you double crossing me?" I said dangerously low, turning my attention on Danger Dog.

He stepped backwards, pressing himself into the wall again. He shook his head, his eyes wide. "I didn't do anything."

I stalked casually towards him, enjoying playing with my prey. "Zane, fuck off, yeah?"

"Please," Danger Dog begged. "We had a deal."

"One that you broke. Say a prayer to your gods, rat, because you'll be seeing them soon."

I rolled up my sleeves, revealing more of my bionic hand and my tattoos. I took his wrist in my metal grip and dragged him into the abandoned building he had pressed himself against.

I'd scoped out the entire place when I first made the mini-DH my home. There was no one here but me, and so many quiet places to deal with those who pissed me off.

Danger Dog squealed like a pig as I threw him down a flight of stairs into the basement of that derelict building. Small lines of light penetrated the dark space, thanks to holes in the ceiling, but it's not like there was anything to look at down here but dust and rust.

"Are we torturing someone?" Zane asked over my shoulder.

"Why did you follow me?" I snapped, my eyes remaining on my

next victim. "You're not doing shit. Go."

"But I've never tortured a person," Zane replied, not at all concerned with my bloodthirsty mood. "You can teach me. I'm a righteous student and if we are going to be working as a team…"

He darted around me and crouched over the rat who was looking equal amounts scared and confused.

"We are not a team," I hissed.

He slapped Danger Dog on the face.

I blinked. "What was that?"

"I'm showing him who's boss," Zane said, beaming, like this was How-To-Torture-Someone-And-Get-Away-With-It and he was my most promising student.

I sighed. "Obviously not you. You're not the torturing type. You're the lovable, fun guy."

"If I'm going to survive here, I need to diversify my skill set."

One blink later and Zane had stabbed a piece of metal into one of Danger Dog's shoulders. I hadn't even noticed him pick it up.

The rat let out a howl.

"I can tell that you have done something to Ace beyond taking his hand, which is messed up, by the way," Zane growled at Danger Dog. "Who steals someone's body parts? Bionic or not, that is fucked up. No one hurts my bestie and gets away with it."

I rearranged the laptop under my arm and took a sip from the flask I'd stolen. "You don't do things by halves, do you? Where'd you get the weapon?"

"Over there." Zane shrugged. He wrinkled his brow, tilting his head slightly to one side as he concentrated. "Am I doing it right?"

"You'll kill him too fast like that," I replied. "The trick is to scare them enough to talk but not hit anything vital. Can't have them bleeding out too quickly. Start small; nail beds, cutting off minor limbs, electrocution … stuff like that."

"I think I have an idea." Zane took the metal shard out and slammed it back in, giving it a twist for good measure. Danger Dog convulsed as his screams rung out.

"Someone is gonna hear you if you keep that up," I chuckled, looking to the ceiling. If anyone was walking by, we'd get caught.

I looked down to see Zane reach into his pocket and pull out a jar of water partially filled with sand and something that looked like a black and white shell.

I raised a brow.

"You said small. This is a marbled cone snail. Found it in the med bay. They were collecting antivenom from the little dude," Zane said, unscrewing the top. He pressed it to the rat's lips. "Open wide."

Danger Dog shook his head, but Zane wasn't deterred. The rat fought him feebly, but Zane was strong and unbothered by the protesting punches he was dealt. It was as though he was in some sort of trance. He shoved, crushing Danger Dog's not-so-pearly-whites as he pushed the contents of the glass jar into the guy's mouth.

I'd seen some messed up shit in my life, but looking at a guy choking on a snail was certainly new. Danger Dog's screams became muffled cries as his face swelled. His chest heaved, his muscles spasming before going unnaturally rigid. He would not last much longer. I was surprised he was still conscious and kinda impressed, if it weren't for the fact the rat was now useless.

"I didn't mean to stop the guy from speaking altogether," I snapped, running a hand over my face. "We won't get anything out of him now."

Zane looked at me sheepishly. "Sorry, I got a little carried away."

"Ya think?"

Zane frowned at Danger Dog; his shoulders slumped. "I thought it would last longer than this. The venom can take days to work."

"Well, it didn't, did it?" I hissed. "End him. There's no point keeping him around now. He's not gonna say shit."

Leaving Zane to it, I grabbed a lighter from my pocket and poured the remaining alcohol from the flask over Danger Dog's body.

Zane rose to his feet, holding the jar in his bloodied hand, the little shell back inside. He seemed concerned the jar had no water for the snail now. He grinned before taking off. "See ya bestie!"

I shook my head at Zane then dropped the lighter. Danger Dog's body instantly went up in flames. Mess with a Drake and reap the rewards. A one way ticket to the grave.

I smiled at the sight. I loved a good fire, especially one that was eating away at a scene. Chuckling, I jogged away to my camp a couple of buildings over. One problem gone and a laptop full of secrets gained.

When I reached my camp, I dumped my stuff on the makeshift bed and blew out a heavy breath. The fire had taken off now, eating its way through what was left of the dump of a building I'd left Danger Dog in. The frames were metal, so I had no fear of them falling or spreading to my camp. When I glanced out the broken window to see its progression, I saw emergency responders had already arrived to put it out anyway. Exactly as I'd predicted.

I dropped the laptop on the blanket beside me, only to remember the last video that I hadn't had a chance to view yet. Opening it, I found the cloaked figure standing in an empty classroom. Nothing of note happened for the first few minutes as I dragged the progress bar. I was about to give up and grab my things to go shower when someone entered the room on screen.

I'd never seen the guy before in my life. His face was as bland and immemorial as milk. The guy wore jeans and a shirt that was unbuttoned to the point of sleezy. Like the other videos, there was no audio, but I didn't need it. Actions most often spoke louder than words. I froze the frame, zooming in on the guy's open shirt.

Unlike his face, I'd recognise that tattoo anywhere.

The guy was marked for the Drakes. The problem was, I didn't know who the fuck he was or why he was here. Cormac had said I was the only Drake nominated for the trial. Looked like he was talking shit and this was just another secret he'd kept from me.

What else didn't I know?

I slammed the laptop shut and stormed across the room, punching the wall until there was a decent dent and blood poured from my split knuckles.

I hated being kept in the fucking dark.

My chest heaved, my rage spilling from me. But as I calmed, I realised there was a silver lining in this. I couldn't say shit to Cormac right now, but I could shove this video in Noah's smarmy face to get him off my case.

I grabbed the laptop and quickly transferred the video to my cuff, then set up another image scan, though this time I set it to look through all past and future videos to find the other Drake.

I was going to find the fucker and get some answers.

I hid the laptop, then grabbed my clothes and headed to the communal bathrooms. There, I showered off the blood and smell of smoke before throwing on my black, ripped skinny jeans, a white t-shirt and sneakers. I washed my other clothes then took a quick detour back to home sweet home before jogging to the caff to find Noah. I rarely picked up my pace for anything, but this was a special occasion.

It was ridiculous how much it pissed me off that Noah didn't believe me, but it fucking did. I was right, and he wouldn't accept it. Now he would see for himself, and I would get a close-up view of his face when he realised he was wrong.

I grinned. Fucker was going to eat his words.

As I reached the caff, I slowed, not wanting to come across as a desperate little bitch. I spotted the little shit walking alone, which was a change considering he'd been spending so much time with Fallon, Zane, and Kendra. Their friendship was obnoxious and made me wanna gag.

I grabbed Noah by the collar of his t-shirt, hauling his ass to the side of the caff out of sight. We didn't need an audience.

"What the fuck?" he hissed, pulling out of my grasp and turning on me. He threw a punch that I dodged easily.

"Chill," I replied with a smirk, ignoring the fact that I'd just sounded like the fucking merman. I cleared my throat. "Those meditation classes are a waste of time for you. You're as edgy as a druggie looking for his next hit."

"Yeah, because it's totally normal to be dragged into a darkened corner by the back of your shirt."

I glanced around and shrugged a shoulder. "Looks pretty fucking sunny to me."

"What do you want?" he asked, sighing heavily.

"I have something to show you."

Noah raised a brow, looking me up and down. "I'm sure you've paid many people to see it, but I'm not interested."

"Mind out of the gutter." I chuckled despite myself. Cheeky fucker.

I tapped my cuff, opened the video from the laptop, then stepped closer to show him. He didn't back away or even flinch like Danger Dog had every time I made a single move in his presence. I played the video.

"There's another Drake here," I said, closing the screen once it finished. "I don't know who that is, but it proves I'm not lying about the helicopter shit."

"That proves nothing," Noah replied, shaking his head. "All you've done is provide evidence of an associate here that you were keeping secret."

"If I was keeping him a secret, why would I tell you?"

"Who knows? A ploy to take my attention away from you so you can work unimpeded? Maybe it's all part of a bigger scheme that you and the rest of the Drakes have going on with House Jupiter, not to mention whatever Mark was up to."

I spat on the grass. "I have nothing to do with that shit, you asshole."

"I don't know what you were trying to achieve here," he said, turning to walk away. "All you've proven is that your gang is a corruption that's spreading, and you have access to files and systems you shouldn't."

Mother fucker. What had I said about a high-ass horse? I ground my teeth. I was done with trying to prove my innocence. Wasn't sure why I'd bothered—call it a brain aneurysm or something.

Noah could think what he wanted. I had more important things to deal with now. And when he finally realised the truth and wanted my help?

He could go fuck himself.

NOAH

"Someone started that fire in the DH arena, didn't they?" Kendra said, coming to sit opposite me in the reading nook beneath the stairs. "Think it was petty arson or another murder?"

Last I'd seen, smoke still hung like a storm cloud over the miniature Damascon Hollow. The fire had been put out, but not before it consumed a good section of one of the buildings, and probably all evidence of a crime scene.

I put the book I was reading down beside me.

"Who knows?" I shrugged. "At this rate, it could be both."

"True," she said, settling back into her seat and folding her arms over her chest. "So why did you invite me to the make out nook?"

"Make out nook?" I repeated, my brow scrunched as I looked around the small space. There were no windows and only a single door for entry, keeping it private. Green cushioned seats lined the walls and a warm light, perfect for reading, shone from the ceiling. "This is the reading nook."

Kendra snickered. "Maybe for you, but that's not what everyone else uses it for."

I froze, taking in the space once more. Dim mood lighting, fluffy cushions, ample privacy… "Well, fuck."

"Told you." She laughed and I couldn't help but join her.

I never said I was the brightest crayon in the box, though I wasn't naïve or anything. I just had never been the kind of person to be solely focused on getting some action. If I liked a girl, I'd go for it, but if there was no one on the cards, I didn't have a radar out searching for my next lay.

"You come here a lot then?" I teased, nudging her foot with my own.

Kendra blushed. "A few times."

I wiggled my brows. "Avid bookworm."

"Alright, alright." Kendra sighed; a grin still wide on her face. "What can I do for you? Why am I here?"

"The Crimson Steppes," I said. I sat up straighter, resting my hands on my knees. "Anything odd going on there? Missing people? Anyone unexpectedly gaining credits out of nowhere? Have you noticed anything out of the ordinary in the last year?"

Kendra chewed her lip. "Let me start by saying I'm no one important back home. That's not me being down on myself, that's the truth. All of us may have trained together, but I've never been privy to information. Kayden would be a better person to ask about the intricacies of the city."

"He—"

"However," she cut me off, "people were leaving. At least that's what we were being told."

"Moving to other cities?"

"Yep," she said, looking down at her hands. "We had more kids arrive at the orphanage because their carers decided to up and leave."

"People are disappearing from my city, too."

She nodded. "I know."

We stared at each other, the weight of our words hanging in the air between us. This was too big to be a coincidence. The Crimson Steppes was, on average, the poorest city in Terrulia. Unlike Damascon Hollow where the gangs brought in credits through crime, the Crimson Steppes didn't have that sort of avenue, so instead, they forged themselves into warriors, biding their time for moments like this. The trials were their ticket to claim the crown and provide for their people.

Whilst other cities were looking for power, those from the Crimson Steppes were fighting for survival.

"Shit," I said, sitting back. "I'd had a hunch, but there was a part of me that still clung to the hope that I was wrong."

Our cuffs buzzed and we froze, looking at each other. Another murder? The start of the second trial? The notifications were never good.

Kendra looked away first and I followed suit, tapping on the screen of my cuff.

Another fire.

No, not just a fire like in the miniature Damascon Hollow.

An inferno.

"It is my unfortunate duty to advise you that a fire is burning through the Verdant Plateau. The world outside the House of Ascension is usually kept hidden from Potentials to ensure those within its walls can give their utmost focus to the sacred trials.

"Alas, a catastrophe of this magnitude cannot be left in the dark. The following news report may be disturbing to some viewers."

The screen flashed then filled with images of the Verdant Plateau. Flames continued to burn as my people cried over their loved ones. My heart shattered in my chest at the sight of a young child, standing alone amongst the ash, their face sooty around the lines of tears down their cheek.

A band along the bottom of the screen displayed short bulletins, describing the location, the number of dead, and the rescue efforts. Thousands died thanks to an explosion at one of the estates that set off a chain reaction in the neighbouring areas.

Thousands.

Panic coursed through me, and I found myself on my feet despite having nowhere to go. Thoughts of my family whirled through my mind. Our home wasn't in the area, but that didn't stem the fear. They could have been visiting someone, gone for a walk, gone shopping. My eyes grew itchy as images of that crying child sped through my mind. The thought of having everyone I loved being ripped away from me made my stomach lurch. My heart ached as a sudden grief filled every inch of my body.

So much death. And my family … my family—

I shook my head, shutting down those thoughts. They were *fine.* They had to be. But the same couldn't be said for others.

The video showed a bird's eye view of the fire, the camera flying over the smouldering debris as flames roared through the town. I felt my insides twist, recognising what remained of the Leroy estate.

My fear and devastation morphed into rage that burned hotter than the inferno that had ripped through my city. This fire was no accident.

"I have to go."

My feet were moving before I'd even decided where to go. I left the nook, ignoring Kendra's concern and the tears in her eyes. I needed answers, and there was only one place I would get them.

———— ✦ ————

I stormed through the academy, seeking out Victoria's usual haunt. She spent most of her time in the communal hall, surrounded by her groupies, and like the certainty of the passing of time, that's where I found them.

They were lounging near the back corner, Victoria at their centre as they all laughed at something she said. Judging by the sound, it wasn't particularly funny, yet that didn't matter to them. The aim of the game was for her to favour them. It was obvious they were vying for her influence, should they survive the trials. If they died, perhaps their family would instead.

It would be pathetic if it weren't so sad.

"I need to talk to you," I demanded, shoving someone out of my way to get to her. I stopped just outside their circle. My gaze narrowed at the sight of her and my chest heaved as I held in my rage.

"I'm busy," she replied, her face impassive as she waved her hand to indicate those around her. I was less than a bug to her, an annoyance that didn't deserve her time. "Can't you see?"

"Now," I barked, getting into her space. She may have tortured me in the first trial, but I wasn't afraid of her. I held my ground, looking down on her now that we were so close. My fingers twitched, readying to lash out.

Victoria glared at me, pursing her lips. I didn't break her stare. Tension filled the room. Then she snapped her fingers. "Go find something to do. Noah and I are going to have a little chat."

The groupies scurried away without a word, and I was left with

Victoria. She stepped back and pointed to a chair. "Sit."

"I'm good here," I said, adjusting my stance and trying to calm my breath. I needed to think clearly and not allow my emotions to get the better of me. "Tell me what you know."

"You'll have to be more specific," she said. "I know a lot of things, though I doubt you're here for pointers on boosting your status." She looked me up and down. "Your lack of education, fashion sense, and credits, are obvious to anyone who matters."

"You know exactly what I want to know about," I hissed, her jibes irritating me close to snapping point. We'd all received the notification. There was no way she was unaware. "My home is being razed and your House was involved."

She studied her nails. "That's quite the accusation, Hawthorn. Be careful throwing that around."

"It's the truth."

"Is it?" She smirked as she lounged like a cat on her makeshift throne. "Where's your proof?"

"It wasn't an accident and you know it," I growled. "Don't you have a heart? Thousands died."

"Very sad," she replied dismissively. "But House Jupiter is a reputable house. The most prestigious in the country."

"Your opinion."

"It's the truth," she hissed back. "I don't have an answer for you because you are seeking to put fault where there is none. But I will tell you this, because I think you have guts coming here after what I did to you in the trial." She leaned forward. "Credits make credits. You don't get rich from nothing."

I looked away, analysing her words, then realised what she was getting at. "The Leroy family were new money."

Her copper eyes burned like the fires in my home. "Mmhmm. How did that happen? Winning the lottery? Borrowing a few credits?"

My gaze snapped back to her, and I shot her a glare. "House Jupiter gave them a loan."

Victoria laughed. "I've heard other Potentials say you were funny, and I believe them after that comment. We're not a bank. We don't lend money. There are other avenues to acquiring the sort of funds the Leroys had."

The Leroy family must have made a deal to get start-up credits. If Victoria was telling the truth and House Jupiter wasn't funding them, then it must have come from the Drakes. They had already proved to be involved with Mark. It wasn't that big a leap to suggest they were funding him, too.

"Such as?"

"Use that little detective nose and sniff around, but leave me out of it. House Jupiter is none of your business," she said.

"Comments like that make it sound like your House has something to hide."

"Don't be ignorant. Every House does—even yours has secrets. House Jupiter has nothing to do with you. I've provided information that will help you as a sign of good faith. Take it."

She had all but told me the Drakes were responsible for the fire. But that didn't absolve House Jupiter of my suspicions. People were going missing, and they weren't going to Damascon Hollow. Victoria had been meeting with the same hooded figure as Mark and tortured me for information about him. Fire or not, House Jupiter was still a prime suspect for the kidnappings in the Verdant Plateau and the Crimson Steppes.

Victoria made to leave but I grabbed her arm. "We're not done here."

"I am," she snarled, clicking her fingers.

I was knocked sideways, my hand slipping from Victoria, as one of her lackeys dove on top of me. The guy wrestled me to the ground, but I'd had enough. The room around me blurred, my focus narrowing to this one Potential trying to impress Victoria by doing her dirty work.

I was sick of her. I was sick of all these people and their bullshit.

Rolling so I was on top of the guy, I threw my punches, swinging wildly as they hit their mark. He fought beneath me, trying to shake me off, but I was stronger. Over and over I hit my fists into his face, blood spraying onto my own.

They'd caused too much pain. Their need for more credits and a higher status came at the price of those who just wanted to live in peace.

My anger fuelled me as I hit him again, knocking a couple of teeth out.

Hands gripped my shoulders and a calming voice pierced through my thoughts.

"Noah," she said. "That's enough."

I let Fallon pull me away and lead me outside as my chest heaved and my shoulders sagged. I was tired. So fucking tired of this game that I'd never wanted to play.

"Noah," Fallon said, taking my face in her hands. Her copper eyes were alight as she scanned my features, her gaze searching as if looking for me within my own skin. "Come back to me."

"It's never going to end."

Tears threatened to spill, or maybe they already had as I felt her thumbs wipe my cheeks. Fallon pursed her lips, her chin set in determination.

"It will. We will bring them to their knees."

ZANE

Master Nolan wanted me dead.

Why? I was a righteous dude, so that was anyone's guess. I'd been nothing but an asset to his classes and he loved having me. He'd even said so multiple times.

"I always feel more intelligent after being in your company."

"Zane, I'm surprised you've survived this long."

"I get why your dad nominated you over all your siblings. Usually he's very meticulous and picky, but it all makes sense now."

The last one was a real heart warmer. The fact that Nolan could see I was the obvious choice for my dad's nomination just proved I was right in coming here. Sure, my dad didn't actually nominate me, but technicalities were always so bogus anyway.

I took a subtle step to my left, giving myself extra space between myself and Kendra. The little murderer had been allocated as my partner for the obstacle course set out before us. It was a gnarly looking thing from what I could see. There were so many places where 'accidents' could happen. Climbing up a three-storey wall only to fall and bleed to death, being caught up in barbed wire and drowning with mud stuck in your gills … I shivered at the last one. That was only what I could see, too. There was bound to be worse shit in there.

Kendra could make use of them all; get as creative as she liked. She was my prime suspect of the murders and this obstacle course would be the perfect cover for her to off me.

Especially after the letter I'd gotten from my dad. We weren't supposed to have contact with the outside, but he'd managed to get a warning to me.

He said I needed to watch out for House Jupiter. Fallon was no threat to me, but Victoria, well, she was a threat to everyone. So that wasn't very helpful.

There had to be more to his letter. It was always a good idea to keep an eye on House Jupiter, that was a no brainer and didn't warrant a letter. So who was he really warning me about? Good question.

Luckily, I was a clever crab.

My dad had signed off with his usual Zale in fancy letters, only this time, his Z looked like a K. A mistake or a clue? Maybe to the untrained eye it was an error, but my eyes had degrees.

The K was for Kendra, I was sure of it.

And luckily I was already on her case.

The worry I was feeling about everyone around me was harshing my usual mellow vibe. Starfish was being accused of the murders, Noah's city had burned and I'd even killed Danger Dog with Ace. Granted it was an accident but I'd still done it.

I needed to chill out.

I looked past Kendra and down the line to where Fallon stood with Kayden. Lucky lionfish was grinning, and I didn't blame him. I would be as happy as a crab at a crustacean's birthday party if I was in his position.

Ace and Victoria stood a few paces behind Starfish and were having some sort of contest on who could look meaner. Victoria was winning, but only because I knew my bestie was no real threat to me. He was my spying partner—the hook to my fishing line—and unfortunately for him, one of the many losers today. Not only did I have to keep myself from being murdered by Kendra, I needed to cross the finish line first, too.

"We can't let Ace or Kayden win," I said to Noah on my other side.

He was partnered with Dick, something that was as funny as a clown fish, though Noah wasn't laughing. The fire in his city had broken something in him. My poor beta fish was drifting in a current of grief. He lashed out at another Potential the other day, and all I wanted to do was wrap my arms around him. Noah wouldn't let me though. He only broke his rage for Starfish.

I could wait for hugs. He'd come to my reef soon. I just knew it.

Noah wasn't the only one hurting, though I cared less about the others. The fire, combined with the murders, had everyone flapping about like seagulls. They were desperate to know what was going on and to get their piece but freaked out as soon as anyone got too close. And everything felt really close right now.

"They'd kill us all if their egos inflated any further," I continued. "I once saw a puffer fish get too big and take out a whole section of reef when he finally burst."

"That didn't happen," Noah replied without looking my way.

"Yeah, dude." I scoffed. "It totally did."

Noah turned and raised a brow. "You're saying a puffer fish exploded like a bomb?"

"Yahuh."

"Underwater?"

I rolled my eyes. "Obviously."

Noah opened and closed his mouth, then sighed. It must be so hard for him, realising he's wrong. He was a smart guy. It would be a blow to the ego for sure.

"So," I began, looking at his partner and frowning. "We should do an old switcheroo. Kendra and Dick can go together, and—"

"No changing teams!" Nolan barked as he strode past us, the whistle around his neck bobbing with the movement.

I threw my hands in the air. Why did he hate me?

"The rules are simple," Nolan began, his voice echoing around us. "You get your ass over that finish line and make sure your partner does as well. Any questions?" A few hands were raised but Nolan looked right through them. "None? Good." He lifted his whistle to his lips and blew. "Go."

My ears rang as I bolted towards the obstacle course, hoping Kendra was nearby. Not close enough to stab me, but enough that we would win. Nolan didn't say it was a race, but I knew better. Ol' Zaney didn't have his head buried in the sand, let me tell you.

I glanced either side to see Noah, Fallon, Victoria, and Ace in line with me. They were my real competition here. The four of them were just as competitive as I was. Kendra zoomed past me like a little rocket, and I grinned despite myself, because Kayden and Dick were nowhere in sight, which meant my team was winning.

I didn't need eyes on Kayden to know he was too heavy to sprint. His muscles weighed him down and he probably made potholes every time he took a step. All that work on bulking his body just to go out in a running race.

Not me though. I had a swimmer's upper-body strength, but I also had strong legs and no giant boulders for biceps. Perfection in human form if I do say so myself.

Ahead of me, Kendra dove into the mud and started army crawling under some low-lying netting. Even in the dirt she moved with speed. No wonder she'd been able to off people without getting caught. I hurried to follow her under the netting and was immediately covered in mud.

I groaned. Mud was not cool. It wasn't like sand and water—that combination was exfoliating and sensual. No, mud was like the ugly cousin. I squelched through it, trying not to gag or get any in my gills because that was just asking for a bad time.

Thankfully, I was out of there in no time. I reached the edge of the netting and pushed to my feet. I searched for my supposed partner, running to the next obstacle in the process.

"Kendra!" I called at the base of the next obstacle. "Kendra!"

"I'm right here," she replied, scaring the shit out of me as she popped up beside me before the giant wall that had ropes hanging from the top. Was that how she was planning to kill me? Giving me a heart attack? "Stop standing there and let's go!"

Kendra grabbed the rope and climbed as though she was still walking on land and not trekking towards the sky. I could hear other Potentials quickly catching up. Fallon zoomed past, smacking me on the ass as she spread her copper wings and flew up the wall. She perched at the top and blew me a kiss before disappearing over the other side.

Cheeky Starfish. She'd pay for that later.

I clutched the rope and hauled myself up. The mud made the rope hard to hold onto, and I almost lost my grip a couple of times. I glanced around to see other Potentials were also having the same problem as me, so at least I wasn't the only one.

"You're dawdling!" Kendra shouted, popping her head over the side to glare down at me. "Stop watching everyone else and move your ass!"

I rolled my eyes because I didn't know what she was talking about. I was making great time. She threw her hands in the air and disappeared from view. I was lucky she didn't try to cut my rope and let me plummet, but then again, there were probably too many witnesses.

A grunt drew my attention to my right, and I saw Kayden dragging himself up the rope. How did he get here so quickly? He barely had his feet on the wall, just using his huge arm muscles to get himself to the top. He caught my eye and grinned, but it was short lived because his eyes widened when a loud crack echoed through the air. His rope snapped. His skin turned into rock as he fell, landing on the ground with a huge crash.

Kayden, or should I say, 'the boulder', got to his rocky feet and roared in frustration before punching the wall and breaking through it like some villain from a comic book. The whole wall shook, and I held on tight to the rope, scurrying up as fast as I could go.

The bricks wobbled beneath my feet when I reached the top, and I grinned like an idiot at the pool below. I dove off the crumbling wall and flipped a few times mid-air for fun before slipping into the water. It felt so good to be back in its slippery wet embrace. I dove deeper, bricks and other bits of wall falling in around me. Then I spotted Kayden on the bottom, still in his rock form.

I chuckled and swam closer to the grumpy boulder. It may have been a competition, but I wasn't going to let him drown. He'd turn into a sea spirit and haunt me for the rest of my life. That was something I definitely wanted to avoid. My great aunt had a sea spirit haunting her. Used to eat all the chocolate and max out her credits shopping online.

I bet if Kayden was a sea spirit he'd spend all my credits on gym equipment and make me get up early to train. I shuddered. What a nightmare.

I grabbed Kayden's rocky arm and dragged him to the surface. I was a real lifeguard, saving his ass. All I needed were some red boardies and a whistle. Swimming past the other Potentials in the pool, I tugged him along, before spotting Fallon at the edge. She looked so beautiful, and my heart ached for not being partnered with her. I was tempted in the moment to release Kayden and take my chances with his sea ghosting.

"Thanks, Merman," Fallon smiled as we reached her. "You're a real peach."

"Anything for you, Starfish." I winked, taking my shirt off and loving the way her eyes dragged over me as I got out of the water. She was getting a good show.

"Zane!" Kendra shouted, ruining the moment. "Stop flirting and move!"

Fallon laughed and I dragged myself away from that sexy sound. I'd made a lot of ground and felt better after being in the water and seeing my Starfish. Those two were a balm to anything and everything. Kendra was just ahead of me, where barren ground was all I could see for ages. Kinda like an old war movie. I sprinted to catch up with the little murderer only to almost be blown into fish food.

The ground shook beneath me, my ears ringing. I stumbled, falling into a trench and getting muddy all over again. Where did the trenches come from?

Kendra appeared above me, her eyes looking me up and down. "You okay?"

"It's in my gills," I groaned, hating the feeling of the mud in my folds.

"You were supposed to watch out for the landmines."

"You could have told me." Or was she hoping I'd die? I gave her my best 'I'm watching you' look.

She shrugged, playing it cool, but I knew she could tell I was onto her. "I'm telling you now. I'll meet you at the end of the trench."

Kendra didn't wait around for a reply and disappeared. For a team exercise, she was quick to ditch me, repeatedly. I took off along the trench in the direction I hoped would get me to the finish line. It stunk and, looking at the walls, it was clear there wasn't only dirt in here. Bits of rubbish and other disgusting items lined the compacted dirt, both at my sides and under my feet. I gagged, holding back the chuck that wanted to escape and staying as close to the centre of the trench as possible. Why did the Masters have to make everything awful? It was bad enough the obstacle was hard but noooo, let's line the trench with trash.

The only upside to being in the garbage disposal was each time I heard a bomb go off, followed by the sounds of Potentials shrieking and yelling before they too fell into the trench. I smiled at that, because at least I wasn't suffering alone.

I followed the winding path and could almost taste the end when I was suddenly shoved into the wall and tumbled to the ground.

"What the fuck?" I half groaned; half gagged. Who knew what I was laying on? I looked up at Ace and grimaced. He was holding me down, though he wasn't looking at me, his eyes were scanning the trench instead.

I followed his gaze, angling my head awkwardly and spotting an upside-down Victoria darting away.

"Ace—"

"Just slipped," he replied hastily, climbing off me then running after her.

I got to my feet; brow scrunched in confusion at first, only to realise what had actually happened. I laughed, shaking my head out. How I could have missed it? It was so obvious Ace was in desperate need of human contact and took the opportunity to get a little up close and personal. It was a shame he had to resort to crazy measures just for a cuddle.

Poor Ace.

I turned to get my bearings and almost knocked into a dagger protruding from the wall. I groaned. The trash wasn't enough? They had to put stabby things in here too? I took off once again, hoping there was another pool after this stretch that I could clean off in. I didn't even want to think about what was currently on me.

"Hey!" a guy called from behind me. "Wait up!"

I didn't because it was a race, but he was quick and was soon running at my side.

"You're friends with Kendra, right?" he said, his breath coming in pants.

"Why do you want to know?" I asked, side-eyeing the guy. I knew him but I didn't know him, you know? He was plain looking—nothing to tell your bestie dolphin friends about. The kind of guy who'd blend into the background.

"Well, if you're friends, you can introduce me to her."

I frowned. Another Potential blissfully unaware of the evil hiding away in the innocent façade that was Kendra.

"I don't cut lunch, so if you're into her," he began, taking my lack of response the wrong way. "I mean, I thought you were into the Auger Bi—ahh, I mean Fallon."

I punched him in the arm, knocking him into the trench wall because I didn't like how he spoke about my Starfish. He stumbled, and at the same time a laugh burst from my lips, an idea springing into my head. I was a fucking genius. Why hadn't I thought of it sooner?

"I'll introduce you," I shouted back at him, forcing more speed into my movements and getting some distance between us.

"Awesome!" he called to my back. "Wait up! When will you do it?"

I didn't slow or look back. I needed time to think because my plan was to make him and Kendra fall in love. She'd be too busy to murder anyone if she was wrapped up in some dude.

I chuckled to myself. Look at me, adding another talent to my resume.

Zane Loch.

King.

Spy.

Matchmaker.

FALLON

"Come on big guy, get that ass moving." I slapped Kayden's sexy butt and smirked as he dragged himself out of the water. Honestly, sometimes he turned rock-hard at the most inopportune times, and I'm not talking the good kind. Although, yeah, he'd done that a few times before too. Like when we were doing physical training, our bodies pressed together, his length grinding against my…

Shit. Now I was thinking about the last time we were wet and he'd rubbed me all the right ways. *Head in the game, Fallon.* We had an obstacle course to win. Losing to a few Potentials, I could handle, but I was not about to let Victoria or Ace shove a victory in my face.

"Gimme … Gimme a minute, Angel," Kayden said between huffs. He pointed at his abs. "Rock skin is still wearing off."

I appraised the second boulder-like skin that was fading back to his tan, then looked longingly at the race we were well on our way to losing. "What if I fly ahead, see what we're up against?"

A soft growl rumbled from his chest. "I love it when you take command." He winked, his lips curving into a cocky smile. "Puts all kinds of filthy ideas in my head."

My lips grazed his as I leaned in close. A teasing brush, little more than a whisper as I conjured my wings and launched into the sky. "We can revisit *that* conversation later."

Kayden chuckled. "Tell my minions I said hi as you leave them in the dirt."

I saluted and turned, flitting left and right as I passed Potentials and all kinds of pitfalls in this death trap of a maze. I mean, really, I was beginning to wonder if Nolan wanted anyone to actually survive or if he was taking out his frustration and forgotten dreams on us by serving it cold in this hellhole.

A high-pitched scream rang in my ears, and I dove, latching on to thin arms before they could fall into a deep hole in the ground. I paused just long enough to drop them to their feet, holding back my laugh at who was standing before me.

"Th-thanks," Dick said, his eyes wide. "I thought for sure I was a goner."

Zane materialised beside me and peered into the hole. "A bit rude, Starfish. You didn't save the girl."

Dick frowned, peering down as well. "Girl? What girl? It was just me."

I bit back a laugh and left them to it. Poor Dick had low confidence as it was, he didn't need me chiming in too. At least Kayden would make quick work of that, having taken it upon himself to train the guy.

On second thoughts, maybe I *should* have let Dick fall in the hole. It'd be easier than what Kayden had planned for him, no doubt.

I caught sight of my partner in crime on a roll—quite literally as he was back in boulder form—and barrelling through any Potentials who were unfortunate enough to be in his way. When the pit loomed before him, he managed a surprisingly agile bump into the air, bypassing it, and me, altogether.

Well, shit. I blinked, shaking my head and returning to my mission. Guess we were back in the game, but there was no harm in scoping the rest of the course out. I flew higher and hissed as I smashed into an invisible forcefield.

Dammit, Nolan had done that on purpose, I just knew it.

Fine then. Low it was. I sped ahead of the group until I was flying solo, the shouts, bangs, and explosions from before all fading behind me. The track narrowed, forcing me to walk on foot and squeeze between craggy rocks and in between tunnels.

My insides coiled. Good thing I wasn't claustrophobic and all. The slick, dirty rock smelled stale and was cold to the touch, making me gasp as I slowly made my way through the tight, dark space. Eventually, the cave swallowed up the daylight, leaving me in pitch-black.

It's fine, everything's fine. You're in a cave with gods only know what lurking in the depths, but you've totally got this.

Blindly, I patted down both walls, cautiously continuing. What was probably only minutes felt like hours. Sweat broke over my forehead, and I forced myself to breathe. To fill my lungs, to let them empty, to clear my mind. It was perhaps the one reliable trick Victoria had taught me that I'd always remember. The piece of her I'd always cling to.

I flexed my fingers, closed my eyes … and breathed.

When it felt like the walls weren't closing in, I opened them and managed one tiny step after another, until the feeling had subsided enough to carry on.

It wasn't the dark I was afraid of, but the combination of not being able to see with the cramped space, the constriction, for me. It reminded me too painfully of my father's training techniques. When I was younger, he'd shove me and Victoria into cells or storage spaces while he would do 'business'. We'd sit there for hours, clinging to each other with nothing but the sounds of screams and breaking bones to keep us company.

I'd thought back then it was to keep us safe from the horrors—protecting us from all the bad men who wanted to hurt us. Now I knew it was to slowly indoctrinate us into that society. Desensitise us. When you are exposed to something for so long, it stops having such an impact. It becomes normal. Screams don't sound as scary after a while. Bones breaking, guns firing, and steel ringing don't seem so bad when you're forced to listen to it, again and again and again. Until one day they're just another noise, and you're the one holding the trigger or wrapping your hands around the blade. Until you're the one making them scream.

So, yeah, it wasn't the torturing or the killing that stayed with me. It was the memory of that small, dark space. The lure and the trap.

As I rounded a corner, I breathed a sigh of relief. Light glowed further down the tunnel. The finish line would surely come soon after the cave ended.

I almost tripped over my feet as I ran out, ready to launch myself into the open air…

Until I saw the bodies.

Four of them scattered around a clearing, with blood pooling around each one.

"Fuck me." I blew out a breath, then immediately dropped into a crouch, alert in case the killer was lingering.

After scanning the area for either a person or camera and straining to hear anything to tell me they were still around, I relaxed enough to tentatively step forward. Three guys and one girl, all of whom appeared to have been stabbed in the back or taken by surprise.

This killer was brutally efficient. Certainly not an amateur at any rate. I frowned at the ruby-red pools growing larger by the second. Another kill, this time in broad daylight with multiple victims. What the fuck was this person trying to prove? That no Potential was safe at the academy?

Hate to break it to ya, blackmailer, but that wasn't exactly a new alert to everyone who'd entered this damn competition. I shook my head and made to turn away to get Nolan or whoever was closest to reaching the cave when I heard a low rasp from one of the bodies.

"Holy shit."

One of the Potentials was still alive? I rushed to the guy's side. He reached out feebly, beckoning me to come closer. I sank to my knees, pressing my hand to the wound in his chest. It was too deep. The gurgles and bubbles coming from his throat told me something vital had ruptured. He wouldn't last more than another minute or two.

"What happened?"

The guy tried to speak, coughed, swallowed, then tried again. "Am … bushed."

I frowned, taking his hand in my free one. "Who was it?"

"D … Drakes. C-C…"

My skin chilled. "A Drake did this to you?" I knew of only one Drake at this academy. Someone Noah had told me to watch out for. Someone I'd even let myself be alone with … among other things. Well, fuck me sideways. "Ace did this to you?"

The guy choked, a spurt of blood dribbling from his mouth. It wouldn't be long now. His eyes widened, seeming to focus on something that wasn't there. Then he shook his head.

"It wasn't Ace?" I asked. Desperate—too desperate—for the resident grump of this damned academy to *not* be the murderer.

The guy let out a long sigh. Then whispered one final word before his body slumped and the last breath left his body. "Camouflage."

Alarms blared in my skull. Could he be referring to someone's adaptation? I frowned, trying to piece the puzzle together. The only Potential I knew of who had that ability was … Noah. An uncomfortable feeling settled in my gut. No way. There had to be another explanation because there was no fucking way.

I stared at the guy for a long time after that. He was a few years younger than me, but it wasn't his age that bothered me. He looked so familiar. He looked like Ethan, my brother. A shiver ran down my spine at the blond hair, tousled and boyish, and the green eyes that I gently closed.

My cuff vibrated, breaking my unfixed stare, and I jerked as a notification flagging a video pulled up on the Acadameet app. A video of *me*. I pressed play, my blood running cold as it showed me sitting over the body, blood on my hands, a vacant expression on my face.

I was up in an instant, looking around for the killer. How could I miss them? There was no way I'd overlooked someone if they'd been there. Was the camera hidden and set up to record when it detected motion?

"Come out and fucking fight me, you coward!"

Only silence answered me.

I searched the area again, looking for anything that might resemble a recording device from the direction the video was taken of me. But I found nothing. There was no point going to find Nolan now. The rest of the Potentials and he had likely seen the video and would be on their way or staying clear of this place. Guess the only thing to do was wait.

So here I was, suspect number one, framed for not one but multiple murders. Not only did this killer have some sort of grudge against me, but several other Potentials would just as happily stab me in the back or let me pay the price for this. Not that I was on good terms with everyone before, but now they'd be actively condemning me.

I never thought these trials were going to be easy, but this was getting out of control. Someone was out to get me, but they'd soon learn I would not go down without a fight. This murderer had made their business *my* business.

And boy was I good at cleaning up.

FALLON

"They let you go just like that? Girl, you are all kinds of lucky."

I snorted, raising my brow in amusement as I glanced at Kendra in the reflection of the mirror. "I think you and I have different definitions of luck."

She rose from the bed, sashaying over like a drunken pirate with a bottle of rum in her hand. When she held it out to me, I accepted eagerly, taking a generous swig before handing it back and returning to finish curling my hair.

"You're free, aren't you?"

"For now," I grumbled.

Since the first trial, things had gone from bad to worse, so we had decided to spend our Friday night by blowing off some steam. In other words, getting blind drunk, dressing up, and maybe getting fucked blind. Something along those lines anyway, and in no particular order. I was well on my way to achieving two out of the three, thanks to the secret stash of alcohol Kendra had stolen from several Masters' studies. Who knew the teachers were such closet drunks?

After yet another session of being poked and prodded for answers about the murders yesterday, I just needed to let loose. Who better to do that with than my partner in crime? And Kendra was right, I was lucky they let me off so easily. Things could have been a lot worse. Blackmail is a bitch. But there was no way in hell I was going down with the Masters and Celeste, so I'd done some threatening of my own. It didn't take much more than mentioning my parents again to get them to back off. Their need to find someone they could claim responsible for the murders and their blackmail apparently wasn't as strong as their fear of my parents. Really, they knew there was no way I could be the murderer. I had alibis and witnesses each time that they couldn't ignore. I had no plans of being their scapegoat.

So I'd stay a free woman for a while longer … at least until the killer decided to set me up again. Whoever it was clearly had a vendetta against me or my House. They might kill me one day, but until then, they wanted my reputation destroyed and for me to suffer. I had to wonder if the killer had something to do with the trials or was simply part of a political mind game beyond the academy.

"Hey," Kendra said, nudging me. "No brooding tonight. Fuck the killer, fuck the Masters, and fuck this academy. We look hot as fuck and we're going to dance our tits off at the party. So forget about all that shit and let's make this night our bitch."

"Heck yes. Gimme that." I snatched the bottle from her and took a long-ass chug. "You had me at fuck everything to be honest."

Kendra took the curling iron from me, finishing the back of my hair. She nodded in approval when she was done, set it down, and joined me beside the mirror with a feral grin on her lips.

She was right. We *did* look good tonight. Kendra had her hair in a high ponytail, her eyes lined with electric blue graphic liner and her lips mega glossy. A mini dress in the same hue as her liner clung to her curves.

My dark hair was loose, the curls falling to below my breasts. I'd lined my eyes with black and painted a bold red on my lips. To finish it off, I'd picked a tight black mini dress in a slinky fabric that plunged slightly at the front, while showing off my whole back, nothing but a skimpy gold chain holding it together at the top. Scandalous, which was perfect, in my books. I was already a villain in everyone's eyes, why not look the part?

It was just Kendra and me in our dorm room tonight. Zane had been hesitant to leave, seeming clingier than ever lately—not to mention shady as fuck whenever Kendra was around—but I'd given him some incentive to let us have some girl time. Incentive that may or may not have involved sexual innuendos for later.

Besides, once I'd mentioned the fight club no one was supposed to know or talk about, he'd just about bowled me over as he bounded out the door. A bunch of guys wrestling half naked? Um, yes please.

"Here," Kendra said, handing me a tissue.

I looked at her blankly. "What's this for?"

"To wipe the drool from your lips, duh."

"Fuck off." She burst out laughing and I bumped her with my hip, unable to help laughing with her. "Such a brat."

"Oh my gods," she gasped between laughs, going so far as to throw herself on the bed. "I was only joking but you were totally thinking about the guys just now! We're having a girl's night and you're busy daydreaming about one of your four amigos' dicks. Honestly, if they weren't so hot, I'd be super offended right now."

I cringed, turning towards her. "I'm sorry, you're right. Girl's night. No testosterone to fuel the fire."

She smirked. "Nah, I'm not going to pussy-block you."

"How generous of you." I grinned. "We can talk about Zane and the others later. I want to know if anyone is on *your* radar. Maybe a certain someone who likes coffee?"

"There ... might be someone."

I put my hands on my hips, frowning. "And you were going to tell me when!?"

Kendra ducked her head. "It's still new. I didn't want to say anything until I knew where it was headed."

"I don't believe it." I squinted at my friend, her pale cheeks reddening. "You're blushing! Who is it? Do I know them?"

"Umm." She peered at the quilt, finding a loose thread suddenly very interesting. "I don't think so. But then again, she's kinda hard to miss. She's very ... pink."

I squealed. "Are you in *lurrvvee*?"

Kendra looked at me in exasperation. "This is why I didn't tell you. You're going to hyper fixate just like the merman does who, by the way, has been acting weird lately." I threw her a look and she grinned. "Okay, weirder than usual."

"Who knows what goes through his head half the time, but I can find out what he's up to. Anyway, who cares about that right now. When do I get to meet her?"

Kendra smiled. "Soon. Maybe. We're just having fun for now. I don't want to make it a big thing just yet. But I think you'll like her."

I huffed. "Fine. But if she hurts you, I'll go full dragon on her ass."

She waved her hand lazily. "I don't want to see another dragon anytime soon, thanks. Besides, I think you've got your hands full already." She propped her chin on one knee, a sly smile growing on her face. "Sooo, on the subject of beasts with bad tempers, any more updates on your boys? Which one were you thinking of just before?"

My cheeks heated, but I grinned deviously. "Is it greedy if I say all of them?"

"Yu*p*."

"Fine, I'm greedy then. Obviously, Zane and I have gotten close, but I'd be lying if I didn't say the others are growing on me as well."

Kendra patted the bed. "I sense there is more to this story. Spill the beans right the fuck now. You know I'm all in for you having your own real-life harem."

I flopped onto the bed beside her, taking the rum she wordlessly held out for me and taking a sip. "So, Noah and I had a moment after I woke up in the hospital bay. Seems our quiet and mysterious little bookworm can take charge when he wants to."

Kendra's eyes widened. "You didn't! After nearly dying?"

"Have sex? Nah. We almost kissed though … and might have since then."

"Psshh." She waved a hand.

"He's more of a gentleman," I protested, feeling the need to defend him. "I think he's sweet."

"I can see that," she agreed. "And I'm sure he'll be worth the wait too. What about Kayden? Have you rocked that boulder's world again yet?"

I grinned, thinking of our hot as heck session post-gym the other day.

"You sneaky shit," she said, elbowing me. "You totally want to. Well, I'm all for it. If the big guy is in our corner, it'll be better for the rest of us. He's a blockhead sometimes, but he'd be a good ally. And, as much as he's a dick to his little groupies, he means well for them. Thanks to his training, a good chunk of them survived the first trial."

"Uh-huh. 'Cause their wellbeing is totally why you're so invested." I shook my head with a laugh. "You are seriously deranged, you know that?"

She shrugged. "Look, if there's a chance we're gonna die any day—and there's a big fucking chance—then I'll get my kicks where I can."

"Should've chosen another bestie."

"And miss out on all the fun?" She scoffed, bopping me on the head. "Fat chance."

"Um … ow?" I rubbed the back of my head. "Seriously though, somebody is out to get me and now everyone at the academy has even more beef with me, what with the framing and all. It's dangerous."

Kendra shrugged again. "Meh. Die in the trial or die in the academy. What's the difference?"

I guess she had a point. With that, I raised the bottle in a full salute to my badass bitch of a friend and took a long, burning drink before handing it over. Kendra took it eagerly, finishing the bottle and throwing it on Mark's empty bed. "Rot in hell, asshole."

"Amen to that," I agreed, pulling her up to stand next to me in front of the mirror. "Ready to face the masses?"

She rested her head on my shoulder. "Girl, I was born ready."

———— ✦ ————

If I'd thought Zane, Kayden, Noah, and Ace couldn't get any hotter, I was dead wrong. As I stood beside Kendra, cheering on the sidelines as they pummelled each other's faces in, all I could do was stare, helplessly, at the number of rippling abs and biceps on show.

Then cry internally at the damage being done to their sexy faces. RIP.

Now, watching men beat their chests and parade around like peacocks wasn't really my jam, but when they were sweaty, ripped, and had jawlines for days, well, I could get around it. Ruthlessly so, apparently, because Kendra and I had placed some bets and, right now, my money was on Kayden.

Noah had destroyed his opponent, which was both hot and alarming at the same time. Clearly, the fire had done a number on him and he had taken it out on the guy now crawling away for dear life. I needed to talk to Noah, but right now, he needed to let off some steam more than anything. Instead of continuing the games though, he'd taken to getting uncharacteristically drunk. I didn't blame him.

As for my poor, sweet merman, he lost his match to Ace, but hey, he didn't drink the crazy juice that Ace did, nor did he have the sheer size of Kayden.

No, I'm not talking about *that* part. Both were equally impressive in that department, thank you very much.

I cringed as Kayden took a nasty jab to the cheek, but the big guy's face barely moved an inch as he took it like a champ. Then, in true Kayden style, he shot me a wink and round housed the smaller guy's stomach so hard the dude had to crawl to the corner of the ring where he vomited over some girl's shoes. Silicone Sally or whatever the girl with the stripper's name was who'd attacked me in the bathroom.

She screeched, slapping the poor guy's face as he wobbled unsteadily in front of her. I laughed so loud she shifted her attention to send me daggers, then she sidled closer to Zane as if that would somehow make me jealous.

Okay fine, maybe I wasn't jealous, but the bitch was asking for it when she started running her talons over his chest. He didn't even appear to notice her as he chatted animatedly to Kendra, which was a drastic change in his recent behaviour. I strained my ears, catching snippets of what sounded like him trying to set her up with some random guy. So weird, but I was not about to fall into the next rabbit hole of whatever he was scheming.

I huffed, turning my attention back to Kayden just as he walked up to me.

"You're bleeding," I pointed out simply.

"A scratch," he replied, wiping the cut on his brow with the back of his hand. Then he grinned, somehow even sexier all bloodied and brutal. "Nice to know you care though, Angel. You gonna kiss it better for me?"

A smirk crept over my lips, but I studied my nails, feigning indifference. "Depends."

"On?"

He stepped even closer, the heat from his chest practically searing through my clothes. Or maybe it was the other way round. It was hard to tell through the haze of alcohol. When I didn't meet his eyes, he tilted my chin, forcing my gaze up to his beautiful brown eyes.

"On whether you win the match. Who's your next fighter?"

Damn, I'd gone from toying with the guy to straight up drooling over him. Kendra was right. I was so fucked. Between him and Zane, whatever was brewing with Noah, and who the hell even knew what with Ace, I had my hands full.

Kayden gave me the biggest shit-eating grin I might have yet seen from him, then jerked his chin over his shoulder.

I followed his gaze to find Ace wiping his bloodied knuckles on his pants, his steely eyes dark and deadly as the bonfire reflected in them. Despite his smaller build, he was utterly ripped. His pale chest gleamed with sweat, his tattoos a smorgasbord of art I wanted to run my fingers over.

I snorted, then tipped my plastic cup back. "Good luck with the angry storm cloud. He's not going to let you off easy."

"I'm counting on it."

Good gods. Girl's night my ass, it was testosterone city out here. I looked around for Kendra, noticing her trying to offer Zane a drink. He wasn't having a bar of it, looking at the cup like it was poisoned. I rolled my eyes. Guess she wasn't keen on his matchmaking, and he'd reverted to throwing shade again.

I looked back at Kayden's beautiful eyes. "If you two want to rip each other to shreds, be my guest. I'm going to have a drink."

"Wait, Angel," Kayden said, grabbing my arm a little forcefully as I turned to go.

I let him, because *fuck me*, he looked good tonight. And maybe a small part of me wanted to see Ace get his ass beat. A large part of me also wanted to kiss Kayden and keep going 'til the sun came up … but he didn't need to know that.

"I win, you finally go on that date with me. No more teasing. Not just the sex." He winked at that. "But a date." In a quieter voice he added, "I'm not asking you to be exclusive with me. I'm a big boy, I learned how to share."

His husky tone sent a shiver down my spine. "Baby, don't promise what you can't deliver."

His eyes turned molten. "I've never played a match I couldn't win. You're mine, Angel. Want it or not, believe it or not, but you were mine the moment I saw you. We're allies now, remember? And I look after my own. If that means the merman is a package deal, I can get around it."

He had no right to go planting images of him and Zane both giving me what I needed. NO damn right. And of course a part of me had to go imagine getting those things at the same time. Ugh. He had me line and sinker and he knew it.

I glanced back at Ace, who was looking at me with murder and something dangerously close to longing in his eyes. And because I enjoyed stirring the pot, I slid my hands up Kayden's chest, kissed him on the cheek and whispered, "Deal."

"What's taking so fucking long? Hiding behind a little girl won't save you."

I jumped as Ace materialised next to us, his usual scowl on his face. "A little girl who could beat you to a pulp," I said sweetly. "I was just telling Kayden what I'll give him when he wins."

"What?" both guys asked at the same time.

"A blowjob." I smiled as Ace's brows drew together. Was that a hint of annoyance? Or jealousy? "It shouldn't be much of a challenge."

"Princess," Ace said, stalking closer. "Don't put your money where your mouth is, or it'll be my cock your pretty lips are wrapped around."

My nostrils flared as I took him in. The little shit knew just what to say to piss me off, even if a part of me knew he'd never do such a thing. Not unless I begged for it just the way his warped little mind would like. Fucker.

"Kayden?" I asked, turning to the big guy. "Don't fucking lose."

He shot me a cocky grin, surprised me by stealing a heated kiss, then stormed towards the ring. Ace watched me carefully for a beat too long, seeming to drink me in, before he stalked after Kayden.

"Ready fighters?" Zane called enthusiastically. "This round will announce our bloodthirsty champion. Will it be the mighty and oh so glorious steed from the Steppes? Or will it be our most devious, most dangerous Drake from the hollow? Let's—"

"Get on with it, Merman," Ace growled.

Zane threw him a dazzling smile, unperturbed, and threw his bottle into the fire. "Fight!"

The fight passed in a blur as both guys fought furiously. Where Kayden was all brawn and power, Ace was quick and agile. Adaptations were against the rules, so Kayden's rocky skin was off limits, meaning blood was splattering everywhere and both guys were getting some good hits in.

The Potentials were screaming and cheering, drunk off their tits and swaying with the adrenaline of the fight. Kendra popped up by my side, louder than any of them and sloshing her drink everywhere.

"Knock his head off Kayden! Tighten your swings Ace!"

"Who the fuck are you going for?" I asked her in bewilderment.

She shrugged. "I'm just enjoying watching them mash each other's faces in."

I pouted. "I like their faces."

She threw me a look that said 'I know full well what you like' then proceeded to hum under her breath and bump into me as she swayed.

Eh. Who was I to tell her to slow down? I chugged my own drink back—anything to distract me from the sight of these two alphas going ham on each other. I wanted Kayden to win, so why did I wince every time Ace got smacked too? Why did a part of me—a teeny, tiny, microscopic spec—want to cheer him on too?

I put it down to hormones. Seriously, fuck the things.

Just as I thought Kayden was going to win the match with a whopping haymaker that probably would've put Ace in the hospital wing, Ace jumped onto Kayden's chest like some sort of wild rabbit and pummelled so hard and fast, other Potentials had to try and drag him off.

"By all the fucking gods," I muttered. "Zane! Noah!"

The guys were there in a flash. Apparently, they were the only ones Ace didn't feel the need to knock out in his rage.

And there he was. The winner of the match. The man of the hour sidled over to me, his lips bloody, his cheek bruised. And he had the nerve to say, "Get on your knees, Princess. I'm ready to claim my prize."

I was deranged. Mentally un-fucking-stable as I appraised those lips a little too long, as well as the abs heaving with each breath. And I considered seeing what would happen if I said yes. But even drunk Fallon had some sense left.

I checked my cuff and tapped my foot. "How about never-going-to-happen? No? We could try keep-dreaming-o'clock."

His lips twitched for a split second. When he slipped into my space and pressed his bloodied lips to my cheek, I almost leaned into his arms. Almost. But when he whispered into my ear a moment later, I shivered.

"You can run, Princess, but I know the darkest parts of you deep inside. I know you're just as fucked up as I am. Because despite how much you might try to put a Band-Aid over your pain, it's festering all the same. We are the same, you and I. It's why you hate me so much. It's why I hate you, too." The cold metal of his bionic hand bit into my throat and I gasped as he tightened his grip. "This chemistry between us, little bird … it's an explosion waiting to go off. Pray that you're not around when it does, because I don't take prisoners, Princess. I take fucking lives. And I want yours. I just haven't decided how yet."

Well, shit. What the heck was I supposed to do with that? I should be running for my life. Better yet, I should end *his* before he decides to follow through on that threat. And yet … a part of me knew it really was just a threat. I didn't think he wanted to kill me at all. Not when his hand on my throat sent heat throbbing between my legs and his violent promises made me wetter than a fucking whistle. Judging by the way his eyes undressed every inch of my skin—not to mention his weird behaviour lately—I'd bet he wanted to do other things with that hand.

Rather than giving him the satisfaction of thinking he'd won, I stepped closer. "For someone with the reputation of a deadly gang member and thief, you sure talk a big game. If you wanted to kill me, you'd have done so already and you sure as shit wouldn't have saved me in the trials."

"That's just the thing. I saved your life, so you owe me a debt."

I clenched my teeth so hard I thought my molars might break. It was just like him to hold that against me. "What do you want?"

"Remember our conversation about your shiny House Jupiter ring? It's time to pay up, Princess."

I stared at him for a long moment, then burst out laughing. "That old thing? I lied. My darling parents never saw fit to give me one. Oh, and before you try taking one from Victoria? I stole hers and hid it somewhere no one will ever find it. Happy hunting, though."

Ace's eyes flashed, and with the reflection of the fire, he genuinely looked terrifying. Which, naturally, only made my pussy throb more. "You're treading a dangerous path, Princess. This isn't some game."

"Aw, but it's so fun." I pouted, then shot him a sly smile. "In fact, I think we should play. If you're really such a big, bad Drake, show me what you can do with those clever hands. Punish me if you will. I promise I can take how dangerous you can be."

He shifted in the dark, making him appear slightly demonic. A low grumble sounded from his chest. "Don't promise things you can't handle, Princess. I don't play nice."

I smiled. "I'm counting on it."

With that, I turned, flicked my hair in his face, and sauntered towards where my friends had moved around Kayden, making sure to swish my hips on the way. I'd probably regret whatever game I'd just challenged Ace to, but that fucked up part of me he mentioned?

Yeah, it was drooling at the thought of all the delicious dark things on offer.

KAYDEN

I lost to a twig. A very angry, psychotic twig with punches of steel and arms that moved like desert cobras, but it was a loss all the same.

I sighed, running a hand through my sweaty hair. And to think Fallon had agreed to a proper date if I'd won. Except life just kept throwing curveballs. Still, she'd practically had hearts in her eyes at the mere thought of there being some possible threesome action with the merman. I was straight as a barbell, but hey, if it kept Fallon happy, I'd be down. And sharing her could be kinda hot…

I shook my head. I was losing my shit in this academy. Kayden Hale sharing his things? It went against everything we fought for in the Crimson Steppes. But ever since I'd lost Flynn, I was all out of sorts. And Fallon had only added to that. I now wanted things I'd never cared for. The throne was still my number one priority, of course, but until I claimed it, a part of me wanted to explore future possibilities.

Possibilities that included opening my circle to new allies … maybe even friends. But it didn't help that my supposed allies didn't really trust me. And the minions were hardly forever material. Allies, yes, but I was their trainer. I had to be tough or else shit went sideways and people started falling out of line. Only, it was kinda hard to stay tough when you lost to metalheads with toys for hands.

Worse, I kept doing embarrassing shit lately. First, the burger incident after lunch. Second, the treadmill exploding in front of Fallon—though that had somehow worked in my favour. And now? Losing to the vicious cyborg in front of almost all Potentials left at the academy. It didn't do much for my standing, that's for sure.

With another long-winded sigh, I took a long sip of my whiskey, not even bothering to shake Zane off and just letting him hang from my rock arm as I swigged. He didn't even question it, just clung to me like a spider monkey and continued chatting with Noah. The merman had taken it upon himself to be my consoling support since I'd lost, and I hated to admit it, but I didn't mind the attention.

"You might've lost the fight, but I learned a lot from watching you, sir," Dick said as he approached me, a sympathetic smile on his face. He'd combed his blond hair and dressed in his Sunday best. I had to wonder if the guy had ever been to a bonfire party before. Judging by the nervous glances he gave everyone, I was betting no. "I hope to fight as well as you one day."

"Thanks, man." I slapped him awkwardly on the back. "It was a good fight," I admitted. "The Drake won fair and square."

"He's crazy." Dick shivered, then leaned in close. "Like, I think he needs some serious help. Maybe I could convince him to join me in magic class for some calming."

I scoffed. "Sure, if you want to get your teeth knocked out."

"Right." Dick's face paled. "Well, maybe—"

"Dick!" We turned, finding a pretty girl weaving through the crowd, her friends giggling in the background. "Wanna grab a drink with me?"

"I—I—I—"

For the love of sand dunes, the guy was going to have an aneurysm before he got a word out. I bumped him towards her, then grinned. "He would love to, wouldn't you, Dicky boy?"

She laughed and took his hand, and Dick looked back over his shoulder, pure terror etched into his blue eyes.

"Don't stay up too late!" I called, chuckling to myself.

"Ah, the fledgling turtle leaves the beach at last," Merman said, leaning on his elbows from where he perched on my arm.

"Err, sure, I guess?"

"So anyways," he said with a beaming smile. "It's about time you slunk back to your pod. There's some serious bad juju going on between you and the angry one and it's giving off negative energy in our circle. You gotta fix it, but we'll tackle that line once you've had enough time to drown in your shame."

"My shame?! You wanna say that again tadpole?" I growled, lifting my arm so he dangled higher in front of me. I opened my mouth to continue when I noticed Zane's cheeks getting redder by the second. "Err, you okay man?"

"Am I okay?" he repeated, blinking at me several times as if I was the one sputtering and choking on my words. "Am. I. Okay?" I could almost see the steam coming out of his ears as he pinned me with what was admittedly a kinda frightening stare.

"Zane…" He held up a finger and I winced, waiting for what I sensed was an incoming rampage. I put him on his feet and Noah tried to steer him away, but the merman was having none of it.

"Here I am trying to repair the kinks in what was the beginnings of a beautiful super pod, yet you continue to insult me! How many times do I have to tell you, tadpoles are freshies! Now, unless you plan on sinking this friend-ship, I suggest you learn your aquatic life!" He slapped me three times then huffed. "That's for the tadpoles!"

"What the fuck?" I roared. "Not cool man!"

That was strike fucking four, and I'd had enough. But before I could square off with Zane, Fallon came stalking over, a bunch of supplies in hand.

"Zane, eat this, you're hangry," she said, handing him a chocolate bar. "Kayden, here's a whisky. Noah…" She wobbled on her feet a little, kissed him on the cheek, then grinned. "Nothing. You're perfect. Just … just keep being your sweet self."

We all blinked at her, watching as she bounced around cheerfully, then started singing—terribly, I might add—to a rock song that started booming over a speaker someone had set up. And because she was Fallon, she jumped onto a log, took a shot out of shoe with Dick, and jumped back down with a huge grin plastered on her face.

"That's my girl," I said, looking at her in awe. I swore, if angels ever really existed, they'd be crying at how beautiful she was. That black skintight dress she was wearing was wrong in all the right ways.

"Our girl," Zane corrected, seemingly over his momentary hissy fit. If that's what hangry looked like on him, he had some serious issues. I wasn't even mad about it though. It just felt normal, hanging out like this. Weird, but normal.

Fallon hugged Dick, then came sashaying back towards us, a huge grin on her face. "Am I mistaken, or do you three appear to be getting along like good human beings?"

I set Zane down and tugged her into my arms, but she shook her head adamantly, pulling away. "No. Mm-mm. I distinctly remember saying to win the match."

"Ouch, Angel," I replied, clutching my chest above my heart. "And here I was thinking I'd taken enough hits."

"I dunno," she teased. "I see room for more bruises."

I growled, pulling her in again. This time, she didn't pull away, instead craning her neck to stare into my eyes. "If a bet is what it takes to spend some more time with you, I'd happily take them all."

"Fuck it," Fallon said, grabbing my hand and leading me deeper into the forest. "After that fight, you deserve a freaking badge of honour. But as I don't have one of those, I'm giving you something else."

"Which is?" I asked, enjoying the view of her ass as she paraded me through the trees. "I'm not good with surprises, sweetheart."

She laughed. "What I'm going to do is anything but sweet."

My cock twitched to attention. "Angel, you just answered all my prayers."

"Kayden?" she asked softly, stopping in a clearing far enough away from prying eyes but still close enough to hear the thumping music drifting through the woods.

"Mmm?" I hummed, enjoying the feeling of her fingers as she placed them against my cool chest. She slid them higher, wrapping them around my neck as she kissed me deeply. Her tongue curled around my own, feeling like fire. Gods, she was perfect.

When she pulled back my cock was well and truly at attention. She smirked; her copper eyes alight. "Have you ever seen an angel in prayer?"

I barely had time to think as she unbuckled my belt with practised fingers and took me in her mouth. "By all the gods, woman, open wide and show me what that dirty mouth can do."

I groaned as her lips tightened around my cock, sucking hard around the tip before she loosened her jaw and took me deeper into her warmth. It was an effort not to blow my load at the mere feeling of her wet mouth on me. Every touch was pure bliss, the pressure of her tongue easing from rough to soft, slow then back to full speed. She was unpredictable. Un-fucking-believable.

An angel. *My angel.* I slid my hands into her silky hair and guided her movements up and down my throbbing cock, loving the way she let me manipulate her. She took every inch of my cock like a champ. The erotic sounds escaping those luscious lips only made me groan louder.

When she looked up at me, those copper eyes sparkling like sunlight, I almost came undone. "Take me to the stars, Angel. Show me what heaven looks like."

I could see the amusement glimmering there—the hunger. And fuck, did she deliver. I came hard and fast, my cum shooting down her throat. She licked up every drop, opening her mouth seductively to show me she'd swallowed it all.

I grumbled in approval, tipping her chin back and kissing her like it was my last day alive. My hands worked their way down to her ass and I cupped her cheeks, pulling her to me until eventually, we were just standing there, her head against my chest and my chin on her head.

"Fallon?" I said after a while, breaking our quiet solitude. "What made you change your mind?"

She pulled back, wrinkling her nose at the question. "About?"

"Me." I shrugged and shot her a crooked grin. "We didn't exactly start off on the right foot."

Her brows rose. "No thanks to a certain someone thinking he owned the joint and everyone in it."

I grinned. "If the boot fits."

"You're such an ass." She laughed and elbowed me in the ribs. "So how is this ally thing going to work if we're all working towards the same goal?"

"I wouldn't ask you to back down from the crown," I said seriously. "I'm not as stupid as I look."

"What a relief," she said drily. "So we help each other out, and then what? Go our separate ways when this is done?"

My heart stuttered. "Is that what you want?" I asked carefully.

She chewed on her lip. "No," she admitted after a painfully long minute. "No, it's not what I want. It's … I— "

I pulled her closer again. "You gotta learn to trust, little one. I don't know what happens in your house on high, but I'm not going to stab you in the back and I'm not going to leave you behind when all is said and done. We're a team now." I rubbed soothing circles over her back, then blurted, "We're a super pod."

Oh, fucking hell, Kayden. When she didn't reply, I pulled her head back gently to look into her eyes, only to find the biggest smile on her face.

"You've been talking with Zane," she stated simply.

"Do I have a choice?" I asked with a huff.

"No." She laughed again. "No, you really don't."

"Am I going to regret this?" I said with a groan.

Fallon tapped her lips. "Most likely. But I think this—whatever this is—is just getting started. Don't think I've forgotten about what you said about a certain threesome."

"Oh? Given it some thought, have you?"

"A little." I raised a brow and gave her a knowing look. "Okay fine, a lot. And I have so many wonderful things planned."

At her devious little smile, I dragged my hand down, then up her dress. "You're practically dripping, baby. So wet for me already."

"At the thought of our bodies pressed together, you and Zane both filling me up at once? Too right I am."

Fuck me. I really was losing my shit, because the thought of Fallon pressed between me and another guy, naked and moaning and so fucking full? All the images ran through my head at once, and I was beginning to think I was pretty keen for it too.

ACE

I felt like someone had hit me over the head with a baseball bat. Scratch that. A baseball bat would have been less painful than the real cause. Kayden's rocky fists and all the alcohol I had downed the night before were the real culprits. I groaned, rolling onto my side and opening my eyes, only to have the sun's rays almost blind me and add to my throbbing headache.

It was the price I paid for my fucking stupidity.

First, I'd made the dumb-as-shit decision to fight the rock boy and, despite winning, I'd walked away feeling like a loser because Fallon had straight-up rejected me in front of everyone. Princess flashed from angry to fuck me eyes and back in a heartbeat. She'd fit in well in DH with the way she toyed with people and went back on bets.

And deals.

Fallon had lied about having the House Jupiter ring too, though I was taking that with a grain of fucking salt because she most likely was messing with me.

Princess was a fucking tease.

Which was the second reason I had a pounding headache.

Women had been draping themselves all over me last night, keen for a ride, and I couldn't even fake interest. All I could see were copper eyes and the blatant fucking truth that none of those women were *her*.

And, oh, the things I could do to her.

Fallon wasn't afraid of the dark. She relished in it because she was just as fucked up as I was. She'd walk the fine line between pleasure and pain with me. Not hand in hand like some cute-as-shit romance, nah. She would be on her knees, crawling and begging as I led her down that twisted path.

Unfortunately, she'd chosen the boulder. Once I saw the princess go off with Kayden, I'd decided to drink the human rock's weight in booze. I don't know why it pissed me off so much, but it had, and then I had been pissed at myself for even giving a shit in the first place.

Fallon Auger was the bane of my existence. I'd grown up having enemies—rival gangs or cops that were out for my blood. Fallon was a different beast. She was a sharp dagger held to my throat that bled me out drop by drop.

She would bleed me dry, and I would fucking let her.

I hated her.

I hated myself more.

The self-loathing was worse than my headache. I groaned. Since when had I turned into such a needy bitch?

The head fuck had been reason enough at the time to down a few drinks because there was no way I was going to sort through that shit like some well-adjusted person.

Drown it out with alcohol and push the fuck on. I didn't have time for this shit. Not the mental mess or the fallout, which was taking shape as a hangover.

I sat up, rubbing my head with the palm of my bionic hand and willing the world to stop spinning me around. Finally, I could open my eyes beyond a squint and searched around my makeshift home for a water bottle and some painkillers.

Finding the water and stolen meds, I downed them both. I would have happily crashed here for a few more hours. Unfortunately, the fighting and party that had followed last night had not been an organised academy event, so we were still expected to attend our lessons today. I doubted the Overseer would let us have a day off even if it had been.

As I waited for the drugs to kick in, I tapped on my cuff to check my timetable, praying I didn't have any physical classes today. Instead, I got sidetracked by a message from an unknown sender.

Confirm you have the ring.

Kill the daughters.

Proceed with the original plan.

I stared at the message from Cormac, uncertainty running through me. Something that I rarely, if ever, felt when it came to his orders. He'd planted that fucking seed though. The helicopter during the trial, and the other Drake walking these grounds with me.

I'd always believed what was best for the Drakes was in my best interests too. Now, I wasn't so sure. I'd been sent in blind. Cormac was treating me like a low-level pawn, and I didn't fucking like it.

Speaking of pawns. I dragged Luna's stolen laptop towards me to check on the security footage. I was supposed to be focusing my attention on getting the weapon I'd originally been sent here for, but that could wait.

Right now, I was more interested in finding the other Drake.

I wasn't doing shit for Cormac until I had answers.

Clicking on the security camera feed, I searched through the footage my program had collected. The other Drake had been playing on my mind, so much so that I had my image recognition program running on all camera feeds, trying to find glimpses of the guy. I'd yet to see him in any classes, or even in the caff for that matter, but he was here.

The slimy bastard wouldn't evade me for long.

There were a few videos capturing the guy's mug, though the shifty fucker mostly slipped from sight. He knew the weaknesses in the security camera system and was exploiting it to a tee.

"Where are you, cockroach?" I whispered, checking to see which cameras he was appearing on and finding all feeds of him coming from around the caff. "Gotcha."

I jumped to my feet, quickly changed my clothes, and headed downstairs. Classes would start in a couple of hours, and I wanted to get this situation dealt with, with enough time left over to grab a bite before my lesson.

The caff wasn't too far from my mini-DH home. I took a wide berth from the front door when I saw Victoria and her pathetic little gang striding towards it, followed by a naked Noah, who saw me spot him and instantly went invisible.

I didn't bother giving him a second thought. Jogging around the back of the caff to use the staff entrance, I found the metal door locked, but locked doors had never deterred me. I clicked off the top of one of my bionic fingers, using the blade inside to pick the lock.

There was nothing overly important in the caff to warrant keycards or proper locks like in the other buildings, so it was no surprise that the lock clicked within seconds. I swung the door wide and stepped straight into the kitchen.

Music blasted loudly amongst the chaos of the place. I wove through the kitchen staff. No one acknowledged my presence, too busy preparing breakfast for the Potentials.

My gaze ran over every face, but the guy I was looking for was nowhere to be seen. I checked several doors, then stepped into a storage cupboard. A washing station sat at the back, out of sight.

"Good morning," I drawled, tapping my bionic hand on the metal benchtops as I strolled towards the dish pig. I picked up a knife, twirling it in my other hand. "I'm looking for someone."

"You found me," the guy said, turning to face me. He dried his hands on the towel in his apron pocket, casual as fuck. Then looked up at me, a wild grin and a spark in his eyes. "Guess it's my turn to count while you hide."

Yup, definitely a Drake. A crazy one, but aren't we all?

"What are you doing here?"

"Straight to the chase, we're in a race," he replied, jogging on the spot. "Let's play a game. One, two—"

"You're gonna tell me why you're here," I growled, "or the game we play will only be one I enjoy."

"You know it doesn't work that way." He shook his finger at me.

"Don't say I didn't warn you."

I lunged, my fist hitting him square in the jaw and knocking him back into the sink. The thing cracked from the wall, water spraying everywhere, not that I gave a shit. The guy was already on me, cackling like a fucked-up clown as he gripped my t-shirt, twisted us, and shoved me back against the bench.

He smashed his head into mine, drawing blood and rattling my hungover brain as music echoed around us. My vision blurred and I rubbed my eyes, only to get punched in the ribs. One cracked due to my stupidity of lowering my guard.

I wasn't gonna let that happen again.

I ignored the pain shooting through me as I reached back, grabbed a pot, and slammed it into his head. Blood poured from the fresh open gashes on his face, yet he didn't seem to care. Still laughing like a madman and punching me in the gut. He could have given Kayden a run for his money.

The guy was a machine. Just way more insane.

He was kneading my gut like the bread dough I'd passed in the kitchen. My hand searched beside me as I groaned at another of his hits. I was about to fall, my legs ready to give way, when my hand landed on a second pot. I gripped it tight and smashed both pots together like I was on the cymbals for the rock band currently blasting over the speakers.

That did the trick.

He dropped to the ground, blood seeping from his ears. I kicked him brutally in the side, shoving him onto his back. The guy's eyes darted erratically as he looked at the fluorescent lights above.

"Why are you here?" I growled, looming over him, spotting the Drake tattoo that peeked out from between his half-unbuttoned shirt.

"Spring clean, daisy dream," he sang. "Naughty maid wants to get laid."

I slapped him hard across the face and the guy laughed. Bloodied saliva dribbled around his lips.

"Why are you here?!"

"I'm a cleaner." His blood pooled around him, mixing with the water still flowing from the broken sink. "You're a wiener."

He snickered at the last part. Fucking idiot.

"I don't need a cleaner," I snapped, insulted by what his presence insinuated. Cleaners were there to remove evidence, but I wasn't some hack job. Didn't Cormac trust me? "I know how to do my job."

"Scrub Ace," he sang. "Don't leave a trace."

I shook my head and gripped his t-shirt, pulling him close. "Clean me?"

The guy burst into laughter, nodding excessively. This couldn't be fucking right. He had to have been sent by someone else.

"Who sent you?"

"Same as you," he replied with a slow-motion wink that ended up with both his eyes closed. "Cormac, boss daddy, that's who."

"Fuck!" I shouted, spinning and kicking a pot at the wall. Ingredients tumbled from the broken shelf, jars shattering as they hit the floor.

Drakes were loyal. They didn't pull this shit. At least, they weren't supposed to.

My fists clenched at my sides. Cormac had taken me in when I was just a kid. We had history. Years of training, of fighting side-by-side, doing what was needed to improve the gang. I had elevated the Drakes. Without me, they'd still be a low-level gang pulling off petty, small-scale jobs.

I was his second, for fuck's sake. The most loyal Drake in Cormac's arsenal. Shit, he was the closest thing I had to a fucking father.

I shook my head. Cormac had betrayed me. Too threatened by my position and too cowardly to face me himself. The fucker was using me, and then he was going to wipe me.

Well, I wasn't going to let that happen.

Fuck him. Fuck his betrayal. And fuck the Drakes.

"Swayed by a pretty face, now Cormac no longer wants Ace," the guy said with a pout. "Don't worry. Once I clean you, I'll clean her, too."

I grabbed a knife from the bench and leaned over the crazy guy. I slid the blade through the opening of his shirt, popping the buttons, then sliding the pointed tip along his chest, pushing the fabric away to reveal his Drake tattoo.

My orders were to take out two Auger women, but I didn't need to clarify which one he was talking about.

"You will not touch her," I said, a cool calm falling over me.

I'd surpassed anger. A line had been crossed. As if sensing the change, the guy's eyes widened and he tried feebly to free himself, but I pinned my knee on his arm and slammed his left wrist to the ground, holding it down.

I pressed the tip of the knife to the head of the inky dragon and pushed down slowly into his chest, staring into his eyes. He gasped, his flailing ceasing as his gaze fixed on mine in his final moments.

I held it, watching as the light left him, then slowly rose to my feet and pocketed the blade.

"She's mine," I whispered to no one.

Slipping out of the kitchen with even less attention paid to me than when I arrived, I jogged to get a change of clothes, making sure to delete any footage of my time in the kitchen as I did.

Determination pushed me forward. My plans hadn't changed. No, I would follow through with most of Cormac's orders, but I wasn't going to hand over the House Jupiter ring—if there even was one anymore—or the weapon I'd originally been sent to steal.

They were mine now.

And while I was here, I might as well win the trials too.

King Ace had a nice ring to it after all.

FALLON

"Is there anything better than coffee in this world?" I asked Kendra with a contented sigh as I warmed my hands around my latte.

The sun was shining, the meadow full of pink and purple and blue wildflowers that were in bloom, I had my best friend beside me, and I was in a damned good mood. Total. Win.

It had taken considerable effort and a whole lot of caffeine to get me up today. After Kayden and I had our fun in the woods last night, we'd rejoined the party where I'd taken getting blind drunk very literally … along with the rest of the group. Even Ace's grumpy ass had partaken, though he'd thrown me daggers all night long.

Still, hungover or not, I was super excited. Today, I got to meet my best friend's girlfriend. And anyone who made Kendra smile as much as she was lately must be a good egg.

Kendra sipped her own coffee in quiet contemplation. "Sex. Definitely sex. And chocolate."

I hummed in agreement. "Touché. You know your priorities. Speaking of sex though…"

She raised both brows. "No. Before you ask, no. A lady never tells."

"Who said you're a lady?" I scoffed, then choked as she elbowed me in the stomach at the same time I took a sip.

She laughed as I chortled and spluttered, then leaned back on her palms and tilted her head to the sun. "Bitch. But I guess you're right. And no details but … yes, we've had it. And yes, it's good."

"Yeah?" I grinned.

Kendra opened her eyes and turned to me, and I knew she was fully invested. "So fucking good, Fallon. Oh my gods. She's addictive. When she kisses me, it's like the world stops. And she's smart and funny. She's like the fucking sun if you bottled it up and carried it around."

I straightened. "Wow. You really like her, huh?"

"I guess I do." Her brows pulled together, then she scooted closer to me and crossed her legs. "I really do. Shit. Is that bad? I know it's not smart when we're all likely to die here anyway."

"So what?" I shrugged and shot her an encouraging smile. "If we're going to die, you may as well make the most of living first. Being happy is never a bad thing. Besides, I'm not really one to give you relationship advice right now."

"Good point," she said, nodding. "But your goss is everything."

I laughed, then swivelled to face her, crossing my own legs. "Okay, so you're never going to believe this but, the other day I was with showering in the locker room and—"

"Kendra?"

I almost jumped at the sound of a feminine voice. Kendra and I had scooted so close together our heads were practically touching, and I'd been so invested in our conversation I'd let my guard down. But when I turned my head…

The first thing I saw was pink. Head-to-toe, sparkly, glittering, pink. From the high heels fitted with adorable lacy socks, to the toned, sun-tanned legs, to the short boucle mini skirt and matching sleeveless top.

My eyes found her face at last, and my jaw almost dropped. She was gorgeous. Drop-dead, cute-as-hell gorgeous. Full lips, a button nose, elegant bone structure, and blue eyes that sparkled. Her blond, shoulder-length hair was styled in soft waves, shimmering in the sunlight. To top it off, from where she stood above us, the sun seemed to frame her body, giving her a halo effect.

Kendra wasn't wrong. Lou was so bright and beautiful; she really was like sunshine.

Oh my gods. You are so freaking cute!

Apparently, I'd said that out loud, because she blushed, and shot me a dazzling grin. "Thank you! You're quite the peach yourself."

My own cheeks warmed, and Kendra took one look at me and laughed.

I glared at her, then got to my feet and held out a hand to Lou. "It's so nice to meet you."

She clucked, batted my hand away and drew me into a warm hug, which I awkwardly returned. She smelt like fairy floss, which was totally unfair.

"Fairy floss," I mouthed at Kendra, whose amused grin only widened. Little shit.

"Kendra has told me so much about you," Lou said as she pulled away to kiss her girlfriend.

"Has she now?" I raised a brow at my bestie, then smiled at Lou. "All bad things, I hope. Ditto, though. From what I've heard, I'm sure we're going to get along just fine. Are you from Stormcrest?"

Lou tilted her head. "How did you know?"

The preppy style, the expensive clothes, the perfect hair and makeup … "Just a guess," I replied instead.

She lowered her head. "To be honest, I was a little intimidated when Kendra told me who her best friend was."

"Because of my family and what they do for a living?" I snorted. "If I were you, I'd be hesitant too."

She offered a sheepish smile and nuzzled into Kendra's side. "Actually, I think it's admirable why you're here. It takes a lot of courage to stand up to your family and protect the ones you love."

I smiled, a little relieved at her admission. "Do you have siblings?"

"Only child," she said. "But let's just say that I'm not here because I want to be. My parents decided my creative tendencies and dreams of being an artist wouldn't pay the bills. There's a lot of things we disagreed on. I think they found dumping me into the trials was an easy alternative."

I frowned. "Shit, I'm sorry. That's really rough."

Just another example of elitists concerned with credits and reputation over their own daughter's dreams. We knew it had absolutely nothing to do with paying the bills. Her parents obviously had a mould they wanted her to conform too and were adamant about keeping her in it.

I understood that feeling all too well, which was maybe what made me like Lou even more.

"Regardless of why you're here, I'm glad you two found each other," I said, glancing between her and Kendra. "There's not a lot of light during these trials. I don't know shit about relationships, but I think what you both have is something special."

Kendra gave me a bone-crushing hug, then we all sat and talked for a good hour or so longer, just enjoying the sunshine and the simple pleasures of coffee and girl talk. It's something I'd desperately needed.

I didn't know it at the time, but it was also the last time we'd do so before shit got even crazier.

My eyes opened slowly, and I smiled instantly, hyper-aware of the man wrapped around me. Zane's breath rose and fell in comforting movements, his heated chest pressed against my naked back.

Sensing I was awake, his fingers explored my body, gently tracing every dip and curve in lazy, slow circles. When his calloused hands skated over my breasts, I sucked in a sharp breath. He was hard, his big dick pressed against my lower spine. My mouth watered at its presence, and I turned my head, looking into his sea-green eyes.

"Hi Starfish," he whispered, proceeding to nip at my neck, then kiss his way up behind my ear.

I shivered, leaning into his touch. "Hi Zane."

He shoved his arm between my legs and lifted me so I was half under him, our bodies intertwined. When he kissed me, I opened to him fully, loving the way his lips moulded to mine, our tongues melting together.

My pussy was already dripping wet, immediately needing him. Zane seemed to notice and grinned against my lips. "Is my baby hungry for some sea cucumber?"

I nodded. Gods, yes. Fucking starving for it.

His chest rumbled as he worked his way down my neck, over my breasts, sucking and licking each one, then he kissed down to my pussy. When he got there, he licked my clit just once in a single, teasing stroke.

"You'll have to wait, beautiful girl. I'm feeling a little peckish myself. Open those legs up."

I glanced over at Kendra's bed, wilting in relief when I found it empty. We had the whole dorm to ourselves, and I didn't know what time it was, but I planned to make every second of it count the rest of the night.

As commanded, I shifted to give him better access and squeaked as he grabbed my thighs, lifting them over and around his head. Then he began to feast like it was his last meal. I moaned as he worked my body, unable to stop myself from writhing against him.

He laid a palm on my stomach and pressed, keeping me still and at his mercy. When he looked up, my juices spread around his lips, he grinned with wolfish delight. The moment he slipped two fingers, followed by a third, into my pussy while his teeth grazed against my clit, I was gone.

My orgasm rushed through me, making me arch my back as he lapped at me all the while. I grabbed his hair in my fist and squeezed, needing something to ground myself as my whole body shivered in the comedown.

I barely had a moment to breathe before he grabbed my legs, pressed my knees to my chest, and sank inside me. I was already so wet, he slid in easily, but the angle of my body squished up made everything feel tight. He groaned as he slammed inside me, then withdrew slowly, repeating the process several times until I was already wild with need once again.

And the way he looked at me … Those green eyes alight with admiration and reverence—worshipping every inch as he thrust into me again and again, not once taking his eyes off my own.

It was slow at first, but our cadence grew faster, harder, as his name spilled from my lips and he growled in response.

"Say it again, Starfish," he commanded, thrusting so deep inside me I cried out. "Scream it as you come."

"Fuck, Zane."

"Louder," he demanded. "I want you to scream it as I come inside you."

My pussy tightened around him, and I trailed a finger down to my clit, circling the sensitive bud as he pounded me so hard I almost forgot my own name. The euphoric waves of pleasure rippled through me, and then I was there, my orgasm ripping my mind to shreds.

"Zane!" I screamed, not caring who heard. Only caring about this. Me and him and the connection of our bodies.

He let go with me, his cock shooting hot cum into my pussy, his hand on one breast as he claimed me—all of me, with this moment.

When we were both spent, we folded into each other, our breathing heavy, as sweat beaded down our temples. After a few moments, he went to the bathroom and returned with a cloth, cleaning me tenderly before returning and rinsing it out.

Then he flopped back onto the bed and shot me that winning smile I adored so much.

He pulled me towards him, and I nestled into his warm chest.

"I missed you," I whispered.

Zane kissed my temple, then started stroking my back. "I missed you too, Fallon. I missed you before I even knew you."

I pulled back and smiled, that motion faltering a little at the unusual seriousness in his eyes. Guilt poured through me at that look, and I suddenly felt awkward as fuck.

"Zane—" I began.

"Shh, Starfish," he said, placing a finger to my lips. "You don't need to explain. I already know everything that's going on."

"You … do?" I crinkled my nose, studying the relaxed lines of his face. "How? I don't even know."

"I know you're hot and bothered for my besties, and it's okay. I am all for keeping your needs satisfied, and if that means an orgy with the other little rapscallions, I'm here for it."

My jaw dropped open. "I—what?"

He leaned in and stole a slow, lazy kiss. "I mean, you're free to date other dudes, Starfish. I'm a righteous guy, and I'm not afraid of a little competition. If riding a sea of dicks is what you need, I fully support your sexy self."

"Oh my gods." I covered my face with my hands, then peeked out from behind them. "You're really not bothered?"

"Nope!" He flashed his white teeth at me. "The more the merrier. And once you tackle the seal, our pod will be complete."

I studied his face, looking for any sign of doubt, but he was serious. In fact, he almost seemed hopeful, like this pod thing was really important to him. And just knowing he was happy to respect my desire for freedom and still not give me up meant the absolute world to me. I think I fell for him just a little more in that moment. This wonderful, wacky man that I was getting dangerously close too.

And as he pulled me into his arms, cuddling and kissing me, I realised I didn't even care.

I thought about what I'd told Lou earlier that day, about happiness and *living* before we met our ends. So fuck it. I wanted Zane, and I wanted the others, too.

Maybe we'd die, but there were worse ways to go than riding a sea of dicks.

NOAH

Following Victoria had been a waste of time. Luckily, I had so much of it to throw away … not. I groaned, rubbing the back of my neck. A guy walking past jumped in alarm, looking around him fearfully for the source. Not that he'd find me, being invisible and all.

I'd been on Victoria's trail since the first trial, hunting for the answers I so desperately needed. Most of which remained unanswered thanks to Mark's death. I'd been spending so much time naked and invisible; I was starting to feel uncomfortable in my clothes.

It had all been pointless though. Victoria had given nothing away, not that her silence was a sign of innocence. She was clever and careful, something that made me even more suspicious, especially after the fire that ripped through my city.

She'd been forthcoming when I'd confronted her, but she'd held back, too. Which I assumed was all part of her game. Victoria only told me what she wanted me to know. Which meant I had to read between the lines and interpret her words carefully. Unfortunately, spying on her hadn't filled in any of the gaps she had left out.

Slipping out of the caff, I jogged towards the dorms to dress and get ready for class when I spotted Ace coming from around the back.

I ran my gaze over him. Someone had been busy this morning.

His clothes were wet and torn. Blood splattered his face. Red dripped from a gash on his head, and he clutched his side. His steps were not as smooth as I'm sure he'd have liked either. Ace had clearly gotten into a fight. Suspicious, but not exactly surprising. I'd hazard a guess he pissed off everyone at some point during the day.

I switched my plans and took to following him to the mini-DH.

Clothing could wait.

Like Victoria, Ace was another one to watch. He had been adamant about having nothing to do with kidnapping people from the Verdant Plateau and the Crimson Steppes, but his gang certainly was.

Guilty by association, despite his words.

It was hard to trust someone who knew how to manipulate people and was in the business of screwing others over for a credit or two. His boss wouldn't have chosen him to come here if he wasn't ruthless.

I followed him into one of the crumbling buildings when he spun around and shoved me into the wall. Dust plumed around us as bits of debris fell to the floor.

"You may be invisible to the eye"—he smirked, pushing his bionic hand into my chest—"But that's not the only way to tell if you're being followed. You need to work on your footwork."

"Maybe I wasn't aiming for stealthy," I replied, raising my chin as I dropped my invisibility. "Maybe I wanted you to know I was watching you."

He released me, stepped back, and chuckled. "Sure you did."

"What were you doing?" I asked, pointedly looking at his bloodied clothing. "Or should I ask who you were beating up? You look like shit."

"Had a run-in with a pig," he said. He folded his arms over his chest. "But you probably don't believe that. I can't be trusted, after all."

"Oh, but you're such an upstanding, overwhelmingly honest person," I said, rolling my eyes.

"You want honesty?" he snapped, getting into my face. My body reacted instantly, my muscles preparing for the blow he'd deal me. He'd hit me before; he'd do it again. "I had nothing to do with the helicopter in the trial. I just learnt that I am blind to about everything really going on right now, and you know what? I'm fucking done with it."

He looked me dead in the eyes. And so help me, behind all that anger and aggression, I could see the truth there. And the hurt.

"The Drakes betrayed you," I realised.

"Looks fucking like it." Ace grunted, turning to walk away.

I reached out to touch his shoulder, earning a snarl from him as he spun to grab my wrist and slam my hand against the wall. I kept my face impassive, not betraying the throbbing of my nerves.

"Touch me like that again," he said, a blade appearing at the end of his bionic hand, "and you'll lose it."

"I have a glass slide," I replied calmly, despite the sharp blade moving closer to my wrist. "I'm pretty sure it was Mark's and I want to know what's on it."

To my surprise, Ace released me. "What makes you think I will help you?"

"The kindness of your very large and warm heart," I deadpanned. "Or maybe a chance there is information you want on the slide, too."

"Fine." Ace chuckled, patting me on the cheek. "Come back tonight." He made to leave, pausing only to glance briefly at me. "Oh, and Noah, you tell a soul anything about what I've said, and I'll gut you. You tell the princess or the merman, or anyone else in that little gang of yours, I'll wrap your insides around your neck and hang you from the top of this building. I haven't said shit to anybody, so if I hear a single word about it, I'll know it came from you."

I nodded. "My lips are sealed."

I watched him climb the stairs before turning and leaving the building. I'd only taken a few steps when Fallon landed in front of me, tucking her copper wings away. She folded her arms over her chest and blocked my path.

"There's something that's been on my mind, and it can't wait any longer," she began, eyeing me almost apologetically. "I want to preface this by saying I don't think it's you. But I need to ask anyway."

I said nothing, waiting for her to drop whatever bomb awaited me.

"You know the group of Potentials I found in the obstacle course in Physical? Well, one of them was still alive when I arrived. Before he died, he said the word 'camouflage'. It's like he was trying to warn me."

"So you instantly thought of me?" I raised a brow, catching her gaze sliding up and down my naked body. She quickly focused back on my face and nodded once stiffly. "You do know camouflage isn't rare in the

Verdant Plateau? There are others here with that adaptation." I grinned; partly from having a concrete reason for it not being me and partly because I liked that she was checking me out. "It takes training to hold the camouflage as long as me, but there are definitely Potentials here who have some form of camouflaging ability."

Concealment was a broad adaptation. I was able to become entirely invisible, but there were those who could partially disappear or make a body part blend in with their surroundings. And that was just the physical camouflage—some people could alter their voices.

"I know," Fallon said, looking at me sheepishly and dropping her arms by her sides. "It's too big a lead to drop, so I guess my next move will be narrowing down the pool of Potentials with that ability. I am sorry I even had to ask Noah, especially with everything that's happened lately. It's a stupid question I know, but are you okay?"

"I get it, I do." I ran a hand over my cropped hair. "And to answer your question … No, I don't think I am. I came here to find out who has been kidnapping Terrulians from the Verdant Plateau and to get Katie and Rena back. Instead, I feel like I'm going in circles. First the disappearances, now the fire? My family could have died in that blaze and I have no way of knowing while I'm here!"

I started storming back and forth, my blood heating as snippets of the footage showing the fire roared through my mind. I thought of that little girl crying in the street, and my hands curled into fists.

"You have every right to be angry," Fallon said quietly, watching me pace. "So use it. You're always the nice guy, Noah, but someone out there is ripping our world apart. We're not even safe within these halls anymore, so now more than ever we need to stick together. You haven't failed me yet, and if tearing these walls down means protecting our friends, I'm all fucking for it. I've got your back, Noah. I'm here for you."

I stopped pacing and stared at her as I tried to regain control over my breathing. Hearing those words from Fallon's lips was … it was everything. I hadn't known how badly I needed someone in my corner. How much I needed *her* right now.

My voice was deep as I asked, "As a friend, a fellow investigator, or something more?'

"A combination of all those things, perhaps." She stepped closer until we were almost chest to chest, placing a hand on my bicep and smiling coyly up at me. She was so beautiful. Heartbreakingly so. "I'm very thorough with my investigations, Noah. I can tell you how if you'd like."

I trailed a hand across her cheek. "I'd rather you show me instead."

Fallon pressed up onto her toes, her chest now flush against mine. Her lips brushed against mine ever so softly. "Best idea you've had all day."

My skin tingled where she touched me, and everything inside me demanded to take her then and there. Fallon was right. I was sick of being the nice guy. I knew what I wanted, and she was standing right in front of me.

Before I could claim her mouth though, everything went black.

———— ✦ ————

I thought waking up mid-air after being thrown out of a plane was the most terrifying thing to ever happen to me.

I was so fucking wrong.

My breathing came quickly, chest heaving as I searched the pitch-black space. I reached out, desperation coming over me as I tried to work out where the fuck I was. My skin felt cold and hot at the same time as I ran my hands over the wood in front of me.

And then it dawned on me.

I was in a wooden box. A box that felt more like a coffin.

That realisation made the sleepy skydiving feel like a walk in the park.

I gasped rapidly, the air too stuffy and thick and *silent*. Dread filled me as my hands darted around the place, searching for a way out. We had to be underground.

Fuck.

Fuck.

My hand landed on someone to my right, and I swear I almost pissed myself. I wasn't the only one in this thing.

"Calm the fuck down," came a familiar voice, speaking as though this was just another ordinary day. I wouldn't say it to his face but knowing he was there had my heart rate steady slightly. Very slightly, but it was still something.

"Ace?"

"Looks like we'll have to check out that glass slide when we get back," he replied, casual as anything, because of course the guy wouldn't be bothered about waking up buried in the ground. "Now relax or you'll use up all the air. There are others here, too."

I snatched my hand back. Right. He was right. I closed my eyes, though it would have been the same as keeping them open, and drew in a deep breath through my nose before letting it out slowly through my mouth. Repeating the process a few times, I was able to calm myself and let my mind think clearly on the problem at hand.

"Is this the second trial?" I asked, opening my eyes.

"Presume so."

A heads up from the Overseer would have been nice," I grumbled. "How do we get out?"

"We have our magic back, so I assume we work together to get out," Ace said.

"I can shift the dirt," a voice said from somewhere past Ace. "But someone else will need to break open the box."

"Anyone here from the Crimson Steppes?" I asked. They were renowned for their strength magic.

"Maybe this asshole snoozing beside me," Ace replied, followed by a shuffle and a curse from an unknown voice.

"What the fuck, mate?" some guy grumbled. "Where am I? What is this?"

His question ended with his voice pitching a high note, and after the sounds of scratching and scrabbling against wood, Ace was suddenly shoved into me as the guy went into full-blown panic. I couldn't see shit, but dust plumed on my face as he thrashed around.

Next thing I knew the wood above was creaking and I had to throw an arm over my face as it crashed down around me. I thought I was a goner as I readied myself for the full weight of soil, but the dirt never fell on us. Instead, it was lifted away, and I stared up at a rocky ceiling.

The guy must have been from Stormcrest City, with telekinetic magic like that.

I jumped up and pulled myself out, eager to be out of the grave. There were more graves around us that Potentials were climbing out of, and more still where heaped mounds of dirt were still waiting for those trapped inside to escape.

"They don't do things by halves," Ace commented, standing beside me and looking around at the cave we were in. His teeth were gritted, his grey eyes scanning the graves. Then suddenly the muscles in his jaw eased, and his shoulders dropped. "Catch you later."

He strode away, but not before I caught sight of what had made him relax. Fallon was standing before one of many passages presumably leading further into the mountain, given how cavernous the cave was.

I clicked my tongue.

Ace wasn't as immune to Fallon as he pretended. Didn't stop him trying to resist though. He took the passage farthest from her, disappearing into the dark.

I focused my attention back on Fallon who was joined by Kayden, Zane, and Kendra. I sighed, feeling my chest lighten. They were all okay. Fallon looked over at me, our gazes connecting, and my mind went instantly back to just before I woke up in the box underground. We had been about to kiss. The moment had been stolen from us, but I'd be happy to steal it back. She waved me over then turned her attention back to the others as they pointed at the passages, seemingly deciding between them.

Coughing came from the grave I had been in, and I spotted Dick climbing out from beneath a pile of dirt.

"Dick, let me help you get up," I said, then barked a laugh at how ridiculous that came out. His parents must have really loved him to give him that name.

"Thanks," Dick said, followed by a series of coughs once he was standing by my side. I slapped him on the back, helping to clear his lungs of all the dirt.

"Don't mention it." I glanced over his shoulder, spotting Zane as he waved his arms at me in front of a passageway. He pointed to it eagerly then gave me two thumbs up and disappeared down it. If I jogged, I could catch up easily.

"What do you think they have in store for us?" Dick asked.

"Who knows," I replied, looking around. I had no idea what the Overseer and Masters had planned, but I knew one thing for sure, it would be anything but good. "I have a feeling it's not going to be sunshine and rainbows."

"It would be a good plot twist."

I chuckled. "Yeah, it would be."

"Want to stick together?" Dick asked as I stepped away, ready to catch up to my friends.

"Yeah, why not." I shrugged and the two of us headed towards the passage Zane and the others had gone down.

It was dark and narrow as we followed the winding path, but I hurried, keen to be with my friends. We turned a corner and Dick let out a yelp beside me. His hand wrapped around my wrist as the ground disappeared beneath him. I twisted, gripping his hand, and dropped to my stomach.

"Don't let me go," Dick begged as I could feel the dirt moving, swirling around him as it sucked him into the ground.

"I've got you," I said through gritted teeth. The ground pulled harder on him, desperate to take him, and I could feel my grip slipping.

One minute I held his hand, the next Dick was sucked into the dirt. The ground solidified once again. I slammed my fist onto it.

"Dick!"

We were only a few minutes into the second trial and already it had claimed its first victim.

FALLON

The cavern was vast and eerily quiet as we walked, but I barely took note of our surroundings, still too damn angry and shaken to think clearly.

They'd buried us alive. Put us in coffins like some sort of horror movie. I could barely contain my tremors as we progressed through the underground maze, so I jammed my hands into the pockets of my jumpsuit and gritted my teeth.

I could still smell the stale air, still feel the dirt beneath my nails and the suffocating silence of that small space. The thought of it sent fresh beads of sweat trickling down my back and flashes of memories locked up in my bedroom closet running through my mind. I couldn't be back there again—couldn't face it.

You're out, you're out, you're out, a little voice reminded me, as if repeating the mantra would make the past go away. A warm, calloused hand reached out and grabbed my wrist, his fingers sliding down to link with my own.

Zane.

I looked at his sea-green eyes, then blinked several times at the encouraging smile that said, 'I'm here, Starfish, I've got you.' Warm, solid, safe. It was all I needed to take a grounding breath and focus on the task at hand. Celeste and House Jupiter wanted to weed out the weak, but I wouldn't be dying today. A House was only as strong as its unit, and the same could be said for the teams in this trial. My team members were strong and gifted. We were *survivors.*

Something creaked up ahead, and I tilted my head as we approached a rickety bridge swaying gently. Below it, a chasm dropped to where I assumed a maze of deadly sharp rocks awaited.

Down the narrow chasm on either side, multiple bridges lay broken and trickling down the cavern sides, leaving just ours and the one to the right intact. I spotted one other group of Potentials, looking as happy to be here as I was.

Kendra threw me a look. "Doesn't seem ominous at all," she muttered.

I snorted a chuckle. "It's not like we have any other options." Then I noticed the tension in her shoulders and the worry in her eyes. "Hey, we'll get through this together. We've got this."

She bit her lip. "It's not me I'm worried about."

Understanding dawned, and I squeezed her hand tighter. "Lou will be okay. If she's anything like you, she'll be too stubborn to let anything stop her. We'll see her at the end, maybe even sooner."

Kendra let out a shaky breath, then nodded. "Sooner, if I have anything to say about it." She took the first tentative step onto the bridge, and we all held our breath in anticipation. The wood held. "Good enough for me," she said with a smirk.

"Wait," I said, putting a hand up. It's not that I was scared, but I *really* didn't like the look of the bridge of doom. "Maybe I should go first. If it snaps, I can just fly to safety."

"Yeah, okay. Better to be safe."

"Be careful Starfish," Zane called.

His brows bunched together, but I shot him an encouraging smile and began the crossing over the vast chasm. The bridge swayed slightly, but otherwise didn't protest too much. Once I reached halfway, I turned and shot him a grin.

"Nothing to worry about! Zane, why don't you come next?"

He shook his head. "I'll take the rear, make sure nothing comes at us from behind and keep that ass of yours protected."

I rolled my eyes. "I can watch my own back just fine."

"I insist."

I looked him over. He was paler than usual, a small bead of sweat dripping down his temple. His hands were clenched at his sides, his knuckles white. I flew back over and landed lightly beside him. His hand was clammy as I took it in mine, so I leaned in close to whisper in his ear.

"You okay?"

"Gnarly," he said a little too chirpily, even for him. "Never been better."

"You guys go ahead," I called to the others, never taking my eyes off Zane. He looked down at the chasm, his eyes wide when they returned to me.

Kayden and Kendra moved ahead, glancing at Zane but thankfully keeping their mouths shut.

I squeezed his hand before gesturing at the bridge. "Just take one step at a time okay? I promise, if you get to the other side, I'll make it worth your while later."

That got his attention. "For you, Starfish, I'll do anything."

His hesitation was still clear though, so I took a small step onto the bridge and held my hand out. "I won't let go," I promised.

He nodded, then took my hand once more. We'd only made it a few steps when a large rumble vibrated throughout the cavern, making our bridge groan and sway. A scream followed shortly after, followed by the sound of a *snap*, then more screams as Potentials on the next bridge fell to their deaths.

Fuck. Zane's hand gripped mine even harder, and I winced.

"We'll be okay," I whispered, unsure if that was more for him or me. "We'll make it to—"

Something hissed behind us, and a strange scuttling noise echoed from the dark. More shouts sounded from the tunnel behind us. My instincts screamed at me to get moving, so I tugged on Zane, but his body was like stone, rooted to the bridge floor.

"Angel," Kayden warned from ahead. "If you don't get him on that bridge right now, I will. We can't stand around and wait for whatever is in this cavern to find us."

"He's right, Zane," I whispered. "We've gotta go now. Please. I can fly you over."

"No." He shook his head and frowned as Kayden smirked at him. "I can do this."

He began walking once more, still slow, but steady enough … until the sea of Potentials swarmed out from behind us.

"Oh my gods," I whispered. The bridge was unsteady as it was. All that weight rushing at once would surely kill us. "Run, Zane. Run!"

We bolted, going as fast as we dared on the now violently swaying bridge. The Potentials behind us began pushing, so desperate to escape whatever was after them that all logic went out the window.

"Woah, guys, too much weight at once," Kendra shouted at the others. "For fuck's sake, one at a time!"

"Fuck. Off," I groused at some Potential elbowing me as Zane started some weird sort of keening. "You heard Kendra, slow down."

"It's coming," the guy pushing us said, his eyes filled with terror. "There's no time."

My first instinct was to fly up and away from the crowd, but one look back at Zane and I knew I'd never leave him.

I took another step and a crack sounded immediately after, followed by a long groan of wood.

"Stop!" Kendra and I both yelled. All the pushing Potentials froze, and I stared at the darkness below in alarm.

"Kendra," I said slowly, looking up. "Run."

She made it a few steps before the cables snapped at the far end and the wood plummeted violently, sending us all surging to our deaths.

"Fuck, fuck, fuck!"

I conjured my wings and flapped furiously, managing to grab Zane by his jumpsuit collar and then hurtling forward to slap my palm into Kendra's. Kayden shot past me in a blur, and I screamed his name as the ground rushed up to meet us. At the last second, he shifted into his rock form and smashed into the darkness below, falling still.

I managed to slow our descent considerably, allowing us to jump safely to the ground before I rushed to Kayden's side. I ran my hands over his rocky skin. His adaptation receded, and I pressed my ear to his heart, sighing in relief as I heard its steady rhythm. Still alive, just knocked out.

The same couldn't be said for many other Potentials. Most had landed with crooked limbs, or broken necks and spines, their eyes still open wide with fear. Thanks to their magic, some had been quick enough to conjure dirt platforms from the soil beneath our feet. The ones with wings had flown to the other side, but judging by the shouts up there, it was still anything but safe.

Kendra hunted around the space, then came back with a glum look on her face. "No way out but up. What now?"

"I could fly us?" I offered. But even as I said it, I glanced at Kayden. Kendra and Zane, I could probably manage, but Kayden's muscle mass? I grimaced. "Or maybe not."

I thought about using my telekinesis to float them up, but I didn't want to risk it. The concentration required to safely navigate the high walls would quickly sap my energy. Not to mention my talents were aggressive in nature. Moving people required finesse and patience, lest I risk harming them.

Zane opened his mouth again, but Kendra slapped a hand over it. "Quiet. Do you hear that?"

I ignored the way he stared at her like she might strangle him and strained my ears. Sure enough, a low buzzing seemed to be growing louder by the second. And it sounded like it was coming from…

"Move," I shouted, shoving Zane out the way just in time to save him from something that launched from below foot.

The creature that spewed from the earth was born from nightmares. It looked like a centipede crossed with a crab, with hundreds of skittering feet and a hard brown shell around its abdomens. But it wasn't the body or even the feet I couldn't look away from. It was the two dagger-like pincers crooked up by its face, not to mention the rows upon rows of fangs in its mouth.

I shrieked as it lunged towards us, batting my hands before me instinctively as Zane bellowed, ducked beneath its pincers, and grappled its body. I blinked in awe as his muscles bunched, his long blond hair streaming as he tackled it to the ground. It was roughly the size of a large dog, and it was *angry*.

Chittering echoed around the chamber, and soon more of the bug things erupted from the soil, surrounding us.

My hands moved faster than I could think, splattering insects against the walls with my telekinesis or impaling them on the sharp points of rocks as they swarmed the ground. Green blood and slime exploded everywhere, and I scrambled to Kayden's side before they could reach him.

"Why did it have to be bugs?" Kendra groaned.

Her magic power was utilising the earth around her, which was useful as fuck given the soil we stood upon. She syphoned the dirt to form hard chunks to smash the creatures' heads in.

I grunted in agreement, not having the breath to spare as I panted from the fight. Zane found his way back to my side, covered head-to-toe in goop. He snarled as he fought with bare, bloodied hands to keep them at bay. Well fuck, even slimed as he was, I could appreciate the view and the primal way he fought to keep us safe.

"There's too many of them," he shouted, his face strained as he fought. We could really use his magic right about now, but as handy as his calming power would be, it was too weak to work on so many. Not to mention it was slow to conjure. Mind over matter, and all that.

"Now would be a good time to wake up, Red," I cried as I smashed two bugs' heads into each other's skulls. "Wake up!"

He didn't stir, and I gritted my teeth, feeling like the end was looming right as a voice called down from above.

"Fallon?"

My brow crinkled. "Noah?"

I looked at Kayden, then at Zane, who nodded immediately, a twinkle in his eyes.

"I've got him, Starfish. Go get the seal."

My wings burst from my back and I flew up, grabbed Noah's outstretched arm, and hurtled back into the fray. He didn't waste a second, rushing to Kayden's side to heal him. His fingers moved quickly, and I watched in fascination, wondering how his magic knew to find the source of Kayden's injury.

Kayden roared awake, took one look at the chaos, then immediately turned into a boulder. I grinned. Super strength as a magical gift sure came in handy. Everything in his path splattered or crunched as his rocky bulk smashed all bugs in his way. At this point we were practically swimming in green slime, and I breathed hard with every bug I tossed into a wall.

"The damn things keep coming," Kendra cried. "We need to get out of here or we'll be a bug buffet in no time. I've got an idea, but I'll need someone to watch my back."

I didn't need telling twice. I waded through exoskeletons and brain matter to stand behind her, guarding her in case anything came in proximity. Zane took her front, and together we fought off the never-ending tide of creatures that burrowed out from beneath our feet.

Using her magic, Kendra created a staircase in the rock wall that led to where the bridge had been minutes ago.

"Kayden, Noah, you first," she yelled.

Kayden returned to his human form, pulling to a stop beside me. "Not without you, Angel."

I smirked. "Very gentlemanly, but I'll be fine." I kissed him, meaning to peck him quickly on the lips but finding myself pulled in for something even hungrier.

"Not fucking now," Kendra hissed, tugging at his shirt with one hand. "Go!" How she managed to concentrate on the stairs while yelling at him was beyond me, but it did the trick. Kayden hurried up, followed by Noah, then she ran to the middle of her makeshift staircase and held her hand out. "Fallon, you next."

I looked at Zane, finding him holding the fort just barely, and scrambled up the earthen steps she'd magicked.

"We're almost there," I breathed. "Hurry Zane!"

Grunts and shouts sounded from above and I screamed as Kendra lost her focus and the stairs crumbled beneath us. My wings beat hard at my back as I caught Kendra and boosted her towards the ledge where more creatures awaited on the surface.

"Are you freaking kidding me?" I groaned.

To nobody's surprise, I'd spoken too soon, which was an absolute shocker.

"Err, Starfish?" Zane called from below. "Not to rush you or anything, but I'm about to be the seafood special down here."

Gods. I took a deep breath and dove back into the fray, grimacing at the number of creatures that had stacked up against him. He was standing on the highest step of Kendra's broken stairs, his jumpsuit ripped and his arms bleeding from numerous gashes. Zane was usually pretty Zen, but I had to give it to him, my man could fucking fight when it came down to crunch time.

"Jump," I barked as a creature took a giant leap right at Zane's head. My arms were open, the jump would've been perfect … if it wasn't for something pulling my ankles down abruptly.

I screamed as he disappeared into a throng of bugs, then found myself drowning in a sea of legs. I wanted to vomit and scream, scream and vomit, as they brushed over my face, cut my arms, buried me. For a moment I was back in that coffin, back in that closet, as air failed to reach my lungs.

Drowning, drowning, drowning, in bug guts and slime and the stench of death. Except I wasn't that little girl anymore. I was Fallon fucking Auger, and I had a job to do. With a roar of fury, I pushed my mind to its limits and sent a shockwave cascading out, using my telekinesis to send bugs flying in every direction and slamming against the walls. Their legs twitched and kicked, but they did not move again.

I jumped to my feet, then blinked in surprise. All at once, the remaining bugs stopped moving and simply sat still, their faces blank as the chittering fell silent. At the centre of a ring of them, Zane sat with crossed legs and a serene face, fucking chanting of all things.

"Your nullifying power? But … how?"

"You gotta get deep down in their brain stems and manipulate their thought patterns. Using my power on too many minds at once is like swimming in the dark—too many brain waves and I lose control. But with smaller groups? It's more like diving into a pool and watching the water ripple." He opened an eye and grinned crookedly. "It's about inner peace, Starfish. We all need to mellow every now and then. These silly little critters just got a little hangry, is all."

A laugh bubbled out of my throat, and I flung myself into his arms. "You are so fucking strange," I whispered, then took his face in my hands and kissed him like it was my last day on Terrulia. He kissed me back just as passionately, his tongue twirling with my own, our mouths crashing against each other's.

Gods, this man's fucking touch. He kissed me like he laid claim to every inch of my soul, and I let him, soaking in his warmth and the scrape of his hands against my skin. When we broke apart, I was panting and a little wet as I felt his arousal nudge against my pussy. Damn trial getting in the way of my fun.

After the first trial, it felt like I'd had less time than I wanted to connect with Zane, much less continue exploring whatever it was we had together. With Kayden now in the picture, and something sparking between Noah and me, I was in way over my head. Would I have it any other way? Fuck no, I was enjoying my freedom to pursue what I wanted without the threat of my parents, but it was all so new and damn confusing.

It was silent above, which I'm guessing meant the creatures were taken care of up there too. But as much as I could really go for some stress relief right now, I didn't want to remain down here any longer than we had to.

"Ready to fly?" I asked. Zane grimaced, but he nuzzled his face into my boobs and sighed, somewhat content. I laughed. "Roger that."

I flew us up to the top in no time, finding the others a little bruised and scraped but otherwise in one piece.

Kendra hugged me once she managed to detach Zane from my chest. She sighed once she pulled back. "Remind me to put Celeste's head on a pike when we're done?"

My fingers curled into fists. "Girl, I'll be first in line. But we gotta get out of here before that."

"Let's keep moving through the tunnel," Kayden suggested. "Anything is better than being around these bugs."

It was the most logical assessment, and I didn't mind one bit as Kayden took my left hand and Noah squeezed in by my right, his shoulder brushing against my own. I leaned my head against Kayden's sturdy chest and sighed, letting his warmth seep into my skin.

"Not the most ideal way to start a trial," Noah said on a long-winded sigh, "but at least we are together."

We walked for all of five minutes before we reached a junction in the tunnels, and something began rumbling above.

"What—"

"It's collapsing," Zane cried. He rushed forwards, then shoved me hard onto the ground, right before a giant rock smashed where my head had been. The cave shook violently as more rock matter crashed down, and I coughed and sputtered as dust circled and enveloped my vision.

At some point Kayden grabbed me. His rocky skin protected me as he curved over my body and practically lifted me while he sprinted along. When it had settled and I looked back, the entire tunnel had been sealed off and Zane and Kendra were nowhere to be seen.

My heart rattled in my chest, fear pumping through my veins. I had to believe they were okay. I couldn't fucking bear the alternative.

Silence settled as we stared at the cave-in.

Noah uttered another weary sigh, his tone dripping with sarcasm. "Yeah … At least we are together."

ZANE

Never thought I'd experience ass burn yet here I was, friction lighting my butt on fire down a stone slide. It would be a miracle if I still had a jumpsuit covering my sweet cheeks when I got to the bottom.

My stomach dropped as the slide abruptly ended, and I yelped like a seal as I fell off the edge and landed on the hard ground. Rising to my feet, I dusted off my jumpsuit and rubbed my ass for good measure. I looked around the room to see flaming torches on the walls lighting the place up. Unlike the part of the cave I was just in, this room had walls made from big red stones, kind of like Kayden's rocky skin. He probably would have felt right at home in here.

A whoop sounded from above, and the next thing I knew, I was on my sore ass again with Kendra sprawled out on top of me.

"Thanks for the catch," she said, scrambling off me and placing her hands on her hips as she assessed her surroundings. Stray dark hairs were loose from the two buns that sat just behind her ears, and dirt was smudged over the bridge of her petite nose. "That was a bit of unexpected fun."

Trust the little murderer to find that death trap of a slide fun. She probably aimed for me when she slid off it. I held in a gasp as the realisation dawned on me. Was that an attempt at my life that she was now trying to play off? Were we alone because she'd purposely drawn me away from the others to silence me? I wouldn't put it past the little sea snake. She must know I'm onto her. I narrowed my gaze, watching her intently as I rose to my feet, keeping my distance.

"How do you think we get out of here?" she asked, her gaze settling on me.

"I dunno, you tell me," I replied with a knowing look, folding my arms over my chest. I wasn't falling for her games. I'd tried setting her up with that dude to get her to fall in love so she'd put her killing days behind her. It hadn't worked. If anything, she only seemed more murderous.

"Uh, okay." She huffed, frowning in my direction before moving to press her hands against the walls. "Maybe there is some sort of hidden mechanism to open a door. If I could sense something I could manipulate with my magic…"

"Or someone," I mumbled.

"What?" She frowned at me, her hands still trailing along the stone, searching each crevice. "You could help, you know."

"I'm lookout," I said. She wanted me to turn my back, but nope, I wasn't a silly sea slug.

Kendra spun, turning to face me fully with a scowl. "What's your problem?"

"Me?" I placed a hand on my chest. "I don't have a problem."

"Yeah, you do," she snapped, pointing a finger at me. "You've been acting weirder than usual lately and stalking me like some kind of creep. Enough is enough. Cut. It. Out."

I gasped. "Is that a threat? Are you going to cut me?"

"Why the fuck would I do that, Zane?"

"I dunno, you tell me."

Kendra threw her hands in the air, her nostrils flaring as she clenched her jaw.

I called my magic forth to mellow her murderous rage, only for her to charge forward and slap me on the chest.

"Ow!" I exclaimed, grabbing her wrists so she couldn't hit me again.

"Don't use your magic on me!"

She squirmed in my hold, tugging her wrists free at the same time as stamping on my foot. My magic instantly disappeared, my attention going to my poor toes.

I quickly dodged out of her way as the feisty murderess tried to hit me again.

"Don't murder me then," I said through gritted teeth.

Kendra paused, blowing out a breath and scrunching her brow. "Why would I do that?"

Should I tell her I was onto her? Fuck it. I was no cowardly sea lion.

"I know you're the one behind the murders back at the academy."

Kendra's mouth popped open. Her eyes widened. "What? You think *I'm* killing people?"

"Don't try to deny it. I've been watching you," I replied, pointing a finger and waggling it in her direction. "I saw you slip that guy in the med bay something! And Seb! How could you? He was a righteous little dude."

Kendra tilted her head to the side. "I didn't kill your crab. Some guy…" She winced. "Stood on him."

I gaped at her. "Stood on him?"

"I thought you already knew," she groaned, her face falling into a frown.

I shook my head. "What about the med bay dude? He was unconscious in bed and you poisoned him."

"I didn't poison him."

"I saw you giving him something," I said, pointing a finger at her.

"Water? He called out for help and I gave him a drink." She rolled her eyes. "Fluffed his pillow for him too."

"His eyes were closed."

"They were damaged in the trial. The nurses had sealed them shut while he healed."

"Oh yeah? Well, what about you disappearing all the time. You've been acting weird, not telling us where you are and then turning up right where the murders happen. *AND* I found your souvenirs. That's some real bogus shit right there, keeping creepy treasures from your victims. All those pink clips and bows, among other things…"

Adrenalin was pumping through me as I waited and watched Kendra take in all the evidence against her. She may have been able to give answers to some, but there was a lot, and the rest was flawless. I was an excellent spy, after all. There was nothing like the high of being right.

"You are the biggest idiot." She burst into laughter, clutching her stomach as she bent over. The sound echoed around the room as her shoulders shook.

She'd officially lost the plot. About time her murdering ways had made her go loopy.

"Name-calling won't change the facts, Kendra."

"I have a *girlfriend*," she said with a gasp, straightening. She wiped tears from her eyes and smiled at me. "That's who I've been going to see and who owns the pink stuff in my room."

I must have looked like a telescope goldfish. "A girlfriend?"

"Yahuh." Kendra nodded, a blush on her cheeks as her smile widened.

I stared blankly at her as my brain tried to catch up with what she said. Kendra had a girlfriend? Cheeky sea snail.

"Well, why didn't you say so?" I raced towards Kendra, scooping her up in my arms and lifting her off her feet. "I can't believe you kept it a secret! You pesky pelican!"

"I didn't want to jinx anything!" She giggled as I bounced her around the stone room. She was so light I was tempted to throw her in the air and make her do flips.

A loud clanging noise came from above, ruining our fun, and I froze, bracing my legs to stop us from falling over as the ground shook beneath me. We stared at each other; our smiles washed away. Like a pair of synchronised swimmers, we slowly looked up into the darkness above.

"That can't be good," Kendra said as sharp, gleaming blades in the ceiling headed our way.

"Son of a sea urchin!" I exclaimed, releasing Kendra and rushing over to the wall, slapping my hands all over the stone. My heart pounded in my chest, feeling like a wave crashing against a bluff. "No time for dilly-dallying, Kendra."

She joined me, and we both spanked that wall like our lives depended on it. Which, funnily enough, it did. There was no way I was going to die here.

"Anything?" Kendra said, shoving her tiny hands into crevices as she searched.

"No!" I shouted, panic rising in me like the tide. I glanced up, the blades drawing nearer with each second. Finally, my sweaty fingers hooked onto a stone, and I pulled. "Wait! Here!"

Kendra rushed over as the stone I was pulling slid out of the wall, revealing a glass box filled with bright yellow-and-blue patterned bugs, as well as a bunch of furry rats. There was a hole in the middle, and the bugs and rats were already trying to crawl out. Worst glory hole I'd ever seen.

"Stick your hand in; there's probably a key in there," Kendra said, grabbing my arm and shoving it towards the hole.

"Oh yeah, I'll just put my hand in there with the beetles. Don't you know that the brighter the animal, or in this case insect, the more poisonous it is? And how do you even know there is a key?"

"Every action movie ever made," Kendra replied, her eyes darting to the ceiling and the spikes of doom. I gulped, following her gaze. They were getting dangerously close. "Hurry up; we are running out of time. Do the thing you did before we slid into here. Make them all friendly so they don't poison you."

I grimaced, shoving my hand into the hole and feeling the little critters running all over my fingers. I summoned my magic, mellowing the little dudes out so that I could find some kind of key to get us out of this gnarly mess.

"What can you feel?" Kendra asked, biting a nail. She looked from me to the bugs behind the glass. "A switch or handle, maybe?"

"Nothing but stone and beetle butts," I replied, my fingers trailing along the stone on the other side of the glass. One slipped into an indent, and my eyebrows shot up like water from a whale's blowhole. Relief flooded me. "Wait, there's something here!"

"And?" Kendra hung over my shoulder, her loose hairs tickling my face as she tried to get a look at where my hand was.

"I dunno, dude," I pulled my hand out of the hole in the glass and picked a strand of her hair out of my mouth. The bugs started wriggling around again, like some weird bug orgy. "Maybe use your magic?"

Kendra grimaced at the bugs, then looked up at the spikes and our impending doom, her frown deepening. "Shit."

I crouched, not able to stand anymore and shook her arm. It was now or we were going to become fish kebabs. "Kendra. Put your hand in the glory hole, now!"

She shoved her hand into the hole with a squeal, and then there was a loud click. The bottom two rows of stone slid away in the wall, revealing a recess to our right. With a deep groan, the spikes increased in speed, hurtling towards our skulls. I shouted and dropped to the ground, tugging Kendra with me. I shoved her through the darkened gap, then scrambled after, hissing as I rolled over a sharp rock. It cut deep into my arm, blood wetting my jumpsuit. I pushed on. The sound of the spikes slamming into the ground behind me echoed as it shook our little alcove, filling it with dust.

I coughed, clutching my bleeding arm.

"Zane!" Kendra exclaimed next to me in the darkness. "Are you alright?"

"This cave is out to get me," I groaned, shimmying along the tight passage. "Nothing compared to a shark bite, though."

"Is it bad? Can we keep moving?"

"Give me a sec." My jumpsuit sleeve was wet and sticky as I felt the damage, hissing as my fingers touched the wound.

"How many times has a shark bitten you?"

"A few," I replied, pressing my hand to the cut on my arm to stem the blood flow. "Pip and Delilah love to ride the waves out in the deep, and who am I to say no to their cute faces? Have you seen a dolphin do puppy dog eyes?"

"Dolphins can do puppy dog eyes?"

"Yeah, dude. Breaks your heart."

"I can imagine." She chuckled. "Come on, let's get out of here so we can patch you up and find the others."

ACE

Celeste and the rest of the Masters knew how to fuck a person up; I'd give them that. Maybe there was a reason King Theo had lost his marbles leading up to his demise. If he hadn't walked out of the House of Ascension with PTSD, then it would have been a miracle.

Buried alive.

That shit was brutal.

Shook me up a bit at the start, but luckily no one else had witnessed it. By the time the others around me woke up, my feelings on the matter had been locked down. Didn't mean I didn't appreciate getting out of that wooden death trap.

I breathed in deeply, revelling in the space around me. I was still underground, but I had room to move, and my attention was fixed ahead of me. Victoria and I were in a tunnel, our way illuminated by glowing blue crystals on the ceiling that were leading us to fuck knows where. There were no other Potentials around, so I had to assume they'd taken other passages. Even her little groupies weren't scrambling along in her wake. Victoria didn't appear to give two shits—her shoulders back and head high as she strutted forward like she owned the place.

Probably did. The crystals above my head weren't like those they farmed for their enterprise, but I wouldn't put it past them to own every crystal site in the country just in case they could be used somehow to eliminate any competition.

Fingers in all the fucking pies.

If I could place a bet on the one person who was going to fuck everyone over in the trial, I would put my credits on the woman striding through the cave in front of me.

Victoria Auger could not be trusted, so she had to be watched. I kept my distance, trailing behind her quietly.

It wasn't that I was trying to protect anyone. Don't get me wrong, I didn't give a shit about the other Potentials. You wouldn't find me standing in her way if she felt the need to slice and dice a few idiots. Nah, I was watching her because I liked to have eyes on a threat.

Just like back in the DH, you kept tabs on those who were out for your blood. Which is everyone when you are a Drake. There are always people looking for glory or to enact revenge. Much like this place, come to think of it.

Keeping an eye on the one person who could take me down was all part of the strategy to get me a crown. Deciding to split with Cormac and go for the throne was like a weight lifted off my shoulders. I'd always been loyal to the Drakes, but only idiots would remain so once they'd learnt it wasn't a two-way street.

Cormac was up to some shady shit. I didn't care what it was, only that I was being treated like some low-level pawn. Fucking Danger Dog level shit, and I was pissed.

So what's a little revenge? The good ol' eye for an eye.

Victoria stopped abruptly, crouching over. As I drew closer and stepped out of the tunnel into a wide-open space, I spotted the lake she was appraising. Black water stretched from one cave wall to another as far as the eye could see.

"I know you're there," Victoria said, rising to her feet. She didn't bother to look my way, the cocky bitch. "I'd have thought you'd be better at stalking."

I barked a laugh and made to stand beside her at the water's edge, crossing my arms over my chest and widening my stance. "Stalking requires some sort of obsession; trust me, there is nothing about you to obsess over."

She narrowed her gaze, making herself look like some villain in the limited light. "Where is my sister? And all your other little friends? I thought you'd be teaming up like some pathetic group of comic book heroes. Did they kick you off the team?"

"I don't play nice with others." I turned to face her, staring her down. "Unlike you, who enjoys using people. Where are your groupies?"

"I don't need anyone," she snapped, wringing her hands in front of her. "I'm perfectly capable of winning the trials on my own."

I smirked, enjoying the way she faltered. Victoria didn't usually take the bait so easily. Truth be told, she looked worse for wear. Her usually immaculate hair and nails were dishevelled, which was expected given how we were buried, but this seemed like more than that. The anxious motion of her fingers and the slightly frantic glean in her eyes gave me pause. The oh-so-scary Auger bitch wasn't in the building right now. All I saw was a scared little girl hiding behind a mask, and that was interesting. *Very interesting.*

"You're not so high and mighty without others to stand on. Maybe you should have been nicer; they might have stuck around."

Victoria scoffed. "You're one to talk. Noah was devasted to hear of the Drake's involvement in the fire that killed so many people in the Verdant Plateau." She stepped closer and ran her fingers up my chest, looking up at me through her lashes. "Naughty Ace, how could you let something like that happen to your friend?"

I snatched her wrist, holding it tight in my bionic hand and squeezing until she let out a whimper. I lowered my voice, my words coming out slowly, taking my time to pierce her with each word.

"It must fucking suck to try so hard, only to have your little sister get all the attention. She walks into a room and is instantly noticed. You, on the other hand, without mummy and daddy's money would be nothing."

I released her, leaving her to rub her wrist as I strode into the water. I was hip deep in when she decided to pluck up the courage and retaliate.

"Shut up!"

"Your parents fucked you up good." I chuckled.

"I said, shut up!"

I was thrown forward by her telekinetic magic, landing deeper in the water. I spat, shoving my wet hair back, and glared at her.

"Oops." She pouted her lips dramatically, a twisted gleam in her eyes. And *there* was the cold killer again. "Don't pity me. It's you I feel bad for. Cormac doesn't tell you anything, does he? I bet you didn't know about the fire. Poor puppy, does your master not let you play with the big boys?"

The fire in the Verdant Plateau that took out the Leroy estate. If Cormac *was* behind it, then he was getting bold. It was one thing for him to scheme in the background, but a fucking huge fire? That was an announcement to the world. The Drakes were no longer aiding and abetting when it came to shit outside of the DH.

Cormac had outgrown the city.

I ignored Victoria's jab, turning and swimming farther into the water. With each stroke, I put more space between us. I probably shouldn't have had my back to her, especially after she'd so blatantly attacked me, but I didn't give a fuck.

I was pissed.

Pissed at Victoria.

At Cormac.

At myself.

The lake rippled, and I pulled up as a fin emerged from the water. It travelled in an arc, followed by a row of more fins, and I glimpsed part of the scaly body they were attached to. I stilled, doing my best to make as little movement as possible without sinking, and surveyed my surroundings. The ripples were gone, but that didn't mean whatever was causing them wasn't nearby.

Or underneath me.

Fuck.

As if it read my mind, something grazed my leg, and the next thing I knew, I was being launched out of the water into the air. A roar filled my ears, and I spun mid-air, narrowly avoiding razor-sharp teeth. I landed on the giant water snake's back, grabbing hold of a fin to stop myself from plummeting into the water below.

It wasn't happy about that. It shook wildly, trying to throw me off like some bucking bull ride on steroids. I held on tight to the fucker, digging my fingers into its flesh to secure my hold. It howled, diving back into the lake and taking me with it. I was dragged through the water, the force slamming into me. It pulled me deeper and deeper into the dark depths, my lungs screaming at me to take a breath.

Releasing my hold, I pushed myself upwards, using all my strength to get to the surface. The lake was messing with my senses. I couldn't see shit and all I could hear was the pounding of my heart as I swore it was trying to rip itself from my chest. I had no idea if I was swimming in the right direction, but I pushed on, my arms and legs aching as they begged me for any scrap of air I could give.

I felt the water move around me, and my strokes turned into thrashing. Fuck. Desperate, I finally broke the surface and gasped for air. It burned, but I gulped it down greedily. My relief was short-lived because that was my fucking luck. A giant mouth with long blades for teeth came shooting towards me. I couldn't see the rest of its head, let alone its body.

The shore was too far away and there was no chance I'd make it to safety before this monster got me. Screw it. If I was going to die, the monsters in the lake were coming with me.

I summoned my magic, readying to unleash my electricity into the water and light us all up when the giant mouth reared back and slumped sideways. I was thrown backwards by the wave it caused and cursed as my back hit something hard. I grasped the slippery rock I'd slammed into and wiped my face, looking over to see the toothy fucker immobile in the water. Behind it, Victoria stared at me, her hand raised as her telekinesis magic held sharp fragments of rock mid-air.

The bitch saved me.

Must have been a cold day in hell.

It went against my better judgement to leave the rock but fuck it. I swam towards her, hauling myself onto the makeshift raft she had created and spat water as I gripped my side and caught my breath.

"Why?" I grunted, crouching on the raft.

"Fallon," she replied softly, her features dropping like she was about to cry. Then she shook her head, the hard edge to her face and eyes returning, her voice coming out more forceful with her following words. "I'm not dying in here. Our odds are best if we cross this thing together.

So don't start thinking I give a shit about you."

"Thought never crossed my mind."

Yet her erratic mood swings were giving me whiplash. If I didn't know better, I'd think Victoria was becoming unhinged, and that was fucking dangerous.

Shouts sounded, then Potentials were rushing into the water like they were running from the scariest fucking thing they'd ever seen. Idiots didn't realise that they were running from one monster into the jaws of another. The water rocked our raft and a giant mouth surfaced, latching onto a Potential and dragging them down. Their shriek was quickly drowned out, literally, by the water. The other Potentials finally caught onto the shit show they had gotten themselves into, but it was too late. More sea monsters arrived at the feeding frenzy.

Magic filled the cavern as rocks flew around us, water rippled in waves, and electricity cracked overhead. Victoria and I remained on the raft, weathering the storm, until a roar rattled the cave walls as the giant water snake burst from the lake. I was fed up. We were ending this now.

"Keep out of the water," I shouted, my eyes never straying from the monster charging through the lake towards us. It ignored the other Potentials, but they were just bloodied and soggy corpses now. "Can you move us?"

Victoria scoffed. "I'm not an amateur."

"On my call then." I dropped my hand just above the surface of the water.

The monster drew closer, and a calmness settled over me even though the raft wobbled from the waves as it headed toward us at a rapid pace.

"Ace!" Victoria screamed my name like a curse.

Three.

"Use your magic, you asshole!"

In my peripheral vision, I could see her throwing her hands in the air. She was getting real pissed off, but my focus stayed on the monster in the water. The one behind me currently swearing colourfully would have to wait.

"You're going to get us killed!"

Two.

"I should have left you to die," she hissed, her hatred lacing her words.

One.

"Now!"

I let my magic loose and the raft began to move.

Sparks shot from my fingers into the water, and a grin spread wide on my face as I watched the way my electricity moved through the lake. The water snake roared, its body jerking as it was electrocuted. It was a sight to behold.

Lit up like a firework.

The raft was thrown about on the waves the snake created as it collapsed into the water. But Victoria kept us from falling off, speeding us to the other side of the lake.

"Barely broke a sweat." I chuckled and, to my surprise, Victoria's mouth twitched up at one side, but our little victory was short-lived.

The water shook beneath us as more sea monsters rose to the surface.

KAYDEN

"It's not going to open with brute force," Noah pointed out dryly as I hurled my weight against the wall for the tenth time. "This is a trial by magic, so your strength will only get you so far."

I scowled, relaxing just a little as Fallon put her hands on my shoulders. "Sit," she demanded. "Let's just take a minute to rest and come up with a game plan."

"There's an idea," Noah grumbled.

Rather than pummelling his snarky mouth shut like I was tempted to, I did as Angel commanded and heaved to the ground, smirking as the resulting dust cloud made the chameleon cough.

We'd been stuck in here since the cave-in, but I had *no* plans to die in this gloomy rat warren, much less with brainiac and his unhelpful commentary.

The tension was high after our fight with the monsters, and I could practically see the cogs turning in Angel's mind as she fretted for Zane and the others. I grabbed her and hauled her into my lap, shooting Noah a satisfied smirk at the fleeting scowl on his lips. Just to rub it in, I rested my hand on Fallon's leg, drawing small circles that crept higher and higher.

She slapped my hand away, which I ignored and put right back where it was. The slight arch of her back and the wriggling told me she was all for it, and I was all for putting a show on and making Noah squirm too. His face revealed none of his irritation, but I saw how stiff his body was. The guy obviously had a thing for her.

"So, smartass, what brilliant ideas do you have to set us free?" I asked sarcastically, arching a brow.

Noah assessed our surroundings and shrugged. "We go up, of course."

"You want us to climb out of here?" Fallon asked, following his gaze. "That's suicide. If someone falls…"

"Actually," he replied, "I'm a decent rock climber. I should be able to navigate these walls with ease. You can fly. The boulder, on the other hand…"

The muscles in my arms twitched. "Are you suggesting I'm too incompetent for the task?"

Noah's lips quirked ever so slightly. "The thought never crossed my mind. Besides, your magic will allow you to teleport to the top, right?"

I scowled. "I can't teleport to a location I've never seen before. I might end up stuck in a wall or impaling myself on a rock."

Noah hummed. "What if Fallon flew up and described the top? How many metres high and wide it is. You could take me with you, and we'd be out of here in no time, unless of course, that's too much maths for you."

"You want to run that past me again?" I growled, shifting Fallon slightly and shooting him a glare.

Brainiac thought he could insult me and get away with it. Not on my watch. The truth was his idea wasn't bad. If it was just me, maybe I could risk it, but I wasn't about to have the nudist's death on my hands if I judged incorrectly and killed us both. Not that I'd ever tell his prissy ass that. I also didn't want to admit how tiring teleporting could be, which is why I rarely used it. If I transported both of us up fuck knows how high, I might be tapped out well before we finished the trial, and that would only worsen my odds of survival.

"Would that help your small brain process it better?" he snapped. "Or is too much of your blood going to your dick with Fallon in your lap?"

A muscle in my jaw ticked, but I leaned back and threw him a lazy grin as I lifted Fallon's waist and eased her fully onto my lap again where my dick was, yeah, okay, a little hard. "Would it piss you off if it was?"

"Okay," Fallon said, getting up and planting her fists on her hips. She glared at us both. "Enough throwing your dicks around and dangling me like a piece of freaking meat. It's not worth risking the teleportation, so do you think you can climb or not, Kayden?"

Before I got a chance to answer, a strange hissing sound drowned out my snappy retort, and I groaned. Not ten minutes since fighting the bugs and this fucking cave was throwing something else our way. I transformed my skin to hard rock, ushering Fallon and Noah behind me as I smashed my knuckles together.

These bugs were gonna regret being born.

"Uhh, I don't think we're facing any enemies, big guy," Fallon said grimly.

"Not ones we can fight at any rate," Noah supplied.

They were right. It wasn't another wave of the creepy monsters, but a magical ember that shimmered and floated down. When it hit the cave floor, it instantly flared into a fire that rippled along the ground and formed a circle around us.

"Well, fuck," I grumbled.

Noah slapped me on the shoulder. "Guess we're gonna find out if you can climb, big guy."

What the fuck? I glared at him, turning my gaze on Fallon, who was trying not to laugh. Now Noah was taking the piss with her nickname for me? I was going to have words with my little minx later. For now, I had to focus on putting one foot in front of the other. Not that I'd ever admit it, but Noah was right, I had no fucking clue how to rock climb. Becoming the rock and smashing everything in my path was much more my style.

"I'm going to search for an exit," Fallon called as she conjured her wings and hovered on the spot. "I highly doubt we'll be climbing or flying all the way out of these tunnels today. The Masters are too fucking ruthless to allow that."

I nodded grimly, watching her soar higher in search of safety. It would be just like them to tease us with blue skies smiling down on the odd cave. I'd bet more than one Potential had found themselves burnt or zapped by some sort of magical barrier preventing them from escaping that way.

I'd made it a metre up the wall when I looked down and noticed the chameleon hadn't moved an inch. "Noah, the fuck are you doing?"

The fire was blazing harder now, and the heat of it fanned my cheeks in sizzling nips. If he stayed down there much longer, he'd be roasted. Puzzled, I looked up to freedom longingly, then huffed and jumped back down.

"Noah," I barked as I hit the ground with a thud. I waved my hand in front of his face, but he stood frozen to the spot, his muscles locked up tight. The fire roared higher still, and Noah flinched as it crept closer. I gritted my teeth, entirely stumped about what to do.

For a moment I was tempted to just leave, but then Fallon would never forgive me. Yeah, that's entirely why I was down here, risking my ass while Noah just stood there like a stunned fucking mullet. Internally, I groaned, cursing the merman and his stupidly catchy language.

I wasn't stupid. I knew why he was frozen right now. The fire in his hometown had done a number on Noah, and I didn't blame him. If that was my family at risk, I'd have found the person responsible and ripped their fucking throat out. But we weren't in the real world right now, we were in a trial. And we didn't have time for this. Not when he was about to become roast chameleon.

With a sigh, I grabbed Noah by the shoulders and got in his face. "Look, any other day I'd be up for a bonfire and beers, but unless you want to die a horrible death, you need to move. I know you're going through some shit, and I'm really, truly sorry you have to deal with that, but whatever trauma you're dealing with right now, shove it in a fucking box for later. Fallon needs you to get through this trial." At her name, his brown eyes slowly drifted to mine. I licked my lips, trying to ignore the increasing heat burning at my back and taking that small gesture as a win. "We need you in this trial, Noah. You with me?"

He blinked, then released a long, heavy breath as his body shuddered and he seemed to take in his surroundings. "Y-yeah. Yes." He nodded, his expression hardening. "I'm with you."

"Good." I nodded firmly, then grabbed him and tossed him onto the wall where he clung like a spider monkey. "And if you ever fucking repeat what I said, we're gonna have problems."

"Whatever you say, big guy."

My nostrils flared, but the fire actually lit under my ass and I jumped onto the wall with a hiss. Angel had better damn well thank me later for risking my life for that jackass. The cavern was cloudy now, and my eyes stung with the heat and rising smoke. It was so fucking hot. My hands began to blister as I clung to the rockface.

Sweat coated my back in a sheen, and I cursed the Overseer for the millionth time as I climbed higher and higher. Noah was already far above me, his body agile and his limbs nimble as he navigated the crevices with ease. Fuck. My heart beat erratically, my stomach twisting with the sudden thought that I might not make it out of here alive.

"Hurry up, Kayden," Noah called, like I wasn't going as fast as I could.

"Not. Fucking. Helping," I snapped between my panting.

Okay, so, rock climbing was damn hard. My huge, muscly frame was only hindering my movement. I felt … weak. Something I'd never experienced and never wanted to again. Panic rushed through my veins, making the world tilt on its axis. I made the mistake of looking below, which only made me more nauseated and dizzier. Sweat coated every inch of my body, and I had to squint to concentrate on latching my slippery fingers into one crevice after another.

Somewhere in the distance, screams rang out as another group of Potentials undoubtedly faced their end. I gritted my teeth so hard I could have broken a tooth. This magic was insane and, for a moment, I just paused. My muscles barked in protest, my skin stinging from the heat.

I was going to die. The harder I climbed, the faster the fire seemed to rise.

"Keep going," Noah called insistently. "Move your ass, Rocky, or I'll have our girl all to myself."

Oh, hell fucking no. I squinted above, finding my Angel circling frantically. So close yet so far. A bit of light glimmered off her copper wings, and in that moment, she really did look like one of those fabled winged creatures from Earth's old religion.

"I found an exit," she cried. "It's—"

A molten rock fell out of nowhere, plummeting into her shoulder. She screamed, the sound raw with pain as her wings faltered and she dropped into the smoke.

"Fallon!" I roared along with Noah.

Desperately, I searched for her, but I couldn't see shit in the smoky chamber. She had to be alive. She had to fucking be there when we got out of this. Seeing her in trouble gave me renewed energy, and I scaled the wall quicker, ignoring the cracking of my skin and the blistering heat.

"Here, Kayden," Noah called above. He was perched on the edge of a ledge, presumably leading to safety. But instead of fleeing he was … waiting for me? "Just a little further."

"Alright, shit head. I'm coming," I growled.

Secretly, I was grateful for his encouragement. Sure, maybe it was corny and cringy as shit on my part, but his voice was like a beacon. It was so fucking smoky now. I could hardly see more than a metre ahead of me. I needed his guidance because I was climbing blind.

"That's it," he said, his voice closer now. "You're almost here."

I moved faster, eager to find Angel and get out of this hellhole. My muscles were so exhausted, I was perilously close to falling to my death. More meteor-like rocks surged from some invisible spell above, and I swayed, narrowly avoiding a hit like Fallon had taken.

The fucker still burned like a bitch as it dropped though, and I hissed as the heat of it sizzled through the material on my arm into my skin.

"Almost. There," I grunted out.

"I see you," Noah said. "One metre to go. Hurry!"

I shifted my hand, pulling my body up higher. Again. Until finally Noah's hand was stretched just before me, and I had one last handhold to shift to before I could take his palm and haul myself up that last ledge.

We both saw it at the same time. A giant motherfucking meteor crashing toward where I was on the wall. Noah looked at me, and it happened so fast I barely registered what he said as I took a leap of faith and jumped.

Our hands each extended, and for a moment there I thought I was going to fall into the fiery chasm below. Fear pounded through my stomach, my heart clenching at the realisation that this was it.

Just when gravity began pulling me down, Noah's hand clamped around my wrist, and I swung into the rockface, latching on with my free hand. He'd saved me.

I'd never been more thankful for the nudist in my life.

24

FALLON

The cave was a riot of fire and smoke as I cracked my lids and groaned. My shoulder throbbed where the rock had hit, but thankfully my wings were okay, if not missing a few feathers on one side. I risked a peek at the wound and hissed as a fresh bout of pain zinged through me just by looking at the damn thing. It was raw and oozing with blood and plasma.

Apparently, I had a knack for starting trials off with a bang. Ignoring the pain as much as possible, I slowly stumbled up from the ledge I'd fallen onto. I'd been lucky. So freaking lucky not to have dropped into the magical fire that now resembled somethiag like a volcano as it bubbled and popped below.

Celeste and the Masters weren't fucking around. Clearly, they were out for blood. Probably taking some of their anger and stress from Mr Blackmailer out on Potentials. Where the first trial had been one long, slow battle of survival, this one was a *constant struggle*. I wasn't sure how much time had passed since we'd started, but I had a feeling this one would only last a few days at most given the speed and intensity of the obstacles we'd faced so far.

All well and good, if I could get out of this mess in one piece. I flexed my wings, checking the membranes were unharmed. Tender, but intact. I coughed into my arm, squinting through the haze to the ledge above that would hopefully lead to safety.

A jolt of pain surged through my shoulder as I took flight, but I managed to flap up to the top without incident. Everything *hurt*. My throat felt like someone had poured scalding water down it, my eyes were burning, and my skin continued to blister and crack in the gods awful heat. I refused to look at my shoulder again. Once was more than enough.

"Kayden, Noah," I called, but my voice was raspy, and the raging fire and rockfall above swallowed the sound. No one answered, of course, so I just had to hope they'd taken the passage before me and were somewhere safe on the other side.

"Here goes nothing," I mumbled, getting on my hands and knees so I could crawl through the tunnel. The very narrow, very dark tunnel. Fuck. My pulse started pounding double time, and my already sweaty skin dripped even more at the thought of going in there.

I tried to take a deep breath, but the scorching air only resulted in a huge coughing fit that felt like nails scraping my tonsils.

You're out. It's not that place. You. Are. Out.

With that little pep talk, I magicked my wings away, squared my shoulders, and entered the tunnel. It didn't take long for the light of the fire to snuff out the longer I crawled and, eventually, I was left in utter darkness as I shuffled on my hands and knees.

My heart thumped against my ribs, and it took everything I had to make myself breathe steadily. In. Out. In. Out. Just one step at a time, or knee and palm, in this case. *Breathe, Fallon. Fucking breathe.*

I closed my eyes, willing myself to just keep going. By this stage my hands were raw and bloody, the blisters on my palms popped and now oozing across my cracked skin. I could feel a warm trickle drip down between my breasts, and I focused on the path it trekked across my flesh.

Surely, not much longer? With a huff, I put another knee forward, then halted abruptly as the tunnel vibrated and some debris crumbled from the rocky ceiling. Something landed on my leg. I grunted in pain and wriggled my foot. I wriggled it again, and sheer panic flooded through me as I tried and failed to keep going.

My boot was stuck.

The walls closed in, dizzying and stifling as I struggled to get a hold of myself. My breath came in short pants, harsher and rougher as terror filled my senses and locked up my muscles. A pitiful whimper escaped my lips as I wriggled again and again to no avail.

I clawed at the passage, my nails tearing and splitting on the rock, my palms now bleeding heavier as I burst more blisters and cut my skin. Hot tears filled my eyes, leaking down my dirty cheeks as it dawned on me that this was how it ended.

In a fucking tunnel, haunted by the ghosts of my past. Oh, I bet my father would just love that.

I'm not sure how long I lay there, but after a while I registered a voice. No, not one. Two voices, echoing down the tunnel.

"Fallon," they called. "Fallon!"

A sob wracked my chest. "Zane?" It took me a moment to realise that it wasn't him, and I shoved aside the thought that his was the first name on my lips. The one apart from Kendra that I perhaps trusted most in this academy.

"It's me, Fallon," a soothing voice called. "It's Noah. Can you hear me?"

The breath shuddered out of me. Gentle, kind, Noah. Strong in so many ways.

"Yes," I croaked. Then swallowed and tried again. "Yes. I can hear you."

"Follow the sound of my voice."

A fresh tear rolled down my cheek as my chest tightened again. "I can't. My—my foot is stuck."

There was a pause, followed by some voices arguing. Then, "Listen to me, Fallon, I know it's scary, I know you're in pain, but I want you to take a big breath. Is something trapping your foot?"

I nodded, then realised my stupidity. Obviously, he couldn't see me because I was trapped in a fucking tunnel. My panic was making me damn delirious. "Some debris fell; my boot is lodged under a rock."

"Do you have a knife on you?"

Oh, sweet, sexy Noah. I did. A shitty butter knife I'd stolen from the caff and stashed in one of my boots, but a tool, nonetheless. I cottoned on to his plan immediately, curling my body inwards so I could reach to pull the flimsy blade out.

It was barely sharp enough to slide through butter, much less my shoelaces, but I could leverage it to slide my foot out perhaps. With some wriggling and manoeuvring and after much swearing and grunting, I managed to ease my foot free at last.

"I got it," I yelled excitedly. Hysteria bubbled up my throat and I laughed like a madwoman as I set myself back on my hands and knees.

I swore I could hear the sighs of relief from the guys, and it was Kayden who called out next.

"Get that sexy ass over here, Angel. You're almost home."

Home. It sounded weird coming from his lips, but I kinda liked it. Anything was better than this place. Anything was better than the memories in my so-called home with my so-called parents.

"We're here, Fallon," Noah said softly, his voice carrying in the small space. "We're here."

Determined to get out, I scrambled on my hands and knees until I could see light at the end of the tunnel. At that point I practically rolled out and into Noah's outstretched arms.

A stupid, unflattering noise of distress escaped me, but I didn't care as he held me and stroked my hair, saying sweet nothings into my ear. I felt Kayden's comforting presence at my back, and I just let myself have a minute before pulling myself together and getting my boss bitch back into place.

"You're hurt," Noah said as he peeled away and pressed his fingers to my shoulder.

I groaned in a way that sounded sexually charged as cooling energy spread through the burns, healing my skin as good as new as he moved from one injury to another. His brows flicked up at the noise, his fingers tightening a little where he touched me, but he said nothing.

Kayden's gaze grew heated when I looked at him, but concern won out and his eyes hardened as he saw all my injuries. Yeah, I didn't think the Masters and the Overseer would be getting off easy once all the trials were said and done. Sucked to be them.

"All done," Noah said. Before I could move, he grabbed my chin gently, tilting it up so I had to look into those gorgeous brown eyes. "Next time … next time be more careful."

My lips quirked in amusement. "Aw, is touching me so bad, Noah?"

He blinked, then ran a thumb over my lip, pressing it into my mouth slightly. "Is that the impression you get? Maybe I didn't show you just how much I enjoyed touching you last time."

I opened my mouth to speak, but he stole the words as he swooped in to steal my lips in a crushing kiss. I melted against him, gripping onto his jumpsuit. Fuck, he was a good kisser. His hands slid over my ass, then back up again. It took me several moments to realise Kayden was watching, and I pulled away, sucking in a breath as I found Kayden's hungry gaze upon us.

Shit. Was that against the rules? Then I remembered that I did whatever I damn well wanted but … maybe I should have waited? Judging by the tent he was pitching, though, he didn't seem to be angry. If anything, the knowing smirk told me he was expecting it.

"So, I guess we should get moving," I said after awkward silence filled the chamber.

Kayden threw me a shit-eating-grin, to which my cheeks heated, and Noah just smiled at me knowingly. Somehow it felt like they were ganging up on me, which was obviously not acceptable. It was confusing, whatever this was, and I wasn't ready to unpack whatever the fuck I was doing with my love life. Not yet.

I huffed as I followed the guys, who seemed to be looking pretty chummy as they walked side-by-side ahead. Had I missed something? I shook my head. Fucking bro code.

With effort, I dragged my gaze from them and took in our surroundings. We'd made it to the largest cavern I'd seen yet, with a giant pool in the centre. The water was so dark it was almost black, and I eyed it cautiously, expecting a monster to jump out at any minute. Instead, lights flashed ahead, and I tilted my head as Ace and Victoria of all people ran into the chamber from a different tunnel.

I blinked several times. "Um. Is anyone else seeing this?"

"You mean the angry twig and the ice queen working together? Yeah, my eyes are still burning from the smoke, but I see it," Kayden responded.

"Should we…?" I asked as they ran, magic blazing and monsters piling after them.

"Nah," Kayden said, folding his arms behind his head and enjoying the show. "Let them suffer."

I smirked, inclined to follow suit and revel in the grunts and shouts that echoed as they fought.

"Really, guys?" Noah levelled us with a look. "We're just going to stand here? I don't care about Victoria, but she is your sister. And Ace did help save you in the first trial."

I pouted. "You're really going to hit me with that card, huh? Fiiiine." I rolled my eyes. "Gear up, buttercup."

Kayden's laugh boomed through the space, alerting some of the strange fishlike creatures to our presence. Damn, the poor things were ugly as fuck, with giant, goggle-like eyes and mouths full of serrated teeth. The blank look on their faces made them appear severely lacking in intelligence, which proved true when Kayden threw a rock in the water and they bounced after it like overgrown puppies. Then they proceeded to gnash the rock to bits, and my amusement was shattered.

I shrugged. Okay, killer fish puppies, nothing too outrageous. Gathering my telekinetic energy, I thrust my hand out and sent a score of them slamming into a nearby wall. Guts splattered over the path, and fish heads literally rolled as Kayden's boulder form separated them from bodies.

My stomach twisted with the smell, but I sprinted on, diving into the fray. Ace looked to be thoroughly enjoying the battle. He had a blade stashed from fuck knew where and was having a field day slicing and dicing the monsters into sashimi samples.

Victoria was fighting with a blade too, though her telekinesis was doing most of the heavy lifting. She sneered at me as I approached to help, hateful as ever towards me. "Nice of you to drop in," she hissed.

"Choke on some scaly fish balls, Victoria," I said.

Together, we managed to push the oncoming monsters back and send them flying left and right, but I yelped as one managed to escape the invisible blast and leapt towards me.

Kayden grabbed its tail out of the air, transforming from boulder to man in an instant and ripping its body in two. It was a little hot. Okay, a lot hot, as his muscles rippled and his red hair glimmered. I frowned. I could see the colour clearly when there hadn't been much light in here before…

Now, the dark water was glowing on either side of the narrow path dividing the chamber in two, and I looked at the ominous water with narrowed eyes. "I think it's time to move," I yelled, backing up slowly.

Kayden's warm, bulky frame hit my back, and I let him shield me as a wind howled out of nowhere, gusting and ice cold as it tried to sweep us from our feet.

"What the fuck now," I grumbled, crouching behind Kayden's arms. The wind picked up speed, reaching the intensity of what felt like a freaking tornado. I gasped as Kayden half-transformed into his adaptation, his boots turning to solid rock as he grounded himself and wrapped his arms tightly around me.

"Grab on," he called to the others. The screeching wind tore his words away, and all I could do was watch with wide eyes as a monster lunged at my sister and she fell screaming into the now glowing whirlpool.

"Noah," I screeched as he, too, lost his grip on the stone path and was sucked into the water.

It took every effort to turn my head towards Ace, who'd stabbed his blade into a crack in the stone and was holding on for dear life. His arms bulged as he latched onto the hilt, and his brows were down pulled, his mouth a feral slash as sheer stubbornness kept him in place.

There was only so long he could hold, so when the violent surge of wind flung him towards the water, I sucked in a surprised breath when Kayden lashed out and grabbed his wrist, pulling him into the shelter of his arms.

Ace panted beside me, his cold, hard eyes glinting in the glow of the whirlpool. Reluctantly, he wrapped one arm around Kayden, then surprised me by holding me tightly with his other. I could feel the corded muscles of his arm flex, tightening to the point of bruising where his fingers held me. Like he was afraid I might fly away…

I shoved that sentimental thought aside and just gritted my teeth, riding out the wave. I found my eyes pinned in Ace's gaze as he stared at me. It could have been seconds, or minutes, but I couldn't look away.

Not as he seemed to see down to my black soul. Instead of shying away, he only looked hungry to dive deeper. To exploit me for my dark secrets? Or to explore them for his twisted pleasure?

As suddenly as it arrived, the wind died and I gasped as Kayden deemed it safe enough to let me go. Ace happily shoved out the moment the danger seemed over.

"I didn't need your help," Ace spat at Kayden once he'd righted himself.

Kayden smirked. "Someone had to make sure the twig didn't snap in half from the light breeze."

The glare Ace shot his way was loaded with pure violence. "Fuck you, Kayden. You're lucky I lost my blade, or you'd find it lodged in your throat right now. Would save me having to listen to all the crap your shit for brains comes out with."

"That's an odd way to say thank you," Kayden said. "I guess that's as good as gratitude gets where you come from, huh."

"Careful, Red. Do you know what my magic is?" Ace smiled coldly as he cocked his head. "I could fry your brain with little more than a thought. That utter mess of neurons in your head would simply … stop."

"Aw, someone never learnt to play nice," Kayden said mockingly as he rolled his neck until it audibly popped several times. "Come a little closer, I can show you how."

"Give it a rest," I said, rolling my eyes as I shoved them both back. "You can go fuck each other up later."

"So eager, sweetheart," Ace said darkly. "I'll drop the dead weight and then I can fuck you right after. We both know you like a bit of blood and fighting. It warms your body in all the right places."

I grinned, stepping close and running a hand over his chest. His muscles tensed under my touch, and my smile widened. "I'd rather your blood on my fists when I break your fucking teeth on them. But we'll see how the evening progresses."

Slowly, he ran his tongue over those teeth, and I had to stop myself from shivering at the dark look in his eyes. Gods, I was beginning to enjoy this game. I knew he was too.

But fuck him, his twisted mind could dwell on whatever happy scene was playing in his head. Right now, we needed to find safety, and I needed to find the others.

I turned to Kayden, reaching out to grab his arms. "We need to find Zane and Kendra. And I'm worried … about Noah. With my sister around—"

Kayden leaned in and kissed me. Probably in part to piss Ace off, but I was totally on board with that if it meant I got to taste the sexy man in front of me.

"Noah will be okay," he said when he pulled back. "He won't let his guard down around Victoria again. Not after the first trial."

The maze rumbled, then something that sounded like a drum beat five times until everything fell quiet. Any lingering monsters watching us from afar scuttled away, and the cavern went as still as a graveyard.

I wasn't sure if that was good or bad, but whatever it was, it could suck my dick. This maze damn well wasn't going to kill me. I glanced at Ace, who was staring at me again.

Not before he did, anyway.

NOAH

When I had thought about how I wanted to spend my day, it was definitely not buried alive, followed by fighting fanged sea creatures and being thrown around in a whirlpool.

I mean, who wouldn't want to be traumatised, attacked, then left feeling like they were in the spin cycle of a washing machine?

The whirlpool spat me out, and I flew before landing hard on something.

"Snapper in a sandal! First Kendra, now you." Zane groaned, shoving me off him.

We were in another cavern. This one was much like the other, at least from what I could tell. LED lights shone above us, looking completely out of place as they provided light to what I could only assume would have been a pitch-black space.

"If Kayden falls on me next," Zane continued, "make sure to give me a gnarly eulogy."

"Shit, so—"

I didn't get to finish my apology as a sharp pain coursed through my leg, and I was suddenly pulled away from Zane by what could only be described as a puppy with a bad attitude. It was the epitome of adorable: fluffy fur, a small snout with big round eyes, little paws, and an enthusiastically wagging tail.

In any other circumstances, I would have bent down and given the cute little guy a belly rub, but its retractable tongue currently hauling me across the ground was an obvious deterrent. Not to mention there were sharp barbs on its tongue digging into my calf.

I hissed as burning pain coursed through my leg, causing my foot to spasm. My magic rose to the surface, attempting to heal me, but it was useless whilst the evil puppy's spiky tongue was still embedded in my skin.

Carefully, I dragged it closer, then pulled back my other leg—hesitating only a second before I kicked out and hit it square in its adorable nose.

It released my leg with a whimper that shattered my heart and made me feel like I should have just let it eat me.

With round, sad eyes, it raised its head to the LED lights and howled.

More demon puppies came running, and I found myself caught in a battle with the little things. They lashed out, using their tongues as whips and either grabbing hold of my limbs or cutting my skin with their barbed tongues. I punched and kicked, my magic working with me to heal the injuries as I received them.

Not once did the puppies growl—they went from viciously playful to tear your heart into shreds sad. It went against every instinct to fight them off, but I pushed on, determined to think logically about the situation rather than with my gut instincts.

Adrenaline coursed through my veins, and I managed to get a look at the battle around me. I spotted Kendra fighting with a few puppies, tears running down her cheeks and a miserable cry escaping her lips every time she hurt one.

In contrast, Victoria, who must have come through the whirlpool with me, was busy sticking a blade into the chest of the puppy closest to her. She didn't appear to give a shit about the emotional arsenal the puppies were fighting with. Not that I expected she would.

I grabbed the tongue that was hurtling towards me, avoiding the barbs, and swung it around above my head, letting go and sending the creature flying off with a gut-wrenching whimper. I choked back a sob of my own and turned my head, not wanting to see where the little beast landed.

Then I spotted Zane laughing, surrounded by the creatures.

They were jumping all over him, nuzzling their noses onto every surface of his skin they could find as he scratched their ears and rubbed their bellies.

"Zane! Think you can use your magic on the others?!" I called out to him, dodging the attack of an angry pup.

Zane didn't acknowledge me, instead getting onto his hands and knees and play-wrestling with the puppies.

I lifted my hands to cup my mouth and shout at him again when a tongue lashed out. The barbs dug into my wrists, and the puppy pulled hard. I tripped over another creature at my feet, and the next thing I knew, I crashed into the ground. My chin split where it hit the ground, my teeth rattling in my jaw.

"Zane!" I shouted from where I lay sprawled out. Demon creatures bounded in my direction, the tips of their long tongues hanging out of their mouths. I never thought I'd die at the paws of a bunch of puppies, yet here I was.

The closest little beast stumbled, the tongue around my wrists loosening, and then they were all on me. I braced myself for bites but instead was given licks from smooth, sloppy tongues. I grimaced as one tongue delved into my ear, leaving saliva to dull my hearing. Little paws bounced on my back, and I couldn't help but laugh as noses nuzzled my sides and neck.

A loud tolling noise filled the cavern, the paws and tongues disappearing. I looked to see the demon pups running towards a darkened corner, the area we were in now void of happy yapping.

I hurried to my feet and surveyed the area as Zane's emotion-influencing magic faded. The others, too, were looking around with uncertain faces, apprehension filling their gazes as we awaited what came next. The tolling continued, but none of us moved as we waited for some horror to make itself known.

Knowing these trials, the probability of something worse than the demon puppies coming out to attack us was high.

"Now what?" Kendra asked eventually, moving to stand by my side.

"Maybe we have to fight each other," Victoria suggested, pointing a blade in our direction.

"Or maybe we can all just chill," Zane said, raising his palms. I felt his magic wash over me, the tension leaving my shoulders as I instantly felt calmer. "And find a way out of here." He turned his attention to Kendra. "Should we spank the walls again?"

I scrunched my brow at him, but what did I expect? The guy was always saying weird shit.

Kendra shook her head. "They aren't manmade like the other chamber we were in."

"Can we go back the way you came?" I asked.

"Not unless you want to hang out surrounded by a bunch of sharp spikes or in the confines of a very tight dark tunnel," Zane replied. He cocked his head. "No judgement if that's your thing, but it doesn't float my boat."

"So we follow the puppies," I said, looking to where they had disappeared and finding Victoria already crouched there.

"The tunnel they went through is sealed," she announced, rising to her feet. "But even if it weren't, we wouldn't fit." She eyed Kendra. "Maybe she could."

"Nope. I'm not sending Kendra into the dark depths without a lifeguard," Zane said, dropping an arm over Kendra's shoulders. Surprising, given he'd previously been acting like Kendra was going to kill him. "I vote we rest for the night … or day … or whatever time it is."

Kendra rolled her eyes but didn't argue. Instead, a smile tugged at her lips as she leaned into his arm. Dread filled my chest. We were getting too close. Statistically, we would not all survive these trials, meaning we were destined for the inevitable heartbreak of losing one another.

"I agree." I nodded, pushing the morbid thoughts from my mind. There was no point dwelling on something I couldn't change. "We should take advantage of whatever respite we are given. We can take turns on watch."

Victoria quirked a brow. "Not worried I'll kill you in your sleep?"

"Let me clarify. The three of us will take turns," I said, pointing between myself, Kendra, and Zane. "What you do is not my problem."

I ignored Victoria's scowl and made my way to the nearest wall.

Even if we only got a five-minute break, I would take it. We had no food or water, and even though I had magic that could heal me, it would eventually become less and less effective as my fatigue, thirst, and hunger grew.

"That was awful." Kendra sniffed where she sat between Zane and me. "I'm going to feel guilty about that until the day I die."

"I know," Zane said, shaking his head slowly. "Those little gnarly faces are burned into my brain. They remind me of the baby piranhas I used to have."

"You kept piranhas?" I asked, instantly regretting it because Zane didn't need encouragement to tell one of his many obscure stories.

"Yup, misunderstood little dudes. They just need love. Unfortunately, my dad made the bogus decision to send them off to the sea farm after Zara got bit, but she shouldn't have been splashing about in their tank."

"She was in the piranha tank?" Kendra asked, eyes wide. Even I couldn't hold back the shock at that. Who in their right mind would willingly get into a tank with fish known to be aggressive?

"Somehow, her favourite shoes got in there," Zane replied, dismissively waving his hand. "But that's not important. Those righteous little dudes had to go, just like those weirdly long-tongued puppies."

Kendra shot me a look, and all I could do was shrug. I'd heard a few of Zane's stories about his family before. From what I could tell, they were always messing around with each other. I was surprised there were so many of them still, considering the number of times they had put each other in dangerous situations—according to what Zane has said in passing, at least.

"Here, I'll heal you both," I said, laying a hand on Kendra's arm. My magic pushed into her, seeking out and healing her injuries. She sighed, her expression softening beside me. "Then you should get some rest. I'll take first watch."

Neither of them argued, and after I'd used my magic on them, I was soon staring out into the cavern, listening to the sound of their even breathing. Victoria sat at a distance, looking a little worse for wear after her fight with the demon puppies. She had cuts on her skin, which I could have healed easily, but I didn't offer. It may have been cruel but after what she'd done to me in the first trial, she could live with a few surface-level injuries. She didn't seem bothered by them anyway.

Her gaze ran over the cavern as though she were analysing every inch. In the time I'd known her, I had never seen her relax. Even with her groupies around, she was always on high alert, calculating her moves.

"I won't hurt you," she said without looking my way. "I think you've been through enough these last few days, right?"

I raised a brow. "Your track record doesn't exactly boast trust."

"I guess not." She chuckled, though it sounded defeated, rather than humorous. Her shoulders slumped, her head falling back as she looked towards the darkness above. "I'm so tired."

"Then rest," I replied, sighing heavily.

"He won't let me," she said, just above a whisper.

"Who?"

"Hindsight can be so cruel," she said, ignoring my question. She looked to her hands, rubbing her thumb over her palm. "I think I would be happier if I could push forward without the ability to look back at what I've done. The mistakes I have made."

"I thought you didn't make mistakes?" I asked, my words biting. Victoria was manipulative. For all I knew this was some act; a way for her to lull us into a false sense of security. "Aren't you the perfect Auger daughter?"

"Perfect," she spat. "I'm what they made me. That doesn't mean when the world goes dark and still that I have no regrets. I did everything right. Everything that was expected of me. All it has done is leave me with a hole inside that I have no way to fill. I hurt the only people who might have cared." She dropped her head into her hands.

Whether she was being truthful or looking to manipulate me, I felt a twinge of pity for Victoria, nonetheless. Even if her admission was some scheme, it was still true that her parents had raised her to be more machine than a person. Dutiful and always looking for an advantage over those around her. It must have been exhausting.

I could tell Fallon had difficulty with being second best to her sister in her parents' eyes. She still struggled with their treatment of her and alienation as the 'spare' daughter. I had a feeling, however, that being the favourite was no walk in the park either.

"Why don't you talk to Fallon?" I asked, breaking the silence. "Tell her about your regrets?"

"What regrets?" Victoria snapped, narrowing her gaze at me as a sneer tugged at her lips. She sat up straighter, jutting out her chin. "True Augers have no regrets. We own our actions and move forward with intent. Lingering in the past is for the soft. House Jupiter weeds out the weak. Just ask my sister."

She sprung to her feet, storming off into a darkened corner where I could only make out her silhouette. I blinked at the sudden change in behaviour, questioning what had just happened. One minute she was opening up, and the next, she was back to her awful self.

It was like I'd been having a conversation with two different people.

FALLON

My bones felt brittle and my legs like jelly as we finally slumped down in a cave we decided to rest in. After today's events, sleep was calling to me, and even the stony ground looked like a freaking bed of feathers. Fortunately, we hadn't come across any monsters on our walk here, so it seemed everything in the cave system was settling down for the night … I hoped.

Once that strange drum had sounded, everything disappeared, so I assumed it was a planned respite for Potentials. How very thoughtful of the Masters to give us a moment for some sleep. Fuckers.

I shivered, wrapping my arms around my knees as I sat. The cold stone seeped through my jumpsuit and into my skin, or maybe it was the stress and lingering anxiety from the day.

Try as I might, it was hard not to think of the dredged-up memories that being buried alive and stuck in a tunnel had resurrected. The hairs on my arms stood up, and a deep shiver raced down my spine at the thought. I gritted my teeth, because fucking hell, I wasn't a child anymore. I was stronger now, forged from pain and fury into a weapon of my making.

A little claustrophobia wasn't going to stop me from winning these trials and, ultimately, the crown. After this, only one trial remained, and despite the cosy little relationships I'd developed, I couldn't forget the real reason I was here. Win the crown, claim the kingdom, and kill my fucking parents.

Or, you know, maim them at the very least. I hadn't decided if that was too kind or if I'd rather them rot in a jail cell for the rest of their miserable lives. It was the least they deserved, not just for what they'd done to me, but to my sister, too. They'd effectively killed the girl she used to be. All that was good in her had died a long time ago. That's not even mentioning the hundreds—thousands—of citizens they'd tortured and killed ... or forced me to.

I remembered each one with cold clarity, and I knew one day I would pay for my sins. But before I rode the highway to hell, I would crumble the Auger Enterprises empire on the way. If what Noah had said was correct, it would mean freeing all those innocent people forced to labour in the mines. A bonus because it wasn't just about my parents anymore. It was about freeing the people from the other cities.

I also wanted to help Noah get his friends back. It was obvious Katie and Rena were close to his heart, and that just made me think about how horrifying it would be if Kayden, Kendra, Zane, and Noah, even Ace—not to mention my own younger siblings—were taken. Different families or circumstances, and we all might have shared that fate.

My eyes squeezed shut. Just the thought of my parents offering empty promises or simply swiping people from the streets made my blood boil and my stomach twist. Good. Anger could warm me up from the inside while we bunked down in this shithole overnight.

"Angel," Kayden said as he flopped down beside me, nudging me with his knee. "Where were you just now?"

I looked into his brown eyes, grateful for the interruption to my spiralling. I still found it hard to believe how far we'd come since joining the academy. Kayden fucking Hale, bully and brute, was now part of my squad. Tentatively, perhaps, but he'd already proven more than useful, even if his temper and impatience often got the better of him.

I knew now, his jock nature was more a mask than anything. Yes, the cockiness and arrogance was still very much there, but I believed his strict regimens and hard-ass training for his minions was not only for his benefit. His training helped keep many of them alive in that first trial. This one, though? I suspected it would only go so far.

Not really in the mood for strolling down memory lane, I shrugged and offered him a small smile. "Just thinking about what queendom will look like." Ace made a scoffing noise, and I glared at him. "Some of us actually want to change things for the better, rather than rule with power and pain."

"Must be a good view from Mount Virtuous, Princess. But your dreams are just dreams. When I win these fucking trials, I'll have you begging for your life at my feet." Ace paused, looking at me thoughtfully.

"What?" I gritted out.

His lips curved cruelly. "I just can't decide."

I waited impatiently for him to elaborate, but he'd gone back to pretending to ignore me as he lay down and put his arms behind his head. Oh for fuck's sake, I knew he wanted me to ask but my curiosity got the better of me. "Decide what, asshole?"

He grinned. "If I'll keep you when I win the crown, or if I'll throw you away with the rest of the garbage. But I'm a merciful man, baby. If you treat me nice, I might just spare you."

"She isn't yours, scum," Kayden growled, jumping in front of me.

"She isn't yours either," Ace snapped, on his feet in an instant and getting in Kayden's grill.

Kayden threw the first punch, and I gasped as blood splattered the ground. Slowly, Ace looked up and licked his bloodied lips, his eyes alight as they met mine. So fucking help me, why was I turned on by the sight of that savage look? It only grew worse as Ace calmly rolled his zipper down and shrugged the top half of his jumpsuit off, exposing a muscled torso lined with tattoos.

"I guess you didn't get the message the first time I beat your ass into the dirt," he hissed at Kayden.

The big guy rolled his neck. "That? Just a warm-up. You won't be able to move once I break your fucking legs."

Okay, probably time to step in now. But my feet were rooted to the spot, my breathing shallow as they threw fists. You know what? Fuck them. They could murder each other if they were so hellbent on it. Rather than give them the satisfaction of watching them fighting like I was some prized freaking pony, I turned around, lay down, and curled into a ball, ignoring the grunts and yells as I yawned loudly.

It only took a minute for them to realise I'd long stopped paying attention … at least in appearance. The sound of scuffles stopped with their panting replacing it.

I looked over my shoulder with a small smile. "Oh, are you done? Great! Maybe now we can act like adults and get through this fucking trial." My smile turned into a scowl as I glared at them. "Perhaps instead of beating each other to a pulp we can get some sleep, cool? Cool."

"Angel," Kayden muttered placatingly, running a hand through his hair.

I ignored him, turning my head and trying to curl in on myself to keep warm. A moment later, he settled beside me, wrapping a giant arm around my waist. I was still annoyed by his need to fight for my honour and with Ace for … well, just being Ace, but I was damn cold, so I allowed it.

After five minutes, the shivering still hadn't stopped.

"Baby, you're freezing," Kayden said, running his hand up and down my arm. "What can I do to warm you up?"

"She needs body warmth, obviously," Ace said, surprising me by gracefully dropping and stretching out beside me. The bastard had the nerve to face me, his warm palm landing on my leg.

"Hands off, fuckface," Kayden said possessively, shoving Ace's arm away.

"Would you rather she freeze?" Ace pointed out, a smirk on his lips as his hand crept back to my thigh.

I bit my cheek to stop my teeth from grinding. He knew exactly what he was doing, and the only reason I hadn't grabbed his hand and snapped every bone in his fingers was because I was freezing my tits off on the cold stone.

Gods have mercy. I could get through one night of this bullshit … right?

After trying and failing to sleep for what felt like hours, I found myself pleasantly surprised when Kayden shifted his arm, unzipped my jumpsuit scandalously low, and started trailing his warm hand over my body.

A small sigh escaped me as his lips trailed up the back of my neck and to my ear. "Shh, baby," he whispered. "Let me warm you up. It will help you sleep."

His husky voice made me shiver, and not because of the cold. In a matter of seconds, sleep had become the furthest thing from my mind as his big hand skated over my body. I was now hyperaware of the path his hand was taking, my scattered nerves calming and fixating on his touch.

Small circles over my hip bones and along the sensitive line of flesh above my panties made me suck in a breath, and I pressed my ass into him, silently asking for more.

His chuckle heated my cheek. "Perhaps there's something else you'd like me to do?"

His hand slid up my ribs and under my bra where my nipples were already hard. I squeaked as he tweaked one, then suppressed a moan as he turned my head and kissed me, his tongue curling around my own so deliciously I curled my toes.

I was instantly wet, my underwear practically soaked as he continued teasing my panty line until his hand shoved the fabric aside and he slid a palm over my slick folds.

"So wet, baby," he whispered. "So naughty to do this in front of our guest."

I blinked, shifting wide eyes to Ace, who was still lying on the ground facing me. His chest rose and fell steadily, the hard lines of his mouth softened in sleep. Fuck me, it was so risky, but the thought of getting off with Ace right beside me was insanely hot. I ground harder on Kayden's hand, indicating how on board with this I was.

"What's the magic word?" Kayden teased, nipping my ear and circling my pussy.

I was practically writhing by now, so I didn't hesitate for a damn second as my needy, breathless voice muttered, "Please."

He slid two fingers in, and I moaned as he worked me, pumping his fingers like I was some drug he couldn't get enough off. He slapped his other hand to my lips, clamping down. "Quiet, Angel. I don't want the angry twig to know when you come."

Oh, fuck. I squeezed my eyes shut and bit Kayden's finger, feeling my release building quickly. He pumped inside me, my pussy so fucking wet that I was dripping down my legs. I arched my back even further, riding Kayden's hand harder. Adrenalin filled me, pulsing through my core like I was on a damn ride at a fair. He angled my head and kissed me deeply, devouring every inch of my soul like a man possessed. When he pinched my clit, I moaned louder and writhed, turning my head back forward as I opened my lids.

I yelped as I found steel grey eyes staring back, a dark hunger lining that gaze. Kayden didn't stop, didn't even slow as I continued writhing on his hand. And Ace … he didn't look away for a second. It was so fucking hot I almost exploded right then and there. The tension between Ace and me was sizzling as he watched quietly. Only after a few seconds did I realise he'd taken out his damn dragon dick—it was that big—and was stroking it.

My eyes just about bugged out of my head, but I licked my lips and smirked. "Are you just going to watch?" I asked huskily. "Or are you going to join in?"

"I want to see you come first, Princess. Then I want to see that pretty mouth wrapped around my cock."

Kayden grumbled something about wanting to snap a twig's neck into my hair, but he didn't stop, and my orgasm came rushing in one delicious wave as I came over his hand. I turned to see him grin, then he slipped each finger into his mouth and sucked my cum off them. It made me fucking wild.

I barely had a second to breathe before Ace grabbed me roughly and hauled me up. His grip was bruising on my arms, but his confidence was so hot, I just rolled with it.

Kayden growled at him for handling me, but Ace shot him a dark smile.

"She likes it rough," he said, then looked at me, jerking my head towards him with one hand and swiping a finger through my wet cunt with the other. I squeaked at the sudden motion, then let out a breath as he lifted it to his lips and sucked. "Don't you, Princess?"

Yes. Fuck yes. I didn't care how the hell this had started, but I was so here for it. Kayden grumbled behind me, but he didn't interrupt.

Honestly, I'd probably have bitten his head off for trying. I looked between him and Ace. "You boys are always fighting … consider this a lesson in sharing."

"You don't deserve anything from her," Kayden snarled at Ace, but he didn't turn away, and his dick looked rock hard from where I was standing.

Ace ignored him, his eyes pinned only on me.

Was this really happening? I bit my cheek, unsure how far I wanted to take this. The guys might be up for watching me, but I knew there was no chance in hell that they'd participate in actively sharing … at the same time, at least.

Ace rolled his jumpsuit down further, then stood slowly and crooked a finger. "Get on your knees, baby."

"Don't tell me what to do, fuckhead," I argued weakly, but at least he had the tools to back that up. My knees hit the ground before my head could say no, anyway.

When I was eye level with his cock, he didn't hesitate to slide his hand under my hair and grip it tight. "Open wide, Princess."

I'd barely parted my lips when he shoved inside me, rocking his hips and shuddering as I choked on his length. When my muscles had relaxed, I rolled my tongue over his shaft, licking up the pre-cum beading there. Then I grabbed his ass cheeks and dug my nails in deep, enjoying the way he hissed at the pain.

He talked a big game, so I was damn well going to make sure he lived up to it. I moaned around his cock, taking him deeper. Ace was relentless as he moved my head, bobbing me on his giant cock until tears were streaming from my eyes.

I could take it though. He wasn't wrong when he said I liked it rough—I enjoyed the wet noises and the grunts, the way his cock fully filled my mouth. More than that, I enjoyed looking up at his face and the primal noises that came from this killer's lips.

In fact, I was so consumed with taking every ounce of pleasure from Ace that I barely noticed the hands grappling at my jumpsuit and shoving it down past my waist. I did, however, notice when Kayden spanked my bare ass hard enough to make me yelp. I cried out, and Ace took the opportunity to sink his cock impossibly deeper, nearly making me gag.

Kayden nudged his dick against my entrance, and I wiggled my ass, knowing how slick my cunt and the back of my thighs would be.

Ace stilled as he realised what Kayden was doing, some part of him at war with allowing another man to play with his toy. I hollowed out my cheeks and sucked harder in encouragement, sliding my tongue up his cock in a way that made him groan. His grey eyes shuttered, and I knew when he started thrusting again that I had him. Both of them.

It didn't stop me crying out around Ace's dick as Kayden shoved in to the hilt, stretching my inner walls. I moaned, and Ace groaned along with me as the sound vibrated along his cock.

Fuck me, I'd never been so turned on. Never felt so deliciously full with not one but two men's cocks inside me. Now if only I could get a third to fill me one of these days…

Kayden spanked me again, my ass stinging, and he pounded deeper, changing angle to hit just the right spot. I moaned again, loving the way both men were worshipping me.

Ace was close now, his speed increasing almost impossibly until his cum shot down my throat. I swallowed every drop. His abs heaved as he breathed heavy. When he was fully finished, I flicked my tongue down the side and over the shaft.

"Open wide," he repeated, and I opened my mouth and lifted my tongue, showing I'd taken it all. He nodded approvingly. "Good girl."

Ace withdrew and watched me with a smirk, his cold, calculating eyes drifting over all my curves as Kayden took me relentlessly. The sound of balls slapping against my skin filled the cave, but I didn't care.

I'd never even considered exhibitionism, but the way Ace's eyes roamed over my body … it made me feel incredible. Made me feel *sexy.*

This was gods damned bliss. I felt every ridge of Kayden's cock, giving as good as I got by arching back into every thrust. "Kayden," I moaned in a garbled plea.

Instead of going harder and faster, he withdrew his cock back to the tip, circled slowly, then repeated the process several times. I growled in frustration, and he laughed smugly as he toyed with me, drawing out what was going to be a mind-breaking orgasm.

"Kayden," I snapped, writhing against him.

"Patience, Angel," Kayden said huskily, then he nudged my legs as wide as they could go, grabbed my arms, and pinned them behind my back. He held me tight as he sank in roughly, making me cry out as electricity fired through me.

I was so exposed, so helpless as the angle made me hang limply. My tits bounced with every movement, and Ace was suddenly there again. He slapped my boob so hard it stung, then he sucked my nipple into his mouth and bit down before lapping and sucking at me.

I was so overstimulated. I was … "Fuck!"

My orgasm hit me hard and fast, making my eyes roll back in my head as I arched my back and shivered, my body trembling like a leaf as Ace's tongue only drew out the wave.

Kayden came shortly after, his cock thickening before he pulsed inside me. When we were both done, I crashed to the ground in a boneless heap, exhausted.

Who knew a few orgasms was all a girl needed to sleep like the fucking dead in a magic trial?

ZANE

Noah was a really good-looking dude. Even now, as he looked at me like he wanted to slap me around, it only made him more attractive.

I could see why Fallon was into him.

I reached out a hand to run along his jawline, only for him to shove it away. Hmm, did I like that?

"Wake up!" Noah shouted, shaking me roughly before moving out of my line of sight and giving me full view of my surroundings.

White bulb flowers covered the ground like a blanket of snow for as far as I could see, except for the small patch we were in. Kendra, Noah, and Victoria stood around me, looking out at the unexpected garden. I guess the flowers would have been pretty on a good day, but here, inside a cavern where they technically shouldn't have been able to sprout, as well as the sheer number of them, gave me the heebie-jeebies.

"Where did they come from?" I asked, rising to my feet and grimacing at the flowers.

"They grew unnaturally fast," Kendra replied with a shudder, and I was happy to see I wasn't the only one getting bad vibes from them. "The ground shook from it. I'm surprised it didn't wake you."

Curiosity got me like a fish on a hook, and I reached out to touch a flower, only to have Victoria punch me in the bicep.

"Hey!" I gasped. The woman had the audacity of a seagull.

"Don't touch them," she hissed, pointing at the flower closest to her. "Those are Frost Tulips."

"They're what?" Kendra asked, crouching to inspect the flowers in question. She kept her distance though with her hands flat on her thighs.

"Frost Tulips. They grow in cold climates, hence their appearance and name," Noah explained. Here we go; my dude was about to quote the encyclopaedia. "Dormant like this, they are harmless, but when the petals open, they emit a toxic gas that burns and eats away at the flesh. The number of casualties has declined over the years as people have become more aware of the plant and its effect. When humans first arrived in Terrulia, Frost Tulips were unknowingly used as decoration or given as gifts. Now we know better and leave the species untouched in its habitat. If Zane had touched the tulip, we would have all been hit by its gas."

"Idiot," Victoria snarled, eyeing the tulips like they personally offended her, which I supposed they did. I wasn't happy about them being here either after hearing Noah's little explanation.

A rumble shook the cavern, and I braced myself as the far wall opened, revealing a passageway.

Please, no demon puppies. Please, no demon puppies.

It wasn't that I didn't like the righteous little dudes; the problem was I didn't want them to get hurt by the gas from the tulips. No, thank you. The puppies were so misunderstood. Morally grey and super cute, like every male love interest in a romance book.

Oh, and Ace.

I huffed a laugh, earning a confused look from Kendra. Yeah, I wasn't going to explain what I'd been thinking to her. It would get back to Ace, and I'd get a punch in the face.

Light flickered on in the passageway, and then we were plunged into darkness.

"We go through there," I said, pointing at the bright lights.

"Really, Zane?" Noah replied. "What makes you think that?"

I frowned, though he wouldn't have seen my face because I couldn't see anything either, besides the passageway. It was unnerving, like when Zuri and I took the mini sub for a joy ride. The thing went flat about an hour into our ride, and we were stuck in the pitch-black depths of the ocean. We nearly froze our asses off trying to swim back home. Luckily an anglerfish rocked up. It scared the shit out of us and tried to snack on our toes, but it helped us with direction, and we didn't die, so that was a bonus.

Zuri lost one pinky toe.

That was a bummer, but there were worse things.

"How about we cover our noses and faces and make a run for it?" Kendra suggested.

"The gas burns flesh," Noah replied. "Not breathing it in is smart, but it won't be enough to get you to the other side, and I won't be able to heal myself, you, and Zane immediately. We'd need to have another break, which I doubt we'll get any time soon. It would be painful."

"Gnarly." I grimaced. "Kendra, can you do something with dirt? Make a bridge?"

"I'll try, but it will be hard because I can't see shit and I don't want to disturb the flowers. I'll have to take from the walls and hope that I can make the bridge strong enough to hold us over them," Kendra said.

We stood in silence, waiting for something to happen. Finally, my feet were shoved backwards, and I stumbled into Noah as Kendra sighed deeply.

"Okay, I can't promise you that it's overly stable, but it's better than nothing."

"Hold hands," Noah said, his firm hand slipping into mine. His skin was so soft. I'd have to get the name of his moisturiser. "Kendra, can you lead the way?"

"Yep," she replied, and I was tugged forward.

"Victoria," I said, holding my hand out for her.

"I'm not Fallon." She sneered. "Keep your hands away from me."

"Suit yourself," I said, climbing a set of narrow steps. "You know, you can catch more whales with plankton than harpoons."

"You're under the assumption I want to befriend the whales."

"Who wouldn't want to be friends with a whale? They are majestic creatures," I replied. "And don't get me started on their songs—"

The earth bridge cracked, and I yelped as it crumbled. I prepared myself to fall onto the tulips when I was suddenly suspended mid-air.

"Get your ass over here," Victoria ordered, using her telekinesis to haul me back to the bridge with the help of Noah. I was surprised to find my feet landing on a solid path.

"You saved me."

"I'm saving myself," she replied coolly. "You falling into the tulips would have had them releasing gas. Stopping you from falling was purely self-preservation."

"And you fixed the bridge."

"I need a safe place to step," she said, snatching her hand from mine. Sweat beaded on her brow, and she gritted her teeth. "You need to move. I'm not wasting my magic holding this bridge up for you to dawdle to the passageway."

We moved at a faster pace, speeding across the bridge. The thought of it collapsing and sending us into the death flowers drove us faster than Victoria's order.

It felt like we'd been moving forever when Victoria stumbled and slammed into my back. Her magic disappeared, and the bridge beneath us crumbled away.

I landed on my side, the tulips cushioning my fall, but that was as far as their help went. My skin started burning immediately, my eyes on fire as they released their toxic gas. I jumped to my feet, getting one quick look at where I needed to go before shutting my eyes and mouth and covering my face with my sleeve. I bolted towards the passage like a swimmer finding a crab in his pants. There was no grace as I ran, just pure desperation to get away.

My limbs wobbled with each step, every jolt heightening the sense of burning until my skin felt like it was peeling from my bones. I could hear the others crying out in pain as they were assaulted by the fumes, but I couldn't help them. I was having enough trouble as it was. This was going to be a shitty way to die.

Crashing into a wall, I stumbled back and opened my eyes for the briefest of seconds. My vision was blurry, but I could see the passageway to my left. I ran into it and gulped down the fresh air, looking like a fish on a pier. The tulip gas didn't enter the lit area, and I slumped against the wall, inspecting my exposed skin as I panted. I was covered in painful welts and bubbles, my skin an angry red.

Kendra was sitting on the floor opposite me, sucking in deep breaths as silent tears ran down her face. "This is worse than the puppies."

"Totally." I nodded, carefully sitting down by her side. I looked back the way we came, searching in the darkness for any sign of Noah.

He appeared seconds later, Victoria resting on his shoulder as she limped into the passageway. She was so red she was almost unrecognisable, like a piece of raw salmon on a dinner plate. Noah eased her onto the ground and then came over to Kendra and me. He placed his hands on my skin, and I could have kissed him for the way his healing magic spread through me. The welts on my skin started easing before my eyes. They didn't completely disappear, but at least the pain was manageable. Noah had said he couldn't heal us entirely if the tulips attacked, but this was bliss compared to a minute ago. I slumped back, laying on the ground and flopping my arms over my head as he moved to help Kendra.

"What about me?" Victoria asked.

"What about you?" Noah said, looking down at her. "I could have let you die, but I helped you through. That's more than you deserve after all you've done to me."

Victoria narrowed her gaze at him. "Fuck. You."

"I can see you were raised with such lovely manners," he replied, offering his hand for Kendra to stand.

I groaned, rising to my feet, and followed my friends through the passageway, clapping a hand on Noah's back and grinning. The odds were against us in these trials, but together, we were an unstoppable team. I'd thought I'd been a goner back there. Yet here I was, alive and flapping my fins.

As we continued walking, my vision blurred, and I frowned at Noah. We stopped moving, and I looked between him and Kendra. They looked as confused as I was. My vision got worse, and the next thing I knew, I was alone. I couldn't feel, see, or hear anything. The world was black.

Was this an effect of the tulips? Had Noah healed me at all or was I still lying on the ground amongst the white flowers, slowly hallucinating as I died?

"Noah! Kendra!"

The darkness consumed my voice until tiny blue lights reminding me of angler fish popped up throughout the cavern. I braced myself as the ground I was standing on shook and broke away from the wall to form a large platform that floated out over the abyss.

Nope, I wasn't lying on the ground dying while surrounded by tulips, but I might be dead soon.

There was no way off but to drop into the depths below. Looking left and right, I found myself in some sort of circle with the other Potentials in the same bogus situation.

I searched for Fallon and my friends among them, spotting her on a platform in the distance, surrounded by others in similar positions on platforms dotted around the place.

A screen lowered into the centre with large numbers reading twenty: zero: zero glowing on it.

A siren blasted.

Movement rippled below me, and a humming noise filled the cavern. My gut clenched, adrenalin shooting through me, and time stood still like in some cliché movie.

When I was an ankle biter, Christmas morning at the Loch house was chaos, thanks to having so many siblings. Us kids would race towards the tree in the early hours of the morning, shoving each other out of the way like sharks during a feeding frenzy. Most of the time, we would get hurt, and someone would break a bone, but no one cared because we'd be caught up in the excitement. We would descend on the presents beneath the tree, tearing the wrapping apart to see what the old dude in red had given us.

Right now, I felt like one of those presents.

I often considered myself a gift to the world; this was not how I imagined it.

The humming grew to buzzing. Time sped up, and giant bees swarmed around me. Not adorably fluffy bumble bees. Wasps. Their evil cousins. They dove for me, angling their stingers in my direction like spears attached to their butts. I dodged some and shoved others, trying to not fall off my podium at the same time.

I couldn't see any of the other Potentials, the wall of wasps around me blocking my sight. My magic surged forward but there were too many of them, my calming effects only working on those closest.

One swooped ass first, its stinger stabbing into my shoulder, and I let out a feral growl, snatching the thing from the air and throwing it like a beach volleyball into one of its friends.

I'd survived too much to let these angry dudes kill me now, especially when there was so much more I still needed to do.

Kiss my Starfish.

Tell Ace he reminded me of a demon puppy.

Meet Kendra's girlfriend.

Find out what moisturiser Noah used.

Teach Kayden how to tread water.

And of course, become the most righteous king Terrulia had ever had.

KAYDEN

I was exhausted, hungry, thirsty, and beyond ready to get the fuck out of this damn cave. When Fallon, the grumpy dickwad, and I ran into the biggest cavern we'd seen yet, a tiny part of me dared to hope we might have finally made it to the finish line.

Should've fucking known better.

Small, glowing lights sparked into existence, casting an eerie electric blue light over our faces. It was still dark, but at least I could see my own damn hands and several metres in front of me now. The ledge we were standing on rumbled and rocked violently, until the damn thing cracked away from the wall entirely and started floating in mid-air. Well, shit, no escape now. We were all in.

With the lights now on, I got a slightly better look around the room as our platform floated towards the centre. Six floating discs filled with Potentials from different groups. They were a little scarcer on numbers, but still a threat. I'd have to watch my back not only from the monsters, but from the Potentials, too.

Never stopped me before.

The screen that had counted us down shifted, the numbers dialling until what appeared to be a timer set for twenty minutes. Twenty minutes, presumably, to stay the fuck alive. Fine by me.

When the first second ticked over, a siren boomed and chaos erupted.

A loud droning hummed in my ears. Wasps … and we'd been

brought right into their nest.

The wasps sped out from the abyss in droves, and I grunted as I ducked a stinger from one, watching as it sailed on to impale another Potential's stomach. Bro looked at me in shock, blinking rapidly before the wasp did it again and again until the guy's stomach was riddled with gaping holes that poured blood.

Another came zooming toward Fallon and I gritted my teeth as I jumped in front of my angel, blocking the stinger meant for her with my rock form.

"Get your damn jabber away from my girl," I roared, enjoying the satisfying crunch of its appendage breaking. Just to remind it of its place, I grabbed its wings and ripped them in two. It let out a defeated rumble and curled in on itself. I kicked the oversized bug over the edge and into the abyss. My actions were instantly met by increased angry buzzing, and I covered my ears.

I guess they weren't a fan of me killing their friend. I grinned. Well, I was feeling a whole lot more murderous. Just like the first trial, I'd do whatever it took in the final moments before victory, and I had a feeling this was it. Blood baths seemed to be stock standard for the grand finale as far as the Masters and Overseer were concerned.

There was no room to transform into a boulder on this narrow platform, so rock fists it was. I threw a roundhouse at the closest wasp, watching as it plummeted into the darkness, then uppercut another's abdomen, its guts splashing yellow blood and body fluids all over my face.

Fallon's telekinetic powers smashed groups of them together, going as far as to shift their stingers to impale each other's bodies. Fucking brutal. We worked in tandem, keeping our backs together to lower the threat from all angles.

Then I saw Ace's true power and had to stop my jaw from dropping. The guy was grinning like someone who belonged in a padded room of a penitentiary. He was barely even moving except for the occasional smooth sidestep or duck. Everywhere around him, wasps just ... dropped, instantly dead from his electrical magic. Which didn't really make sense now that I thought about it. It was rare. Really fucking rare for anyone to have magic allowing one to manipulate electrical currents. The last person I'd heard of having that ability was some prissy, posh dude from Stormcrest who'd died in a bombing.

Stashing that train of thought away for later, I watched in grim awe as magic flashed all around me. What remained of my minions were all fighting viciously, and I nodded my head, pleased with how far they'd come. Pride filled me as I spotted a very sandy looking Dick leading the crew, his battle cry enough to raise the hairs on my arms. He might be little, but he was one mighty son of a bitch.

Kendra vaulted onto our platform, kicking a wasp out the way before clasping hands with Fallon quickly and giving me a smug look. Stupid flexible ninja and her sassy ways.

I ignored her as the two of them faced off a fresh wave of wasps together, then grunted as something clinked against my thick skin. A Potential leered up at me from where they'd shoved a dagger made from ice into my leg. Unfortunately for her, my rock armour stopped the blade and I was unharmed. I raised a brow, and their victorious expression quickly shifted as they realised who they'd come up against.

I grabbed the girl by the nape of her neck and lifted her to my eyeline. Wide blue eyes bulged, and she clawed with dirty nails, trying feebly to fight me off.

"Wait," she croaked between gasps. "I'm sorry. Please, I didn't—"

"Big mistake," I said darkly, offering her a feral grin. "Big fucking mistake." Then I dropped her over the edge.

Her scream echoed through the chamber. I shrugged. I wouldn't lose any sleep over it. Not when she'd come for me first.

But when I turned, I couldn't help but cry out myself. I crossed my arms in front of my face as a swarm of wasps descended on me. Wings and stingers and furry, spiked stripes flashed before my vision. Everywhere I looked, all I could see was flitting body parts. Vaguely, I could see Fallon and Ace banding together on the other side, their hands too full to help.

Why wasn't my rock armour working? Then the wasps' red bodies started glowing, and I knew. Whatever these creatures were, I was going to guess they'd been magically enhanced, because nothing got through my rock armour … until now.

They whittled away at me, the coating over my skin chipping away like it was little more than hardened dirt. Fuck. I threw punches blindly, mincing and mashing at their bodies until my biceps were stained yellow.

It only made them angrier.

I cried out as the first full chunk of rock armour dropped away and a stinger stabbed through my shoulder, followed by another to my thigh, forcing me to drop to my knees. The ground rushed up to meet me, and I gasped as blood poured from my wounds, hot and sticky. All the while I kept on punching, until a sharp pain had me reeling forward.

"Kayden," Fallon shrieked. I could just make her out, fighting furiously, but she was shoved back by another wave of wrathful wasps.

Surprised, I glanced down slowly, finding a stinger poking out from my stomach.

"Huh, that's not supposed to be there."

Adrenaline raced through me, every nerve ending on fire as my mind identified the foreign invasion to my body.

Then pain. Blinding, shocking, pain, which quickly shifted from hot to cool by the second. The hairs on my arms stood on end, and I blinked rapidly, in a daze as scarlet dribbled from the wound. Reaching over my shoulder, I found the wasp responsible and snapped its damn neck, killing it instantly with its stinger still inside me. I was too scared to take the damn thing out.

I spat out a glob of blood and grimaced. Well, that wasn't fucking good.

The world went hazy, and the last thing I saw was the shadow of someone racing toward me, their roar bouncing off the walls.

Against my will, my knees buckled and, slowly, I slumped to the ground.

FALLON

"Kayden!" I screamed, unable to do anything but watch as the wasps stung him again, again, again. Until the big guy fell to his knees and finally slumped to the ground, unmoving. My stomach twisted violently, every instinct telling me to run to him. I shouldn't have left him. This man that had done a 180 from bullying me to becoming someone I hadn't realised until now just how much I was coming to care for.

Kendra made to run to Kayden but stopped suddenly, her face draining of colour as a blood-curdling scream echoed through the chamber. I turned, spotting Lou about to be skewered by a wasp. My best friend looked between Kayden, Lou, and me, her eyes full of anguish.

"Fallon," she whispered, looking back at her girlfriend. "I…"

"Go, Kendra!" I nodded encouragingly, though I felt anything but confident. "We've got this."

Kendra nodded and leaped to another platform, leaving Ace and me to guard Kayden.

Ace swore beside me, his sharp jawline gritted tight as he fought off the wave of wasps surrounding us with vicious accuracy. He was beyond powerful—strong enough to rival the likes of my father—but even his electrical manipulation wasn't enough to stem the swarm.

We worked in a strange, synchronistic tandem as I used my telekinesis to hurl one cluster after another into his line of sight, only for him to short circuit their brains without even breaking a sweat. But

I could see his strength waning, even if the stubborn look in his eyes meant he'd not back down for a single second, exhausted or not.

"Fuck this," I spat, grabbing hold of Ace's hand. "Kayden, turn into your rock form, now!"

"The hell you think you're doing, Princess?" Ace grunted, but his hand only tightened to the point of pain, as if anchoring himself to me. I welcomed the bite of his fingers crunching against mine, not missing the thumb that caressed the top of my hand in the briefest motion.

I ignored the shiver it sent through me and mustered every last drop of my power until I could feel myself overflowing with telekinetic energy.

"Hold tight, grumpy butt," I said under my breath.

I bent over, and with a war cry that could rival an army's, I *unleashed*. A shockwave slammed out of me, sending everything in my platform's radius blasting so hard against the walls that wasp abdomens splattered, cartilage crunched, and everything around me died instantly.

Everything but the two men I was trying to protect. Ace's painful grip had kept him level and Kayden, thankfully, had turned to rock as much as possible with his injuries, keeping him on the ground. Gasping, I straightened, finding myself staring into Ace's eyes. Eyes filled with … awe? He looked at me like I was his last meal, his gaze burning with hunger.

"The princess shows her teeth at last," he said huskily. Slowly, he lifted a hand towards me. "You are…"

"Angel," Kayden croaked.

Instantly, Ace's face hardened, and he dropped his palm. I didn't have time to work out what the damn Drake was trying to do, so I ignored whatever the fuck had just happened and ran to Kayden. More wasps were advancing, their stingers sharp and deadly in the fae-like blue light. Fuck. I had to get there in time, had to—

Before I could make it, someone else bellowed, swinging towards our platform on a vine magicked from a Potential. I blinked, not quite sure what I was seeing. At first, I thought it was Zane, then realised the guy was too small and skinny. When the light shone on their face, I had to blink several more times.

"Dick?"

The guy vaulted off the vine like some kind of superhero, then batted the surrounding wasps away like they were little more than mosquitos. "Your Little Dick will save you, Big Red!"

A bubble of hysteria climbed my throat at the adorable nicknames they had given each other, but the feeling quickly washed away as I stumbled towards Kayden. The power I used had left me lightheaded. I was strong and had more stored up, but hell, I'd need a freaking vacation after all this shit. Preferably with a crown as my new accessory and servants giving me mimosas whenever the damn hell I pleased.

My little escape mechanism immediately evaporated as I saw up close the condition Kayden was in.

"Oh my gods." I put a finger to his pulse, swallowing hard at how faint it was. How *slow*. "Dick, can you help?"

He shook his head, a sad look on his timid face. "I don't have the power to heal. But Noah does."

I looked over to where Noah and Zane were fighting together. Shit, the two of them side by side was a vision for the spank bank, but I didn't have time to wipe away my drool. Dick placed a hand on my arm, his blue eyes earnest as he gazed at me. "I'll protect him, Fallon. With my life."

My lips quirked slightly. I'd give this guy a badge of honour just for being nice as fuck, but still, I gave him a no-nonsense nod. "I'm trusting you."

He banged a hand to his heart. "On. My. Life."

That's all I needed to hear. With a gust of my wings, I took to the air, swerving bugs left and right as I landed beside Noah and Zane.

"Starfish!" Zane cried, slaughtering a wasp with a strangely sexual thrust of his hand without even looking at it. "I knew the currents would send you drifting back to me. I missed you."

He kissed me deeply, then pulled back with a lopsided grin. I shot him one of my own. "Missed you too, handsome. But I need Noah, now."

"I'm here, Fallon," Noah said a little breathlessly. "What do you need?"

"I..." I looked down, only just realising he was fully naked, his dick swinging in the wind like a flag. "Holy shit, Noah. You're naked."

He grimaced, looking around awkwardly. No one was watching, the rest of the Potentials still in full blood bath mode. "I need to be naked to camouflage," he said with a world-weary sigh. "One of the joys of my adaptation."

"Never mind that. It's Kayden. He's dying, Noah. I need…" I swallowed my damn pride and forced the words from my mouth. "I need your help."

We both looked at the now crowded path back to my original platform. "Take me to him," he demanded. "Quickly."

Any other time I'd have thought Noah giving me orders was kinda hot. As it was, I took his hand and grunted as I used my wings to give us an extra boost of air as we jumped back to the other platform. It took everything in me to ignore the fact his cock was bouncing along beside me as we ran back to Kayden. Damn chameleon was saving lives like no tomorrow in these trials. Once I became queen, he'd be on the royal medical response team for sure.

He leapt out of my arms before we'd even landed, settling over Kayden and assessing the work needed.

"Help me roll him over. Good. Now I need you both to hold him down as I pull the stinger out," he said. Dick and I looked at each other, feeling all kinds of helpless. "*Now*," Noah barked.

Dick squeaked, going to Kayden's thighs and pressing down. I took his shoulders, my heart skipping a beat at the vague expression in his brown eyes. He tried to speak but no words came out, and I nodded grimly.

"I know, baby. But you'll be better in no time."

Noah looked at us and nodded. "On three," Noah said. "One, two—"

He pulled the stinger out in one swift motion and Kayden jerked violently beneath us, groaning. His eyes rolled back in his head, his tanned skin paling by the second. Immediately, Noah's hands were on the gaping, bloodied hole in his stomach, and I watched as the wound slowly began to close.

I wanted nothing more than to comfort him and shower him with kisses, but the hairs on the back of my neck stood on end, a cold shiver of awareness trickling down my spine. Looking around, I found nothing moving on our platform. Ace had launched himself onto the one Zane and Kendra now occupied, the three of them fighting together.

Still, the feeling didn't leave. Something splattered on my cheek, and slowly, I looked up.

"Dick!" I shrieked. I shoved him out of the way as a gigantic shape descended from a string and scuttled backwards. Its fangs wriggled as eight massive black eyes were staring at us.

"What fucking next?" I growled, rising to my feet and shifting my stance. Dick just stood there like a limp noodle, his arms like pin rods at his sides. "What are you doing, Dick? Move!"

"I can't," he said quietly. "I'm terrified of s-s-spiders."

"Well, it likes you just fine, so fucking move!"

I sprinted forward, tackling him to the ground to avoid having his head bitten off. Then I commando rolled back into a run. I heard Dick's shrieks behind me, then found him running like a freaking athlete and passing me with flying colours. The little guy took a hurtling leap across the platforms. I grinned wildly as I took a rounding arc back to Kayden and Noah.

Both were on their feet, though Kayden didn't look ready for much action. He was still deathly pale, and I'd be willing to bet those stingers might have been filled with some kind of venom, because he was damn near wobbling off the ledge. How we were going to get him onto the other platform, I had no idea.

"Our odds of survival aren't looking good," Noah drawled.

"So helpful, Noah," I sassed. "You're the smart one, figure it out!"

With a huff, I turned to the spider, using my power to push it back, but it was a strong mother fucker. The clicks and clacks of its fangs turned my blood ice-cold, and it took everything in me to stand my ground and fight. I wasn't going to run, but I'd be lying if I said that spiders and I were good friends.

To make matters worse, a few Potentials jumped onto our platform, looking ready to spill some Auger blood. I groaned. "Guys, not that I don't love a good fight, but I'm kinda busy right now. Noah!"

I glanced over my shoulder, but he was … gone. My heart sank into my stomach. He'd left us when we needed him most? I hadn't thought he was the type to turn and run, but maybe I was wrong. Maybe he was done with all the bullshit that my family name pulled him into, not just with Victoria, but possibly beyond with his investigations into his missing friends. Fuck. It's not as if he owed me anything. I wasn't even sure if Noah and I could even call each other friends. He'd owed me a debt, and he'd paid in full. The kisses were probably just a meaningless distraction, so why did it hurt so much to know he'd left?

"We came to help, sweetheart. Let us do the heavy lifting," one of the newly arrived Potentials said.

I raised my brows at that weird remark but didn't argue as they turned to the spider and dispatched it easily. Static shifted through the air as one punched a hole through the creature's leg, making it stumble to the ground. The rest threw wind and earth magic at it, binding its other legs and then shooting it off the edge to fall into the black depths below.

The Potentials chuckled amongst each other as they turned to me. I stood my ground, though every instinct in me screamed to *run*. Despite what they'd said, they weren't here to help me get out of this trial. I didn't know these people, and no one went out of their way to assist strangers for no good reason in these trials. You didn't win trials by being nice.

I threw them a winning smile. "Looks like the spider's gone, boys. Thanks for the assist."

"Where did your friend go?" one asked, looking around pointedly.

"Looks like he didn't think you were worth the effort of sticking around," another guy said, his smile widening. He glanced at Kayden, who had slumped to the ground, clutching his stomach. "The rock isn't in a position to save you either."

"I think you're mistaken," I said sweetly, flexing my hands. "I'm not the one who needs saving."

Their faces shifted into sneers. Bingo. Four losers with some kind of vendetta against the Augers … or just me. Either way, what's a little more blood to spill?

"We know you're the one who did Mark in," one said as he stepped forward. His short black hair was greasy and matted, the muscled arms of his jumpsuit covered in blood. The leader, I was guessing. The cruel look in his eyes told me everything I needed to know—not that his taste in friends hadn't already.

"I did," I admitted with a shrug. Then I let them see my own violent smile. "I enjoyed every fucking minute of it."

"Bitch," the leader spat. "You'll be drowning in your own blood when we're done with you."

"I've already had my fill for breakfast," I said sweetly. "But thanks for the offer."

Before they could move, Noah flashed into existence behind the leader, his brown eyes so dark they were almost black as he held a knife to the guy's throat. Where he'd gotten that from, I had no idea, but it looked suspiciously like Victoria's illegal weapons.

"Move and I'll slit his throat," Noah hissed at the others. They backed away instantly, hands lifting in the air. "Not only are you gunning for the crown, but you're also dabbling in human trafficking." He clicked his tongue. "Quite the resumé."

"That wasn't—" the leader spluttered. "We didn't mean to—"

"Uh-uh," Noah said, pressing the blade tighter to the guy's throat. "I'm willing to forget your poor judgement if you can give me information. I'm looking for two girls, Katie and Rena. Do you know of them?"

"We traffic hundreds of girls from all cities," one of the other dudes interrupted, and Noah shot him a withering stare that made him instantly clamp his lips shut.

"They're twins. Olive skin, brown eyes. One has cropped hair and the other's is long and curly. Beautiful women, both from the Verdant Plateau. Ring any bells?"

"No," the leader began to say, but Noah shifted the blade up under his cock, to which the guy immediately stiffened.

"How about now?"

Holy shit. Whoever this Noah was … he was ruthless. Hell, if someone had taken Ethan or Hadley, I'd do whatever it took, too. Had done from the moment they'd been born. For a second I wondered if he'd really go through with it, but one look at the determination in his eyes and I knew he would. You don't know how important things are until you lose them, and Noah would not stop until he had them back.

"Please..."

The sharp sting of urine filled my nose, and I crinkled it as I tilted my head. I wasn't going to lie; I was loving every minute of this interrogation. These sick fucks had been willing to take Potentials and farm them like cattle. They deserved everything they got, just like Mark had.

Shouts and screams rang out across the platform, but I couldn't look away.

"Katie and Rena, where are they?"

"I don't know!" the leader screamed. "If they're from the Verdant Plateau they were most likely sold to Stormcrest. That's where the bulk of them go. Just ask your pretty little plaything over there. That's all I know, I swear."

"Then we're done here," Noah said matter-of-factly. He withdrew his knife and moved around to stand between the leader and me, casual as a cucumber.

"You're letting me go?" the guy stammered.

"Sure," Noah said with a shrug. "I have no use for dead weight."

He kicked the guy over the edge with a savage kick, then crouched and sliced the femoral artery in one's upper thigh and slammed his blade into another's throat. The other two barely had time to blink before they turned tail and ran, making to leap across to another platform.

I lunged after one, grabbing his ankle and twisting so the guy fell to the ground. He turned and grappled at my shoulders. I punched him, once, twice, three times until his nose broke under my fist. Someone grabbed me from behind, and I shrieked in anger, almost punching Noah in the face as he lifted me.

"We've got company," he shouted, jerking his chin at the spiders quickly descending their webs from high above.

A loud gong sounded, and I covered my ears and grit my teeth against the vibrations in my ear. Instantly, the droning of wasps grew louder, but they weren't swarming towards the Potentials anymore, they were fleeing back into their nest far below the surface in the abyss. Which meant the spiders were the next main course.

I glanced at the clock. Only three minutes remained, so the Masters were throwing a curve ball into these last crucial minutes. A white light suddenly flashed at the far end of the cavern, and I yelped as the platform we were on jolted and began shifting towards the other floating islands. One by one they merged to form one long path to a finish line that revealed itself in the rock wall. And along the way … spiders landed at every interval.

"Run, Fallon!" Noah shouted as he went back for Kayden. "I've got him."

I nodded, because after the grit he'd just displayed, I didn't doubt him for a second. My legs had never moved faster as I sprinted towards that finish line, my eyes taking in the chaos around me.

A girl screamed ahead, the sound cut off as a spider gripped her in its furry limbs and bit her damn head off. *Fuck.* Bile climbed my throat, but I forced myself to keep moving. Another group of Potentials fought spiders to my left, and I ducked as one shot a web that effectively netted the group in its grasp and hauled them in. The giant creature began spinning a web of death around the screaming men and women.

My conscience fought with my survival instincts, and in the end, logic won out as I scrambled on. There was no saving those people and trying now would only get me killed. Who would Ethan and Hadley rely on then? Swallowing my guilt, I ducked and swerved. Sweat dripped down my back as I exerted my muscles to the point of burning and pushed on. The finish line was so close, so fucking close. I could practically taste safety as I fled towards it.

To my relief, Zane, Kendra, and Lou crossed the line together, their hands held tight. Zane let Kendra go, muttering something in his usual chaotic, full bodily way as he turned back. My heart dropped instantly. For me. He was coming back for me, and for Noah and Kayden, probably even his grumpy care bear Ace.

As he tried to step back into the ring though, he bumped into an invisible wall, his gorgeous face instantly turning furious as he banged against it.

No, Zane. Stay fucking safe behind that line.

His eyes scanned the cavern, flooding with relief and softening the instant they met mine. That look alone gave me the strength to go on, and I mustered what remained of my energy and ran faster, faster.

Just metres away now. I held out my hand, ready to hold onto Zane's, when something slammed into my leg. I looked back, registering the furry limb sticking through flesh and pinning me to the ground. White hot pain burned up my body, setting my blood on fire. My power burst out of me, but what remained was little more than dregs, and the spider simply leered at me with its many eyes. I saw my death in them. Quick and painless if I was lucky, or slow and agonising like those captured in webs would no doubt be.

A frustrated growl ripped through me as I turned and clawed at the rocky ground, splitting nails and tearing my skin as I struggled to grip onto something. I lifted my gaze, finding Zane frantic on the other side of that wall, fear like I'd never known etched in the lines of his face. This was it. Fallon fillet. Fallon mignon. Fucking done in by a grossly enormous and magically enhanced eight-legged freak.

I closed my eyes and waited for the final blow. When none came, I cracked one lid. I found Victoria standing above me, huffing and panting with a scowl on her beautiful face.

"Are you fucking coming or what?"

She pulled me to my feet and supported me with an arm around my shoulder while I limped.

"Victoria," I said, working through my muddled brain. All I managed was, "Why?"

"Because I owe you a debt," she said, refusing to look at me. "Because I'll never finish paying it."

NOAH

"Why are you naked?" Kayden panted, stumbling beside me as I dragged him towards the finish line.

Around us, the cavern was filled with the sounds of people fighting for their lives, the buzzing and scuttling of monstrous-sized wasps, spiders and dying. So much dying.

"Didn't you get the note about the dress code?" I replied, stepping over a mangled body, a web restraining their limbs in unnatural directions. "Pretty embarrassing for you."

Kayden huffed, and I angled my head to see him cracking a smile, only to have it drop into a frown. Tears welled in his brown eyes, and he became a dead weight on my shoulder. He'd already been an effort to move when he could amble, but now I had no way of shifting him. The guy was all muscle and as heavy as the boulder he turned into. Sobs racked Kayden's body as he turned into a bumbling mess.

"Shit, Kayden." I groaned, stopping, because there was no way I could get him to the finish line like this. He crumpled to the ground, curling into the foetal position and proceeded to suck his thumb as tears fell from his eyes. "We don't have time for this."

I spun around, searching through the fighting to see who was doing this to him. Someone was using their magic to affect Kayden; there was no way he'd be acting this way in the middle of a fight otherwise.

A spider launched at me, swinging on a thread of silk like some jungle man. I dodged its first swing, then when it was on the return, I hit the spider square in the face, launching it towards a lingering wasp that was heading for a nearby Potential. I continued searching for whoever was assaulting Kayden with their magic, my gaze snagging on a guy with dark brown hair who looked like he'd stepped out of a women's hair salon in the Pre-Terrulian 1970's. The guy made eye contact with me and smirked before his gaze quickly returned to Kayden.

"I want to go home," Kayden cried, drawing my attention back to him. He began rocking, whimpering like one of the demon puppies I'd faced earlier. "I want my angel."

"You'll be with her soon. I'll be right back," I promised him, then darted towards the Tritosan without letting myself second-guess. I had to stop the magical assault, or we both wouldn't make it to the finish line.

Those from Zane's city were renowned for their ability to manipulate emotions. Most Tritosans weren't very strong with their magic, but I'd read that sadness wasn't hard to draw out of someone. On the other hand, making someone happy was considerably hard and required an immense amount of power.

I summoned whatever strength I could, turning invisible and zig-zagging between the other Potentials and the spiders. I gritted my teeth, focusing on staying hidden and ignoring the feeling of exhaustion wanting to crash over me. I was pushing myself to my limits, and though my mind wanted me to keep using my adaptation and magic, my body was having difficulty abiding by my wants.

Narrowly avoiding a spider's scrambling legs as it tried desperately not to fall over the edge, I reached my destination, appearing before Kayden's attacker and punching his surprised face with my invisible fist. His head snapped around, blood splattering from his mouth. I didn't ease up, throwing another fist and following him to the ground. He tried to fight back, but I didn't give him any opportunities, blocking his attempts with my own barrage.

I had been a dormant volcano, holding onto my rage and letting it simmer, but no longer. I'd erupted, and this guy was getting the brunt of my wrath.

I was sick of people using others to get what they wanted. Greedy people who only wanted to exploit those around them. And this asshole was just like the ones who had burnt my city and all of those innocents in it. He didn't see Kayden as a person; no, he was an obstacle in his way to a crown.

Well, not anymore.

My hand stung, the blood on the guy's face mixing with my own from my split knuckles as I hit repeatedly. Eventually, he went still beneath me, and I dropped my invisibility. My shoulders slumped as I panted and slipped off him. My anger calmed to a simmer once more.

A spider scurried towards me, and I deftly lifted the guy's torso, his head dropping forward and rolling around as I used him as a shield. The spider pushed forward, hissing. I fell back, the dead man on top of me. I continued to use him as cover, keeping him between me and the spider's dripping fangs. Blood from his crushed face spattered my own and my bare chest. I had so much adrenalin coursing through me that I could not process that I was using a man I'd just killed as a shield. It would come back to bite me later, as all traumatic things did.

A growl rumbled from the spider. I didn't think they could growl. But on the other hand, I knew there were aggressive members of the arachnid family, so that part of their behaviour was expected. The one above me thrashed around, another growl spitting from it, then it sunk its fangs into the dead guy, spilling more blood onto me. It must have torn the carotid arteries as blood poured, coating me in the sticky substance.

With a snarl, I shoved both off me whilst the spider's fangs were still embedded. They tumbled to my side, and I jumped to my feet, kicking them in order to maintain their motion until the duo fell over the edge.

Gasping, I wasted no time rushing back to where I'd left Kayden, only to find him on his feet again and fighting. His moves were sloppy, but he was skilled despite his deteriorated health. The wasps fell prey to his attacks, partly thanks to the help of Dick. The guy was by Kayden's side, stepping into the gaps that Kayden missed.

Dick squeaked when I appeared beside him and grabbed hold of a wasp's wings, tearing my fingernails through its flesh. It buzzed loudly, trying to fight me, but I wouldn't let go. My muscles strained; luckily, Dick regained his composure after seeing my current state and stabbed the wasp, killing it.

"We need to get to the finish line," I shouted over the frantic noise of the fighting.

"I'll lead the way," Dick offered, and we made to follow, only for Kayden to be tugged backwards.

I swung my hand out, grabbing onto him and wrapping it around his wrist as he did the same to me. We were pulled up into the air, and I was helpless as every part of me dangled, but I couldn't focus on that now. I needed to work out how to detach the web currently stuck to Kayden's back without us falling to our deaths in the process.

Think, Noah, think.

Heart beating at a rapid pace, I scanned the cavern for some way out of this mess. Beneath us, Potentials fought chaotically, some succeeding in escape whilst a fair few died in their attempts. It was a massacre. One that I refused to be part of.

"I'm going to let go!" Kayden shouted at me. "You'll fall onto the platform, but you can heal. Yeah, bro?"

"Can you teleport?"

Kayden shook his head, grimacing. He was still feeling the effects of the wasp stings and the fighting. I hadn't been able to heal him to the degree I would have liked, and after using my invisibility, I was tapped out.

"We can figure something out!" I called back, my eyes going wide at the sight of the spider behind Kayden.

It crept out from the darkness and put all the other spiders below to shame. It was huge, its beady eyes glossy as it took us in. Its furry legs crept forward ever so slowly like it had all the time in the world.

I shuddered.

It was cocky, and I was man enough to admit it scared the shit out of me. The monsters in the first trial—heck, even the others from this one—had been fearsome, but there was just something about spiders that could bring people to their knees.

"Don't fight it," I shouted at Kayden. "Lull it into a false sense of security. Make it believe we are easy prey; then we attack together."

Kayden locked eyes with me and nodded.

Please let this work.

The spider's legs reached out, drawing us into its web.

ACE

"Ace!"

I sent bolts of electricity through the spiders hurling themselves towards me, electrifying their asses and dropping them into the darkness below. The Overseer and Masters were in sight, the finish line so close I could taste it. Unlike the first trial, this one had been less than 24 hours, though they'd managed to pack more punch.

I turned, seeing Dick Jobs rushing towards me, covered in blood and sporting some injuries. He had a determined glint in his eye, reminding me of a newbie Drake, looking to impress Cormac by beating the shit out of anyone disrespectful. I was surprised he was still alive. If you had asked me who would be the first to die in our first few days at the House of Ascension, I would have put my credits on Dick. The little fucker had defied the odds, that's for sure.

"Ace!"

"What?" I grumbled, flicking a jolt of electricity into the nearest spider. If Dick wanted my help, he had another thing coming.

He pointed above us as he bent over, catching his breath. "Kayden and Noah are in trouble."

I glanced above, spotting the pair getting pulled into the darkness. A spider had been fishing with its web for Potentials and now had quite the catch. I couldn't see them for the life of me now, but I could see the giant hairy spider that had caught them. It was one huge motherfucker.

I threw a fist at a spider who thought it could sink its fangs into me, my metal hand propelling it into another and knocking them both out. Then shot a bolt of lightning at the spider above us.

The lightning cracked through the air, the cavern shook, and rocks fell around us like rain. Why was I protecting Noah and Kayden? Apparently, that's what I did now.

The bullshit with Cormac and working with Zane and co, not to mention the princess, was messing with my head. Impulse drove many of my actions, like my little rendezvous with Fallon and Kayden. I don't know what had gotten into me. It was like I was under some kind of mind control.

Fallon was a drug. An illicit temptation I kept going back for. I rose to her baiting, literally. I was an addict and there was no way I'd be able to quit her now. No group meeting, pill, or therapy could stop me from pursuing her. The princess was mine. She just didn't know it yet.

"Thanks," Dick puffed.

I ignored him, already focused on where Noah and Kayden were. My gut dropped at the thought of my magic having hit them along with the spider, but then I caught sight of Noah's naked ass and Kayden's flaming hair and blew out a breath.

"You're not as bad as everyone makes out, are you?" Dick said in a way that was all too chummy.

For fuck's sake.

I hauled ass away from Dick and his doe eyes, letting my magic fill the air around me. My hair stood on end, the electricity shocking anything that got close as I made my way towards the finish line. The electricity didn't deter them for too long, which I'd expected. I didn't have much left in the tank, magic-wise, but I didn't need a whole lot of time. Killing the spiders and wasps didn't help me pass the trial. Crossing the finish line did.

I sprinted over the line, running right past the Masters before smacking my hand against the cavern wall and grinning like a madman. Coming to the academy had been for the Drakes. Enduring the trials was all because Cormac wanted me to steal some shit for him. I'd only cared about survival, but now that I wanted to win, crossing the line was all that much sweeter.

Potentials were in varying shades of fucked up around me. Some of us may survive these trials 'til the end, but we would pay a high price.

Zane had his arms wrapped around Fallon, the latter patting his back. Blood coated her skin and she looked beyond exhausted. Despite it looking like she was consoling him, she was still sagging in his arms.

The sight of her so vulnerable and weak sent a rage simmering inside me, and I lashed out, punching the guy closest. His head snapped back, and he hit the cave wall with a crack before sliding to the ground where he lay motionless.

Movement at the finish line caught my eye and I saw Noah stumbling through with Kayden. My fists unclenched and I released a sigh.

Not of relief … I was just exhausted.

I shook out my shoulders. The second trial was done and dusted. Now the bodies would be counted, bones mended, and we'd be sent back to the House of Ascension to recoup under the pretence of safety.

Nowhere was safe when competing for a crown, and now that I wanted it for myself, there was another threat walking back onto the grounds.

——— ✦ ———

I was starting to regret my decision to come down from my camp in the DH setup. The lure of beer had me leaving my solitude and attending this poor attempt at a party. Some might have thought it bad taste to throw a party the same night of finishing a trial that had killed so many Potentials, but where I came from, that's exactly what you did after surviving a fight—got pissed to forget.

Whoever was hosting had chosen the communal room for this little event. Groups hung out in their usual areas, missing a few of their members but otherwise still intact. Noah was right about sticking together. Potentials who worked alone were becoming a rarity.

A few faces were yet to turn up. One being the princess. I was far enough down that rabbit hole to know I'd be instantly aware once she stepped through the door. I'd been taught growing up to be aware of all threats, which was exactly what Fallon was, but not in the way that would result in me ending six feet under.

She was a threat to my sanity and everything I'd ever known.

I stepped away from the wall and headed to the drinks table, dropping my empty beer bottle into the trash and reaching for another in the bucket of ice. It looked like someone had just brought out a fresh batch of punch, but I steered clear of that sugary shit. I felt a hand on my back and angled my head to see Zane grinning at me.

"Survived another one."

"You doubted me?" I asked, popping the top of my beer with my bionic hand.

"No way, dude." He chuckled, shaking his head. His long hair flowed around him, the shells clinking with the movement. He helped himself to some punch and took a sip of his brightly coloured drink. "I also didn't doubt that you'd help save Kayden and Noah. Can't let the pod lose a single member. Starfish needs us all."

We moved away from the punch, where a line of Potentials was waiting impatiently.

Zane continued rambling on before I could chew him out for touching me. Or for his comments about rescue and some fucking pod.

Oh, and the Starfish shit, too.

Fuck, I was in deep.

"Speaking of which, I wish they'd hurry up," he continued, "Kayden was taking too long to get ready. For a dude who wears mostly gym clothes, he takes a bogus amount of time choosing between singlets. So, I decided to ride this wave solo for a bit." He stuffed his hands into the pockets of his board shorts. "But you're here, so I guess this fish won't be swimming alone anymore."

"Isn't that Kendra over there?" I asked, looking to where she sat on a couch with a woman dressed in a bright pink skintight dress. Her blond wavy hair fell to her shoulders and the glittery strands were lined with highlights that matched her outfit.

"Sure is," Zane said. "And her girlfriend, which means she's no longer a suspect. But don't worry, we don't need to go back to the drawing board to figure out who has been killing people here at the academy. I know who our new suspect is going to be."

"And?" I asked, raising a brow. There was something about Zane. Once you let him in, even the smallest amount, you suddenly found yourself playing along with his crazy shit.

"Victoria." He leaned in. "Did you notice how she was suddenly a team player during the trial? Spent the whole night near Noah and didn't try to murder him, then saved Starfish too. She's up to something."

"I would have thought she'd be at the top of your list from the get-go?"

"She was too obvious before, but now with her weird behaviour, it all makes sense."

"She's not here tonight," I said, looking around the room. Her groupies were in their usual hang-out, but Victoria was nowhere to be seen. "Her absence is definitely a choice because, as you said, she made it through the trial, even without the help of her groupies. I'm starting to think the woman can't be killed. She's like a—"

"*Turritopsis dohrnii.*"

"Huh?"

"Immortal jellyfish," Zane replied, his words slurring. He reached for my shoulder only to miss it entirely as he spun in a slow circle on the spot, mumbling something about a sea slug.

Zane collapsed to the ground, his body convulsing at my feet. I dropped beside him, checking his vitals and searching for something to explain what was happening. Suddenly, Fallon appeared at my side, her copper eyes wide as she cradled Zane's head to prevent further injury. He stopped shaking, but his eyes rolled back into his head, and froth spilled from his mouth, followed by a trickle of blood.

"Zane! What happened?" Fallon asked but didn't wait for an answer as she looked up to where Noah now stood. "Can you heal him?"

"Our chips have been activated again."

I reached up, dragging him down beside me, then flicked out the blade from my bionic hand and dug it straight into the flesh of his arm.

"Fuck!" Noah shouted. I ignored him. Kayden appeared and must have understood my train of thought because he grabbed Noah's arm, holding him steady for me.

"Hold still, and it will be quicker," Kayden said, and Noah nodded before looking away and gritting his teeth.

Efficiently, I worked my blade into his skin until I saw the chip and plucked it from his bloodied wound with my free hand. Instantly, Noah began to heal, and Kayden released him with a chuckle.

Noah wasted no time, his hands hovering over Zane to heal the merman. I couldn't see Noah's magic working, but it must have been, because Zane's mouth no longer resembled the head on a beer. Fallon leaned against me, her eyes never leaving the merman, and I relished in her nearness despite everything going on around us. Zane wasn't the only one-half dead on the floor. Other Potentials had fallen, but unlike Zane, they had no one to help them magically.

Screams filled the common space as bodies convulsed in pools of blood, some surrounded by friends whilst others were left abandoned as Potentials backed up, afraid to catch whatever was causing them to hit the deck. Blood dripped from the eyes of one woman, her mouth agape as she stared at nothing.

I slung an arm over Fallon's shoulders, drawing her closer to me, and turned away from the blood bath to watch Noah work. It was a tense few seconds that felt like hours, and then the merman gasped. Fallon dove forward, wrapping her arms around his neck.

"Zane," she groaned, then pulled back and slapped him on the chest. "Don't ever do that again."

"It wasn't intentional, Starfish," Zane replied, tugging her close to his chest once more. "I don't even know what happened."

"You collapsed," I told him, rising to my feet now that the commotion was over. At least for Zane. Noah hurried off to help the other Potentials, so we'd soon see whether the merman would be the lone survivor or not. I knew Noah was tapped out, so he'd be lucky to save many. "Looks like poisoning."

"Coward's weapon," Kayden growled.

I nodded stiffly.

"What did you have to eat and drink since getting here?" Fallon asked, looking up at Zane. "Did someone give you something?"

Zane shook his head. "I ate in the med ward earlier. And I've been drinking here, but Ace has been too."

“The punch,” I stated. “You’ve been drinking that coloured shit.”

“But it was so tasty.” Zane frowned.

“We need to be more careful.” Fallon gripped his shirt and drew his face close to hers, forcing him to focus on her alone. “We’re getting to the pointy end of the trials. We can’t trust anyone.”

I ran a hand through my hair. She was right. Everyone would be out for blood now that we only had one trial left. We couldn’t trust any Potentials. Not even each other.

FALLON

Gods damn. Going to a party was the last thing I'd felt like after that trial, but after getting ready with Kendra and Lou, I'd started looking forward to winding down and letting loose after the trials. Not to mention spending time with my guys and making sure the night ended on a high. And by that, I mean getting screwed so hard I wouldn't be able to walk properly for days.

Instead, we'd gone from one brutal battlefield to another. My heart was still racing as I stomped towards my dorm. First Kayden, then Zane. My little black heart couldn't take the freaking stress. I guessed this was what opening it up meant, though. Pain, heartache, and maybe worst of all, vulnerability. If they were smart enough, anyone who wanted to hurt me could do so by picking off the people around me. It's what I would do if the roles were reversed. How fucked up was that?

Let's not forget the sociopath serial killer who was both blackmailing the Masters and, oh yeah, framing me for the damn murders. How convenient that the Masters had pinned it on Danger Dog. The guy was dead, it's not like he could defend his honour. Plus, tonight's poisoning only proved the murderer was still around. I felt no closer to finding answers.

Fuck. At least this time, no creepy camera snapped me alone at the scene and there had been ample witnesses. So whoever it was, either their agenda had changed, or they were simply getting tired with their old tactics. Unless this time it was someone else who wanted to wipe out the competition…

I wrinkled my nose. Who decided to poison punch these days? Fucking coward. With a long sigh, I opened my dorm room door quietly and cautiously, checking every shadow and dark corner. Couldn't be too careful with a killer on the loose. I did, however, find a note scrawled in my sister's handwriting.

We need to talk. Meet me in the auditorium. Then, hastily scrawled after that … *I need you.*

Well, shit. What next? I didn't know what to think when it came to Victoria anymore. She tried to kill me in the first trial, then saved me in the second. Girl was giving me whiplash from her newly developed personality disorder lately. Something was up, and I wanted to find out what.

It was probably a trap, but hell, she was still my sister. I wasn't stupid enough to go without backup though, so I sent a quick message to Zane, Kayden, and Noah, asking them to standby near the auditorium just in case. After a little hesitation, I flicked the same one to Ace too. I didn't trust the guy, but he was an efficient killer. Plus, he could deny it, but I had a sneaky suspicion he actually liked Zane and Noah. Kayden was … a work in progress. Me? Hell if I knew.

I shrugged a leather jacket over my slinky black short and top combo and swapped my stilettos for some chunky combat boots. Then I slid the trusty knife I'd found in the med bay into my sock. Victoria would be pretty damn stupid to try anything on me now, but a girl could never be too sure. We were both spawned from the same demon parents, after all, and Victoria was their spitting image. For all I knew she could be playing mind games to reel me back in and finish what she'd started.

On that note, I clamped my jaw tighter and headed out the dorm and towards the auditorium. The grounds were dead quiet, and I kept all my wits about me as I shied away from the well-lit path, keeping to the shadows. Everyone was likely hiding in their dorms or still at the party helping with damage control. Call me over-cautious, but after seeing Zane choking on his own spit and blood and convulsing like a zombie, I wasn't painting any more of a target on my back by being easy to find.

I slunk through the darkness like a monster of night, treading lightly and breathing silently. Nothing reared out to get me, but the tension in my shoulders didn't ease as I approached the auditorium doors. The room within was dark, bar a flickering light through the frosted glass. Cautiously, I slipped my blade from my boot. The cold metal kissed my skin like an old lover, and I narrowed my eyes as I stepped forward to push the doors open.

The breath caught in my throat as the dim glow of a fae light glinted off a dagger. A dagger dripping blood, angled in the hand of someone in a hooded cloak as they stood and watched the Potential at their feet choke and gurgle.

The Potential who was my sister.

I shrieked, sprinting towards the attacker and sliding along the varnished wooden floor, spinning to narrowly avoid a swipe at my throat. When I turned, I plunged my dagger into the side of their stomach. They grunted, but it did nothing to stop them from punching me in the jaw, swiping my legs out from beneath me and slamming my head down on the ground.

Pain vibrated through my skull, and I groaned as the world tilted on its axis. I saw the knife come at my eye in the nick of time and clasped their hand with both palms, the muscles in my shoulders locking and burning as I struggled with my attacker. They hissed, and I sucked in a sharp breath as that knife came closer, closer. So close I could see the tip primed to stab me through my socket.

A soft whimper escaped my throat. They were strong, and despite my surprise attack, they seemed to know their way around a blade. My body shook with effort, trembling, burning, fighting with everything it had to stay the fuck alive.

It wasn't enough. The knife crept closer, and just before the hooded killer could claim their next victim, the doors burst open, and shouts rang out as the guys flooded in. Something flashed through the room and embedded itself in my attacker's shoulder. They jerked backwards, giving me time to scramble away.

I spared a quick glance at the guys and shivered at the terrifying sight. I wasn't afraid, but the killer damn well should be. Their faces were filled with fury, and Zane and Noah had blood speckled over them. I'd seen many gangsters before, but none of them had displayed such primal savagery. They were out for blood and so was I.

A gurgling noise drew my attention and, suddenly all distracted, we looked to Victoria. The killer took that moment to flee, but I didn't even bother looking his way.

"Follow him," I barked. "Bring him back alive. Noah, help me."

Only Zane hesitated, and I looked up, softening at the tender expression on his face. He bent, took my face in his hands, and wiped away the blood from the split lip I'd gained. He kissed me gently, his tongue curling passionately, his hand sliding into my hair.

"Go," I whispered when he pulled away, his green eyes alight with fire. "I'll be okay."

He nodded and joined the chase like a big cat hunting its prey. I turned back to my sister.

Noah shifted his hands over Victoria, his brow creased and his lips thin. When he looked at me, eyes sad, I knew immediately it was too late.

"She's lost too much blood, Fallon," he said softly. "I'm tapped out, I can't…"

I smiled weakly at him, too exhausted, too horrified by the pity on his face. I put a hand on his cheek. "It's okay. Help the others."

He nodded and joined the hunt, but my eyes were already on my sister.

"Fallon," Victoria croaked, reaching for me blindly.

My blood was ice cold, my stomach a knotted mess as I shuffled closer. I gasped, my heart damn near thumping out of my chest at the sight. Her body was riddled with stab wounds, each of them uglier than the last and bleeding profusely. So much blood, it would be impossible to stem the tide.

"I'm here," I said softly, tucking a strand of her blond hair back. "I've got you."

"Fallon," she rasped again, her copper eyes finding mine in the low light. They looked clearer than I'd seen for a long time, almost feverishly so as she stared at me with true remorse. "I'm sorry. For everything."

"Victoria," I tried, but she shook her head.

"I tried to tell you so many times. I tried to show you, but they wouldn't let me."

"Who?" I coaxed gently. "Who wouldn't let you do what?"

She spat out a glob of blood, then licked her lips. "House Jupiter. They're … they're working with the Drakes. They're responsible for enslaving the people from DH, the Verdant Plateau, and the Crimson Steppes."

I nodded slowly. There was never really any question about my House's involvement. Hell, I could even understand why the Drakes might get involved. They were one of the most notorious gangs known for violence and drugs. What was a little human trafficking as the cherry on top? It made sense for them to take a handout and an opportunity to step up. Did Ace know? Was he part of this whole operation like Noah suspected? I swallowed, taking Victoria's hand in my own. It was cold as ice, the pulse in her wrist fading by the second.

"The trials were rigged from the start," Victoria said, quieter now, her eyes glazing over. "The throne was never in reach."

"House Jupiter rigged the whole thing?" I asked, my brows knitting. "But if they wanted you to win, then why…"

Why kill the leading candidate? My eyes said what I didn't voice, but she shook her head just once, seeming to understand my train of thought.

"Not me. I was just a puppet for him to manipulate."

"Who?" I asked desperately, but she was fading fast, her focus wavering.

"I never … I never wanted to be a monster. It was all to protect you, Fallon. You, Ethan, and Hadley. He made me like this … brainwashed me."

I shook my head, trying to process everything. If Victrus was responsible for rigging the trials, it made sense he would want Victoria to win, giving House Jupiter access to her reign as queen of Terrulia. So why, then, had someone jumped her? Was another player on the board? I tried to quieten all the thoughts rambling on in my mind, then fully realised what else she'd told me.

"You're telling me," I said slowly, licking my lips. "That Victrus—Father—brainwashed you into being his puppet? Into doing anything and everything he asked?"

Victoria's nod was barely perceptible, and she coughed violently, hacking blood all over the floor. Pain wracked up my body. Pain and *fury.* Violent, unyielding, vicious fury. Our father had done this to her, moulding her into his very image not by her choice alone, but through sheer force.

Suddenly it all made sense.

Why she'd changed the moment she'd come home from initiation into his inner circle. Why my loving, kind, protective sister had grown cold and distant and always hungry for pain and suffering. Why she'd never batted an eye when Victrus abused me or forced me to do his biddings—why she'd seemed to enjoy it.

He'd made her into a monster, and he was going to fucking pay.

"Fallon," Victoria croaked, leaning into me. "I'm sorry I wasn't stronger."

"Shh," I whispered, feeling my eyes burn with hot, prickly tears. I took her bloodied palm in my own, squeezing gently. "You have nothing to be sorry for. I'm going to make this right. I'm going to end their empire, Victoria. And I'm going to keep our siblings safe. I promise. But you need to tell me. Who did this to you? Who is killing all the Potentials?"

"His name…" She grunted, her body wracking violently as pain flooded through her. "His name…" Her body jerked suddenly, then slumped. A long sigh escaped her lips, and she fell still, her pupils dilating.

I stared at my sister for long moments, clutching at her hands with my own. "Please don't leave me," I whispered. "Don't leave me again."

She didn't answer.

My pleas fell on deaf ears in a silent room, and it took me several moments to realise my cheeks were wet. One perfect tear fell onto her perfect face, and I wiped it away, hating myself for the bloody marks I left on her skin.

Memories of my childhood flashed through my mind—running through the halls of our home, learning to fly, and nights cuddled beneath our blankets together as rain fell outside.

I had forgotten the sound of her laugh and the way her eyes would crinkle when she was happy. I had truly loved her once and I would never forget what Victrus had taken from me.

That pain in my heart hardened, and I fisted my hands over my sister's chest, letting out a scream. I'd already planned to take down my parent's empire and to destroy the corruption in House Jupiter, but they weren't my only targets now. I didn't know who this mysterious murderer was working for, but they'd crossed the wrong fucking girl. Killing Potentials and blackmailing the Masters was one thing, but murdering my sister? I'd have their fucking head.

These trials were just the beginning. I would wear that crown, but not before I got my hands even dirtier first. They were already stained. But I wouldn't be satisfied until they were coated in the blood of my enemies.

My father hadn't just taken Victoria's life from *her*, he'd taken a sister away from *me*. All this time I'd thought her cruel and corrupt, but she'd never had a choice. I didn't know how the fuck he'd done it. Maybe by experimenting with his telekinesis or some sort of mental conditioning.

Either way, it didn't matter. There was a reason people feared my family name. There was a reason people back home feared *me*. Only this time, I wouldn't be working for House Jupiter.

Victrus Auger was a dead man, and I would be the executioner.

WANT TO KNOW WHAT HAPPENS NEXT?

Well, shit. It got a little hectic and heavy at the end there, didn't it? We're sorry about that, but hey, at least all our main babies are okay, right? … For now ;)

Two trials down … hell to go. What might you find in the next instalment? Death, obviously, but maybe a twist or two and a whole world of hurt for our main lady. It's only going to get more wild from here, so you won't want to miss out on Book Three, A Sea of Secrets, which you can pre-order Amazon.

Can't wait until doomsday with the next book release? We got you. Join our FB group to chat all things Terrulia! You'll get access to a bunch of goodies, like updates, sneak peaks, ARCs and more.

www.facebook.com/groups/asosdiscussiongroup

You can also follow our reading groups for teasers, freebies, and to keep up to date with all our bookish content!

Chloe Hodge's Reading Coven - www.facebook.com/groups/chloesreadingcoven

Rebecca Camm's Reader Group - www.facebook.com/groups/rebeccacammsreadergroup

Acknowledgements

The brain child is growing up, and we couldn't be more proud. We loved writing A Sky of Storms, but we adored A Forest of Fire. When you work with the right people on the right projects, it doesn't feel like work. It's cuppa teas over video calls, laughing at Zane's nonsense, plotting Ace's next move, or daydreaming spicy scenes. It's two friends working on something more than just a book.

And it's nice when things come together, isn't it? When all the little threads start intertwining to form the bigger tapestry. The best part? We're just getting started.

We started this series on a bit of a whim, but you, lovely readers, make this a continued possibility. Thank you to all the bookstagrammers/tokers/tubers, our amazing beta readers, the street team, ARC readers, the shout-from-the-rooftop book dragons and the loyal supporters in our corner.

Thank you to Fran for another beautiful cover, to Emily for the editing, to the artists for their amazing pieces, to the creators for bringing merch to life …

A big thank you to our families for supporting our dreams.

The journey is just getting started. See you in the next trial.

Much love,
The Overseers xx

About the Authors

Chloe Hodge has always had a fondness for the fantastical. Before her love of books led her to publish the Guardians of the Grove trilogy, she completed a Bachelor of Journalism and Professional Writing and worked as a journalist. She currently lives in Adelaide, Australia, crafting new worlds, running editing business, Chloe's Chapters, drinking copious amounts of tea, and playing video games.

Stay in touch!

Instagram
@chloeschapters

TikTok
@chloehodgeauthor

Website
www.chloehodge.com

Reading Group
www.facebook.com/groups/chloesreadingcoven

MORE BOOKS FROM CHLOE

The Cursed Blood Duology

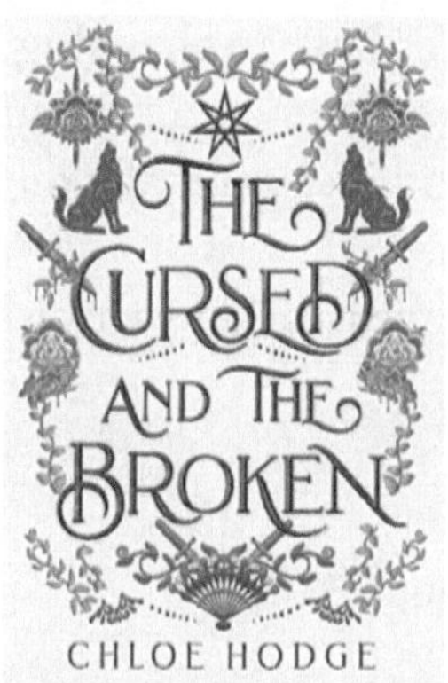

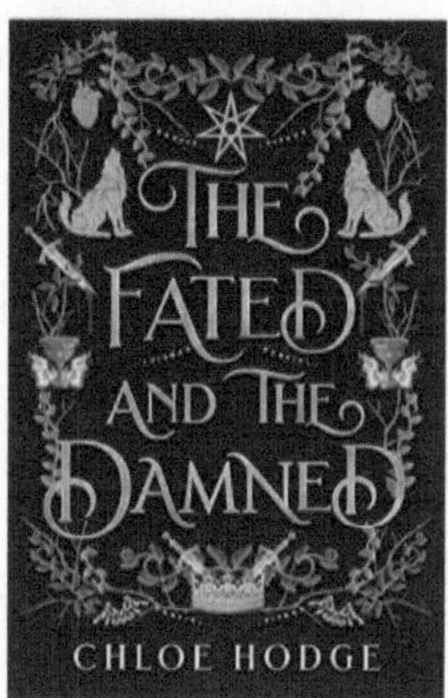

The Guardians of the Grove

About the Authors

Rebecca Camm is a Melbourne writer who loves reading and all things magical.

She strongly believes in the power stories have in changing lives. Just like her, Rebecca's characters are flawed, yet they are continually learning. Unlike her, they are confident, witty, and just generally more exciting.

When her children allow her free time, she is either writing or attempting to conquer her ever growing tbr pile.

Stay in touch!

Instagram
@readingwritingdaydreaming

TikTok
@readingwritingdaydream

Newsletter
www.rebeccacamm.com/contact

Reader Group
www.facebook.com/groups/rebeccacammsreadergroup

MORE BOOKS FROM REBECCA

The Valmenessian Chronicles

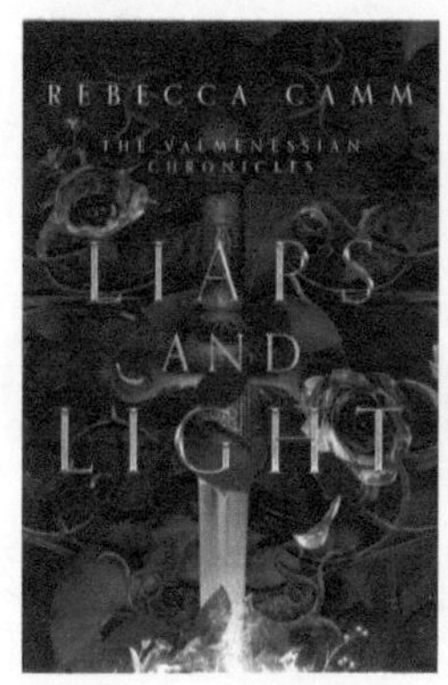

Novellas

www.ingramcontent.com/pod-product-compliance
Lightning Source LLC
Chambersburg PA
CBHW020457310726
48979CB00016B/2684/J
* 9 7 8 0 6 4 5 6 2 5 0 6 6 *